Award-winning  elve years in the most unromantic career ever – divorce lawyer. After dedicating all that effort to helping people terminate relationships, she is thrilled to deal in happy endings and write romance novels for a living. Her books have been featured in *Cosmopolitan* magazine and *E!* online. HelenKay loves hearing from readers, so stop by her website at helenkaydimon.com and say hello.

Jennifer D. Bokal penned her first book at age eight. An early lover of the written word, she followed her passion, becoming a full-time writer. From there, she never looked back. She earned a Master's in creative writing from Wilkes University and joined the Romance Writers of America. Happily married to her own alpha male hero, Jennifer and her husband live in upstate New York with their three beautiful daughters, two spoiled dogs and a kitten who aspires to be a Chihuahua.

The Sinful Sleuths Club

December 2025
A Date with Death

February 2026
A Reunion on the Run

January 2026
A Trap for Two

March 2026
A Midnight Mystery

A REUNION ON THE RUN:
The Sinful Sleuths Club

HELENKAY DIMON

JENNIFER D. BOKAL

MILLS & BOON

All rights reserved including the right of reproduction in whole or in part in any form. This edition is published by arrangement with Harlequin Enterprises ULC.

This is a work of fiction. Names, characters, places, locations and incidents are purely fictional and bear no relationship to any real life individuals, living or dead, or to any actual places, business establishments, locations, events or incidents. Any resemblance is entirely coincidental.

Without limiting the exclusive rights of any author, contributor or the publisher of this publication, any unauthorised use of this publication to train generative artificial intelligence (AI) technologies is expressly prohibited. HarperCollins also exercise their rights under Article 4(3) of the Digital Single Market Directive 2019/790 and expressly reserve this publication from the text and data mining exception.

® and ™ are trademarks owned and used by the trademark owner and/or its licensee. Trademarks marked with ® are registered with the United Kingdom Patent Office and/or the Office for Harmonisation in the Internal Market and in other countries.

First Published in Great Britain 2025
by Mills & Boon, an imprint of HarperCollins*Publishers* Ltd
1 London Bridge Street, London, SE1 9GF

www.harpercollins.co.uk

HarperCollins*Publishers*
Macken House, 39/40 Mayor Street Upper,
Dublin 1, D01 C9W8, Ireland

A Reunion on the Run: The Sinful Sleuths Club © 2026 Harlequin Enterprises ULC.

Under the Gun © 2010 HelenKay Dimon
Texas Law: Undercover Justice © 2022 Jennifer D. Bokal

ISBN: 978-0-263-42109-5

Printed and Bound in the UK using 100% Renewable Electricity
at CPI Group (UK) Ltd, Croydon, CR0 4YY

UNDER THE GUN

HELENKAY DIMON

To Ethan Ellenberg for convincing me to give romantic suspense a serious try.

Chapter One

Luke Hathaway scanned the surveillance monitors set up in the nondescript Washington, D.C., office building's underground security headquarters. The wall of television screens showed every inch of public area and private offices of the financial firm on the eighteenth floor.

He and partner Adam Wright had flashed a fake subpoena ten minutes earlier. The official-looking paper convinced the guard to give up his comfortable seat and call someone in charge for guidance. That provided Adam with just enough time to slide into the chair, tap into the system and send the feed directly back to Luke's office across town.

Luke put his palm on the console and leaned in close to the monitors. The move blocked the guard's line of sight and gave Luke a good look at every angle of the business on the small screens. "Seems only the bathrooms are sacred in that place. Every other square foot has a camera hidden somewhere."

"Yeah, no paranoia there," Adam said.

The security guard covered the phone's mouthpiece. "What are you two doing? You can't touch the equipment."

"Just looking." Luke smiled at just how easy it was to infiltrate a company in supposed lockdown.

Adam had tried to tap into the computer's hard drive from back at the office but needed direct access to the financial company's internal system. One cover story and a stack of forged documents later, they were in. Just proved Luke's theory that when the back door refused to budge, you used the front. He found that most people with something to hide spent their time covering all the tough routes to information and missed the obvious ones like an overweight fifty-year-old security guard who nearly wet himself at the sight of a sheet of paper with a big seal on it.

"Now *there*'s something worth watching." Adam let out a low whistle and hitched his chin at the screen to Luke's right. "The lady with the fine—"

Luke saw the flash of jeans out of the corner of his eye. "Yeah, I can see."

Adam laughed. "It's your lack of enthusiasm that has me concerned."

Even in black and white Luke saw long dark hair and an impressive shape. Still, he needed Adam to focus on the job so they could get out of there before the guard hung up the phone and figured out what was going on.

"Drool on your own time." Luke returned to memorizing the area around the receptionist's desk in the financial office upstairs. But a prickling sensation at the base of his neck pulled his attention back to the image of the woman at the elevator.

There was something familiar about her. Something about her perfect posture with shoulders back and chin lifted high, almost daring anyone to question her. That curvy shape, from her full breasts to her slim waist to the way her dark jeans hugged her hips.

Something…

Just then she turned around and stared straight into the security camera. Didn't even pretend not to notice the device in the black bubble hanging above her head. Big eyes. Flirty smile. Hands resting on her hips in a way sure to highlight the rocking body underneath that slim-fitting T-shirt.

The hair was darker but Luke would know her face anywhere. Hard not to recognize the woman who dumped him right before their wedding two years ago. The same woman now on the run and wanted for murder.

"Is that…?" Adam came up out of the chair and pressed his face close to the screen.

The woman always did have the worst timing. "Yeah."

"Man, it can't be."

Luke fought off the urge to throw something. "Definitely is."

The security guard dropped the phone and joined Adam at the desk. "Who is she?"

Adam shook his head as if unable to believe his eyes. "Claire Samson."

Luke mentally skipped ahead to his next move. Analyzing how and why Claire had dropped right in front of him could wait. Catching her was the priority here.

He reached into his jacket pocket, grateful he'd worn a suit and brought the microphone just in case. "Got it."

"What are you doing?" Adam asked.

"Washing my car. What do you think?" Luke slipped the tiny disk in his ear and tapped it to test its strength. "We're good to go."

"Care to fill me in on where?" Adam asked.

Luke pointed at the screen. "You are staying here and watching her. I'm going to get out there and grab her before she runs again."

The guard looked back and forth between them. "Isn't she an escaped convict or something?"

"The official term is 'person of interest,'" Adam said.

Enough talk. "Adam, your job is to tell me exactly where she goes. If she moves, I want to know it. You're my eyes on this."

The guard shook his head. "Her photo's been all over the news for the past two weeks. We need to call someone or...wait. Are you the guys we call?"

Luke knew better than to sit around and debate the

issue. The one thing he was an expert on was watching Claire leave. Give her a couple of minutes head start and she would slip into a crowd and disappear.

Adam grabbed Luke's arm before he could take off. "She clearly knows you're on-site. She wants your attention."

Oh, she has it. "Looks that way, yeah."

Even now while working this other job, watching an idiot businessman who made his chief financial officer disappear, Luke had been thinking about Claire and where she might be. About how he could drag her back to Virginia and put her in jail.

"It isn't our job to go after Claire. We're on this…" Adam shot the guard a scowl before lowering his voice. "We have another assignment, Luke. We need to stay here and let the police handle Claire."

Luke had tried that. He had sat back and watched law enforcement lose her trail. No way was he letting her walk out on him again. There was only one reason for her to be in this building, a place she didn't belong, on this day. She was following him. She wanted him to notice and come after her. He was happy to oblige.

When she hit the elevator button Luke knew his time was up. "I'm going after her. Do not call anyone official about her, hear me? She's mine."

He waited until Adam nodded before pushing open the door and hitting the emergency stairs at a run. Claire chose some millionaire over him—fine. Killing the guy, taking his money and trying to disappear—not fine.

"She's on the elevator," Adam said.

Luke adjusted the small speaker in his ear. "Bring up the schematics and tell me how many exits there are to this building."

"You don't know she's leaving. She could duck into an office on another floor and wait you out."

"Wrong." Luke made the prediction as he took the stairs two steps at a time. "She's headed for the street. Her plan is to blend into the lunch crowd and metro commuters roaming around McPherson Square."

Then she'd be gone. The woman was playing some kind of game. Luke knew that much. Why else was she hanging around the D.C. metro area, instead of taking the money and heading for a country that wouldn't extradite her back for trial?

No, Claire had some sort of plot in mind. Something that involved him. Boy, would she be disappointed, because once he had her he was done running around after Claire Samson for any reason other than to turn her in to the police.

"She stepped off on the second floor and is headed toward the stairwell on the east side," Adam said.

"Exactly what I would do." It was the smart thing to do, and Claire was not dumb. As she came down the stairs, he went up. After one flight Luke stopped and stood at the door to the garage level. "Where next?"

"She's out on the first floor walking toward the west-side stairwell now. Looks like she's zigzagging."

Luke took the stairs to the lobby floor two at a time. "Can she get outside?"

Computer keys clicked before Adam answered. "Once she hits the lobby, she can turn to her right and take a service exit that dumps her in an alley off K Street."

Luke pressed the disk tighter against his ear. "Gates, locks, people? Anything there to stop her?"

"Once she's outside her only choice is a long alley to the sidewalk. She won't be able to turn around and reenter the building without a code."

Busy downtown street and one with loads of business traffic at this time of day. *Definitely not dumb.* "Got it."

"She's in the lobby now," Adam said.

Luke shoved open the door to the opposite end of the large area. The force sent it banging against the wall. Heads turned. Two people standing nearby stopped talking. Luke ignored all but the brunette at the other end of the lobby. She didn't even glance around, proving she had her escape route planned.

"Claire!" His voice bounced off the stone walls.

When their eyes met, Claire went still.

He pointed at her. "Do not move."

A hush fell over the businesspeople gathered at the elevators. Everyone glanced around and shuffled their feet as if embarrassed by being caught in the middle of a private conversation. Despite that, they listened in, but no one seemed to notice a notorious fugitive standing right there in front of them.

"Help! He's following me." The words barely left Claire's mouth and she was off. She threw open the door to the exit and let it slam shut behind her.

The race was on.

Luke ran past a security guard, ignoring the shouts to stop. Using a shoulder, Luke knocked a twenty-something male Good Samaritan to the floor when he tried to block the path to Claire. People crowded around Luke to slow him down. He dodged, even jumped over a chair someone threw in his way.

A high-pitched alarm blared through the building as he hit the door Claire had used for her escape. The piercing sound echoed throughout the lobby, making it impossible for Luke to hear Adam screaming directions in his ear.

But Luke didn't need any help from here. Even through the harsh scent of the alley, he could smell her familiar flowery shampoo. He was right behind Claire. As long as he grabbed her before she got to the street he was good.

He looked around for anything to stick in the door and slow down any do-gooders who decided to follow him out there. The piece of wood under his foot wasn't perfect, but it might buy him some time. He shoved it through the door handle, then raced down the pavement, following Claire and getting closer with each step.

She kept her body toned, probably from hours of aerobics like before, but he was still faster. Only a few feet away now, he could see her on the other side of the Dumpster, hear her heavy breathing and watch her hair fly around in the warm October breeze. Then she slid to a stop. Actually lost her footing and fell back on one hand.

Instead of getting up and breaking out of the dark alley into the sunshine and possible freedom, she scrambled to her feet and ran toward him with her cheeks puffing and eyes wild. She landed with a thump against his chest but didn't stop moving. With her hands wrapped in his shirt, she tugged him toward the door and back into the building they'd just left.

"We have to move," she said. "Inside. Now."

Luke planted his feet to stop the slide across the loose gravel under him. "Claire, stop."

She grabbed his jacket sleeve and pulled hard enough to rip the fabric at the shoulder. "No time. We have to get out of here."

Luke looked at the shadowed figure standing near the distant sidewalk. From the bulk, Luke knew it was a man, but that was all. "Who the hell is that?"

"I don't know," she said, her usually husky voice interrupted by huge gulping breaths.

Luke knew there was no way back into the building without a code, and he sure didn't have it. They had to go through the guy at the other end.

"Tell security to back off!" Luke yelled the order

loud enough for Adam to pick up through the honking horns and other sounds of the nearby street.

"Who are you talking to?" Claire asked.

The shadow at the end of the alley moved closer. The figure took his hand out of his windbreaker pocket. The sun behind him glinted off the metal of his gun. The baseball cap pulled over his face hid his identity, but the casual clothes and quiet stalking told Luke they had a problem. This other guy was no cop.

Luke positioned his body in front of Claire's. A bullet or knife or anything else would have to go through him first.

He could hear people on the other side of the building's door and a dull thud as they pushed against it. He needed backup and a way out that didn't involve fighting through an angry crowd that viewed him as Claire's attacker.

"He with you?" Luke asked her over his shoulder.

"Does he look happy to see me?"

Adam's voice crackled in Luke's ear. "Luke, there aren't any security guards outside. They're all standing around the lobby with their thumbs up—"

"Then who's this guy I'm looking at?" Luke heard a short buzzing and saw the outside camera switch position to aim at the end of the alley.

The other man pulled his cap even lower. The gun pointed down, but Luke knew that could change in a second and didn't wait. He shoved Claire behind the Dumpster, ignoring her squeal of surprise. The mystery guy's footsteps fell faster against the pavement now. Luke ducked and squeezed in next to Claire.

Her eyes grew wide when he slipped out the gun he had tucked at the small of his back. "Where did you get that?" she asked.

"Not important."

"You told me you sold art for a living."

"I find antiques." That was his cover and he was sticking to it.

"Find them or shoot them?"

Luke ignored the sarcasm and checked his gun. "This is your last chance to tell me the truth. Do you know how to do that?"

"You may want to remember I'm wanted for murder. Ticking me off might not be your best move."

As if he could forget that fact. "Who's this guy coming after you?"

"Don't know." Her skin paled. "Probably someone Phil sent."

Phil Samson. Her husband. Make that her *dead* husband. Luke vowed to deal with her lies later. Now he needed to get them out of there alive.

The other man's steps stopped. Except for the soft rustle of his slick jacket, he didn't make a sound. But Luke could feel the tension radiating off the guy. He motioned for Claire to stay quiet as he peeled her fingers off his shirt. The last thing he needed was her slowing him down.

Glaring at her one last time, Luke mentally started the countdown. In one swift move he stood up and pivoted around the Dumpster, gun raised, to face the other man head on. The guy's eyes bugged out the second before he lifted his weapon. The slight hesitation gave Luke the opening he needed. His bullet hit the man's shoulder, sending him stumbling backward.

At the sharp bang people gathered at the end of the alley. Someone shouted for the police. Another person started yelling about a robbery. Luke heard it all, but his focus remained locked on the man in front of him. The guy refused to go down easy. Instead, he held on to his weapon and stayed on his feet.

Claire ran for the back door to the building and yanked on it. It took her a few tugs to see the wood Luke had shoved there. With a growl of frustration she ripped it out.

When the door still refused to open, she hammered it with her fists. "Open up!"

Luke lunged for her. "Claire, no! It's—"

The other man's roar cut off the rest of Luke's warning. Everything moved in a blur. Claire jumped away from the door, holding the stick in her hand like a bat. At the same time the mystery man lurched, shifting his gun to waist height.

When the man pivoted toward Claire, Luke didn't hesitate. No way was he going to let the guy get a shot off in her direction. Luke shoved her against the wall as he fired a second shot at the attacker. The explosion from the gun mixed with a second crack Luke couldn't place. For a moment all he heard was the whir of distant sirens and screams from the street.

As he watched the man drop to his knees, the twitching began. Luke tried to flex his hand to keep it from going to sleep, but the muscles fell limp. Heat raged in a line down to his fingers as if every nerve ending had caught fire under his skin.

Claire picked that moment to run out of her hiding place with the stick held high. She slammed it into the back of the other man's neck, knocking him face-first into the gravel.

"Claire, what are you—"

Grunting with a mania Luke guessed was fueled by adrenaline, she finally faced him. Her gaze zoomed in on his arm and her cheeks blanched even more.

"Are you okay?" Her question came out in a voice both breathy and uneven.

He had no idea what she was asking or why. "Fine."

"You've been shot."

"I...what?" Luke caught her around the waist to keep her from running. His head spun and his vision blurred, but he knew he had to hold on. No way was he losing her this time. Only thing was, she didn't struggle or try to break away. He couldn't figure out that part.

"Luke, stop moving around."

"You recognize that guy now?" Luke asked, forcing the words out over the sudden searing pain radiating through his shoulder.

She stared at the man lying at her feet with the bullet hole in his back. When she glanced back at Luke's face, her hand tightened on his forearm. "You have to sit down."

"Why?" With the noise at the end of the alley and police sirens blaring, Luke knew they had to move. "Doesn't matter. It's time to get out of here."

As the whirring screech from the approaching police cars grew louder, two men started down the alley. Luke guessed the body sprawled on the ground grabbed their attention. He couldn't blame them for wanting to check it out. Still, he had his fill of knuckleheads rushing in and trying to save Claire.

"Stay back." Luke tried to lift his hurt arm, but a new bolt of pain blinded him, forcing him to let it fall uselessly to his side. He finally looked down and saw the blood. "What the hell?"

"You can't feel that?"

The thumping increased. "I can now."

"You're injured." She ripped the bottom edge of her T-shirt and held it against his shoulder. "Badly."

The pressure of her palm knocked the breath out of him. He bit back the shout rumbling around in his throat and forced out the words he needed to say. "Adam, get here now."

Claire glanced around. "Who are you talking to?"

A white van appeared at the end of the alley a few seconds later. Adam got out, flashed his fake badge and started issuing orders.

"Our ride is here," Luke said through teeth tight with agony.

"Where are we going?" Claire shifted her attention from the commotion back to him.

"Out of here."

"Not to the police."

"Not yet." He vowed to get the real answers first.

It was about time Claire Samson learned there were consequences to her actions. He was the perfect person to teach her—as long as he didn't pass out first.

Chapter Two

A half hour later Claire heard Luke hiss as he shrugged out of his suit jacket and got the material caught on his watch. He sat on his kitchen table with his legs dangling and his dress shirt unbuttoned down to his stomach. The only blemish on his bare skin came from the dark red stain spreading across the white material.

Slumped shoulders and face drawn tight with pain, Luke looked ready to drop. Claire half hoped he would. If he fell over she could run. Well, she could if she somehow managed to knock out Luke's friend. Mr. Blond, Big and Ticked Off. Yeah, that guy looked ready to kill someone, namely her.

Both men had chests and shoulders broad enough to make football players jealous. Luke's light brown hair with bangs that brushed his eyebrows gave a boyish quality to his handsomeness. But in the two years since they were together he had changed. He now possessed a lethal air, making him more like his tough friend than the charming man she once thought would be her future.

Neither man gave off the upper-crust snootiness she expected from guys who supposedly spent their days locating precious works of art. She doubted Luke could tell a Chagall from a cartoon. The comfortable gunplay made her think his work was something more along the lines of law enforcement, but he lacked the clean-cut government-man look she associated with FBI agents. Now that she had experienced the great misfortune of being questioned by a few, she recognized the beast.

One thing was for sure. Luke, the man she followed from a distance and tracked to the office building—the same one who ran her down in the alley and kept a gun in his waistband—did not spend much time behind a desk. She'd bet her life on that. In fact, that's exactly what she was doing.

She needed Luke's help and cooperation, wanted to get him interested in her case and set him loose to find the truth. She just had the tiny problem of earning his trust first. With their history that was going to take some time, and probably some begging, which was not her strongest skill.

Luke focused on his friend. "You can get me the whiskey. The rest of the supplies are in the bathroom."

"You're thirsty?" she asked. "Now?"

Luke ignored her and kept talking to his friend or partner or whatever the other man was. "Then you've got to get back to the scene and help clean up the mess with the police."

The guy shot Claire a blank stare. "I'm not leaving you alone with her."

"My name is Claire."

The man made a face as if he'd tasted something sour. "I know who you are."

"Adam, meet Claire, and vice versa." Luke peeled off his shirt, gasping when the blood-soaked material caught on his skin. "The supplies? And now would be good."

Adam nodded, then headed down the hall.

The second they were alone Luke pinned her with the same green-eyed gaze that used to make her forget what she was saying.

"If you even try to move out of this room, I'll stop you," he said.

"You only have one good arm."

"I can do a lot with that."

Which was exactly why she hadn't yet made a run for the door. "I'm not leaving."

"That's not my experience," he muttered under his breath.

Adam stalked back into the room and dumped a small box on the table, along with gauze, some medicine, a knife and a bottle. "What are we looking at in terms of injuries here?"

Luke tried to lift his arm but groaned, instead. "It's a through and through. Not serious. Just bloody and stings like a son of a bitch."

She eyed the whiskey. "Which is cause for a celebratory drink?"

Both men stared at her but only Luke answered. "I'm going to use it to clean the wound."

She noticed his husky voice had cleared and his swaying had stopped. Still... "Shouldn't you be at a hospital? I mean, how bad is this?"

Luke picked up a bandage packet and put the edge between his teeth and ripped it open. "It's a gunshot, so it doesn't feel good. But unfortunately for you, I'm not going to die."

She forgot how dizzying his stubbornness could be. "You are if you don't stop with the attitude."

He peeked up at her through his mop of hair. "I'd like to remind you how I got shot."

That was an easy one. He refused to stick with the mental plan she had worked out for him. He might hate her, but his rescue tendencies hadn't dulled.

"Have we figured out who it was you two killed?" Adam asked.

Luke nodded in her direction. "Ask her."

They both stared at her, but she ignored it. Her mind wandered back to that alley. The acrid mix of blood and sweat filled her nose. For a second there Claire had forgotten this death was on her. She actually had killed a man this time. It was in self-defense and in an effort to save Luke, but someone was still dead.

She swallowed hard to keep from gagging on the

bile that rushed up the back of her throat. "He was following me. I don't know who he was."

"Your partner?" Luke crumpled the empty packet in his fist. "I'm betting you weren't really the victim out there today."

If she thought for one minute Luke intended to save her when she walked into that alley...yeah, not the case. He hunted her down for one reason only—to turn her over to the police. She could see it in the intensity of his eyes.

He had been in that building for a job of some sort. Hung out on every floor until the security cameras finally flared to life. She showed up hoping to get his attention, but she'd miscalculated. She expected he would catch a glimpse and get the bug to start digging into her story. She hadn't been prepared for a multifloor rundown that ended with a shoot-out.

The entire situation made her want to scream. Phil did this. He set her up, pretended to be dead and now had someone on her tail. Marrying him had been the worst decision of her life.

Adam spilled the alcohol on Luke's wound, earning an impressive string of yelled profanity in return.

Men. "You're going to kill him. Here, let me." She pushed Adam out of the way. Kind of felt good to surprise the guy with a shove.

Then she stepped between Luke's open legs, resting her thigh against his. The reality of being separated by only two thin pieces of material made her freeze in place. An accidental brush against him shouldn't mean anything. Certainly shouldn't send her stomach into flip-flop mode.

"What are you doing?" Luke asked.

"Helping." She sucked in a few deep breaths as she struggled for control. Even after all this time he had the power to shatter her into a thousand useless pieces.

Instead of dwelling on her weakness to a man so determined to forget her, she went to work. Grabbing the gauze out of his hand, she rubbed the swab over the jagged wound with infinite care. When his lips stayed pinched, she knew the whirling in her stomach only went one way.

Adam plunked down in the chair beside her. His gaze never left her hands. It was as if he expected her to injure Luke with a cotton ball.

"You have a problem with me?" she asked.

Adam's eyebrow lifted. "Other than the fact you killed your husband?"

Nothing like being found guilty without a trial. "Allegedly killed."

"Does it sound better to you when you make that distinction?"

"Answer this, Adam. Do you always judge people you don't know?"

Luke exhaled. "Maybe you two could spar another time. Like when I'm not bleeding to death."

"I see you've taken up exaggeration." She worked on Luke's arm, ignoring the pain that flashed in his eyes as she swiped the pad over his injury with delicate care. "Not a very attractive quality, by the way."

"Yeah, well, it's a hobby." Luke leaned over and tried to grab for something from the table. The move put his head right by her cheek and close enough for his breath to tickle her ear.

As soon as his hair brushed her skin, he sat up straight. Even grunted.

The quick move broke her trance. "What now?"

"Hand me the needle and tape." He barked out the order.

And she ignored it.

He sent her a wide-eyed surprised look. "I'm bleeding here."

"I'll get it." This time Adam did the shoving. Without any fanfare he crowded Claire to the side and away from Luke. Before Luke could argue, Adam started sewing. "You need anything else right now?"

"An explanation from Claire here would be good," Luke said.

She glanced at the syringe and bottles sitting on the table. "I was just thinking the same thing."

Luke's skin whitened as Adam worked. With each tug of the thread and poke through his skin, Luke's mouth stretched flatter into a thin line. His jaw tightened to the point of breaking.

"I'll take her to the police after this." Adam ignored Luke's squirming. "We should end this now and get back to work."

She decided to focus on the latter point. "And exactly what is your work? You were clearly looking for something in that building and it wasn't me. Wasn't a painting, either."

"Speaking of that." Adam put a hand on his hip and stared her down. "How did you know we'd be at that building?"

She'd stalked Luke, of course, but admitting that was out of the question. "I got lucky."

Adam snorted. "Right."

"Don't worry about Claire and her snooping. I've got this situation under control," Luke said.

Situation? She assumed that was his new pet name for her. Interesting how he couldn't use his arm and was six seconds away from passing out but still thought he was in charge. Only the Y chromosome could result in that kind of bent logic.

Luke inhaled. "Just call the office—"

"You mean your antique storefront or your real job…" She hesitated until she knew she had their joint attention. "Whatever that job actually is."

Luke scowled in her direction before turning back to Adam. "Go back to the scene," he said. "Claire and I are going to have a little talk."

She noticed Luke sounded more like police and less antique expert by the minute. "I'm fine, but thanks."

"Then?" Adam asked.

"I'll bring her in."

"Never going to happen." And she meant it. Injury

or not, she would knock Luke down, press against his wound. Do whatever it took to stay free.

The idea of sitting in a cell and depending on the services of a court-appointed defense attorney made her head spin with fear. She knew how the system worked—poor people lost. Despite everything she had done in the last two years to escape her past, she had somehow slipped back into a situation where she had nothing. The exact place she'd spent her entire adult life trying to avoid.

"One more thing." Luke used his good hand to cuff Adam's shoulder. "This all stays between us."

"How exactly do I explain the dead guy in the alley?"

Claire shook her head. Antiques experts. *Right.*

"You'll think of something. I just need a little time with Claire."

"How much?"

"Some. Might need a cover, too." When Adam started to argue, Luke stopped him. "This isn't up for debate."

Silence lingered while Adam just stood there. When he finally spoke again, he sounded anything but convinced. "You've got twenty-four hours."

Luke nodded. "Agreed."

"Not by me," she muttered.

"Just be careful." Adam grabbed his keys but not before shooting Claire one last warning glare.

She waited until the door closed to say anything. "I

get the distinct impression your friend doesn't like me."

"And here I thought you weren't good at reading people."

She picked up a damp towel and wiped the area around Luke's wound before taping a bandage over Adam's surprisingly professional stitching. The process took a few minutes. Rather than haggle and argue, she used the quiet to come up with a plan to leave Luke before Adam's twenty-four-hour deadline expired.

She saw the mess of ripped paper and blood-drenched pads on the table. "You've ignored this question so far, but care to tell me why a businessman keeps a syringe in his bathroom?"

He smiled in a way that was more warning than welcoming. "Why? Want to learn a new way to get rid of your next husband?"

"I see you've decided to be as much of a jerk as possible." She threw the towel on the table and plunked down in the chair Adam had abandoned.

"Some people like me," Luke said.

She didn't doubt that one bit. From creeping around and watching him for the past few weeks, she knew about his dating life. Women came over, stayed the night, and a new one showed up a few nights later. It was an endless parade of blondes and brunettes, each one looking easier than the one before her.

But that wasn't Claire's business. Her focus was on clearing her name. Like it or not, she needed help for that. When the whole town judged you guilty, you had to find someone who didn't. Luke didn't fit in that believer category yet, but she hoped he would.

"What's the plan now?" she asked.

"You tell me what happened to your husband."

She hated that word because it made Phil sound special, and he wasn't. "And then?"

"I'll decide that after I hear what you have to say."

"How is that fair?"

"Do you have a choice?"

She didn't.

Chapter Three

Four hours and two confusing explanations from Claire later, Luke was ready for a handful of painkillers and a bed. But thanks to his unwanted female sidekick, he didn't have the option of the sweet oblivion of sleep.

They stood at the double doors to his office suite. He positioned his body in front of Claire to block her as much as possible from the security cameras he knew were shooting them from all angles.

Following her gaze, he looked at the words stamped on the door: Recovery Project. On the outside, the fifth-floor office on a side street in the Georgetown area of Washington, D.C., housed an antiques salvage operation. In reality it served as headquarters for an off-the-books agency tasked with finding missing people, both those who wanted to hide and those who prayed for rescue. That's what he did for a living. He hunted people.

Since he didn't directly work for the government, he

didn't have to obey its stringent rules. The Recovery Project was the place the guys with the real badges came when they needed the dirty work done. Luke and his team worked outside the law. They flashed fake credentials or whatever else it took to get in the door and never asked for credit when they succeeded in reaching their goals. To Luke's way of thinking, they accomplished more in one day than most law-enforcement agencies could manage during a year-long sting operation.

Lights on the security panel flickered when he swiped his key card through the reader. The doors to the main reception area opened with a click. The place was in after-hours mode, dark except for one small lamp in the lobby area. Just as he expected—quiet and empty. It was about time something worked right today.

He had called seven times on the way over, trying the main number and then each private line to make sure they'd be alone. The idea was to protect Claire's secret for a few more hours. The gun tucked into his sling protected him from her. If she made a move in any direction he didn't like, he was ready.

Not that he could shoot her. Despite everything that happened between them before and everything bubbling under the surface now, physically hurting her was out of the question. But the desire for emotional revenge had not dulled since she'd left him holding a stack of bills for a wedding that never happened.

He had spent those first days dreaming of her coming back to him broken and despondent, begging his forgiveness for leaving. In his fantasy, he turned her away. He would listen, laugh in her face and walk off. That proved to be much harder in real life. Those chocolate-brown eyes and body born for the bedroom were enough to drive any sane man to do something really stupid. She had done it to him. Likely did it to most men unlucky enough to cross her path.

No, he couldn't push her out of his head. But he could threaten. Oh, boy, could he threaten.

"What is this place?" She walked up to the receptionist's desk and fingered the business cards piled there in individual holders.

He started to follow her and groaned when the swift shuffle to the side sent pain rippling down his injured arm. "My employer."

"Ready to tell me what you really do for a living?" She glanced around at the stark white walls that gleamed despite the relative darkness. "Seems sort of modern for a place that supposedly deals in antiques."

"We find them. We don't collect them."

"For some reason I doubt you do either of those things."

When she leaned against the counter, her hair caught the light. Mahogany replaced the rich brown color he remembered. He guessed the longer, darker look was part of her disguise. Little did she know, all the dye in the world couldn't cover her high cheekbones and smooth skin. Purple or green hair, he would know her anywhere.

"Let's move on to a conversation I actually care about. Your missing husband," Luke said.

"Former."

Luke refused to let that distinction matter.

"The divorce is final, but the financial settlement wasn't signed. That's the point of the murder, wasn't it?" When she ducked her head, he lowered his to meet her eyes. "Right? With Phil dead and the money issues not resolved, you would inherit. With Phil alive and the agreement signed, you got whatever the prenup and final paperwork said."

"I see you've been reading the newspaper again." She picked up a business card and tapped it end over end against the counter.

"You would have been a very rich widow." He watched the card twirl faster between her fingers. "You know, if you hadn't actually been caught in the act."

"I was set up."

"Tell me again why I'm supposed to believe that."

"We've been through this. I told you the entire story twice on the way over here."

He folded his hand over hers. The goal was to stop the annoying clicking of card against counter before his head exploded. At the touch, he felt a shot of a different kind. The feel of her soft hand beneath his brought back a flood of memories. Skin against skin, touching her, making love to her. He didn't even have to close his eyes to picture her sprawled naked across his white sheets.

When the image refused to leave his mind, he shook his head to knock it out. He also pulled back his hand, because touching her skin was just plain stupid.

"Let's go to my office," he said.

"This should be interesting."

That was just about the last word he'd use. But rather than debate, he slid his fingers under her elbow and steered her down the short hallway to his room. Letting her peek into an area so private made him nervous, but it was better to bring her here than drag her to his house. Here he would stay focused and he could make sure she only saw what he wanted her to see.

The conference rooms, computer rooms and most of the back half of the space were off-limits to visitors and anyone else who failed to get through the retinal scanner and other security measures in place there. That included Claire. Especially Claire.

He swiped his key card at the second door on the left and punched in his code. When the door unlocked, he gestured for her to move inside ahead of him.

The spare and minimalist look of the rest of the space continued in here. No dark heavy wood or oil paintings featuring somber sixteenth-century faces. He preferred clean lines, a comfortable leather chair and a desk sturdy enough to hold the stacks of documents piled on top of it.

Not that the papers contained anything of value. Everything on his desk was there for show. The actual work files sat secured in his hidden safe along with his removable computer hard drive and every other piece of confidential information from his cases. She would see what he wanted her to see and nothing else.

He waved at the black chair in front of his desk and took his seat behind it. With his computer switched on and his mind engaged, he was ready to hear her story one more time.

"Again," he said.

"You're going to type with one hand?"

Her reminder made his arm ache even more. Thanks to her presence, he had to skip the heavy-duty painkillers and go with antibiotics and aspirin for the injury. The combination wasn't working. Every nerve ending throbbed.

"I'll get by." He stared across the desk right into her dark eyes. In that moment he wondered if he really would survive a second round with her. Last time she won, but he vowed to be the victor this time.

IF HE WANTED to be some sort of martyr and plow ahead with questions when he should be in a hospital, Claire wasn't about to argue. She needed his help. If she tried to tell him how to provide it, his testosterone would kick in and she'd never get through this uneasy alliance.

"It was three weeks ago. Phil called and asked me to come to the house," she explained.

"Is that normal?"

"I don't understand the question."

Luke leaned back in his chair. Held on to his injured arm while he did it. "According to everything I've read, the divorce wasn't exactly amicable."

She had known the accusations would come eventually. Still, the idea that Luke so readily believed the absolute worst of her stung. "You mean because Phil told everyone who would listen that I was a whore."

"I was trying to be tactful."

"Why start now?"

"Fine." Luke tapped his fingers against the space bar on his keyboard. "He accused you of sleeping around."

"I didn't."

Luke hesitated before tapping again. "Okay."

"You believe me?" Something deep inside her chest tightened into a hard ball while waiting for the answer. It was as if every cell waited to see what he would say.

Instead, he waved his hand in a dismissive gesture. "It's not important. Not my business."

Yeah, well, it mattered to her. But she refused to justify or explain. If Luke was so determined to judge her guilty on that point, let him. She knew she had damaged his ego when she walked out. A man didn't forgive that sort of thing easily. But no matter how much he hated her, the important thing was that he believe in her story enough to help her.

"Why did you go to the house?" he asked.

"It was stupid." In hindsight, the dumbest move of her life, even less intelligent than her marriage. "Phil called and said he wanted to come to a reasonable financial resolution. Asked me to come over to talk. I should have questioned the change in him, but I was so relieved. And when I got there everything was wrong."

The scene unfolded in her mind. The dark first floor. Music playing in the background. The strong odor of cleaner. She had called Phil's name from the front door, but no one answered. When she heard a thump upstairs she figured he was moving stuff around and couldn't hear her. She followed the curving stairway to the second floor. There was a light on the landing and more spilling out of the master bedroom down the hall.

"I walked into our old bedroom. Something seemed off. My jewelry was on the bed, the same items Phil insisted I stole when I left the first time. He must have had them all along."

"Anything else? Was anyone there?"

The remembered smell filled her head. It was a mix of sickening sweetness and harsh cleanser. The same wave of dizziness that hit her that night flowed through her again.

She could hear the floor creak as Luke shifted around in his seat. She knew she was safe in his office, but she couldn't pull her mind from the memory.

"Just relax and tell me what you saw."

Luke moved his hand over hers. She didn't even realize she had twisted a business card in her palm until Luke slipped it out from between her fingers and put it on the desk.

As soon as the warmth of his skin came, it left again. His hand was back at his keyboard, but the touch had returned her to the present. She could finish the story. She *had* to finish.

"There was blood splattered on the walls and on the floor. I remember kneeling, looking around trying to figure out what I was seeing. Then I heard the sirens."

"The police."

"Yeah, but it still didn't sink in. Even seeing the cleaning bucket didn't compute."

"And that's where the police found you."

"On the floor by the bloodstain."

"They say you killed Phil and hid the body." Luke's hand hovered over the keys. "That they caught you cleaning up the scene."

"But they conveniently forget that Phil made a call from the house only a short time before that." She scoffed. "I mean, did he turn into smoke or something?"

Luke nodded. "Admittedly, the timeline is going to be the prosecution's weakness at trial."

"Gee, thanks for the vote of confidence. Maybe you should be on my defense team."

"Tell me what happened."

"Phil set me up with a brilliance I didn't know he had in him. He called his brother that night and claimed I broke in." The prosecutor depended on the delay in calls from Phil to Steve to the police to explain the problem. "The theory is that I killed a 190-pound man and hid the body within a fifteen-minute window."

The evidence didn't fit. The fact that everyone refused to see that made her seethe in frustration.

"I'm assuming you deny killing him." Luke said it more as a fact than a question.

"I can't kill someone who's not dead."

Luke began typing. Even with one hand, he moved fast. Images flipped by on his screen. She could see him trying to log in passwords as fast as possible. Probably feared she would somehow break into his system.

A Web site she recognized popped up. "Wait, you're with the FBI?"

He smiled. "Definitely not."

"But you just entered a password to get on their system."

"True."

Lines of information filled his screen. She leaned in closer to see.

He eyed her for a second. "Sit back."

"But that said something about Homeland Security."

"Yeah, I know."

"We're talking about my life here, Luke."

"This is confidential information." He said the words but didn't do anything to hide the monitor from her view.

"Then why do you have it, Mr. Antiques Expert?"

Another window opened. This one had the D.C.

Police logo on it. A few more strokes and Luke entered another password. The page that popped up looked like a bank statement.

"Other than violating about a thousand state and federal laws, what are you doing?" she asked.

"Checking for evidence that Phil is alive. Phone and bank records. Something that would support your theory about Phil setting this up to make it look like you killed him so he had cover to run."

"That's exactly what happened."

Luke's gaze did not leave the monitor. "So you keep saying."

"You don't work for the FBI."

"I already said no."

"Or the police."

"Still no."

Wariness spiraled through her. He had access to all sorts of information he shouldn't have access to. "Exactly what side do you work for?"

Luke stopped typing long enough to stare at her. "Do you really care?"

"Yes." She said the word but didn't mean it. Her question wasn't about following the rules. It was about trying to figure out who he was—the man he claimed to be or the one who carried a gun.

Luke hit a few more keys and then sat back in his chair. "There's nothing on Phil. No sign of life at all. He hasn't accessed any account or anything else in the three weeks since he disappeared."

"The man is a multimillionaire."

"I seem to remember you mentioning that when you left me for him."

She dug her fingernails into the arms of the chair to keep from shaking him. "Phil has money hidden all over the place.

"None of it's moving."

Luke didn't believe her. The fact hit her with enough force to push the breath out of her lungs on a *whoosh*. Desperation bubbled in her stomach. She had to move before it ran up her throat and she embarrassed herself.

She got up and paced the few feet between her chair and the open door to the office. A few steps and she could hit the hallway, run as fast as possible for the door and hope his injury slowed him down enough to let her get away.

"Don't even think about it." Luke issued the threat without moving an inch.

If he worried that she was about to make a break for it, he sure wasn't showing it. Open hand, relaxed shoulders, even a small smile playing on this mouth. Yeah, he was sure he had her under control. She saw it in every line of his body.

He was hiding more than his real profession. Behind the passwords and key cards there might not be an easy way out of what looked like an otherwise normal office. Still, she had to try.

She moved her foot closer to the hallway to test her theory. If the door slammed shut and locked her in, she'd deal with his anger then. It wasn't as if Luke trusted her, anyway. He probably expected her to bolt. Was waiting for it.

She inched the same foot outside the office. Her gaze stayed locked on Luke. He taunted her by leaning back further into his oversize leather chair. With one last deep breath she stepped out of the doorway. She turned her head to look down the hall.

A second later the barrel of a gun pressed hard against her forehead. She bit back a scream as she stared into the blue eyes of a stranger dressed all in black.

Adrenaline pumping, she raised her hands in surrender. "It's okay. I'm here with Luke."

The other man's smile never reached his eyes. "Luke who?"

Chapter Four

Blood thundered in Claire's ears. If her heart drummed any harder, it would come right out of her chest and land on the floor at her feet.

With Luke injured and her without a weapon, she tried to use reason to keep the big guy with the gun from firing straight into her forehead. "Listen to me. We can work this out."

"I doubt it." Black-haired and well over six feet, the guy radiated danger. His arm stayed straight and the gun never wavered. If ever there was a man ready to shoot first and talk later, it was him.

"You don't want to do this," she said, trying to stall for time as she mentally searched for a way out of this.

"I wouldn't be so sure about that."

At this range, there was no way the guy would miss unless he was cross-eyed, and she was just not that lucky. Not lately. If something didn't change, she'd die with the presumption of guilt tied around her neck.

And Luke, injured and vulnerable. She didn't want to think what would happen to him. Her only hope was for the meds to wear off and his brain to kick-start him into action. That even now he had his gun drawn and was working on a plan to free them.

"Phil's just using you." She didn't have any money, her ex saw to that, but maybe this guy didn't know the intricacies of her financial settlement. Only possible if he never watched the news or read a paper.

"Phil who?"

"I can beat his price. Whatever he's giving you to do this, I'll double it." A total lie, but she was desperate to keep the conversation going and the gun's trigger exactly where it was right now.

The guy pursed his lips as if considering the deal. "Interesting."

"Problem out there?" Luke asked from inside the room.

Her heart dropped at the sound of his deep voice. She closed her eyes in defeat. Maybe Luke really was an antiques dealer. Seemed a guy with a badge would be smart enough to understand the benefit of sneaking up on a situation like this rather than announcing his presence.

"Are you going to answer him?" the guy asked.

She thought she heard a touch of amusement in his voice, which made about as much sense as everything else that had happened in the past hour. "No."

"You should."

She took that as an order. "We have company." She shouted that obvious assessment to Luke. She wanted to tell him to bring his gun, but she was pretty sure that would tick off the guy who wanted to put a bullet through her brain.

After a bit of paper shuffling and chair squeaking, Luke appeared in the doorway. He stared down at the gun. Up at the guy. Didn't show an ounce of surprise.

"Ahhh, I see you weren't kidding."

Her hands balled into fists. "That's all you have to say?"

"No." Luke stepped into the hall and leaned against the wall. If the other man's presence worried him, he sure didn't show it. "I saw you two on the monitor."

"What monitor?" she asked.

Luke hitched his chin in the general vicinity of the gun. "Ease up. You're scaring her."

Oh, he was way past that point. "Lowering the weapon would help. I can't go anywhere, anyway."

The mystery man's shoulders relaxed. "I wouldn't let you."

"Looks like we have an agreement, then." Luke rubbed his shoulder. "Holden Price, this is the infamous Claire Samson."

"Wait, you know him?" Her heart flip-flopped at the thought. When she tried to turn her head to let Luke see just how angry she was, the gun scratched her skin. "Uh, could you call your friend off?"

Holden looked her up and down. "When I'm ready."

"Lower the weapon," Luke ordered, his voice suddenly stronger and harsher. "Now."

Holden hesitated before pulling the gun back closer to his side. "What's going on?"

"So that's a yes?" She looked back and forth between the men. What she really wanted to do was knock their heads together as payback for scaring the crap out of her. "You two do know each other."

"We both work here," Luke said.

"Now that we've cleared that up, why is she here?" Holden still held his gun at the ready. A fact that kept Claire on edge.

"We had an incident."

It was as if the testosterone had rushed to Luke's brain and swamped his common sense. She fought the urge to roll her eyes. "It's a little more than that. You were shot."

Luke shrugged on his good side. "Yeah, like I said, an incident."

"I know about the alley. I've already been there to make sure Adam has everything under control." Holden nodded in the direction of the sling. "You okay?"

Since Holden actually frowned, looking as if Luke's health mattered, Claire decided to let the gun threat slide. Luke might not understand how serious his injuries were, but from the way Holden's eyebrows snapped together she assumed he got it.

"Will be," Luke said.

The color had returned to his cheeks, but the dark

circles under his eyes just kept getting darker. She was convinced he'd drop over at some point. Probably right when she'd need him to show off those impressive shooting skills of his, because that was how her life worked at the moment.

"You should be at home resting," she pointed out. "It's not normal for most people to get shot. Not even for supposed art dealers."

"Antiques," Holden muttered.

"Only way I can take the night off is to turn you over to the police. That scenario interest you?" Luke actually smirked as he made the observation. The man knew when he had a conversation won. He knew and she knew.

But she wasn't ready to give up. "Not really."

"Why did you bring her to the office?" Holden asked.

When the barrel of Holden's gun finally pointed toward the floor, instead of at any part of her, she coughed out the breath she'd been holding. "I have a bigger question. What's with all the weapons?"

Luke's hand inched toward his gun as if she had reminded him. "We like to be prepared."

"In case you encounter a dangerous collectibles shop owner?"

Holden nodded. "Something like that."

Only a man bathed in darkness who grumbled more than he spoke could throw out a line like that and make it sound menacing. Without thinking, she shifted closer to Luke. Yeah, he hated her, but he'd had the chance to shoot her in the alley and passed it up. She wasn't convinced Holden would do the same.

"What are you doing here this late?" Luke asked.

"I was in the back when the phones started ringing. The way they went a desk at a time sounded suspicious to me. Thought I'd stick around to see if we had trouble." Holden stared at her. "And we do."

"I don't want to be here, either, if that helps," she said.

Luke talked right over her. "Was just trying to see who, if anyone, was here. I had to use the computer and couldn't exactly leave her waiting in the car."

"Makes sense." Holden's lips quirked in what Claire assumed was his version of a smile. "How'd you manage to trip the alarm?"

Luke went still. "What?"

"You forget to swipe the card or something?"

"No. Followed protocol exactly."

With a suddenness that shocked her, Holden straightened. Both men morphed from relaxed interplay to an on-guard stance in an instant. Holden's gun was raised as Luke started pushing buttons on his big square watch.

She knew enough to be worried. Wide-shouldered macho men didn't spook that easily. "What is it?"

"Quiet," Luke said in a voice that hovered just above a whisper.

With guns out, they surrounded her. She couldn't move or run. The closeness suffocated her as they walked her backward into Luke's office. "What's happening?"

"You have someone with you?" Luke took a position on one side of the doorway.

With his good arm, he pushed her behind him. Since the idea of dying in a shoot-out didn't exactly appeal to her, she stayed put. They'd talk about his tendency to shove her around another time. Right now, it worked for her. "No."

Luke stared at her.

"No, really," she said. "No partners. Nothing."

His facial features took on a nasty sharpness. "We're going to take this guy out, so tell me the truth."

She knew she'd be blamed for what was happening now, whatever that was. "I just did."

"Possible you were followed?" Holden asked from the other side of the doorway.

Luke's concentration switched between his watch and the hallway. "I don't see how."

"Maybe you're off your game." Holden stood on the other side of the open door. "The injury, meeting up with your old—"

"No."

Together they made up a wall of angry brooding male. Claire couldn't hear or see anything. Except for their breathy whispers, a deadly quiet filled the office. But she knew from the way Holden and Luke held their bodies so still that something or someone very bad lingered out there waiting for them.

The reality hit her. *Phil.* Again. He had access to endless resources and a deep hatred for her. Throwing the blame on her for his mess was one thing. Having someone track her every move was another. Years before, she had seen Phil as a safe alternative to Luke. Everything about Luke was shrouded in mystery. Phil had nothing to hide. She never dreamed he would turn into her biggest nightmare.

Luke motioned for her to stand with her back against the wall behind him. "You do everything we say when we say. Got it?"

She nodded, afraid to utter even a syllable and risk having her voice carry back to whoever was out there.

Holden stared at his watch. It matched Luke's perfectly. "He's in conference room two."

She grabbed the back of Luke's shirt and tugged to get his attention. "He who?"

"Whoever is trying to kill you."

"You believe me?"

"I believe someone wants you dead. The 'why' is a question for another time."

She rested her forehead against his back for the briefest of moments. "If we live."

Luke pressed a button on the side of his watch. From over his shoulder she could see the face. Instead of the time, a floor plan flashed in green lighting. She saw four red dots in the outlined rooms. Only one of them moved.

She pitched her voice as low as possible, which was

hard given the way her head buzzed with fear. "Is that him?"

"Last chance." Holden slid his gun along the door frame until the barrel was at eye level. "You know this guy or not?"

If either of them asked again, she might lunge for a gun. "No."

"Then you stay in here while I kill him," Holden said.

"Negative." Luke gave one shake of his head to match his clipped tone. "She doesn't move, but I want him alive. Need to know what's happening here and who's behind all this."

She knew. "I told you. It's Phil and he's—"

Luke ignored her. "The dot is moving."

And so were they. Holden and Luke slipped into the hallway. Back to back they moved, guns up and bodies snapped stiff with tension.

Claire glanced down the hall toward the reception area. Everything in her screamed to run down the dark path and out the front door. She'd figure out her next step once she hit the street. But she didn't know the office building well enough to know where the mystery man could go and how he could get there. She couldn't risk a bullet in the back.

Plus, the idea of leaving Luke while danger swirled around them made her stomach heave. She had dragged him into this mess. She would get them both out. She just needed access to information and a way to hunt Phil down. A weasel like him couldn't hide for long. Sacrifice was not his style. She just hoped her last stand wouldn't be in a fake office with her furious ex nearby.

When shots rang out behind her, she forgot about everything except hitting the floor.

LUKE BIT DOWN on his lower lip as he eased his arm out of the sling. Pain screamed up his shoulder and pounded above his eyes. Letting his muscles hang loose hurt more than he anticipated, but getting tangled up in the material was no way to fight.

Holden raised his eyebrows in question, but Luke waved him off. This was his fault. He'd brought Claire here into a sacred and private place and somehow dragged a stray behind them. He damn well knew better than to risk the agency's cover over a woman with a nonsense story. But it had always been that way with Claire. She walked in and his common sense skipped out.

The red dot moved along the inside wall of the conference room. In a few more steps, they'd be on opposite sides of three feet of shock-absorbing concrete. The construction of the office provided the advantage Luke needed. The barrier would stop a bullet, but their unwanted guest couldn't know that. That split second might give them the window they needed to get the jump on the guy.

Luke motioned for Holden to stop. As the red dot

drew closer, Luke counted down on his fingers. The small movements sent new rounds of thumping up and down his arm. The pain might have stopped him, but the adrenaline racing through his veins proved stronger.

When the red dot came even with Luke's position in the hall, he didn't wait. There would never be a better chance. His third finger rose just as he crashed the uninjured side of his body into the thick wall and shouted. The goal was to make as much noise as possible. His teeth rattled when the hard surface refused to give at all.

The reaction inside the room was instantaneous. The cracks of gunshots reverberated through the quiet office. The man tried to shoot his way through, to take Luke out without ever facing him. The gunfire rang out in wild bursts, the impacts causing the concrete against Luke's shoulder to shake. With each round Luke tensed, waiting for the impromptu blockade to fail. When the wall shuddered but held, Luke knew the first part of his plan had worked.

But that was just the start.

Luke hit the doorway to the conference room a second after Holden. With the visitor concentrating on the sound outside, he failed to guard the room's only access. Holden entered with his gun raised. The first shot hit the man's thigh and he went down shooting. Gunfire exploded around the room. Holden dove for cover behind the conference table. Luke ducked back into the hallway. He peeked around the corner in time to see the attacker skim his gun along the floor, as if he planned to hit Holden from underneath through the legs of the chairs and table.

"Holden, roll!" Luke yelled over the rhythmic beats of gunfire and male grunts.

Surprise flashed across the visitor's face at the sound of Luke's voice. On the ground on his back with blood seeping into the carpet, the attacker tried to shimmy to the side and out of Luke's sight.

Luke wasn't having any of it. He ducked down and got off a shot just as the man fired at Holden. The attacker's shot went wild. Luke's hit straight on, causing the other man's body to jump. It hit him in the stomach, which meant Luke had to move before the man lost too much blood to be of any use to anyone.

"Got him." Luke jumped over to the injured man's side and kicked the weapon out of grabbing range.

Luke need not have rushed. The attacker curled on his side, gasping and gurgling as blood rushed out of him. "I need help here," Luke said.

"Coming." Holden dropped his weapon and hit his knees beside the man. "Man, how bad?"

"Very."

The injured man groaned as his eyes turned glassy. Luke flipped him onto his back. The low keening moan coming out of his throat reminded Luke of a death rattle. Unless help got here soon, the man's last minutes would consist of a series of long painful moments of bleeding out. Luke refused to let that happen.

"We've got to get him stabilized," Holden said as he pulled back the material and inspected the jagged wound.

"I should have aimed for his hand."

"There was no time. I, for one, am grateful you didn't hesitate." Holden balled his jacket and pressed it against the man's stomach to stop the flow of blood. "I can do this. Make the call."

Luke exhaled, trying to calm the unspent energy revving inside him. "Right."

He hit the red button on the other side of his watch. The emergency call would go out and people would come running. They'd never used the office warning system, never had to, but he had no choice now. The man on the floor, whoever he was, needed medical assistance.

And they would all need to protect their cover. That meant calling their boss, Rod Lehman, and preparing him for the questioning that was about to come down on him from above. The real work of Recovery Project might be top secret, but that didn't mean they could hide two bodies and clean up an office bloodbath without someone at Homeland asking a few questions. Luke couldn't imagine the bureaucratic crap storm that was about to hit them. And all because of Claire.

"Is he dead?" Her stunned voice rose over the commotion of Holden and Luke trying to keep the dying man alive.

"Not yet." Luke saw her huge eyes and trembling

hands. He didn't need any more excitement or another chase. "Do not move from this room."

"I can't—"

Luke shot off the floor to stand in front of her. As gently as possible, he brushed a hand down her arm. "Listen to me." He waited until she tore her gaze away from the man on the floor and stared up at him, instead. "You are not safe alone."

"I know, but—"

"Get her out of here." Holden pressed down hard on the material as blood seeped out from underneath. "Neither of you can be here when everyone arrives."

"I don't have anywhere else to go."

Her soft voice spun through him, chipping away at the resistance he had built up against her over the past twenty-four months. "You're coming with me."

"It's not safe." She grabbed his sleeve. "I'm not safe to be around."

"We'll figure it out."

"Do whatever you're going to do now. You only have two minutes before the cars arrive." Holden's words rushed out between rough breaths.

"Sure you can handle this?" Luke asked.

"I'll take this guy." Holden glanced at Claire with a look most would describe as blank, but Luke knew to be one of festering anger. "You get her under control."

Sounded like an easy enough task, but Luke knew better. In the hours since they'd been reunited, he'd been shot at more than he had during an entire year in his current position. "We'll be at safe house two."

"Just watch your back."

Claire's mouth dropped open. "I wouldn't hurt him."

With their history, Luke found the comment pretty hollow. "I won't give you the chance." Not again.

"We don't know how many more are after her," Holden explained.

Maybe not, but Luke now doubted everything he knew about Phil Samson's supposed kidnapping and death. If someone really did murder the man, the least he could do was have the courtesy to stay dead and stop sending armed men after Claire. But that wasn't happening. Someone was gunning for her. Luke would bet it all led back to Phil.

The man ruined Luke's life once, looked like he was trying to do it again. Money or not, Luke had no intention of losing this round.

Chapter Five

It took two hours for Claire to stop shaking. She stood at the kitchen sink and stared at her open hand. Her fingers trembled under the stream of cool water.

Luke stepped up beside her. He leaned his backside against the counter and faced her. "You okay?"

"No."

He glanced around the room. "I know the place is a bit less than what you're used to."

"Do you really think my problem is with the decor?"

"I gave up trying to understand you and what you thought a long time ago."

At first she thought he was itching for a fight. Then she really looked at him. Exhaustion pulled at his cheeks and mouth. From his eyes to his shoulders, everything drooped. "What about you?"

"I dunno. What about me?"

"You look ready to fall over."

"Apparently getting shot wreaks havoc with my stamina." He folded his arms over his chest.

"Was this your first time?"

He leaned in closer and whispered, "Are you fishing for information?"

She was desperate to gain some control over her situation. If all she could manage was an honest conversation about who and what Luke was, that was fine with her. "Yes."

"I'll pass."

So much for getting a little peace. "Either way, you should rest."

"Not going to happen."

She couldn't decide if he wanted to protect her or handcuff her. One thing was for certain, her hours of running and being scared witless convinced her the safest place to be was right by Luke's side. Injured or not, he was determined to find out what was happening to her. That gave them a united purpose. She could go and hide out on her own, but together they might meet their goal faster.

"I'm not going anywhere." For the first time in a long time she said it and meant it.

"You'll understand if I don't exactly trust your word about sticking around."

She didn't have the emotional energy for this battle now. More important, she knew he wasn't ready to listen. He would never understand that he'd unconsciously pushed her away. Yeah, she had made some terrible choices. She hurt him when she didn't even know that was possible. Stability, honesty. He couldn't see it, but Luke refused to give her either when he hid whole parts of his life from her.

She grew up with the burden of dangerous secrets. In another time she would have been called a bastard. That was what happened when a father set up two families simultaneously without enough money to support either. Claire and her mother, the second and expendable family, suffered. He was absent, lying, and loving another woman and child more than he ever loved Claire and her mom. When his double life was exposed, he had to make a choice. He threw Claire away.

Yeah, she knew about the things people didn't say, knew that those never-spoken words could cut and destroy. She also knew what it was like to grow up poor and alone with everyone pointing and laughing. For her mother, cancer came as a welcome relief from the mocking. Claire learned a different lesson: rely only on yourself.

But rather than risk another argument, she switched topics. "Interesting house."

She had no idea where they were. Somewhere in Virginia, away from highways and the congestion of close-in D.C. Luke had driven for more than an hour, in the dark and fighting sleep as his eyes kept trying to close, until they pulled into a wooded area. No road. Just a gate that swung open upon command from his watch.

The one-story, one-bedroom house qualified more

as a cabin than an actual residence. It was clean and stocked with food, so she couldn't complain. A long kitchen anchored the open living room on one end. The bedroom sat off to the right. Claire knew from looking that the only choice of sleeping arrangements was a king-size bed. That and the couch, which she planned to use tonight no matter how much Luke whined about her decision.

The rustic atmosphere and heavy furniture reminded her of hunting and fishing. She didn't associate either activity with Luke. "What is this place?"

"Somewhere safe."

"I don't see any art."

He smiled. "You mean antiques."

"What I mean is that it's time for you to tell me what you really do for a living, and skip the art talk or I'll quiz you on it."

"Does it really matter?" He turned around and poured a cup of coffee.

"I think so."

"Isn't the point that I can protect you?"

He still didn't get it, didn't understand how secrets festered until they destroyed everything. She learned that the hard way years ago. "Maybe I don't want someone throwing himself in front of me every ten seconds."

"You would have preferred I let the guy in the conference room shoot you?"

"Of course not."

"Then you must be talking about your husband."

Everything circled around to that. No matter how hard she tried to steer the conversation somewhere else, Luke brought it back. "My ex, and I rarely talk about him."

"Because?"

"I don't have anything good to say."

"Almost two years of marriage and not one good moment?" Luke took a long sip of his coffee. "I find that hard to believe."

"It doesn't work that way."

"Since I dodged the marriage bullet, why don't you explain to me what happens."

"It's about how those moments string together. For me, they never did." She tipped her head, letting her hair fall back. "I didn't love him. He didn't love me. A quick end was inevitable. I just never expected death and disaster."

Luke watched every move she made with a face pulled tight in confusion and something that looked like pain. "Then why, Claire? Why him?"

No. They needed to discuss this, but not when bullets were flying and unknown men nipped at their heels. "This isn't the right time."

"I've got nothing but time."

"That makes one of us." When she tried to move away, he grabbed her arm. She stared down at his long fingers. "You've picked up a nasty habit of manhandling women."

He dropped his hand. "I don't know how else to get

your attention. You seem to spend most of your time running away from me."

"I'm here now."

"Why?"

"Because my ex-husband set me up."

"Not that." Luke shifted, inched closer, until his mouth hovered next to her cheek. "Why me? I'm not the only guy you know. Why show up in front of me, taunting me?"

Warm puffs of air brushed her skin. "I didn't know where else to go."

"Not good enough." The words sounded tough, but there was no heat behind them.

"I knew you were more than you claimed to be." She'd always known. His unwillingness to tell her was part of what broke them apart.

"Meaning?"

"I knew if you thought I was out there you'd follow me."

Their mouths nearly touched now. "I still don't get it."

"My thought was to lead you to Phil, prove he was alive and let you do the rest. You'd see that he was brought in, that my name was cleared."

Luke's head snapped back. "What makes you so sure of that?"

"Because while I never really knew you, I did understand you. You're one of the good guys. A rescuer at heart."

"I'm not sure the guy on the conference-room floor would agree with you."

"And whether you want to admit it or not, you're law enforcement and I needed a guy who could use a gun."

"So you wanted me for my weapon."

She laughed. Had to. "I'm not sure if there's some macho double meaning there, but yeah."

"That's good enough for now."

"There isn't anything else."

"That's where you're wrong, Claire. There's a lot between us. I don't like it any better than you do, but it's there beating with life and refusing to die."

"Luke, we shouldn't—"

"I know."

Then he was kissing her. Warm lips touched hers, sweeping and tasting until every muscle in her body turned to liquid. His fingers found the small of her back as one arm wrapped around her waist. His mouth slanted over hers again and again. The sensual assault hit her senses from every angle and seeped into every pore.

She wanted to forget all the fear and distrust, pain and betrayal. She wanted him. All he could give her and show her. A repeat of every second of sunshine they ever spent together.

"Yes," he whispered against her lips as his hand moved up to her cheek, then dived into her hair.

She fell into the kiss, returning his sure touches with her own. Hot breaths. Guttural moans. The memories of being with him came rushing back. Not that they had ever truly left. A woman didn't forget being overwhelmed by the joint pleasure of a man's mouth and hands.

Luke had that power over her.

Which was exactly why this moment had to stop. No matter how much her body begged for the familiar feel of him, this couldn't happen. Not now with the world upside down and so much left unsaid between them.

She turned her head to the side and fought for air. "Luke."

He took advantage of the angle, kissing a trail down her neck to the base of her throat. It would be so easy to throw her head back and let him lick and taste. Instead, she slipped her fingers into his hair and gave a gentle pull.

He broke off the kiss. With cloudy eyes and wet lips he stared at her. "What's wrong?"

"This. Us."

His chest rose and fell on hard breaths. He eased back, letting a few inches of air seep between them, but his hand didn't move from her body. "You're stopping?"

Everything she could see in his eyes—desire, confusion, a shocking sense of need—she felt deep inside. "We can't."

His brow knotted. "Because I got shot?"

She thought about using that excuse. "You seemed to be doing just fine with one hand."

"Then is it Phil?"

"It's because of *us*."

Luke dropped his arm until both hung lifeless by his sides. This time he did step back. He stood only a foot away, but his sudden coldness made it seem more like a mile. "Right."

"Luke, I just meant—"

He pointed at the other side of the room. "You take the bedroom."

The abrupt end left her reeling. "We need to talk about this. I want you to understand."

He rubbed his eyes. When he looked at her again, the sexual haze had disappeared. Back was the practical man who liked to bark orders. "We can either keep on doing what we're doing or we can go to bed. Separately. You don't get another option. Not after that lip action."

Her gaze traveled down his body. She could see his frustration in every line and muscle. The stiff shoulders and tight jaw, locked knees and an obvious erection pushing against his fly. Her abrupt halt left his body needing more. He was trying not to show it, not to let her know he felt anything, but the evidence was right there.

"I'm sorry," she whispered.

He dumped his coffee mug in the sink. "You say that a lot. Said it when you gave the ring back and walked away."

"You don't believe me?"

"As usual, Claire, I have no idea how to read you." He walked out of the kitchen area. "Be here when I get up tomorrow."

"Where else would I go?"

"I don't know, but next time I might disappoint you and not come, after all."

Chapter Six

Luke's arm still ached the next morning, but his body thrummed with a very different type of sensation. They stood outside the house Claire had once shared with Phil, and the only thing on Luke's mind was that burning kiss. Not the murder or her leaving. Just the kiss.

Two cold showers failed to knock the vision of Claire naked out of his head. Sure, things hadn't actually progressed that far, but they'd been well on the way. She'd put on the brakes and he respected that. But he didn't have to like it.

"I still don't understand why we're here." She paced the grass in the secluded area behind the three-story brick mansion.

"Nice place."

Her hands were in constant motion and her moves jerky and agitated. "Yeah, well, it's not my favorite."

"I think I saw this in a magazine once." To Luke it

looked like a private prep school only with more security and a chandelier hanging in the window. The eight-foot black iron fence circling the property didn't exactly welcome people to stop by. Luke couldn't see Claire, young and vibrant, locked away in there.

"It's part of The Samson Family Trust," she said.

"What the hell is that?"

"A corporation Phil started with his brother, Steve. They own commercial and residential properties all across the metro area."

"Sounds like a lucrative arrangement."

"I wouldn't know."

That comment caught Luke's attention. "I don't pretend to be an expert, but shouldn't a man own a house with his wife?"

"Phil thought otherwise."

"Isn't one of the benefits of marrying the rich dude that you get the big house and fancy cars?" Luke tugged on a section of gate to test its strength. Even with diminished strength from the shooting, he still had one good hand and could tell the thickness of the metal. Unless there was a weakness somewhere or a blowtorch, no way did anyone break through those bars.

"I guess he was too busy setting me up for a murder charge."

"Well, there is that." Luke scanned the windows and second-floor balcony. No way could he hoist his body up there in his current condition. They'd have to go in through a door like normal people. "I want to look at the crime scene."

"No."

Her emphatic denial made him smile. "Excuse me?"

"The evidence is gone. It's bagged and sitting in a locker somewhere just waiting for me to go to trial."

"Feeling dramatic this morning?"

She sighed. "I don't know a calm way to face jail time."

"You have a point." He walked around the back of the house and away from the street.

Not that traffic was an issue. The property sat on a secluded cul-de-sac in the exclusive suburb of McLean, Virginia. Country clubs and private schools littered the landscape. The yards stretched for acres and cost more than he'd earn in a lifetime of government work.

The area was home to dignitaries, congressmen, the CIA and Claire. No wonder she'd dumped him. It would be hard for anyone to say no to all this wealth and luxury. He lived in a two-bedroom condo off Capitol Hill small enough to fit into one of the property's four garages. Hardly competition for what Phil could give her.

It had always been that way. Luke, the son of an army colonel who picked up and moved his life every few years. Phil, the shiny millionaire who could buy her a house anywhere. Until he settled in with the Recovery Project and proposed to Claire, nothing had ever belonged to Luke. He lost the girl, but he saved the job he'd started around the same time. The job was the only thing that kept him sane when he saw her engagement notice in the paper less than a month after she dumped him.

Luke forced his mind back to the work. He studied the ground, looking for obvious signs of breach. He heard the rustling behind him and then she appeared by his side.

"You could reassure me by telling me I'll never be convicted," she said in a dry tone.

"I need to see inside the house first."

"What are you looking for?"

"I'll know it when I find it."

"That's kind of trite."

He stopped. Without thinking he rubbed his bicep through his thin sweater. The sling was back at the safe house, but the nerves still burned.

"You came looking for me, not vice versa, remember?" he asked.

Her eyes closed on what looked suspiciously like a wave of pain. When she opened them again, the usual sparkle had dimmed. "I know."

Luke's instincts kicked in. She was saying something but not using any words to do it. "What?"

"Nothing."

"Are you trying to tell me something?"

"Yeah. I don't have the security codes anymore."

Luke wasn't sure what had just happened, but he sensed he'd dodged some big emotional scene. He exhaled long and hard. "No worries. I have this." He held up a security card.

"The key to your office?"

"A little 'get in free' insurance."

When they reached the back gate, Luke slid the card into place, then hooked a cable from one end of it to his watch. Numbers and letters flashed on the small screen.

Her toe began to tap against the thick grass. "Still insisting you don't work for the FBI?"

"The FBI doesn't have anything this cool." The lock clicked as the gate opened. "And we're in."

"Won't the police be here?"

"Adam's been watching the place. No one is here but us." Luke checked and double-checked before dragging Claire with him. "Which is why we picked daytime. Don't have to worry about turning on lights and tipping off a neighbor, though I now get that someone would need a telescope to see in here."

"There are cameras everywhere inside and outside."

"They still on?"

She glanced at the brick patio just inside the gate but didn't move closer. "How would I know?"

"You did live here once, right?"

"Phil's brother Steve moved me out the same night I was at the police station being interrogated for seven hours."

"Why didn't they arrest you then?"

"Not enough evidence. They were waiting for the forensics to come back."

"So you ran."

"Wouldn't you?"

"I wouldn't have married Phil in the first place." Luke took the first steps. He walked across the patio toward the set of French doors. When he realized he was alone, he glanced over his shoulder. "You coming?"

"Depends. Are you ready to stop with the digs about Phil?"

"Not quite yet." When she made that face, the one that telegraphed an I'm-about-to-explode urgency, Luke changed tactics. "I need you with me in there."

"It's not easy to walk back in there after all that's happened. After my last trip here."

Ah, there it was. This was about the divorce and memories from the last time she walked through the place.

Luke thought about kicking his own ass over his insensitivity. "I'm not trying to torture you. I really do need someone with inside knowledge of this place. That's you."

She waved her hand in front of her. "Forget it. It doesn't matter."

"Yeah, it does. But nothing's going to happen to you in there. I won't let it."

CLAIRE BELIEVED HIM. And when Luke held out his hand, she didn't balk. She grabbed on and held tight. Walking through the rooms, seeing the bloodstain, knowing now that it was all fake, started a headache pounding in her temples.

But if this was what it took to get Luke to believe her story, then she'd do it. "Let's go."

"That's my girl."

They walked fast and low across the open outside area, around the pool and barbecue pit. When they hit the back door, Luke repeated his covert operative skills. Two seconds later, she stepped into the family room of what was never really her house.

"You entered where that night?" he asked.

She dropped his hand and crossed the room, walking down the hall until they hit the marble two-story foyer.

Luke stared up at the winding staircase. "Damn, that's impressive."

It had all wowed her once. The intricate carvings and gentle slope of the curves. Now all she saw was another reminder of Phil's over-the-top spending on things that didn't matter.

She stood with her back against the double doors leading to the front yard. "I parked in the driveway and came in right here."

"And then you went up the stairs without poking around down here."

"Because I heard noises up there. Yes."

Luke jogged up a few steps and then turned around to face her. "I know this stinks, but I need you to come up with me."

"Why?"

He dropped his gun to his side.

She wasn't even sure when he drew it.

"First," he said, "I'm betting there's more than one bedroom up there, so I might need some guidance to pick the right one." When she started to talk, he raised his hand to cut her off. "And second, I need to see you at the scene."

"That sounds ghoulish."

"The theory is that you dragged a man almost twice your size down these stairs and out of this house—all without getting more than a few drops of blood on the marble, I might add—and then hid him in a place where the police and all their dogs and equipment couldn't find him."

She was afraid to hope, but some pressure was lifted from her chest. "Sounds ridiculous, doesn't it?"

"Looking at the size of this house, I'm thinking that it's impossible, but I want to be sure."

She closed her eyes and let a wave of relief crash over her. She didn't have anyone. All her supposed friends had abandoned her, choosing to chase the money and side with Phil. Steve screamed at her, nearly inconsolable with grief. And her family was long gone. That left…no one to root for her.

"Thank you," she whispered.

"For what?"

"Believing."

He stared at her for an extra beat before nodding his head. "Upstairs."

THE NEXT HOUR moved in slow motion. The bloodstain still marked the carpet. Luke made her wait in the hallway while he walked around the former master suite. He said something about her leaving additional genetic material behind, which probably explained why gloves appeared out of his pocket.

Luke finally looked up. "We're done."

"What does that mean?"

"Unless you threw Phil out the window, and I'm thinking there would be a sign of that, I can't see how the timeline can work. The prosecutor must be hoping he has enough other evidence to overcome that flaw, or that science will provide an answer."

"I didn't do it."

He stripped off the gloves and shoved them in his back pocket. "Yeah, it looks that way. The press has pointed out the timeline problem. The prosecutor says there's an explanation but isn't sharing. I'm guessing the real answer is that they haven't come up with a reasonable story just yet."

She thought about throwing herself into his arms, but his watch started beeping. "What's that?"

"The alarm on my car." Luke joined her in the hallway and showed her his arm. "Recognize this guy?"

"You have a camera in your car?"

"Claire." Luke snapped his fingers. "Focus."

She shook her head to clear out everything and concentrate. A man with dark hair and dark clothes slipped around the side of the car. She couldn't make out his face, couldn't see what he was doing, but now it looked as if he was on his knees under the automobile.

"He's probably planting a tracking device." Luke swore to let her know what he thought about the idea.

"Who is it?"

"Someone who knows you're with me."

"Phil would hate that." The words slipped out before she could stop them.

Luke scoffed. "Why? He won you."

No, he didn't. Claire knew that as well as Phil did. "I'm not a prize to be fought over."

"Is that the point you're going with here? That I said something offensive? Seems to me my assessment was pretty accurate despite my choice of words."

"No." She exhaled, knowing this was the wrong thing to say, but she was going to do it, anyway. "Phil would hate to see me with you because he thought I never got over you."

Luke's eyebrows rose. "Paranoid guy."

"And smart, too."

Luke's eyes narrowed. "What are you saying?"

"Exactly what you think."

"Claire—"

She jumped ahead before he could dissect her words and drag them into a conversation neither of them wanted. "So what does it mean that someone else is sneaking around the house?"

He opened his mouth to say something, but then closed it again. It took another second for him to speak.

"We need another way out of here. They're watching the house."

"You think someone followed us here." The idea made the contents in her stomach roll. It seemed that Phil knew every move she made. The blow to her privacy left her feeling raw.

"I know they did." Luke pointed at the watch. The mystery man disappeared off screen as he headed toward the mansion. "I'm betting he has a key and he'll know which room to search first."

"There's a back staircase we can use."

Luke started shaking his head before she finished the suggestion. "No good. He could have a partner waiting there. We need something less obvious."

"I can't fly, so the windows are out."

"I was hoping a big place like this might have a few secret entrances, that sort of thing."

"If it does, Phil never shared them with me." She tensed when the security system chirped. "He's in."

"Where's the balcony?"

Her mind refused to function. "What?"

"The one I could see from the backyard. Where is it?"

The blueprints snapped into place in her mind. She walked as fast and as quietly as possible into the sitting room to the left of the bedroom. The balcony doors were against the back wall.

Luke didn't waste any time explaining his plan. He turned the lock. The sound of the soft click bounced off the walls. Claire couldn't remember the last time she heard a noise so loud.

As if reading her mind, Luke shook his head. "Imagination."

"Right."

He pushed his gun into her hand. "Know how to use this?"

The cold metal burned her fingers. "You need it."

"I have another. Here." He motioned for her to step out onto the balcony. "Anyone but me comes out here, you scream and shoot. Got it?"

Her pulse danced a crazy beat. "Luke, stay with me."

"Right now we have surprise on our side."

Before she could argue, he shut the door, leaving her alone outside. He stepped into the connecting closet.

And then they waited.

She tried to wait over to the side, just in case the sun cast a shadow in the glass. From her position she could watch the closet. Luke didn't peek out. Nothing moved. She couldn't hear anything but the knocking of her own heart.

Minutes ticked by with a dedicated slowness that made her itch to burst through the doors and run down the stairs to freedom. Every second of standing out there, exposed and hanging on to the railing, passed like a week. Just when she decided to give up and go inside to grab Luke, a floorboard creaked just on the other side of the wall from where she stood.

Her body switched into shut-down mode. Air didn't

flow. Her muscles froze. She stood as still as possible, trying not to breathe.

The outline of a male appeared in the window and close enough for her to see the sleeve of his coat. She had to bite down on her lower lip to keep from screaming in surprise. The gun in her hand started to shake. When her vision started to blur, she blinked to clear it again.

Just as the man turned toward her hiding place, a shout of fury cut through the room. Luke flew out of the closet and launched his body at the other man. Guns clattered to the floor. One spun across the hardwood and landed under the bed as the men fell to the floor. Legs and arms were everywhere, fighting and punching. The men rolled, stopping only when they slammed into the chest of drawers. Then they started the free-for-all again.

Claire stepped inside. "Luke!" She aimed her gun but couldn't get off a decent shot, not with her lack of skill. One wrong move and she could fire right into the back of Luke's head.

Luke yelled in pain when the other man pressed his thumb right into the gunshot wound. It was as if the guy knew where to push and how to inflict the most damage. Luke landed a punch to the man's throat and managed to shift away from the grinding grip. Luke pulled back, rising to his knees, his injured arm hanging from his side like it was no longer attached. Blood dripped from under his sweater and down the back of his hand.

Now that the man knew Luke's weakness, he went for it again. Through grunts and swearing, Luke lifted his knee and popped the man in the groin. The guy dropped on his side. As he writhed on the floor, Luke scrambled on his stomach a few feet away. He snatched his gun from under the edge of the bed just as the other man landed a punch to the back of Luke's knee.

Eyes bulging, Luke kicked out, catching the man across the jaw. The guy's head snapped back as his eyes rolled and his head hit the floor. The shouting gave way to dead silence. With his arms thrown out to the side and mouth hanging open, the guy didn't move.

Claire stood over him with the gun just to be sure. "Is he dead?"

Luke flopped back against the bed. He covered his injury with his hand as he breathed in heavy pants. "It amazes me how you say that as if it doesn't matter."

"He was trying to kill you." As far as she was concerned that meant the guy deserved whatever he got, even if it was an early grave.

"No kidding."

"Do we call the police?"

"Only if you want to be arrested." Luke struggled to his feet.

She rushed over to help him, sliding her shoulder under his armpit for balance. "That was impressive."

"He knew about the gunshot wound. Knew right where to take me. That means someone else was following the guy in the alley. We have a group working together, which is not good." After a few steps Luke stopped.

"We'll worry about that later."

"I'm pretty ticked off about it right now."

"You okay?"

"Will be." He shook off her assistance. After a few more deep breaths he stood up straight, wincing and grumbling with every move.

Claire refused to be offended. It was clear this show of machismo was more about proving to himself that he was fine than anything else. A guy like Luke needed to know he was in charge, so she let him have that moment.

She looked around for a rope or something to use as a tie in case the guy on the floor woke up swinging. Nothing. Someone had cleaned the place out except for the furniture on the floor and paintings on the wall. No knickknacks. No clothing, not even hers. Steve sure did erase her presence in a hurry.

"We've got to get out of here." Luke clicked a button on his watch.

"We're not going to bring him in? Question him?"

"No way to do that since I don't know what he did to my car and I can't exactly carry him to the bus stop."

She stared down at the guy. Other than a small lift of his chest, he didn't even twitch. "But what if he talks?"

"He won't. He's not supposed to be here, either, remember?" Luke crouched down and searched through the man's pockets. He held up a key. "This is all he has on him."

"Travels light."

She watched as Luke scooped up the man's gun with two fingers and dropped it on the bed. With a flick of his wrist, the pillow came out of its case and the gun went in.

"I'll call it in, have my guys try to round him up and tow my car just to be safe," Luke said. "Tell them to check the security tapes and erase them while they're at it so no one sees you."

"Thanks."

"We need to figure out why these guys keep coming, and if Phil is sending them, just where he's hiding."

"Think this one will say anything more than the guy who broke into your office did?"

"They'll crack eventually. Once they realize the help and money aren't coming, they'll turn. They just need time."

She wanted to ask if the office attacker had been arrested, but a tiny voice in her brain told her not to. Luke and his buddies didn't work through regular channels, which meant the men they captured weren't going to be sitting in jail cells waiting to meet with their court-appointed attorneys.

"And, Claire?"

Something about the lightness in Luke's voice had her glancing up at him. "Yeah?"

"I still don't work for the FBI."

Chapter Seven

"We've got trouble." Holden delivered his observation while pacing back and forth in front of the small refrigerator in the safe house.

"You mean more trouble." Luke sat propped up on the couch with an ice pack plastered to his wound. The thing thumped like a son of a bitch thanks to the unwanted wrestling at the mansion. The bleeding had finally tapered off, but not until Adam came over and did more stitching.

Holden grabbed a beer and then plunked on the couch by Luke's feet. "The forensics in Phil's case point to Claire."

"Not possible."

"You sure that's your head talking and not some other part of you?"

"I saw the house, the supposed murder scene. No way could she have managed what the prosecution says she did. I'm telling you that man walked out of there very much alive."

Holden stretched his arm across the back of the sofa. "You think she's being set up."

"There's no other story that makes sense."

Holden nodded. "I agree."

"Thank heaven for smart men." Claire walked into the room wearing the slim T-shirt and pajama pants Holden had delivered. She had scrubbed her face clean and pulled her hair up in a ponytail.

She managed to look both fresh and strong. The combination proved irresistible to Luke. Looking at her now, he wondered how he ever let her walk out on him. Why he didn't tamp down his ego and rush after her when she started talking about needing more than he could give.

"We figure things out eventually," Holden said.

"Not bad for art dealers."

"Antiques." Holden and Luke corrected her at the same time.

"The gadgets I saw today, those kicking and slicing moves?" She imitated the fighting as she spoke. "That ain't like any museum curator I've ever seen."

Luke knew she deserved an explanation. After everything they'd been through over the past day, she was entitled. "We find people for a living."

"Luke." Holden said his friend's name like a warning.

"She's watched me track down attackers and fight. She's not stupid." Luke had fought telling her everything for so long that he was surprised at how right it felt to just spill it. "We're not FBI. We're much better."

"But you're with the government."

"Sort of."

"I'm not sure how one is 'sort of' a government agent."

"When one works undercover at a place with few rules."

A huge smile burst across her lips. It was the kind of pure joy that could feed him forever.

"Now was that so hard to tell me?" she asked in a saucy tone.

"Yes," Holden mumbled. "And it's top secret, so not a word to anyone. You think the boneheads chasing you now are a problem? Imagine having me on your tail if you open your mouth."

She smiled over the threats. "I got it."

Holden plowed on. "You talk and we'll deny. We have an entire backstory that will refute anything you have to say. That is, if anyone can find you."

"That's enough." Luke figured his friend had made the point. Claire didn't look scared. If anything she looked excited at having been let in on the big secret.

Her reaction made him wish he could have told her back then. But he'd been new and had understood that the rules didn't bend. He didn't want to blow his assignment or get kicked out during the probationary period. Mostly, he'd thought she should accept his word and leave the rest. Now he wasn't so sure things were ever that absolute when it came to trust.

She sat on the floor in front of them and crossed her legs in the way only women can do. "Your secret is safe."

"You." Holden pointed at Luke. "Shut up before I use some of Adam's thread and sew your mouth closed."

Luke lifted his hands in mock surrender. "Yes, boss."

Claire's eyes grew wide. "Holden is in charge?"

"No."

"I should be," Holden said at the same time.

"So no one is talking, the rope around Claire's neck is tightening, and my real boss is tired of cleaning up bodies after me." Luke leaned back. "Does that sum up your message for today?"

"That and the fact someone is digging around in your financial and employment records," Holden said.

Claire's smile fell flat. "What?"

"Even broke into Luke's house and had a look around."

Luke wasn't happy with that news, but he wasn't surprised, either. Clearly whoever wanted Claire knew she was with him. It was only a matter of time before he became a target. "Anything missing in my condo?"

Holden tapped his beer bottle against his knee. "Not that I could see."

"Then it's no big deal. I don't keep work stuff there or anything that could trace back to the office." When Luke saw the rage boiling behind Claire's eyes, he rushed to soothe her. "We have all sorts of bells that go off when this sort of thing happens. If anything, it might give the computer experts in the office a way to track down the people at the top of this mess."

"And there's one more thing." Holden took a long swig of beer as if prolonging the anticipation. "Steve Samson, Phil's brother."

"What about him?" she asked.

"He wants to talk to Luke."

Claire looked appalled at the idea. The scrunched-up nose and flat mouth gave her away. "For God's sake, why?"

"He knows you two had a past relationship. He wants to know if Luke knows anything about where you are and where you might be going."

Luke saw the news as an opportunity. "Interesting."

"Don't you mean annoying?" Holden asked.

"It opens a door."

Claire looked back and forth between Luke and Holden, the frown on her face deepening by the second. "Can I have the non-spy translation of that sentence please?"

"While Steve is sizing me up, I can do the same to him."

Holden balanced his bottle against his leg. "You think he's involved in all of this?"

"If Phil is dead—"

"He's not," Claire said in a tone that suggested no one disagree with her.

"Humor me." Luke waited until Claire stopped fidgeting to continue. "If Phil is gone, then who would be the one person to benefit? I'm guessing that would be his brother, who is also business partner in several lucrative property corporations."

"Steve." She shook her head. "But we always got along."

"I don't remember him supporting you in the divorce or after the police showed up." And Luke knew because he followed the news with an obsession that scared the hell out of him. Even though she had walked out, even though he hated her, seeing her scared and shaken as the police dragged her in for questioning was a vision that Luke could never shake out of his head.

"That's different."

"Is it?" Luke asked.

Her shoulders slumped. "I hate the Samson family."

"That makes two of us."

IT TOOK ANOTHER two hours to kick Holden out of the house and get Claire to stop spouting off about everything she'd ever heard or known about Steve. She was trying to help, but once she got turned on to a subject, it proved near impossible to turn her off again.

With the lights out and his head balanced on the pillows on the couch, Luke was ready for the sweet oblivion of sleep. He had skipped the serious painkillers in favor of a second beer and an aspirin.

"Luke?" Claire's soft voice slid through the room.

He sat up fast enough to wrench his shoulder...again. He bit back a groan. "What's wrong?"

"I think you should take the bed."

He'd been thinking about the mattress and her on it for longer than he wanted to admit. "I'm fine," he said in a voice rubbed raw from wanting her.

"You're not."

"Nothing that a few hours of rest won't cure."

"I'd rather you skip the rest and share the bed with me."

In the darkness he couldn't see her face, couldn't read her motives. The only thing that was clear was the glow of the short white nightgown she now wore and the outline of her body underneath.

This sounded like an offer, but he'd been down that road with her before and didn't plan to take that turn again. "I'm comfortable here."

Which was a damn lie.

He heard the shuffle of bare feet against the floor. Then she was on her knees beside the couch. Her hair spilled off her shoulders and onto his bare shoulder. "I want you with me."

He shut his eyes and struggled for control. "Claire, I'm not really up for a night of cold showers."

"You aren't understanding me."

Every muscle in his body tensed. "I'm trying."

"Then listen."

"Just say what you want."

"Sleep with me." And she didn't mean sleep. This time the message got through. Probably had a lot to do with the way she pressed her palm against his stomach.

"Be sure."

"I am."

There were a thousand reasons to say no. He ignored every last one of them. "Then yes."

He tried to cool the churning inside him and not run into the other room to get started. Instead, he threw back the covers and sat up nice and slow, giving her plenty of time to change her mind and take off. That was her specialty, after all.

She stood up and held out her hand to him. "Ready?"

No. He wasn't sure he'd ever be ready for this. All those fantasies about pushing her away crumbled under the weight of his need and the brush of her fingers down his cheek.

"I'll be gentle with you," she whispered against the back of his hand right before she placed a kiss there.

He could hear the smile in her voice. He almost laughed at the thought. When they'd come together in the past, it was fiery and passionate, a wreck-the-bed-and-roll-on-the-floor type of thing. They'd acted as if every minute could be their last. Eventually it was.

He waited until they crossed the threshold to the bedroom to pull her into his arms and match his lips with hers. Over and over he pressed until the feel of her consumed him.

The kissing ignited something deep inside him. This part always felt so right. And those moments right before he entered her tortured him as much this time as they did before. The waiting and wanting, he could barely contain it.

She slid the straps of her nightgown off her shoulders and let the light material slip to the floor. Naked and ready, not an ounce of shame as she wound her arms around his neck and pulled him closer. Her bare breasts rubbed against his chest and he was lost. Only a flash of common sense saved him from being reckless.

"Wait," he said as he broke off the kiss. "Protection."

She nibbled on his neck. "On the bed."

"Holden brought condoms?"

"Apparently he's a *very* good friend." She pushed Luke down until his butt balanced on the edge of the mattress.

When she straddled his lap, he forgot about everything else. All his doubts and concerns slipped away. All that mattered was her.

His mouth moved over hers as their hands went exploring. His back hit the bed and he rolled them over, careful not to put any pressure on his weak shoulder.

"No." She shoved against his chest. "Let me."

The words refused to compute in his head. It wasn't until she turned him onto his back again and stripped off his boxer briefs that he understood. She would be in charge tonight. He wouldn't have to worry about his weak arm because she would guide them through.

A rip echoed through the quiet room and Luke knew what was next. Her hand covered him, putting on the protection and bringing him to a fullness that had his back arching off the comforter.

"Claire—"

"Now, Luke." Then she slid down over him.

His body shuddered when she started to move. The steady rhythm pounded through every part of him. Then she shifted positions and he lost the ability to breathe.

Chapter Eight

Claire stared at the laptop screen and waited for something interesting to happen. If someone had told her a month ago that she'd be sitting in a safe house watching Luke have a chat with her former brother-in-law, she would have found the nearest mental-health professional for a prescription pad.

"How did you manage to get a camera in the coffee shop?" she asked Holden. If he was going to stay stapled to her side while Luke was gone, the least the guy could do was answer a question or two.

"There are cameras everywhere. It's a simple matter of tapping into them."

"Adam?"

Holden flipped a chair around and sat down next to her. "It's his specialty."

"Adam has computers. Luke has guns. You're, what, head of sarcasm?"

"Tactics and strategy."

"Aren't those the same thing?"

"No."

She gave in to an eye roll. "Okay, but wouldn't it have made more sense to use your office downtown for this meeting, instead of some random Georgetown restaurant? You would have had more control. Seems to me you guys are all about control."

"It's been compromised."

She tapped her fingers against the table. "Because of me."

"Yes."

The plan seemed so simple a few days ago. Now everything was twisted. Luke got hurt and they ended up in bed. She had no idea how to pull back and reassess.

"Sorry," she murmured.

"You don't sound it."

She pointed at Luke's image. "I still don't understand what Luke hopes to accomplish with this meeting."

He sat slumped over a cup of coffee. The cell phone on the table beside him was actually a speaker so they could hear and record every word. So far, the men had only managed polite introductions. At this rate, she'd be on death row before Luke ate his muffin.

"Information." Holden said the word and then let it sit there.

"Are you just throwing out words, or is that supposed to mean something?"

"Steve's pretty sure you killed his baby brother. He's been all over the news calling for your arrest. It's not exactly a stretch to think that he's angry enough to send someone, or a bunch or someones, after you." Holden turned up the volume.

She figured he hoped to drown out her questions. Not like she was going to let that happen. "Phil is at the bottom of this."

"I know you think that."

"He's framing me."

Holden folded his arms over the top of his chair and leaned down. "See, that's the part I don't quite get. I know you've got Luke staking his reputation and job on this…"

The allegation rumbled through her. "That's not true."

"Sex will do that to a man, but I don't understand what *Phil* gains. It's easier to cut you a small slice and get rid of you through a nasty divorce, especially since he has the upper hand in public opinion."

"You sound like my lawyer."

"So why go through the big scene? Why walk away from everything?"

She had turned that question over in her head a thousand times, dissecting it and breaking down the facts. The logic of Phil's actions eluded her. If he wanted to prove he hated her, he did that when he filed the paperwork accusing her of infidelity, a charge he knew wasn't true.

"He must be hiding something." It was the only explanation that made sense.

"I combed through the financial records. I'm not an

expert and couldn't get very deep, but on the surface the company looks solid. Times are rough everywhere, but he's got some cash flow. Enough to pay the bills and keep everything afloat. Certainly shoveled a lot of money in his attorney's direction to get rid of you."

"Thanks for the reminder."

"So why dump it all? Why is setting you up so important?"

A loud thumping caught her attention. She realized the drumming of her fingers grew louder the more frustrated she became.

She flattened her palms against the table. "I don't know."

"Think, Claire. There's got to be something."

Holden's sharp tone surprised her. "You believe I'm holding out on you? I don't gain anything by doing that."

"You get Luke back."

"That's not what this is."

"I have eyes. I know you still want him."

Holden had been waiting to drop that little insight. She could tell by the way he froze as if waiting for a denial. Well, she wasn't going to let him think he won on that point. "This is about clearing my name."

Holden studied her as if he was memorizing her reaction and analyzing it in some internal computer. At last he nodded. "I hope for your sake that Luke can weasel something out of this little rodent."

"Or what?"

"Just hope he can."

Luke tried to hide his contempt for the forty-something, balding millionaire sitting across from him. Maybe if Steve hadn't driven up in a car that cost as much as Luke's condo, they could have found some common ground. But between the expensive business suit and general air of disgust for the chosen rendezvous spot as reflected in his sour look, Steve Samson made his position quite clear. He viewed himself as above it all. This was a task he had to perform. It was less about real concern than it was about familial duty.

Luke found Steve's oversize ego laughable. The man came off as the older, less attractive, less polished Samson brother. Extra pounds sat around his middle and disdain dripped off him. But the reality was simple. In a competition with Phil on style and public opinion, Steve lost.

In the ultimate insult, Phil was even blessed with a full head of hair and a chin that didn't dissolve into the rolls on his neck. It had to suck to be outshone so brightly.

"I know this is a sensitive topic." Steve used a napkin to wipe the crumbs off the table and onto the floor.

"How so?"

"You have a...history, shall we say, with Claire."

Luke glanced around the empty shop. No one would notice or complain if he punched Steve in the face. If the conversation kept going like this, that was a significant possibility.

"We were engaged."

"Yes, that's right." Steve leaned his elbows against the table before sitting up straight again and brushing off his sleeves.

"And she picked your brother over me. So?"

Saying the words made Luke bite the inside of his cheek. His job was to pretend to give a crap about what Steve had to say. To suck it up and play along. Still, talking about Claire with a family member who welcomed her, then discarded her made Luke want to flip the table over.

"In light of the circumstances I would think you'd be grateful."

"For?"

"Being left behind."

Luke hated this guy more with each passing second. "Interesting choice of words."

"My brother is dead. You could be, as well, if you had been Claire's true target." Steve made the statement with a detachment that left Luke cold.

Luke didn't have a sibling. He had never really known his mother. She'd skipped out of the military lifestyle long before he was old enough to become attached to her. But he had his dad. They moved and shuffled, but belonged to each other. When his dad died, Luke lost something. A piece of him broke off inside. Crumbled. Yet Steve sat there thinking his baby brother was gone and talking about it with all the emotion one would normally reserve for reading the sports page.

"Has Phil's death been confirmed?"

"There isn't another explanation." Steve touched the top of Luke's phone. "Why, if Claire has nothing to hide, is she running?"

Luke fought the urge to pull his cell out of reach. "Why are you asking me?"

"I thought it might be possible that you'd spoken with her." Steve's eyes gleamed.

The guy reminded Luke of a trapped animal. A feral one. "We didn't exactly break up on good terms."

"Of course, but I thought it conceivable that…" Steve shot Luke a man-to-man look, one that suggested a deeper familiarity than they would ever share. "Well, please understand that how you lead your private life is not my concern."

Luke felt the heat rise in his cheeks. "I think we can agree on that much."

"There was some suggestion that Claire might have continued to see you after she married my brother." Steve held up a hand. "I'm not judging. She is a beautiful woman. There's something about her that worms its way into a man's life before he can build a wall to keep her out."

"Ouch."

"Certainly you agree with my assessment of Claire, what with the way she discarded you. Unless, of course, the rumors are true and she never did."

Hearing this man say her name made Luke's hands ball into fists. "Who's been suggesting that?"

"That's not important."

"It is to me."

"My point is that after all of her maneuvering and lies, you might be of a mind to tell me where she is."

"Uh-huh."

"If so, I might be in a position to help you in return."

"You're talking money." Luke was surprised it took Steve this long to whip out the checkbook and compare balances.

"You strike me as a practical man, Luke Hathaway."

"True."

"And I am someone who appreciates information. I think we could make our objectives work together, don't you?"

Only if your objective has something to do with being punched in the face. "I'd think with all of your resources, Steve, you would have been able to track down one woman by now."

"She is well financed."

There was news. From what he could tell Claire didn't have enough cash to buy a pair of socks. "I thought she walked out of the marriage without anything."

"There is some information the public doesn't know."

A familiar rumbling started deep in Luke's gut. The sensation rose inside him whenever he hovered on those last few steps before gaining the information he needed. "Such as?"

"This is confidential, you understand."

Like he would ever share a confidence with this guy. "Understood."

"Money is missing."

"From?"

Steve glanced around and then leaned in as if sharing a trade secret. "This is the difficult part. You see, in addition to a family trust, Phil and I run a very successful commercial real-estate-development company. We're responsible for most of the new construction you see in the Maryland suburbs. We develop—"

Enough with the advertisement. "What does this have to do with Claire?"

"The company employs over four hundred people. People with pension funds that are now missing."

Luke had not seen that allegation coming. He didn't believe it one bit, but he gave Steve credit for dropping it at just the right moment. "You're saying Claire stole money out of office accounts without anyone knowing it?"

"Yes."

"Did she even work there?"

"She is a very enterprising young woman. Convinced Phil to discuss vital business facts with her, shared the paperwork. That sort of thing."

"And somehow she wrote a big business check to herself without anyone seeing?"

"She has those skills. I would venture to say if Phil had understood her background before they got married…" Steve sat back in his chair. Made quite a scene of pretending to be buddies, as he shook his head. "Well, let's just say it's unlikely we would be in this position."

"Her background?"

"Her father was a con man. Look how she caught Phil."

Luke wasn't sure what bits of information grew out of a truth, but he suspected the one about Claire's father did. "Why isn't the news about the theft all over the press?"

"We're holding back those pieces, hoping to flush Claire out. It is possible, at this point, that some of the money can be recovered. We need to tread carefully for the sake of our employees."

"And you think she's still in town?"

"I know she is. There have been sightings."

And shootings. In Luke's mind, the only thing missing at this point was a car chase. "Have you checked the house?"

"Phil is the owner of several properties. The only one that's open and not being watched is the family horse farm out in Loudon County."

"She doesn't strike me as the farm-girl type."

"Except for staff, no one else goes there. It's actually a fairly recent purchase. Phil bought it for Claire when they got married. As a surprise he had it remodeled, and that's only recently been completed."

"Claire owns a farmhouse."

Steve scoffed. "Well, no. The Samson family owns it. I doubt she could even find it. Once Phil suspected there was a problem in the marriage and with Claire's honesty, he took great pains to make sure she never knew of the property except as a business investment."

"So he bought her a house and then didn't tell her about it." Yeah, that made about as much sense as everything else Steve was saying. Luke just wondered how much more he had to hear.

"To my knowledge he never took Claire there or let it be known that it was to be her legacy. We quietly folded it into the business. You see, Phil didn't trust his wife."

"Obviously."

"Turns out he was right to be troubled."

"Sounds like it, but look, I can't help you. I cut my ties with her a long time ago."

"All I am asking is that you be aware. If she does come to you, please contact me." Steve reached into his jacket and pulled out a business card. He slid it across the table. "My deal is always open."

"Good to know."

HOLDEN CLEARED his throat. "You can let go of my arm now."

Claire eased her fingernails out of his skin. She didn't even know she had him in a death grip until he mentioned it. "I'm sorry."

"I could be wrong, but I think Steve doesn't like you."

She pushed the chair back, letting it squeak against the wood floor. "Because he accuses me of theft and low morals?"

"Yeah, that's about where I sensed the dislike."

"I had dinner with that man every week." She pointed at the empty screen. "He was decent to my face and...and..."

"I get it."

"Do you think he believes that garbage?"

"I think he trusts his brother."

She snorted. "So did I."

"Right now we have bigger problems." Holden tapped on the keys.

"What?"

"Someone, probably someone who took Steve up on his big money offer, is following Luke."

The laptop switched to a street scene. Claire could see Luke's dark sedan. When Holden split the image, she saw the second car. "What are we going to do?"

"Wait an extra half hour for Luke to get back while he loses the clown."

"But he—"

"Have a little faith, Claire."

That's the one thing of which she'd always had a very low supply. "I do."

Holden smiled. "Nah, not yet. But you'll learn."

Chapter Nine

The next morning Luke stood by his car and stared down at the map of Loudon County spread out on his hood. From Adam's digging through court records and corporate shell companies, they knew the top-secret Samson property sat a mile to the west.

Luke knew he wanted to get in there and poke around. Putting an end to this mess for Claire moved farther out of reach the more they worked. The evidence kept stacking up against her. Much more and it would fall right on top of her.

But that wasn't what ate at Luke on this cloudy fall morning. A day later and he still hadn't brushed off the stench of sitting at a table with Steve. The guy's words lingered. Not that Luke believed the garbage about Claire stealing pension funds. He didn't need Adam to trace that one. If money was missing, she was not the one to blame. He refused to believe her faults extended to embezzlement.

Besides that, the facts just didn't fit. If she had that kind of cash, counting into the millions, and really had no compunction about taking what wasn't hers, then she'd be gone. Her integrity wouldn't have forced her to stay. Sticking around for the sole purpose of driving him nuts and taking another tumble between the sheets didn't make any sense. No, Claire didn't take the money.

That left Phil or Steve. Luke hoped that something in this house would point to one of them. Finding Phil alive and kicking back by the fireplace would do it. With that information, Luke could go to the police and prosecutor. Until then, he had a bunch of theories and a bullet wound and little else to prove Claire's innocence.

"Why are you frowning?" Claire asked as she fought with the cool breeze to hold down the edge of the map.

"I still don't like this. You being here. It feels wrong."

"It's always nice to spend some quality time together. Happy to know you appreciate it."

"You know what I mean. This is dangerous."

"Too scary for the little lady?" She skimmed her fingers over the red circle outlining the acres the Samson family owned. "Get over the macho garbage. This was your plan, if you recall."

His temper flared to life, licking at the inside of his skull and begging to get out. "To come out here, yeah.

But my scenario had you back at the safe house listening to the radio—"

"Like that would happen."

"—while we carried out the surveillance."

She stared him down even though she had to lift her chin to do it. With hands on her hips and the skin of her cheeks pulled tight in anger, she treated him to a tsk-tsk sound.

"You know I'm right," he fired off before she could launch into whatever diatribe she was cooking in that head of hers.

"This is my life."

"And this is my team. Hell, we don't even know if we're at the right place." Luke looked at Holden for support. His friend of more than two years just shrugged.

So much for having his back.

Claire poked Luke's arm to get his attention. "Luke—"

"Easy. That's still sore."

"Steve is right. No one comes out here except the help. Look around you." She swept her hand out to the side, across the acres of crisp, green perfectly mowed grass and gentle hills. "It's the perfect place for Phil to hide."

"It's not exactly roughing it, either." Adam set his laptop down on the car and pointed at the photo of the front of the Samson manor home, then clicked through a series of other pictures. "This thing should be on a hill in Europe somewhere. There's an actual helicopter pad on the far end of the property. And what is that, like, ten thousand square feet under roof?"

To Luke it looked like five times that much. Beige stone reaching at least three stories high. There was an extra wing coming from the main house in a diagonal to the right and a row of garages to the left. He was surprised he didn't see a moat and a drawbridge.

If Phil was in there it could take a year and an entire police force to track him down. Luke knew he needed to shortcut that process.

"Have you tapped into the security feed?" Holden asked as he chugged the last of his coffee and squashed the cup in his fist.

"That's where this gets interesting." Adam clicked on a button and four images filled the screen. Four blocks, four big guys with even bigger guns.

"There a lot of crime out here?" Holden asked.

Claire made a clicking sound with her tongue. "He's in there. Leave it to Phil to live in greater luxury and with more security while in hiding than he did during his regular life."

Luke couldn't disagree because he knew she was right. Somewhere in that mass of firepower and maze of rooms sat Phil. Waiting, scheming, ready to pounce on Claire the minute he saw her.

Steve may not have figured it out, but Luke had. The minute the other man mentioned the house, a fissure of knowledge moved through Luke. Claire must have felt the same way, because she announced her discovery the second he'd walked into the safe house last night. They didn't talk about the other things Steve had said, only the house.

"I need to get in there and look around without getting my butt kicked or shot at. Again," he said.

Claire puffed out her chest. "I'll get you in."

Adam groaned as he turned away from the car.

Luke decided to make his dismissal of the idea even clearer. "That is never going to happen."

"I know the house plans. I know where Phil might be. You can't do this without me."

"Watch me."

"You said yourself the place is huge. I am the only hope we have to make it past the front door, with Adam's help on the alarms, of course."

"I thought you'd never been here before," Holden said.

About time his friend stood up and helped out. "Exactly. You have as much information as we do. None." Luke said.

"Steve was wrong about that." She folded the map. "You don't think my attorney found this house? Look at it. Even my budget lawyer could look through records. This house was on the table at the time we started working on our divorce settlement agreement."

"Your attorney has some good contacts, then, because this was not easy to track," Adam said.

"My point is that Steve didn't know everything his brother was up to. If he did, that pension money might still be in its account."

"All good arguments, but no." Luke plucked the map out of her fingers. "It's too dangerous."

"I am the one Phil wants."

"That position does not work in favor of your argument." Luke slipped a microphone into his ear and glanced at Adam. "You're going to have to steer me through."

Adam shook his head. "I'll try."

"Since when is that good enough?"

"We have a disadvantage." Adam flipped the top of his laptop closed.

"You mean another disadvantage," Holden said.

"Yeah. See, the house plans on file with the county are interim plans and they don't match the house I'm looking at. That whole right side is new. I can't find anything about the construction and what's in there now. I can rig something through the camera feed, but I can't guide you from room to room."

"Which is why I am going in," she said.

Luke didn't think the pounding in his head could get any louder, but it did. "Absolutely not."

Holden laid a hand on Luke's shoulder. "Luke, she's going."

"Thank you." If she smiled any wider her eyes would disappear.

"It's not a compliment. I just know that unless I tie you to the steering wheel, you're going after him." Holden threw Luke a pitying look. "So just accept it and get moving."

Luke felt the ground shift beneath him. "You can't keep one woman in her place?"

Holden glanced at Claire and then back again. "Not this one."

"Then it's settled." She snapped the map out of his fingers before he could stop her. "Do I get a weapon?"

"I'm already regretting this," Holden said.

Luke frowned. "That makes two of us."

CLAIRE CROUCHED DOWN behind a hedge cut into the shape of a diamond. A four-foot diamond. Yeah, because having a big ol' house didn't make a strong enough expression of wealth. The Samson family went one step further and cut the rows of greenery that divided the garden from the pool in the shape of symbols from a deck of cards.

She wondered how she survived almost two years with Phil. And how she lived through the same time without Luke.

He ducked down beside her. He scanned the area, his eyes constantly taking in the surroundings.

"What's that building?" He pointed to one of the many structures sitting in the back half of the property.

She had no idea what it was. She had never been here. Didn't even remember Phil mentioning the place. Kind of hard to believe he just forgot he owned a multimillion-dollar property in the middle of horse country.

"The pool house." Because of its location, she engaged in some deductive reasoning. But really, the answer didn't matter. Phil wasn't hanging around outside. He lurked somewhere behind the heavy draperies.

"Where do you think he is?"

"Phil?"

"Who else would I be talking about?"

She knew, but she was stalling, trying to come up with the most logical response. "I think he could be…"

Luke's face fell. "You have no idea, do you?"

"Of course I do. I was married to him." When Luke didn't move, she gave up. "Okay, no."

"All that stuff about your attorney?"

"That wasn't true. I only said all of that so that you'd stop arguing about me coming with you. But how exactly could my attorney miss a house like this when he went searching for Phil's assets?"

"The part about you knowing the house?"

"A complete lie."

"Steve was right. You didn't know it existed."

"Didn't have a clue."

Luke sighed heavily enough to part her hair. "What's with all the subterfuge?"

"You were going to leave me behind."

"I still might."

"It's too late."

"Is that why you're telling me the truth now? You think I can't have Holden come in here and get you?"

"I'm saying it because it matters now. It was irrelevant then."

Luke smacked his lips together. "That pretty much

sums up our entire relationship, doesn't it? You make whatever decision is best for you and screw me."

The abrupt turn in topic sent her stomach in free fall. "This probably isn't the right time for a 'what happened to us' discussion."

"I'm starting to think there's never going to be a right time."

"Then why did you bring it up?"

"I regret that I did." His gaze went to the speakers mounted around the outside area. "We know there are cameras out here somewhere because the Samsons love that sort of thing and the house plans we do have show a significant security operation downstairs. I'd bet they're hidden in those mountings."

As he droned on about wiring, something sharp and painful broke loose inside of her. The dam holding back all of the frustration and loss burst.

"You want to know why I left you?" The question was rhetorical because she sure as hell intended to tell him.

His eyes shifted to the side. "Uh, Claire…"

"I grew up with a man who hid the truth. He avoided questions and pushed my needs aside to focus on his own. When I woke up one morning and realized I was about to marry a man just like him—that's you—I panicked."

Luke's mouth dropped open. "Wait a second. You're comparing me to a con man?" Luke muttered under his breath.

She had suspected Luke wouldn't let that tidbit Steve delivered about her past slide by. She hadn't shared all that much with him about her parents. When Luke refused to open up, she returned the sentiment, closed off her emotions and prepared to leave. It took her longer than expected because despite it all, she loved him so much, but she knew she could not stay with a man just like her father.

"I didn't know, Luke. That's the point. You took a new job and started skulking around. You were out half the night."

He tapped on his ear. "We'll talk about this later."

"No, now. See, I didn't need to know every single detail about your past, but your present mattered."

"You were my present."

She refused to let that heartbreaking comment push her off task. "Do you know I followed you once? I was so sure you were cheating on me. I could close my eyes and smell perfume on your shirt."

"That's not true. I would never do that to you. To any woman. That is not who I am and you should have at least trusted me with that much." His harsh whisper carried the force of a punch.

"Don't you get it? I had no idea what you were capable of." When she realized how much her voice had risen, she swallowed and started again. "I didn't know you. You wouldn't let me in."

"Like how you didn't tell me about your dad?"

"I wanted to open up and tell you everything. I tried,

but you kept cutting me off. You were always running out the door for your new job, the fake one." She snorted. "I always knew the antiques thing was a front. But when I asked you about it, about your life before me, you brushed me off."

Luke's fingers clenched around the tree branches. "So you ran off and married the first rich guy you met. Or maybe we overlapped."

"That is not true."

"The timing was awfully close."

"Because I saw what I thought was a sure thing and grabbed it. I found someone safe and stable who didn't remind me of all of the insecurities that came with living with a man I didn't know."

Luke's jaw hardened. "Okay, let's calm down."

"I had been through enough secrets and lies with my father. Watched him walk out never knowing when or if he'd come back. Then it all repeated with you." The words poured out of her. She wanted to pull back, but they kept coming. "I didn't like everything about Phil, but I knew who he was."

Luke sputtered. "Clearly not."

The bubble of emotion inside her popped. "Yeah. That's where I screwed up. My radar misfired. I ended up with the exact man I was trying to avoid."

"Is that my fault, too?"

She wanted to say yes. A few months ago she would have. Now the blame exhausted her, sucked the energy right out of her soul.

"No."

A sudden calm washed over Luke. His features changed from sharp to flat. "You still think I'm a risk?"

She didn't. Not anymore. Not after watching him on the job, seeing him in protector mode. She knew the truth. He thrived on secrets but not the type that would destroy her. He was a good man, driven and sure. Leaving him had been the biggest mistake of her life. One she would pay for every lonely day until she died, which, if people kept shooting her, could be today.

"I think you're careful and guarded," she said.

"I don't know what that means."

"Ah, kids?" Holden's voice boomed in her right ear.

Claire's heart actually stuttered to a stop. "Oh, no."

Luke nodded. "Yeah."

She had forgotten all about the microphone and their audience back in the car at the end of the half-mile-long lane. Heat flashed over her entire body. If it was possible to blush from head to toe, she just did.

She glanced at Luke. When he threw her a half smile, she seriously considered throwing him in the bushes. "You could have warned me."

"In my defense, I tried," he said.

"When?"

"I pointed to the microphone in my ear."

"I thought you had an itch."

"This is interesting, really, but could we focus on clearing Claire of a murder that probably didn't happen before you two start throwing punches?" Holden didn't laugh, but she could tell by the lightness in his voice that he was fighting it off.

"Of course." She slugged Luke in his good shoulder. "Idiot."

"None of this would have happened if you hadn't married Phil," Luke shot back.

"I only did that because I was scared and you wouldn't tell me the truth."

Luke blew out a long breath. "Okay, look. I'm thinking Holden is right."

"Always," Holden said into the mic.

"Stop talking." She tried to clear her head of everything but the plan. Hunt down Phil and drag him into the precinct to clear her name. It sounded so simple. "Where next?"

Luke watched her for an extra second before getting back to work. "Adam?"

"I'm in the security system and can keep the screens on their end set to my picture long enough for you to slip in. Just let me know where and I'll set an infinite loop to give you the time you need."

"We want the easiest angle in." Luke's gaze went to a single door.

She followed his gaze. He managed to find the least impressive entrance. "Nothing fancy and no furniture in front of it."

"Probably means it leads to one of the least-used rooms, which is exactly what we need." Whatever Luke saw must have satisfied him because he brought the house blueprint up on his watch. "Adam, there's a door off a small patio on the far right."

A tapping sound filled the earphone. "It's a music room and it's clear."

Luke frowned at her. "Phil plays the piano?"

"I never saw it. Of course, I never saw this house, either, so what the heck do I know?" The fact that Phil hid all this from her didn't matter now, but it sure did tick her off. Nothing about Phil turned out to be real.

"How many exits once we're in?" Luke asked.

"Just two. Door to the patio and one to the hall."

"That will work." Luke scanned the open yard one last time. When he looked at her again a certain seriousness had washed over him. Gone was the confusion and arguing. "Stay down and follow me."

"You're in charge." She wasn't about to argue.

"About time you recognized that."

Chapter Ten

Luke smelled another setup. Getting around a wall of security, past the open space between the back patio and the house, and through a series of gates and locks should have been excruciating. He expected to dodge and hide, possibly fight off one or more of Samson's guards. Instead, they breezed through it all as if they'd been invited in the front door.

Alarms didn't blare. Cameras didn't shift to capture their movements. The back lock clicked open with very little pressure.

Too damn easy.

"What now?" Claire asked as she quietly shut the door behind her.

Luke stopped in the center and turned around in a full circle, hearing only the swoosh of his feet against the carpet. "Listen."

"I don't hear anything."

"Exactly. It's too quiet."

Except for the huge black piano sitting in the middle of the room, there wasn't much in there. A bunch of crystal bowls and figurines that only the rich would find interesting gleamed under a series of small lights. It all reeked of money, but none of it told a story about the people who lived there, except to say they spent money on useless junk.

"You think they left or we got it all wrong?"

"We weren't wrong."

"We seem to be alone in here."

The warning bell in his head tripped. "Where are the guards now, Adam?"

"Two out front by the entrance. That's about four miles from where you are right now, by the way."

"The other two?"

"One is on his way down the stairs. The other is in the kitchen. No one is near you. And from what I can tell, no one is manning the security station, either."

It all felt wrong.

"Holden? What do you think?" Luke asked.

"It's pretty relaxed at the moment. A good time to go in."

"I'm not so sure." Luke's voice didn't even rise to a whisper. He didn't want to raise the alarm prematurely.

"I went ahead and disabled the camera in your room just in case. You should be clear until you hit the hall. I can pick up again then. Just give me the signal," Adam said.

"I'm guessing we got lucky and the house is too big for them to hear one downstairs door open." Claire's voice filled with excitement as she spoke.

Luke didn't share her enthusiasm. He didn't believe in luck. Sometimes things worked out. Sometimes they were planned to happen. This smelled like the latter. "Maybe. Maybe not."

She stopped checking out the room and faced him. "What are you thinking?"

That they had walked right into the middle of a trap. Steve dropped a reference to this house, and Luke picked it up, thinking he'd found a piece of gold. He let the concerned-brother act fool him, even though it wasn't all that convincing.

"Talk about a con man."

"What?"

Luke pushed the coffee-shop memory from his mind. "Are you sure Phil never mentioned this place to you?"

She spread her arms. "I'd remember all this. Why?"

White-hot energy pumped through Luke. His body prepared for what his mind already sensed. "Something's very wrong."

Adam chuckled. "You always—"

His voice cut off.

Damn it. "Adam?"

Claire's eyebrows snapped together. "What's going on?"

The low buzz of static filled Luke's ear. "Adam. Check in."

"Why isn't he responding?" An edge of panic moved into her voice.

Luke let the anxiety spin until it fueled him. "Holden, you there?"

Nothing.

Claire tapped on her earpiece as if that would make the sound come out. "I can't hear them, either. What happened?"

Luke tried his cell but couldn't get a signal.

He peeked out the door to see if they had company. He knew that was inevitable now. "If I had to guess I'd say someone is jamming the signal. Trying to trap us in here without any eyes to the outside."

"That answers the question about whether we're alone."

"Exactly."

She gestured toward his wrist. "It's good we have your—"

Luke motioned for her to stop talking. He had downloaded the house's schematics, the only ones available, to his watch. Announcing that small advantage would steal any chance they might have to sneak up on someone.

He leaned down and whispered against her cheek, "Careful. Ears are everywhere."

Her gaze darted to the side. "Phil?"

Luke conducted a visual inspection of the room, looking for anything that might function as a secondary camera. Something Adam didn't know to scuttle.

"That's why we're here. Chasing your not-so-dead ex all over the metro area."

"But how would he know we were coming?"

That was the simple part. "Because he was expecting us. He let us come right to him."

"I don't understand."

Luke could see the adrenaline pumping through her in the way her body trembled and her weight kept shifting from foot to foot. She didn't panic. Not his Claire. But she did look ready to bolt.

If Phil walked in right then, she might have choked him. Luke probably would have let her. The manipulative bastard of an ex-husband just kept crawling out and screwing her. Now he added Luke to his list of enemies. Luke viewed that as the other man's biggest mistake.

"This is part of the setup, Claire. Phil lured you—us—out here."

"Why?" Her mouth twisted in confusion.

The last drop of doubt in her story evaporated. Luke felt guilty that any still remained. "I'm not sure."

"That's not very comforting."

"What I mean is, I'm not sure what he has to gain here. It's all part of the plan."

Luke didn't have time to soothe or explain. Phil had been a very bad boy. This went deeper than hating his ex. The embezzlement and team of protectors suggested that Phil had a much bigger crime in mind. Probably hoped to skip out with the pension money and hang all that on Claire, as well.

Luke's gaze moved over the room looking for the one thing that didn't fit. A bulky statue on the piano grabbed his attention. The few pieces of art in the room were made of fragile crystal. All sat perfectly arranged under individual lights on the built-in bookshelves. The clay form of some unknown man was twice the size of anything else and totally out of place. Looked cheap, too.

"Phil knows exactly where we are." Luke wanted to hit something. Despite all the careful planning, Phil had stayed a step or two ahead.

She stared up at the ceiling. "He can see us?"

"Not if I can help it." Luke grabbed the statue and rubbed his thumb over it, checking for a seam or any evidence that it was something other than a priceless piece of art.

"You pick this moment to show an interest in antiques?"

"It's junk."

"No offense, but despite what you claim, you're not really an expert in that sort of thing."

"Don't have to be. I know a cover when I see one." He turned the item over and slid the bottom plate back. "Here it is."

The opening led to wires and a switch. And there, in the base, was a tiny window. A camera.

An image of every step they made traveled through the house and landed on a screen planted in front of Phil. When Luke found the guy, he planned to shove the camera down his throat. Let him choke on it. Until then, it was time to shut the information highway down.

He didn't need both arms for this. With a tight grip and a wide arc, he cracked the statue against the shelves. A sharp *thwack* sounded the second before the wood splintered, sending chips flying. The fake head rolled to the floor as the rest of the casing crumbled in Luke's hand.

"That's my kind of fine art," Luke said.

"Did you cut yourself?"

"No." He dropped the pieces to the floor and crunched them under his foot. "And so much for eavesdropping."

"I thought we were being quiet."

"Why bother? Phil already knows we're here. He's waiting. Watching. The object is to give him something he doesn't expect. Now that his mirror into this room is gone, we have that chance."

"How?"

"I don't know yet, but we need to get out of this room."

"Outside?"

"Too open. I don't know where Phil's men are. We could walk right into an ambush. And if I know Adam, he's doing double time trying to get the feed back up. Until he does, the key is to stay out of the camera range and get moving before the goons come sniffing."

"Claire."

Luke jumped at the sound of the deep voice bouncing

off the walls. It echoed in the hall as if a loudspeaker blasted the message in every room.

"What the hell?" Luke asked the question of the room. He didn't expect an answer.

Claire had one. "That's Phil."

"He must be on some sort of intercom system. Guess that's one of those upgrades he made that's not on the plans anywhere."

"Does that mean he can still see us?"

"Since the sound's filling the whole house, I doubt it. If he knew we were still in here, we'd probably only hear it in here."

"Come into the entry and I will consider letting your boyfriend live," the faceless voice said.

Luke flashed Claire his harshest scowl. "If you move I'll…"

He trailed off when he realized he didn't have a believable threat ready.

She twisted her hands together hard enough to redden her skin. "Phil knows we're here. He has control over the guns and cameras. We don't have a choice."

"There's always another way. Besides, I'm armed."

"He could have Holden and Adam, for all we know."

Luke pushed that possibility out of his head. He could only handle one battle at a time and didn't need to invite more. "What are you suggesting?"

She pulled in tight to him, her feet planted between his, and held on to his forearms. Leaning in, she spoke in a voice so soft that only he could hear. "Let me."

This close he could smell the subtle hint of her shampoo and the fear that beat in her chest. "What?"

"I can go out there and talk to him."

The idea of that confrontation started a growl low in Luke's stomach. "The last time you tried to reason with this guy on his home turf you ended up as a murder suspect."

"He's not going to give up. Even if we do make it out of here, which I can't imagine, he'll hunt me down. He'll hunt you down."

"And we need to know why."

"Will it matter if we don't stop him? Luke, he's sent men to find us. He has men in the house to protect him now." The pleading in her dark eyes shouted louder than words.

"We've done fine so far." They had avoided and landed a few good shots. Even Luke wasn't sure how much longer that streak could last.

"Claire." Phil said her name in a singsongy voice. "It's time."

Her fingernails dug deeper into Luke's arms. He felt the pinch of pain but ignored it. She needed reassurance. If he could think of a way to fill her with hope, to pour it into her until the raw pain in her eyes disappeared, he would do it. But his mind went blank to anything but empty assurances. "We'll be okay. I promise."

"Don't you see? I can't let anything happen to you." Her tortured whisper battered his will.

"It won't."

"You don't know that."

"In case you haven't noticed, I can handle myself," he said, because he couldn't think of anything better to say.

She cupped his cheek in her palm as her eyes grew soft. "But I can't tolerate the idea of losing you."

The hard barrier around his heart eased up a fraction. "Claire—"

"I picked the wrong man last time. Let me do the right thing now."

Without touching her he could feel the determination radiating off her. There were so many things he wanted to say to her. He didn't even know what the right words were, but he wanted to stand there, staring into those eyes, as he fell for her all over again.

He settled for a harsh order. "There is no way you're going out there."

"Yes, I am. You are going to find Holden and Adam and get help. I'm going to stall for time. It's not a great plan, but it's the only plan."

Before he could protest she flattened both hands against his face and pulled him in closer for a world-shattering kiss. This time his hands slid up to her waist as the soft touch of her lips rocked him. His body shuddered from the impact as his eyes slipped closed.

His mind screamed to shut this down, but the rest of his body took charge. Heat flooded through him. In those precious moments, the seal, a promise, passed between them.

When her hands skimmed over his shoulders, he

knew she was about to break off the kiss, stop the mad mix of danger and longing.

She jabbed her finger into his still-healing wound.

The shock of the violation sent a shout of fury rushing through him as his mouth broke from hers. Before he could push her away, she jammed her finger in harder, driving him to his knees and starting a fresh flow of blood down his arm.

When she finally let go, his body heaved in relief. But he couldn't stay on his feet. He crumpled to the floor, every nerve ending pulsing as his head spun. Random thoughts and slivers of pain assaulted his brain. He tried to ask her why, but the air refused to fill his lungs.

"I had to do it."

Doubled over, holding his throbbing arm, he struggled to clear his vision and shift back to his knees. His mind grabbed for any explanation for her behavior.

"Why?"

She placed a quick kiss on the top of his head. "It's my turn to save you."

The enormity of her actions pounded into him with the force of a car. She'd subdued him, nearly knocked him out with a blow of debilitating pain, so she could sacrifice herself.

He tried to reach out to her, but his arm wouldn't move. "Don't do this."

Worry and regret filled her gaze. "I'm sorry."

"Not this way."

"There's no other."

She blew him a kiss…and was gone.

Chapter Eleven

The walk from the music room to the main hall was the longest of Claire's life. Her legs dragged against the expensive marble floor as if each foot weighed more than the house. The screams of rage and fear in her head threatened to overwhelm her, but she kept moving. She had left her heart broken on the floor behind her. She needed her brain with her now, especially when she was doing something so unbelievably stupid and dangerous.

A bright light bathed the area in front of her. The tall windows drew in the sunshine, filling the round entry with a yellow glow. All that stood between her and the massive double doors to the freedom outside was a place in the dead center of the tile pattern on the floor. That and the determination to deliver Luke out of this mess in one piece.

"Claire." Phil's voice rang through the house once more.

"I'm coming, you crazy son-of-a—" When the uneasy sense of being stared at pricked at her, she stopped. Standing at the edge of the table, she pivoted and looked up at the staircase winding to the second floor behind her.

Stared right into the cold eyes of a dead man. One that was very much alive. Unfortunately. Tanned and fit with the same welcoming smile that fooled everyone, including her, for years. He had the nerve to wear the casual polo shirt she'd bought for his last birthday.

His gaze traveled over her. "I expected you yesterday."

"I had hoped you were dead."

He tsk-tsked her. "Is that any way to talk to your husband?"

"Ex."

"You forced me into that. I was satisfied to keep living separate lives."

"You mean sleeping around."

"I was discreet."

She suspected that last part. Never had the proof, but now she knew. On top of everything else Phil cheated on her. Couldn't even keep his zipper up for their short marriage. There was just nothing sacred to this man. What he showed on the outside clashed so sharply with the lack of substance beneath.

"You were pathetic. Still are," she said, meaning every word.

"If you had stayed I would have let you follow your dream of being an artist. Isn't that what you really wanted to do, instead of working as a property manager? Turn your little drawings into something profitable?"

"Let me?" She was appalled that she ever gave this man control over her life. Disgusted with him and furious with herself.

Phil shrugged. "I was willing to indulge you."

"Lucky me."

"Let you be whatever it was you wanted to be before we got married, and you stopped trying to be anything important."

The harsh words rang true, but she shook them off. Had to. If her mind wandered to the place where she relived every missed opportunity, she would be lost. Worse, she would lose Luke.

Phil wrapped his hands around the railing. "In return, all you had to do was understand that I needed to run my life as I pleased."

"When you put it that way, I wonder why I left. That's sarcasm, in case you couldn't tell."

Phil cocked his head to the side and shot her a look of false sympathy. "We both know the reason you insisted on the divorce."

"Which was?"

"The man who brought you here." Phil looked around and then opened his arms. "Where is your boyfriend? Your Mr. Hathaway."

"Luke is gone."

"You expect me to believe he'd walk away from you after all the trouble he went to over the past few days to keep you alive?" Phil barked out a harsh laugh. "I don't think so."

"I forced him."

"I doubt that. In fact, you seem to have charmed him. That's really the only explanation for why he would risk everything to sleep with a felon."

"I haven't been charged with anything." Not that she could be since the man was alive. But the idea of killing him now sure appealed to her.

"You are free because I allow you to be so."

"You own the police now?"

"You never appreciated the extent of my power."

"And you never realized the limits of your appeal."

"You cannot win here. You actually made my plan easier when you ran." Phil leaned against the railing. "I have to say, I didn't expect that. You always seemed so…practical."

"I guess that shows that you never really knew me at all."

"I could say the same of you."

No kidding. "What do you want from me?"

"You're going to come up here and we're going to have a little talk."

"I'm not moving."

"Oh, you will. I assure you."

She'd once found his self-assurance a sign of

strength. Now she heard only the blowhard meanderings of a crazy person.

"I figure seeing you dragged up the stairs should bring your boyfriend out of hiding," Phil said, his voice low and menacing.

"I told you. He's gone." Part of her wanted Luke to flee to somewhere safe. Anywhere but this house on this day.

"We'll see." Phil glanced over her head and nodded.

Before she could duck or run, strong hands latched on to her upper arms. Instinct kicked in. She threw an elbow into the monster on her right as she tried to shift away from the one on her left. With feet moving, she struggled and thrashed.

The blow came out of nowhere. A sharp knock to the back of her head that caused her legs to collapse under her. Balance deserted her as gravity pressed her down. The men didn't try to hold her. The force of her knees hitting the floor cut off her breath. An agonizing burn radiated through the lower half of her body. She clamped down on the yelp, cutting it off before it could fully form into the traumatized scream rattling around inside her.

She didn't want Luke to come running or for Phil to enjoy her weakness. A few deep breaths helped her to wrestle back her control. When she finally worked up the strength to move her neck again, she saw the confident smile on Phil's face.

He motioned to his men. "Bring her up here."

THEY WERE GOING to kill her.

That thought ran through Luke's mind as he grabbed for the doorknob and pushed to his feet. While the blurring at the edge of his vision started to clear, the throbbing in his arm only increased.

To stem the bleeding he ripped the bottom of his shirt and tied the cloth around the juncture of his arm and shoulder. The tight band didn't do anything to stop the thumping, but at least he could move again without leaving a blood trail behind him.

He managed two steps before he heard Claire's strangled cry. The sound knocked the last of the dizziness out of his system. With his gun in his hand, he whipped around the corner, forcing his heartbeat to slow and his mind to concentrate. Running in at the wrong time could get Claire killed. He had to be smarter. Be patient.

He hit the entry just in time to see two goons pull Claire up the steps behind them. Luke flattened against the wall before they could notice him. But he saw her. The limp. The grimace when she put weight on her left leg. They'd hurt her. In the few minutes it took for his mind to clear, they'd hurt her.

It would take him even less to carry out his revenge for her pain. One bullet should do it.

When the bulky male figures disappeared out of sight and the beat of footsteps stopped, Luke took off. He crept across the entry to the front door. Looking up behind him, he saw nothing but an empty balcony. Luke vowed to find her. First he looked out front. No goons. The two with Claire were probably the two that Adam reported being together. That left two more unaccounted for.

With slow, sure steps he slipped to the bottom of the stairs. He eased his weight up one stair at a time, careful to keep his weight balanced and the chance of creaking to a minimum. With his injury acting up all over again, he leaned his sore side against the staircase railing as he went.

When he got to the top he prayed the action would be to his left. He had the floor plans, or a version of them, for all the rooms on the left. The right was new and a mystery. Getting around there without any intel or assistance from Adam could prove impossible.

Even now Luke hoped that whatever Adam had done to knock out the security cameras continued to work. Since no one showed up to shoot him or push him down the stairs, he held on to that hope.

The low grumble of voices grew louder the higher he climbed. With all the stone and hard surfaces, sound bounced around the cavernous place, hiding its true origin. He stopped, trying to get his bearings and pick out Claire's husky voice. But he couldn't make out the words, could barely tell who spoke.

The hard floor was carpeted on the second floor. The plush pile muffled the sound of his footsteps as he turned first to the right, then the left. From here he could tell that Phil held her on the right.

Advantage, Phil.

The man had planned for this, possibly from the first minute he met Claire. Maybe he recognized the vulnerability under all that sexy strength. It was one of the things that attracted Luke.

Not that he would admit to having anything in common with Phil. Luke refused to believe that. Where he loved Claire, Phil used her. Phil might have said the right things at the right time, but Luke meant them. He just hoped like hell that he had the opportunity to make her believe them this time.

He passed the first two doors, checking his watch for any indication of what was ahead. The internal GPS put him off the grid.

He was on his own.

Chapter Twelve

Claire sat in a chair with two thugs looming over her from behind and one guy staring at her head-on. She knew from a quick visual inventory that she was in some sort of library. Dark shelves filled with books she'd bet Phil never read. A huge mahogany desk and an even bigger red leather chair filled with Phil and his smug smile.

"So," he said, and then let the word just sit there.

No way was she engaging. She was too busy making a mental note of the exits and setting the furniture in the floor plan she'd created in her head.

Phil twisted a pen between his fingers. "Don't you want to know why you're here?"

When she didn't answer, Phil nodded to one of the men behind her. She braced for the shot she knew would come. Just as she inhaled, the man landed a repeat smack to the back of her head. The sudden shock of pain brought tears to her eyes. She grabbed the armrests, digging her nails deep into the soft leather, to keep from crying out.

Phil laughed. "Nicely done."

Her attacker grunted in response.

"Are you ready to talk now?" Phil asked.

Since she didn't know how many hits she could take before she gave in to a concussion or worse, she relented. "What do you want, Phil?"

"You."

The thought of letting him touch her again brought a rank taste to her mouth. "Never."

"Don't flatter yourself. You were good, attractive, but utterly forgettable."

He probably thought the comment meant something. That it would break her, but it just showed how little he knew. The insult struck her as a feeble attempt by a pathetic and desperate man.

"If I'm so unimportant, then why the big need to track me down? These morons are only the latest you've sent after me." She hitched her thumb at the men behind her. "You've got to be running low on henchmen willing to do your bidding."

"When you ran I had to improvise." Phil tapped one end of the pen against the desk blotter before returning to the frenzied flipping in his hand. "It gave me time to refine your role in my murder and the company's yet-to-be-discovered embezzlement."

"I can't believe you actually stole from the people who work for you."

"The money belongs to me."

"Are you insane?"

He flashed her a smile that hinted at malice more than madeness. "I assure you, no."

"It's their retirement security, not yours. You didn't earn any of it. They put their money in accounts for years. They trusted you to invest it and expected—"

He slammed the pen against the desk. "Spare me the lecture. It sounds hollow coming from a woman who climbed into my bed to get her hands on my checkbook."

She looked into his eyes and knew he believed it. That's how he saw her. Only, his opinion didn't matter.

"That is not true, Phil. It was never about getting my hands on your money."

"It wasn't a secret. I knew. My family knew. The people at the club saw through the outer shell of confidence you presented. Sure, you tried to adapt, but underneath you never stopped being the throwaway kid of a bigamist."

She should have guessed he had checked into her background, even though he'd never asked her or seemed to care. After being stung by Luke, she had welcomed the idea of not getting in too deep, of just living in the moment without a huge investment of emotion. Loving without limits had cost her everything. She'd learned that lesson the hard way.

But while she created a distance from Phil, it looked as if he had his own plan. If she guessed right, the entire marriage had been a setup for this moment. That meant finding a victim. She'd unwittingly played the role so well.

"Why did you marry me?" she asked, wanting to know for the first time.

"I thought you might prove useful."

The words slapped against her already bruised skin. She didn't care what he thought, because he'd ceased to be important soon after they walked down the aisle. But the idea that she sold her dreams and crushed her hopes of being with Luke because she was afraid, because her father's actions taught her not to trust or believe in love, made her stomach heave. She ran from her father's image and a man who was good for her to Phil, a man who wanted to destroy her.

Here she'd thought she'd spent her life fighting for control when, really, she let the men she knew determine the roads she traveled. The reality of her missteps pummeled her.

"That's funny because I thought the same thing about the Samson name. Might be useful, but I was wrong."

"If you were really looking for love and forever, why didn't you marry your salesman?"

"My what?"

"Isn't that what Luke does? He trades and sells antiques." Phil's face crumpled in mock shame. "Really, Claire. Did you think he could give you the money and prestige you so desperately craved?"

Claire almost laughed at how far from the truth that assessment of Luke proved to be. "You never said why I'm here."

"I need you to sign some papers."

The hit to the head must have scrambled something. She couldn't think of another explanation for what she thought she'd heard. *"What?"*

"The evidence against you is strong. I should know because I planted most of it, but since I don't want any do-gooder cop who's looking to make a name for himself seeing those big sad eyes of yours and deciding to dig deeper, it would help if your fingerprints were actually on the incriminating documents. Fingerprints and signatures. The e-mails have been planted. This is just something extra."

"You're crazy."

"I'm leaving town with twenty-eight million dollars in my offshore accounts and a pile of debt behind me. I can guarantee you that is the sign of being smart, not crazy."

"I'm not going to help you."

"Yes, you are."

A hand clamped down on the back of her neck and pushed her head forward. The position crushed her windpipe and had her gasping. With each breath the knocking at the back of her skull increased.

When the pressure eased, her head flew up but her brain kept rattling. "Phil—"

"These men are prepared to make the next hour of

your life very unpleasant. Your choice is simple. You can do what I tell you, and in return, you'll die quickly." Phil smiled. "As will your boyfriend. Or we can make it last."

Her throat grew thick and closed at the idea of anything happening to Luke. "I told you he's gone."

"I'll bet he's just a few steps away, waiting to jump in here and play the role of rescuer."

She hoped Phil was as wrong about that as he was about everything else. "What if he does?"

"He'll die fast, but you'll get the slow torture option."

Her mind raced with questions, ways to stall for time. Jumping out the window in a mangled heap would ruin Phil's plans but not bring her one step closer to saving Luke.

And where was he? She knew she'd inflicted damage. Saw it in the raw pain that flashed in his eyes as she put on the pressure and threw him to the floor.

But she knew Luke. Recognized the bone-deep stubborn streak that would keep him from giving up. Somehow he would find her.

"How are you going to pin all these crimes on me if I'm dead?" she asked.

"That part is taken care of." Phil tipped his head to the side. "So what will it be?"

"As far as I'm concerned I've done enough for you."

"Then torture it is." Phil's smile widened. "Perfect."

Chapter Thirteen

Luke wiped the sweat off his forehead with his arm as he stood on the balcony with his back pressed against the brick wall of the house. From two rooms down he could hear pieces of the conversation, mostly Phil's end, since he delivered every word as if he was standing on a stage. But Luke got the gist. Claire's time had just run out.

He slipped back into the bedroom. Picked up the phone on the nightstand, hoping this one would work where the two others he'd found in the house didn't. He had tried to dial and only got silence in return. They were as useless as the cell in his pocket. Phil had some sort of jamming device set up on the property. Luke recognized the technology. He was just surprised Phil had thought that far ahead.

Despite the numbness in his shoulder and the questions spinning in his head, Luke knew he had to move. He would only get one chance to surprise the two gun handlers in the room. Take them out and get Claire to the floor. Then he could go after Phil. No matter how many bullets pumped into him, he knew he could stay on his feet long enough to take Phil out.

Luke stepped closer to the open doorway. Heard the whack of a hand against a face, Claire's face, and checked his gun.

After a silent count of three, he flipped around the corner. "Claire, get down!"

With gun raised and firing, he hit Phil's men in the backs of their legs. Each dropped to the floor screaming like the wounded animals they were as he pumped additional rounds into them.

When the constant banging ended, Luke stood over Claire's curled form. He reached down to scoop her off the floor. Before he could touch her, she jumped off the carpet and slammed against his chest.

"You came." She repeated the mantra over and over again.

"You're okay," he said as he brushed his hand up and down her arm, as if searching for injuries.

Luke noticed Phil hadn't moved. But she was alive. For a few wrenching moments he feared she had gotten caught in the cross fire. Then he realized that neither of the other men had gotten off a shot. Even now, one lay still and the other squirmed and moaned, but the end would overtake him soon.

The jump of surprise had worked.

Luke used his foot to drag their weapons close. He

tried to wrap his arm around Claire, but he had no strength left in his ripped-up shoulder. He settled for bringing her in close to his side, tucking her head against his throat, while he trained his weapon on Phil.

The anxious jumping in Luke's chest slowed for the first time since he'd seen Claire across that lobby days ago. He smiled at Phil. "Surprise."

Luke strained to understand the mumbled words of apology Claire pressed against his neck, but he couldn't truly enjoy the moment. Not with Phil just sitting there. The man hadn't so much as shifted in his chair. He sat with hands folded in front of him and watched the horror scene unfold. He didn't rush for a weapon or the door, didn't even shout a warning to his men before Luke's fury was unleashed.

Phil finally tipped his head. "Very impressive for a salesman."

Claire squeezed Luke's waist with her arm. She continued to shake. "He thinks you peddle art."

"I don't care what he thinks." Luke nodded to the phone next to Phil's hand. "Pick it up."

"I would, but the line appears to be dead."

So calm. Phil didn't act like a man whose world had just collapsed. His breathing remained even and his movements fluid.

Made Luke think the other two of his men were close by. "Get up."

"I am fine where I am," Phil said.

"Just shoot him," Claire said, her voice gaining in

strength as she found her footing again. She stood up straight and stared at Phil with a look that promised pain and retribution.

In that moment Luke wanted the other man dead. Punished and destroyed. The temptation to put a bullet in Phil's head pulled at Luke. He had spent his professional life following the law. This one time, he wanted to break it. He had never craved another man's agony the way he craved for Phil's.

"I said, stand up," Luke said before he could fire that gun and fundamentally change who he was as a human being.

"Let's just grab him and get out of here." Claire made her plea from right behind him.

"I intend to." Luke took two more steps and stopped right in front of the desk.

Suddenly he heard footsteps behind him. He didn't sense the trap until it sprang. He turned around in time to see Steve pointing a gun at the back of Claire's head.

"Were you expecting me?" Steve asked as he kicked at the men littering the floor.

Claire jumped at the sound of her former brother-in-law's voice. She tried to move away, but Steve had her arm and the gun dug into her skin.

Luke bit back the string of profanity sitting on his tongue. He blinked and they swooped. For a second he let his desire for vengeance overtake his common sense. And Claire was going to pay the price.

Phil finally stood up. "Lower your gun or she dies."

Claire's eyes grew wide. "Luke, don't do it."

Luke shifted his gaze between the other men. Steve's hatred for Claire radiated off him in waves. He wanted her gone and he had the will to do it. The dangerous combination made rushing him a poor solution.

"Do it now, Mr. Hathaway," Steve said.

"Do not test me. Just hand it over." Phil extended his palm.

Luke knew the cardinal rule: never surrender your weapon. But the battle between heart and head was an easy one, thanks to the gun aimed at Claire.

Luke turned his gun around and handed it to Phil. "Here."

Claire gasped and reached out. "Luke, no!" She stopped when Steve shook her. The hard action made her head bounce as if barely attached to her body.

Luke took a step in her direction. "Let her go."

"You are not in charge here."

When Steve pressed the gun harder against her skull, Luke had to block the image from his mind. If he saw the dizzying pain in her eyes or heard her moan again, he would lose it. Snap so hard he'd never return to normal.

Instead, he decided to test the brotherhood bond. "So, which one of you is in charge?"

"Me." Steve motioned toward the desk and shoved Claire in its general direction. "Sign."

When her eyes met his, Luke nodded. She walked across the carpet with careful steps, putting more weight on her left than her right. She grabbed the pen Phil offered and signed where he pointed.

"This is never going to work, you know," Luke said, concentrating his attention on Phil, whom he considered the weaker of the two.

Steve answered. "Shut up."

"You have a lot of bodies piling up. You think people are going to believe Claire accomplished all that while the cops were on her tail?"

"That's why it was so convenient for her to run. Took away what otherwise would have been her security. Made it easy for us to continue to set her up."

The pages flipped as Claire signed whatever it was the Samson brothers found so important. "And when the police eventually find us?" she asked.

"We will be far away from here. Even if the police track the money and ignore the trail we planted to Claire's door, it won't matter. We will have everything we need."

"All this for money?" Luke asked, knowing the answer was yes.

She shrugged. "When a house falls, it falls."

"What does that mean?"

"The money is long gone," Steve said.

The pieces finally fit. The Samson family wealth was illusory. "You built your empire on the dollars of investors, but the underlying capital had been spent. Now that the cash flow has stopped, you don't have any money left to pay back the people you owe."

Phil folded his arms across his stomach. "You're quick for a salesman."

The enormity of the situation hit Luke. This was all about something as simple as stealing. People dead and Claire ruined all over money. "This is about a pyramid scheme? You guys committed fraud and don't want to serve any time."

"Do you blame us?" Phil asked.

Luke decided right then that he would never understand the thinking processes of rich people with overdeveloped senses of entitlement. "Why not sell this house or one of the twenty other houses you own?"

"We've taken out all the equity we can without tipping off the authorities. Well, according to the paperwork Claire is signing, she's the one who did it."

When she stopped, Phil shoved her to get her moving again.

"Claire will be held responsible, but we'll take the money with us." Steve brushed aside the curtain and stared out into the backyard. "It is up to the banks to figure out the rest. It will probably take years to sort through it all."

"You're just thieves." Luke could think of other names to call them, but settled on that one.

"You have yourself to blame. After all, you provided me with the perfect ending. All I had to do was mention this house and here you came." Steve shared a hearty laugh with his brother. "It was so easy. I could see the gears grind in your brain as you sat there pretending to drink your coffee."

"Why don't I show you something else I can do?" Luke asked.

"Stay where you are." Steve glanced at Claire, then Phil. "Is she done?"

Phil leaned down to scan the pages. Luke watched as Claire slid the pen down to her palm, grasping it like a weapon.

Good woman.

They had seconds only, but somehow she had figured out a way to squeeze them out of the dire situation. He balanced, ready to jump on Steve. The man looked comfortable with a gun, but that didn't mean he ever left the safety of his desk to shoot one. If his shot went wild, they stood a chance.

Claire looked around the room one more time before lifting her arm. With a *whoosh,* her hand slammed down on top of Phil's. The point of the pen entered the back of his hand. Phil's hysterical screams followed right after.

"What did you do?" Steve roared.

But Luke was already moving. He crashed into Steve using his injured side. There was no time for anything else. As Phil stalked around behind his desk, Luke fell on top of Steve. Their bodies hit the carpet before Luke could brace for the fall.

Despite his superior physical condition, the mix of the injury and awkward position gave Steve the extra second to step back and only endure a fraction of the knock heading his way. In a smart move Luke didn't know Steve had in him, he shook off his daze from the fall and kept moving.

Like everyone else, he went right for the bandage. A beefy hand clamped down on the blood-soaked area. Through gritted teeth, Luke struggled, only stopping when Phil yelled his name. The high-pitched snarl matched the rage in his eyes. Phil held Claire around the neck with the tip of the pen aimed directly at the artery pumping there.

Luke froze. "Don't hurt her."

"I am going to kill her and make you watch."

"It's okay." She repeated the words several times until Luke didn't know if she was convincing him or her.

"Phil, not yet. Putting a bullet in her now will ruin our plans." Due to the extra weight around his middle, Steve grabbed on to the chair to get off the floor. But he never relaxed his hold on the gun. If he had, Luke would have been all over him.

Luke sat on the floor with the dull roar of pain vibrating through every part of his body. He doubted he would ever feel the sweet freedom of a normal moment again.

But he got what he wanted. One of the guard's guns was tucked under his thigh. Hiding it would be the problem. Without a jacket and with Claire still in the direct line of fire, he had to be careful.

Steve pointed the gun at Luke's head. "You have five seconds to get up."

He palmed the weapon, rolling it under his shoe as he made a show of struggling to his feet.

"Luke, please…" Claire's voice trailed off as his head rose above the edge of the desk and into her line of vision. When her face turned milk white, he knew he looked bad.

But inside the fight remained. The left half of his upper body had turned soft and useless, but he had Claire on his side. Together they could get through this. Somehow.

"It's time to go." Steve frowned at Phil. "And clean up that mess."

Phil turned his hand and saw the blood dribbling to his wrist. His reaction was immediate. He tightened his hold on Claire's neck until she gagged and gasped for air.

"Stop!" Luke yelled the command.

When he made a move to follow it up with action, the barrel of Steve's gun pressed into his temple. "No one moves unless I say so," Steve said.

The more she fought and the harsher the guttural scratching in her throat became, the wider Phil smiled.

Steve finally ended his brother's show of unnecessary macho strength. "We have plans for her that do not include bleeding out in the library."

After one more tug, Phil let go. Claire's hand fell to the desk for balance as ragged coughs shook her body. After a deep inhale, she stood up.

Her gaze went right to Luke's. "I'm fine."

Phil laughed. "For now."

Chapter Fourteen

Phil used a tissue to grab the papers Claire had just signed. Touching the edges, he threw them into a briefcase, then marched her around the desk. As they met up with Luke on the other side, he grimaced.

She didn't think she had an ounce of emotion left in her, that it had all been drained away, leaving behind only aches and cuts. But seeing such a strong man brought down sent a new wave of sadness washing through her.

She rushed to Luke's side. "What is it?"

He grabbed his shoulder and bent over, moaning. Before she could comfort him, Phil delivered a blow to Luke's back. Luke fell to the carpet, sprawling on his stomach, and went still.

"Luke!" Seeing him crumple like that shredded what was left of her sanity. She bent down to help him back up.

He could not die like this.

Phil poked Luke's side with his shoe. "Get up, Hathaway."

"Stop it!" She threw out her hands and tried to put her body between them. "He's hurt."

Steve grabbed her by the elbow and lifted her to her feet. "He's going to be a dead puddle on the floor if he doesn't start moving."

Luke held up a hand. "I'm fine. I can do it."

He rose first to his knees and then the whole way up. When he cradled his shoulder across his stomach and blood oozed through his fingers, she knew he had taken too many blows. The constant pounding and loss of blood had made him woozy. She could see it in his staggering steps. His mouth stretched into a grim line as he tried not to wince.

She brushed her palm over his back as she swallowed a sob of regret. "Are you okay?"

"There will be plenty of time for the two of you to say goodbye later." Phil smiled at the comment, clearly proud he'd come up with it.

Claire ignored the Samson brothers. She had wiped them out of her life and now she would clear them from her mind. Her only concern was Luke. She stole a few sideways glances at him as Phil ushered them down a long hall with a gun at their backs.

She regretted every decision of the past week. Heck, of the past two years. She should have stayed and fought for Luke, for them. Having blown up everything good around her, she should have run and kept on running. Not involved Luke in her mess of a life. She had forced him to do this, to risk his life for her, by following his steps and reappearing in front of him long after he had moved on.

And now he would die. The crushing pain of that realization slowed her steps.

"I think you'll like the work we've done here," Phil said. "Added a few rooms, including a special one we've fixed up just for you two."

She blocked out the words and concentrated on sending Luke a silent message. She loved him. In the shadow of what once was, she had grown to love him even more. Gone was the fantasy of a perfect, quiet life. She now understood that Luke had offered her more—a lifetime of commitment and fidelity, love and protection. She had pushed it, and him, away.

Maybe he could no longer say the words or give her every piece of information she needed, but that didn't matter. She would cherish every precious moment she'd ever had with him. Hold them close until the very end.

"Stop." Steve positioned them in front of a locked door. He flicked open the keypad next to the door and punched in a code.

Only these two brothers would have private rooms in their huge private mansion. She tried to see over Steve's shoulder what required so much secrecy.

Phil pulled her back. "That's close enough."

When the wall monitor beeped, Steve shoved the

door open and gestured for them to walk inside. Not knowing what lingered over the threshold, she hesitated. But there was nothing all that special about this place except for what was missing. No windows. No chairs. Just a desk in the middle of the room, a safe and walls painted dark brown. It was the most depressing decor she'd ever seen, and it did not match the overstyled look of the rest of the house.

She glanced at Luke to see his reaction. He stayed huddled over his arm, as if he had lost touch with the horrors of their situation and slipped into a world only he understood. In a way she figured that might be a good thing, because she continued to live right here in reality, dreading every second.

"What is this place?" she asked as she maneuvered Luke to the table and let him lean against it. He needed to preserve what little energy he had left.

Steve stood right behind her, his breath right on top of her. "It was going to be a panic room of sorts. We didn't get a chance to finish it, but it will do for our purposes."

"Now it will be the place where you die." Phil leaned on the door looking satisfied with his plan.

She waited for the shots to come. Instead, the brothers stood there, staring at her.

"Don't you want to know how?" Phil asked.

"I'm sure I'll figure it out in a few seconds."

Steve tapped on the small computer screen just inside the door. "From here you can watch us walk down the hall. We're going to leave."

Phil nodded. "And you're going to stay."

She figured she missed the part where they shot her. "And?"

"We want the authorities to find your bodies intact. Otherwise, your boyfriend would be dead." Phil frowned. "Not that he's all that alive anymore, anyway."

She shifted her weight onto her sore leg. The throbbing started immediately, but she didn't move. She wanted to block any shot Phil might take at Luke.

"The police will find the evidence they need to figure out you died while planning your escape, and we'll be far away. Safe," Steve added.

Phil's smile turned feral. "With all the money."

They could not be dumb enough to leave her alive. She knew there had to be something else. Despite that, hope flickered inside her. If she could rouse Luke, they might be able to break down the door or crash through the wall.

As if he read her mind, Steve started shaking his head. "You will not be able to weasel out of here. It is not fully outfitted, but the room was built for security. And I assure you it is very secure."

"Unfortunately for you, it will function to keep you in, instead of keeping other people out," Phil said.

For guys who needed to leave, they sure were doing a lot of talking. But every second they stood there gave Luke another second to heal, so she didn't question it.

"Why would you even need a room like this?" she asked.

"You never know." Steve pointed his gun at the monitor again. "Just watch this and you'll see when you're about to die."

Phil took a step toward her. "Death will come racing down the hall in a few minutes. I want you to know it, breathe it in and be unable to escape it. Think of it as part of our divorce settlement."

"Not being married to you is gift enough."

"Now, don't be like that." Phil dropped his head to the side in that annoying way only he could do. "How about a farewell kiss?"

"If you come within a foot of me, I will bite you. And there's no telling where I'll aim."

Phil barked out a laugh. "If you had been that feisty during the marriage, I might have cut you in on the deal."

"I don't want anything to do with you."

Phil took another step. "So be it."

"Enough." Steve grabbed his brother by the arm and pulled him back. He nodded his head toward the door. "It's time."

After some silent message passed between them, both men backed out.

"Enjoy your final minutes with Mr. Hathaway," Steve said with a dramatic bow.

She heard their demented laughter as they shut the door, locking Luke and her tight inside. When she turned back to Luke, his head popped up and he smiled.

"Sounds like we need to move fast," he said in a

clear voice. "Not sure what this racing-death thing is all about, but I don't really want to find out."

Her stomach dropped heavy and hollow to her knees. "I thought you were so hurt that you couldn't move."

"All an act to get my hands on this." He held up a gun.

"Where did that come from?"

"One of the guards."

The confusion and fear bottled up inside her morphed into fury. "You mean you were fine the whole time?"

"I was pretending." His voice suggested she should just get over it. "I needed to buy time and grab a weapon. I figure those two would feel more manly and be less likely to attack again if they thought I was subdued. Also gave me time to get in position in the event I had to fire off a shot."

Luke made it sound so simple. She thought it was the exact opposite. "Well, genius, what if they had tried to shoot me?"

"Yeah, that's where I thought they were going."

She took one step, got close enough to smell his earthy scent, and then shoved with all her might against his uninjured shoulder. "You jerk!"

His chest absorbed her hit. "Hey!"

"What?"

He frowned at her and had the nerve to look offended. "What is wrong with you?"

"I thought you were…"

"Asleep?"

"Destroyed, Luke. I thought they'd broken you." The words tumbled out of her. "When you curled up on the floor, a piece of me dropped there with you. I didn't think you could function."

Instead of being reassured, he looked appalled. "Why would you think that?"

Clearly she had struck a blow against his manliness. While she was at it she decided to level one more verbal shot. "You all but wept like a baby in there."

"It's called acting."

"I could shoot you myself right now." She turned away from him because she didn't want to see his smug face. Not when tears pushed against her eyelids and her body trembled with relief.

"Claire." He wrapped his arm around her from behind. "I was ready to kill them both. I would have if they made one move in your direction."

She brushed her fingers over the back of his hand and settled into his warmth. Even through the red haze of her anger, being next to him filled her with comfort. In the middle of complete madness she experienced a second of calm.

But she wasn't ready to forgive. "Why didn't you use the gun and end this?"

"You were right in the middle. I refuse to risk your life even further. The chance of me getting two rounds off before they fired was not a sure thing." He kissed the side of her neck.

She tilted her head to the side to give him a better angle. "You had the advantage. You're in law enforcement. They're just two crooked businessmen."

"With a shooting range at the back of the property."

Her heart fell to her knees. "Oh, I missed that."

"I saw it when I was hanging off the balcony earlier. Either way, I still didn't like the odds."

"Why?" She glanced up at him and slumped in relief at seeing clear eyes gaze back at her.

"Because without the absolute guarantee that you'd be safe, I wasn't going there."

Her heart tripped and fell. Love. The nothing-else-matters kind. The sure sort of love that ignored small slights and reveled in being together. She loved him before, but this was so much more. She didn't need him to complete her. She needed him for life to make sense.

Right now she also needed him to get her out of there. "I don't mean to be negative, but we're stuck."

"Not really."

She broke out of his grasp and turned around to face him. "You plan to shoot our way out?"

"I plan to open this lock like I do every other lock." He held up his wrist and shook his watch at her.

"It can't be that easy."

"They should have smashed the monitor."

"They were pretty clear that there's something out there they want us to see."

Luke stalked over to the monitor and stared. "There's nothing out there." Then he started punching numbers.

"What are you doing?"

"Making sure it's not booby-trapped."

"Fabulous." She walked over to the safe and yanked on the door. It wouldn't budge. "Wonder what's in here."

"Probably whatever it is they think will implicate you."

"Then why have me sign all of those other papers?"

"Insurance." He slipped a small knife out of his waistband and started undoing the panel covering the keypad. "The idea was to leave a significant paper trail."

"How enterprising." She slouched down on top of the safe. "If Phil had put half this effort into his company, he wouldn't have had to steal from his employees."

"It doesn't work that way."

"Meaning?"

"The bad guys always go for the easy solution. Usually they can't handle the hard one."

She threw out her arms. "This was easy? They had this elaborate setup. They hired these men, so that means paying people. And this house is ridiculous."

Luke snorted. "Expendable."

"What?"

"Nothing." He set the panel on the floor. "They were buying time as they looted the funds."

For a guy she thought was near death just minutes ago, he sure did sound chipper. "What are you doing now?"

"Seeing if I can blow this thing."

"I thought you planned to use your watch."

"I don't know where the Samson boys are. If they're still downstairs, I don't want to tip them off. Not if I can just open this the usual way."

"Usual?"

"By figuring out the code." He poked around, then made a clicking sound with his tongue. "Forget it. We'll take the chance."

"Works for me. I just want out of here." Even with Phil and Steve gone, her stomach kept jumping with nerves. She couldn't settle the feeling of anxiety that moved through her and gained speed with every circle.

"Two seconds." He pulled a wire out of the side of his watch and connected it to the panel.

"We don't have that much time."

It was more like a minute, but his shoulders finally relaxed. "There."

The door clicked open.

Neither of them rushed into the hall. Heeding Steve's warning, they waited for something to rise up and attack. But nothing came.

Luke held up a finger. "Wait here."

"No." She slid off the safe and walked over to him. "We do this together."

"I don't know what's out there," he said in a whisper.

"I know what's in here and it's not freedom, so I'll take my chances so long as I'm going in the direction of an exit."

"Well said."

He leaned down and treated her to a quick, hard kiss. Just enough to get her wanting more.

She held on to his shirt, keeping him close for a few precious seconds. "Besides, I watched you collapse once. I will not wait around and then stumble over your body at the bottom of the stairs."

Something sparked to life in his green eyes. "Have some faith."

"In you? Completely."

He winked at her. "Then let's do this."

They got into the hall before she smelled it. She coughed when she tasted the acrid scent on her tongue. It was a mix of chemicals and hot metal.

Her gaze went to the soaring ceiling. Gray smoke hovered along the sloped walls. She was afraid to lean over the balcony to the floor below. "I think I know what Steve wanted us to see."

Luke nodded. "They set the house on fire."

Chapter Fifteen

Luke tried to figure out what else could go wrong. Short of killer bees, they'd survived everything. So far.

The flames licking up the banister could be the final shot. Bright orange filled the downstairs and began the slow walk up the stairs. There was no way through it. They'd have to go around it.

Claire covered her mouth with the back of her hand as a coughing fit overtook her. "I can't breathe."

And it was only going to get worse.

He covered his mouth with his shirt and grabbed her hand. The fire hadn't reached the landing where they stood. He debated crossing to the other wing, the one where he could call up a floor plan and pray for a set of back stairs. But once they were over there, they'd be trapped.

"Do you know if there's another way down?" she asked through her sleeve, which was now wadded up and covering her mouth.

He tried to call up the layout from memory. Nothing came to him. The only sure thing was the long balcony that extended from the bedrooms where he hid earlier.

"Must be, but I don't know where."

She buried her face in his arm. "What do we do?"

Whatever choice they made, they had to do it now. Thick gray smoked swelled, floating higher to surround them. Intense heat cut off the oxygen until every breath burned down his throat and into his lungs.

He grabbed her hand. "This way."

They crouched down, trying to find a pocket of clean air, but smoke covered everything now. The space grew thick and black. Every step dragged as his vision clouded.

He dragged his hand along the wall, counting doors as he went. He depended on his memory to guide him. At the fourth door, they ducked inside.

He slammed the door shut behind them and inhaled the cleaner air. "We should have a few minutes."

"Here." She stripped a blanket off the bed and handed it to him.

As he shoved it under the door, tucking in the corners to block as much of the seam as possible, he gestured to her to open the entrance to the balcony. "We need fresh air."

Since she continued to wheeze, he knew she understood the importance of moving fast. Problem was, the smoke and heat brought on exhaustion. Every gesture and step seemed to take forever. It was as if they moved in slow motion.

With the small space stuffed as tight as possible, he joined her at the open double doors. A sweep of cool air hit their faces, refreshing them. He inhaled as deeply as possible, trying to draw oxygen into his body to feed his muscles and brain. He needed all his strength and wits for the next few minutes. He could not afford to have a weak arm and a stilted mind.

He also needed Claire to trust him. "Listen to me."

"We're trapped in here."

"No, we're not. We can get out."

"How?"

"We're going over the side."

She walked to the front of the balcony and looked at the ground below. "It's a long way down."

"It's fine."

She checked the distance again. "Probably twenty feet."

From what he could tell, more like thirty.

"We'll make it." He used his most assured tone.

If she sensed his fear, they'd never make it. He knew from her reactions of the past that heights made her nervous. Add in the fire and choking smoke and she'd venture into full panic mode.

Besides, he was already worried about how he would support his weight with one good arm. There was no way he could balance both of them and get them to safety. No, she had to do her part.

The two of them. Together.

"I'm afraid of heights." She shook her head so hard that he waited for her to fall over. "Deathly afraid."

"You're more afraid of dying. Trust me."

"I can't jump." Her mouth flattened. "Don't ask me to do this. I can't."

"Stop." He stepped in front of her.

"Please, Luke."

His palm cupped her cheek. With his thumb he rubbed a bit of soot off the tip of her nose. "We can do this. We'll lower our bodies down."

"The fire is down there."

That was his biggest fear. That he'd coax her off the side only to watch the fire steal her away from him. They could choke, miscalculate, fall. The chances for failure were too significant to contemplate. But the probability of death if they stayed in that room was a hundred percent. Even now, small curls of smoke seeped through the blanket and trickled into the room.

The sight revived his stubbornness. He would not die today. She would live to see this through.

"When we get low enough, we'll swing out and jump," he said.

"Luke, I can't…"

He pressed his forehead against hers. "There is nothing you can't do. I've never known a woman with more spirit or heart."

Her eyes turned misty as her lips moved against his.

"And I can't do this without you, Claire. If you stay, I stay. We'll face the fire together, but we will not survive."

She nibbled on her lower lip as she turned her head and glanced nervously over the side. "How do we do this?"

A thunderous roar filled the background. It sounded like ten thousand trains bearing down on them. Luke knew the sound. It meant the flames were growing and devouring. The foundation beneath would soon sway, then crumble into the killing heat.

He ran back into the room and stripped the sheets off the bed. When she saw him struggling with the elastic, she rushed over and helped. They worked in tandem, grabbing the cotton and dragging it back out with them to the balcony.

"Help me with this." He slipped his hand under the heavy bed and pulled.

"What are you doing?"

"We need to anchor the sheets on something."

Together they moved the bed, wedging it in the doorway with one end sticking out into the balcony. He took one last look around the room and decided to try one more thing. "The mattress."

"What about it?"

"We'll throw it on the ground as a precaution." He doubted it would help, but if they fell from ten feet, the padding should help.

"I'll trust you."

He hoped that wouldn't be the biggest mistake of her life. "Good."

They picked up opposite ends. Once more the slice to his shoulder made his one hand useless. But she had enough strength for both of them. She wrapped her fingers around the handles on the side of the mattress and tugged until it almost rolled on top of her. He finished the job by chucking it over the side. It bounced, but was still within aiming distance.

"Do you know how to tie a strong knot?" she asked.

He had to smile at her attempts to stay positive in the face of doom. "I thought we'd use the sheets as parachutes and fly down."

Her hands stopped working. "That's a joke, right?"

"I'm the son of an army man. Spent my youth camping and my twenties in the military. The one thing I can do without trouble is tie a knot."

"That explains a lot about you."

"It's not news to you. You know that much of my background."

"But the context is different now."

"Okay."

"But have at it." She handed him the edges. "Be all you can be."

He tried to keep her gaze on him and her back to the door. She didn't need to see the smoke pouring in and around the makeshift blockage and slowly filling the room. He knew she could hear the house creak and moan beneath them, knew she smelled the fire and felt the heat under them. From all around, flames spit out windows and blackness filled the sky.

They had to go or risk losing their only hope.

He tightened the sheets at every juncture one last time. Unless they ripped, they should hold.

"You're going first," he said.

"No. I can follow."

"If you lead, I'll know you're out." And that would leave him as the one to fight off the flames he knew were about to knock on the door.

He already heard the shocking *whoosh* of fire as it started its race up the hallway. That meant they were dealing in seconds, instead of minutes, at this point.

When she hesitated, he slid her thigh up and onto the edge of the balcony wall. "You've got to go."

Her gaze searched his face. "Promise me you'll follow. No hero stuff."

"Absolutely."

She kissed him then, long and deep. The intensity shook him. He knew she was saying a possible goodbye.

"I love you," she whispered.

Then she lowered her body over the edge. With shaking arms and panic in her eyes, she slipped hand over hand down the side. When her side slammed against the wall, she screamed but held on.

Fear shot through him. "You okay?"

"Yes," she said in a shaky voice.

He knew she could see the fire. Feel the extreme

heat against her clothes and skin. He tried to keep her attention focused on him. "You're almost there."

She had a good thirty feet to go. The poisoned air made her cough.

But she was better down there than up here with him, so he was grateful. Fire danced up the doorway and snapped at the ceiling.

He pulled tighter to the edge of the balcony and inhaled as much air as possible. Even that stagnated in his mouth. The air outside slowly became as polluted as the stuff behind him.

"Luke!"

Her scream had him looking down again. Flames exploded around her. He thought about jumping down there but forced his legs to stay still.

"Swing out," he yelled over the roar of the fire.

"How?"

"Move your body. Get away from the flames." He had to curl his hands around his mouth and yell down to her. The banging and hissing from the fire almost drowned him out.

She pushed, at first barely moving. But when a cloud of smoke engulfed her, she began rocking back and forth. He helped from above by pulling the sheets away from the wall. The motion caused the bed to smack harder against the doorframe, but the knots held and the creaking wood continued to provide the needed counterbalance to her weight.

"Now, Claire. Jump."

She glanced up, her eyes filled with terror, and then nodded. He could see her take a breath. And then she let go. With a yelp, she flapped her arms and fell. When her body hit the edge of the mattress and rolled off onto the grass, he stopped breathing.

He leaned out farther and tried to make out her form through the billowing smoke. "Claire?"

"Get down here!"

Nothing subtle about that. Luke didn't wait for a second command. He curled the sheets around his good arm and threw a leg over the wall. He tugged twice to make sure he still had some leverage. Holding his body up with one hand and shimmying down wasn't going to be easy. He had to depend on open spaces against the wall to jump off and land. Then he had to hope he didn't send his body flying right into the flames.

Smoke filled the bedroom. The flames raced right behind. The bed would go up in the next few seconds.

He hopped off the edge and felt the immediate tug of his weight against the muscles in his biceps and shoulder. His bones strained and his hand blistered as he hung there.

The blaze raged around him. He couldn't even see the ground. The rumble and crack of the fire filled the area as the sky turned black with smoke.

He swung his body against an open space on the wall. With one arm, he couldn't stop his momentum and smashed into the brick wall. His grip slipped, dropping him two feet lower on the sheets.

Claire's muffled shouts reached him through the noise and madness. She was begging him to keep going.

That was the push he needed. He clutched the material tighter in his fist and used his legs to guide him down. As he hit the bottom floor of the house, all he saw was fire. It traveled everywhere, destroying everything it touched.

He hung there, fifteen feet from the ground and unable to locate the mattress, and knew the climb down was over. The fire had scorched the end of the sheets from the bottom and was moving up toward him. He bunched his body, bringing his legs up tight to his stomach, then pushed out and let go.

The tumble through the air took about a second but felt like forever. Boiling heat surrounded him. Flames inched up to touch him. He passed through it all, landing with a hard thump on the far edge of the mattress. Despite the cushion, the whack of ground against bones shocked the breath right out of him.

Claire was there to bring it back.

She gripped his arm and started pulling. "Luke, wake up."

He didn't realize his eyes were closed until she said the words. "Give me a second."

"We don't have one to spare." Her tugging became more insistent.

He looked up and saw the wall of red and orange roaring in front of them. They stood in a half circle of fire. They had a slim path out to green grass and land not seared by an uncontrolled inferno.

Finding a reserve of energy fueled only by adrenaline, he pushed to his feet and ran at a crouch with Claire by his side. The house exploded behind them as they continued to chase fresh air.

Out of danger, they fell to the hard ground and coughed out the smoke filling their lungs. Fatigue dragged at his muscles, but Luke knew they weren't done. He had lost contact with Adam and Holden. They could be anywhere, including in the middle of the hell they had just escaped.

He lost the mic during all the climbing and falling. There was only one other way to check on his friends. He found the energy to lift his arm and stare at his watch. The screen was black.

"Why aren't the fire trucks here?" Claire asked. The question came out in a rasp.

"We're far enough away from other houses that it will take time for anyone to see it."

"There's enough smoke to signal another planet."

"Well, when you hear the sirens don't get too excited."

"Why?"

"We're not supposed to be here, remember?"

"Right." She tapped her fingers against his chest. "Where do you think Steve and Phil are? The goal was to catch them. They could be anywhere."

He wished they were dead, but he knew better.

"They're running."

"I doubt they'll be as good at it as I was."

"I'm hoping they drive past Holden and he rams their car." Luke felt her shift. When he finally found the strength to open his eyes, her expression swam above him. "What? What are you thinking?"

"I've got a better idea."

"For what?"

"I know where they are."

Luke wasn't sure he knew where *he* was at this point. "How is that possible?"

"They're not driving."

"Then what are they doing?"

"How about flying?"

He lifted his head off the ground. "I don't—"

"Adam said there was a helicopter pad on the grounds."

Luke's brain cells started firing again. "Sounds convenient for the perfect getaway."

"Not if we can help it."

Chapter Sixteen

Claire stared out into the distance and tried to figure out where her evil ex-husband would hide a helicopter pad. She strained to remember if the site had shown up on the photo lineup Adam had shared with them on the laptop. She could only conjure up a blank page.

"Which way?" she asked when she couldn't come up with the direction just by willing it.

Luke's gaze wandered over the landscape before settling on the far side of what once was the house. "There."

"Are you guessing?"

"More of a deduction, actually."

"Based on?"

"I know it's not behind us and wouldn't be in the front yard. That only leaves one direction."

"That's good enough for me."

With the world exploding behind them and pieces of flaming wood and paper falling to the ground around them, they kept moving. The jog to the opposite end of the house took forever. The ache in her leg slowed them down. She kept trying to shake it off, but the crack of marble against her knee had done some damage.

Dodging behind the small outbuildings scattered around the grounds and hiding from any eyes that might be watching also limited their progress. The only good news was that the fire hadn't engulfed the older part of the house. That meant their march across the wide yard brought some fresh air and welcome relief for her dry nose and parched throat. But not much. Smoke and the charred smell seeped into everything.

When they reached the edge of the house, he pushed her back against a gardening shed. "Stop."

She didn't mind the manhandling now. Walking into the middle of a new disaster didn't appeal to her. "What do you see?"

"Two idiots loading boxes onto a helicopter."

"The other guards?"

"No, the idiots you were related to."

She peeked around the corner. On the next acre over sat the aircraft in the middle of a concrete pad. There was a small steel hangar between them and the Samson brothers. Other than that, they were looking at a wide-open field with grass that looked as if it hadn't been mowed in a month—very few places to hide.

"Can Phil fly a helicopter?" Luke asked.

"You're asking the wrong person. I didn't even know he owned this house."

"Well, there's not much left of that."

They both glanced over at what used to be a stone mansion. Now it was a ball of fire slowly collapsing in on itself on one side.

"What a waste." She thought that summed up the property, as well as the past two years.

"Yeah, someone could have used it as a hospital."

"Or a college." She left that problem and focused on the human one in front of her. "What are they doing?"

"Packing."

"What's left?"

"Whatever they need to make a run for it. Looks like they stored whatever they needed back here. The money is likely already out of the reach of the U.S. government."

"Why do you think that?"

"They wouldn't take the risk of having it with them. It's been transferred and transferred again to throw off anyone trying to track it down."

"It shouldn't be that easy."

"You'd be amazed."

"So why waste time with whatever they're doing now?"

"This is the getaway part of their plan."

"Even if they can fly that thing out, they're not going to get very far in it. They can't exactly get to South America from here." Not that she knew much about helicopters. She barely knew anything about cars except you got in and started the engine. "Right?"

"They only have to get to a private airport. That's not a problem out here in rich-people country. I'm sure there are airstrips all over the place."

"Convenient."

"And with their money they can bribe people from there, hire a flight instructor or anyone who needs some cash and get out of the country."

"I wish they'd done that from the beginning and left me alone."

"They needed you to buy time and for cover. They've been hatching this for quite some time. Hell, these two likely have had their escape all mapped out ever since they decided to take their employees' money. They knew how to get everything else done without making the police suspect them."

"I wouldn't have said they were that smart."

"Think of it as underhanded."

She watched as Phil heaved a bag onto the helicopter. "So they get to leave with all that money."

"Yeah, they think so."

"What do *you* think?"

"That we're going to stop them."

"Any idea how we do that?"

"They believe their plan worked and we're dead, so we have surprise on our side."

Luke was getting ready to pounce. The anxiety thrumming off him crashed against her. The pure predator in him shone through in every line of his body. Everything in his stance said battle. He had the prey in his sights.

His need to attack sparked hers. "We have to get out there now before they spot us or take off."

"I will."

She closed her eyes to keep from screaming. "You aren't leaving me behind and we are not going to spend two seconds arguing that point."

He nodded. "Wouldn't dream of disagreeing with you."

That was way too easy. She hadn't won a similar battle with him—ever. Now he was acquiescing to her command and smiling at her as if he'd gone simple.

She didn't trust the change one bit.

"So what *are* you dreaming about?" she asked, waiting for him to return to his me-man-you-woman-stay-here ways.

"Crawling over there, getting the jump on Phil and then using him as a shield against Steve. The goal is to keep them from lifting off and grab whatever it is they think is important enough to waste time loading on the plane."

"You think Steve is in charge." For some reason that struck her as odd. She had also viewed Phil as the more suave and sophisticated of the two.

"He's the one with the gun."

"Under that theory you're in charge."

"Yeah, let's see how that works."

Luke could shoot both men for all she cared.

"And what do I do while you're doing your superhero act across the lawn?" she asked.

He nodded to the building situated between them and the escape helicopter. "Circle around by the hangar."

"You think there's another helicopter in there?"

"I only have one gun and I'm going to need it, so you need to find a weapon."

"Like what?"

"A piece of metal. A crowbar. Anything you can carry and use to stab or hit with."

"And just who am I attacking?"

Phil. She wanted to take Phil down.

"Whichever one I leave standing," Luke said.

"Makes sense. I like the plan so far."

Luke drew a diagram on her hand with his finger. "I go in from the front and you sneak around from the back."

When he started to kneel down and winced in the process, guilt struck her. She laid a hand against his hair. "Can you do this?"

"I'm the professional, remember?"

"You've been beaten and you fall about one story to the hard ground. Even professionals are destructible."

"You jumped and you're fine."

"I was almost at the bottom of those sheets when I let go. You were at the top."

He shook his head. "I'm fine."

That was his mantra. She now understood that he said the empty words whenever he was the exact opposite of *fine*.

But they had a bigger problem. A mess she was trying to ignore rather than risk having it stop her. But she had to deal with it. Luke's life might depend on it.

She brushed her fingers over the sticky stain on his now crusty shirt. "You have blood everywhere."

"What?" He glanced at his shoulder and frowned. "I need a new bandage."

The ultimate understatement.

The reality is that he hadn't even realized that blood poured down his arm. She guessed that the mix of danger and adrenaline kept his blood pumping and the pain at bay. Either that or he had moved into a state of advanced denial. His mind had shut off to the numbness moving through him.

His brain might be fighting the extent of his injuries, but hers wasn't. She hadn't seen him move his arm in any significant way since they got into the mansion. When he held her, he only used one hand. And watching him get down that rope while one arm dangled at his side counted as the most harrowing moment in a series of endless horrors.

Swollen fingers. Limp muscles. Blood soaking through what was once white cotton wrapped around the wound. The same material now glowing and stained with dark red.

It didn't take a doctor to know Luke was in huge

physical trouble. She expected he couldn't even close his fist at this point. So she made the decision for him. Her priorities were clear now. Whatever happened to her happened. She could face jail, even a false sentence, if Luke lived. The important thing was to get him to a hospital before he lost his arm...or worse.

"We should forget about this and leave." She pointed at the figures in the distance.

"No."

"Let them get away. They don't matter now."

"Absolutely not."

"I'm sure we can track down a neighbor or passing car somewhere around here."

"I said no. Several times. I mean it. We're finishing this if it kills me."

That was her fear. "We know the truth."

Her biggest concern, greatest relief, was that Luke believe in her. She could face anything or anyone with that knowledge tucked deep in her heart.

Luke refused to listen. He shook his head. "I'm going in."

She tilted his chin so that his gaze was forced to meet hers. "It doesn't matter. Only *you* matter."

The words came from deep inside her. A tiny area she had locked out of her mind two years earlier opened. Now the truth of her feelings pumped through her, overtaking everything else.

His dark frown didn't waver. "If they get into that helicopter, I might not be able to save you."

"I'm more concerned with saving you."

She could see him wrestle with the best way to fight her terror. The tension across his shoulders eased as his palm moved up her leg. "I'm going to be here. But I'm not going to be able to live with myself if we walk away now and let these two idiots escape to freedom without being punished for what they've done to you and all their employees."

Their priorities still clashed because all she cared about was making sure Luke lived. "What if we fail?"

"We won't."

Luke was sure of that part. They had come too far to turn around and sneak off now. He didn't even know where they would go. No one was around for miles, and he didn't have the strength for a hike. He had just enough energy to take out a Samson or two. He'd worry about the rest later, because no more bags or boxes sat on the ground near the helicopter. Liftoff was imminent. Luke could feel it.

"Let's go," he said.

They took off in opposite directions. He went first, not giving her another chance to argue. If Phil and Steve were going to spot one of them, Luke wanted to make sure it was him. He didn't want to give away his position, but he would draw their gazes if necessary to protect her.

As Claire shimmied along the ground with her head down and using only her elbows and knees to propel her across the grass, Luke started jogging. He bent down as far as possible. There was no way his one side would support him long enough to get him close to the helicopter, and for his plan to work, he had to get damn close.

He stopped and dropped down, keeping as still as possible when the brothers faced the house. Their laughter filled the smoky air. Clearly they thought letting people burn to death was hilarious.

It only made Luke hate them more.

Luke used that fury to push himself on. His body ran only on the drive to see these men caught and Claire's name cleared.

When the laughter stopped, Luke lifted his head again. He saw a flash of white off to his right as Claire stood up and slipped behind the hangar. That meant it was his turn to act.

He waited until the brothers turned and looked over the booty in the helicopter. There wouldn't be another chance. Luke inhaled and took off. He ran as fast as he could, using up every energy reserve inside him to get to the two men.

As he shot across the clear field toward Phil, Steve pivoted. Shock registered on the older man's face and he gave a shout of warning. Phil proved slower. He raised his hands to his head as if ducking from a flying object but didn't get out of Luke's path.

Knocking the man down would satisfy the desire to hurt him, but Luke doubted he could get back up once he was down. That would leave him vulnerable to attack by two men who would think nothing of beating him to death with their hands. Instead, he used all his concentration to slam his body to a halt. He slowed his movements in time to raise his gun and shove it into the back of Phil's head. Phil screamed in rage.

When Luke turned his gaze to Steve, Luke saw the gun. So while Luke pointed his gun at Phil, Steve pointed his at Luke. It was a circle of violence that guaranteed at least two of them would end up dead. Luke knew which two he would pick.

"Drop it or I'll kill your brother." The blood pounded hard enough through Luke's body to threaten to knock him down.

Steve's mouth twisted in a snarl. "You don't have it in you."

"You don't know me."

Phil cowered under the gun. "Where's Claire?"

The question proved she'd made it to the hangar without being seen. These two had lied their way through their entire plan, but Luke sensed this was not a trick. So he adopted their skills.

"She's in a room on the second floor of your house. And you're going to pay for her death." He laid the desperate act on thick, playing the role of a heartbroken and deranged boyfriend. It wasn't hard to conjure up the feelings, because he had been toying with them all day.

"He's lying," Phil said as he tried to move away from the gun.

Luke pulled him back, shoving the gun harder

against Phil's skull. "You aren't in a position to question."

"But I am." Calm washed over Steve. He acted like a man in control rather than a man who got caught.

"It's over, Steve. You lost."

"No. Phil did."

A shot rang out. For a second Luke wondered if he had fired by accident. Then he saw Phil lying at his feet. Drops of blood sprayed in a pattern across Luke's shirt. He looked at his stomach and at Phil's still body and realized the blood wasn't his.

Steve's skills were as impressive as Luke feared. Steve had put a bullet right through the center of his brother's black heart.

"You shot him." The idea was so outrageous that Luke's mind refused to grasp it.

"He served his purpose."

The men now held guns on each other.

"Which was?"

"To set up Claire and grab the money." Steve shifted so that the helicopter sat directly behind him, as if he wanted something hard supporting his back.

"You used him."

"He's always been the brother for show. I'm the brother for action."

"You're the murderer."

Steve laughed without amusement. "This, too, will fall on Claire."

"She's dead."

"That's just part of the cover-up. Once again Claire has complied with my wishes and performed in a way that only makes the story better."

"What are you talking about?"

The dead woman in question slipped behind the helicopter. Luke saw a flash of her hair and the edge of her shirt before she disappeared behind her metal cover again. Knowing she was there made his fingers tighten on the gun. She had walked right into the middle of a lethal situation, but having her on his team might be their only chance.

"In my story she dies while trying to get away and everything goes wrong."

"It will never work."

"Sure it will. The public already sees her as a killer. Adding Phil's death now is perfect. It will make it look as if she kept him alive and only now killed him."

Steve's arm stiffened.

"You shoot, I shoot."

"You are a minute away from dropping on top of Phil. Just look at you. How much blood have you lost by now? A pint? More? That brain of yours will shut down soon."

As Steve said the words, Luke's muscles grew weak. "Not before I kill you."

"If you kill me, how do you clear your precious Claire's name?"

"That doesn't matter now."

"Steve!" Claire shouted his name in a quick burst and without giving away her exact position.

Surprise had Steve turning around, which was all Luke needed. He aimed and fired straight into Steve's back. The shot propelled Steve's body forward and his gun dropped from his fingers to the grass.

"No…" Steve slumped over the opening area in the center of the helicopter before falling on his back to the ground.

Luke watched the man's eyes flutter and his chest heave for breaths. A bloodstain spread over his stomach as his face went pale.

Luke took it all in, tried to care. But he couldn't feel anything, didn't even know how he kept standing. He heard bells and whistles and thought he had to be hallucinating. His mind had finally checked out as his body went numb.

Claire appeared at his side. "Luke?"

She was okay. He repeated that fact over and over.

"I'm right here." Her hands traveled over his chest and across his face.

He saw rather than felt her touch. "Claire?"

"The police are coming. I can hear the sirens."

"Were you hurt?"

"No." She wrapped an arm around his waist. "Hold on."

"Can't."

And then his world went black.

Chapter Seventeen

The next few minutes passed in a whirl. The wind kicked up as a fleet of police cars raced across the lawn. They stopped, kicking up dust around Claire and stopping only inches from where she lay covering Luke's still body on the ground.

"Help me!"

Doors opened. Holden and Adam stepped out. When Holden tried to run to her, two officers had to hold him back.

"Get down." The policeman's order boomed across her senses.

His words confused her. The danger from Steve and Phil had passed. Why weren't they coming to Luke? "He needs an ambulance."

"Step away from him."

The command didn't make any sense. She was saving him, keeping him and protecting him from additional pain. Trying to stop the bleeding from his arm.

She continued to kneel on the ground. "What are you saying?"

"Stand up."

"I don't understand."

"Claire, move away from Luke so we can get to him." Holden's mouth pulled tight as he yelled the command.

She could see the tension in the police officers surrounding her with guns raised. Adam practically bounced as he shifted and moved around, his gaze never leaving Luke.

They were here to arrest her.

The thought had her gasping. "Luke needs help!"

An officer approached her. "Put your hands up."

She obeyed even though it killed her to let go of Luke. "Please. He needs a doctor."

"I know, ma'am." The officer motioned for her to stand up. "I'm going to get him in an ambulance right now."

That promise was all she needed. She struggled to her feet with her hands in the air. As soon as she stood, the officer grabbed her arms and wrenched them behind her.

"Careful," Holden said.

"I know how to do my job, sir." Cuffs snapped on her wrists as two ambulances raced into the yard.

An officer checked Steve's pulse. "He's alive."

No, that was wrong. She didn't care about him. No one should care about him.

"Luke goes first," she insisted.

Holden and Adam surrounded their friend until the ambulance crew shooed them away. The world erupted in chaos. Fire engines screamed around the back of the house. Men filed out with hoses and ladders and assessed the burning building. Police and emergency workers filled every inch of the grassy area she'd initially seen as huge and open. A crew worked on Steve and another on Luke.

The relief of having made it out alive made the ground spin in front of her. She almost fell, but the officer caught her against his chest and guided her to the side of his car.

"Are you hurt?" the officer asked.

"Just save Luke." She whispered the plea as she watched the workers load Luke onto the stretcher.

Holden's face appeared in front of her. "Are you okay?"

"Luke?"

"They're working on him." Holden leaned in closer. "Do you need a medic?"

"No." She wanted all their attention on Luke.

The area around Holden's mouth whitened. "I'm sorry."

"For what?"

"I brought the police. We saw the fire and took out two of Phil's men as they ran out the front. But we couldn't get to you. We didn't know where you were in there."

She couldn't grasp what he was trying to say. She got

that he'd called the ambulance. She was grateful for his quick thinking. Luke's safety was all that mattered to her.

Holden put his hands on her shoulders and gave her a little squeeze. "They're going to arrest you. I had to get them here fast and to do that I turned on you."

Now it made sense. He thought she had planned to run and he was willing to look the other way to let her go. "I'm not leaving Luke."

Holden smiled then. "Good."

LUKE FORCED his eyes open to wake up from the floating sensation cocooning his body. He saw Adam and medics. Not the one person he wanted.

"Where's Claire?" When no one paid attention to him, he said it again in a louder voice.

"Luke." Adam rushed to his side. "Are you okay?"

"Claire."

Adam's frown didn't ease. "We have to get you to a hospital."

Why wasn't he answering? "Fine. Tell me about Claire."

"Your sleeve is soaked with blood and your skin is whiter than milk. Hell, you passed out."

Luke swallowed, then pushed more strength into his voice. "I want Claire."

Adam hesitated before motioning to a police officer that Luke could see on the periphery of his vision. The ambulance crew poked and adjusted equipment.

Someone took his pulse. Another guy administered a shot.

Luke didn't feel any of it. He wanted Claire by his side. Now.

A medic stepped back and Claire filled the space. Her tears fell on his face. "I'm right here."

He tried to lift his fingers to touch her lips, but his arms refused to move. "Are you okay?"

"I'm fine," she said, repeating his words.

A policeman appeared over her shoulder. "Ma'am, you need to come with us."

Irrational panic filled Luke's senses. He knew if she stepped away, he might not see her again. He could not lose her now.

"She stays with me."

"Do you have to do this now?" Holden's voice rose above the flurry of sounds and buzzing of people around him. "He needs her."

"There's a warrant out for her arrest. She's a flight risk," the officer explained.

Luke blinked, trying to fight off the lethargy stealing over him. "For what?"

"The murder of Phillip Samson," the officer said in a firm voice.

"That's Phil Samson." Holden pointed at the man's body, which hadn't moved or been moved since Luke dropped him there. "She couldn't have killed him before because he was only killed just now."

"His brother did it," Claire said in a rush.

The officer shook his head. "I have to do what I'm told."

The medic gave Luke another shot. Luke tried to tell him not to, but his tongue went numb, so he stuck with the words he needed to say. "Listen to me."

Claire leaned down and pressed her cheek against his for a second. Then she gave him a soft, loving kiss. "Luke, it's okay."

"You didn't do it."

"I know."

"You aren't going to jail."

With a nod to the medic, Holden slipped his hand under Claire's elbow and pulled her back. "We'll straighten all this out later."

Now, it had to be now. Luke tried to raise his head. The move forced bile up the back of his throat until it threatened to choke him.

The medic eased Luke back down with a hand on his chest. "Sir, I need you to stay down."

Luke let his head fall back. "Not until I know she's coming with me."

The officer started to tug her out of the way. "She has to ride in the car."

"Holden, stop this."

Holden's mouth pinched. "Man, I can't do that. I tried."

"I can't…" Whatever the medic shot into Luke's veins now held his mind captive. Colors swirled in front of his eyes. "Claire."

"I'm here, Luke," Claire whispered.

"Come with me."

"I'll be there as soon as I can." Her voice grew more distant.

"Luke, man, you need to let the ambulance take you," Adam said.

Luke let his eyes close, but he could hear his friends arguing over him.

"Is he going to be okay?" Claire asked, her voice higher than usual and her concern evident.

"There's been a serious loss of blood." Luke didn't recognize the speaker. He assumed it was the medic, but he couldn't open his eyes to check.

"I can go with her to the police station and work this out." Luke whispered the suggestion as his body fought off the start of a gentle sleep.

"You're going into surgery. We'll stay with Claire," Holden said as he squeezed his friend's good shoulder.

"Don't let anything happen to her." Luke's breath turned shallow. "Phil tried to kill her."

"He's dead now," Claire said.

"I can't stay awake." The words came out so staggered that the sentence took forever for Luke to say.

"Don't fight it, sir." The medic slipped a mask over Luke's face.

"Where's Claire?" he mumbled.

"You'll see her soon." Holden cleared his throat. "Promise."

Luke wanted to believe, but his mind went blank.

Chapter Eighteen

Claire sat on the hard bench and dropped her head into her hands. Her fingers snagged on a piece of scorched paper between the strands. She brushed it out but did wonder what else could be caught up in there. It was a miracle she had any hair left after the fire and everything else that had happened.

Not that her looks mattered all that much where she was. After the fires and gun battles, pain and terror, she'd ended up in the one place she most feared and was desperate to avoid. A jail cell.

She had been there all night. They said she'd move to more permanent quarters today, but it hadn't happened.

Now she feared she'd be there forever, lost in the system and discarded.

Metal clanked against metal as doors opened and closed. Officers walked the area, ignoring the women confined inside. Every now and then the loudspeaker would squawk. The announcer would say a name or give an order.

Claire could barely hear the announcements over her fellow inmates' shouting and swearing. There were those who blamed the system and the men in their lives for their temporary homes behind bars. A few threw insults from their individual holding cells. She had been called a whole host of names that she sure hoped didn't fit.

She felt small and alone. Pain knocked against the back of her head, and her lungs still ached from the intake of so much smoke. An officer promised her medical attention, but she knew that would be a long wait. She was not a priority.

The press, public and prosecutor still saw her as a criminal. The arrest warrant had been issued while she ran around the Virginia countryside trying to track down Phil and prove he was alive. He wasn't dead when she got charged. He was very dead now.

She tried to care but couldn't. He had destroyed so much, stolen from everyone and wrecked something very precious about her belief in her own instincts. Innocent people in his company would wake up in a few days and find out that not only was their employer out of business, but their money was gone. Some would blame her, but they would learn the truth eventually.

Adam said it could be months or longer before law enforcement and a host of computer specialists would track down the funds. Even then, most of it could be gone. No one knew how much Phil and Steve had spent, and Steve wasn't talking.

That wasn't true. He kept babbling, insisting that she was in on it with Phil. That he was the aggrieved and innocent party. The man could lie without blinking. He'd tried to kill her and acted as if that little piece of information didn't matter.

But Steve wasn't the man she was thinking about right then. If she could manage it, she planned to never think of him again.

She wanted Luke.

Strapped to a gurney, he had disappeared into an ambulance as the police dragged her away. She could still hear his desperate calls for her as the ambulance door shut. Just thinking about him, about them, about all they had survived and the slogging road to recovery still ahead, brought tears to her eyes. She couldn't let them fall. If her new bunkmates saw her as scared or weak, they'd attack. And she had been battered and bruised enough to last a lifetime.

"You asleep in there?" Luke's voice carried a touch of amusement.

But that couldn't be. He was in the hospital under anesthesia and observation. Adam told her about the surgery and the long recovery ahead. All while she was awaiting transfer to the cell that would become her home until her trial.

She raised her head, prepared to see nothing but bars lined up before her. But the fantasy remained.

What greeted her made everything else slip away. Luke. Standing there in jeans and a clean shirt. Leaning against the open cell door with a sexy, stupid grin on his face.

She blinked a few times to make sure he didn't vanish like the vision she'd had of him so many times during the long night. "What are you doing here?"

"It's visiting hours."

She looked down but she didn't have a watch. "Isn't it after midnight?"

"Yeah." He pushed away from the door and came closer.

She'd forgotten how big he was. His broad chest blocked the view of everything behind him. But that handsome face had never left her memory.

"You're supposed to be in the hospital."

"Holden broke me out."

"Adam said—"

"I'm fine. And this time I mean it."

"Are you allowed to be here?" she asked because she didn't know what else to say.

He had cleaned up and showered. She had fire refuse poking out of her hair and a mix of grass stains and soot caking her pants. Her fingernails were filthy. Basically, she was the least attractive person in the jail. Ever.

He walked into the cell and didn't stop until the tips of his shoes tapped against her sneakers. "I have to say this isn't exactly the response I expected when I paid your bail."

She laughed even though the joke wasn't all that funny. "It's set at a million dollars."

"It was. Not now."

"You're serious."

"I know some people."

"Sure you do."

"You doubt me?" He dropped down next to her, ignoring the catcalls from the cells around them.

"What are we talking about here?"

"You getting out of here."

The words sounded so good to her ears. "Is that ever going to happen?"

"It can happen as soon as you stand up."

He wasn't kidding. She felt that certainty through every vein. "What's going on? I'm supposed to switch to the prison. You're supposed to be resting with nurses buzzing all around you."

"Nurses are overrated. I prefer strong beautiful women who know how to create a distraction in a crisis."

Her mind still couldn't process the barrage of information hitting it. "I don't get it."

"There's a judge who owes me a favor." Luke rubbed his good shoulder against her dirty one. "Found his niece last year, kept her out of trouble and her name out of the news."

"Really?"

"He returned the favor with a reduction in bail."

She didn't understand much about the legal system,

but she knew nothing worked that easily. Not at midnight on a Tuesday. "The prosecutor agreed to that?"

"He's not dumb."

"I'm sorry to hear that, since he'll be on the other side of my case."

"When I gave my statement, when Holden and Adam chimed in, it was hard for the prosecutor to hold on to the theory that you're the bad guy in this scenario."

Hope jumped to life inside her. "He believes I'm innocent?"

"He trusts me, and for now, that's good enough."

"Does that mean he dropped the charges?" She was afraid to hope for such a fantastic ending to such a tragic series of events.

"No. Apparently I'm not that convincing." Luke laid his hand over her knee. "But he will. He just needs a little time to check into everything. He's satisfied that you're done running."

"I am."

"Good."

With those simple words, something important passed between them. Something strong and binding that she grabbed on to and held tight to her heart.

The brush of his thumb on her leg lulled her into a certain peace. "That feels good."

He smiled. "It will take some more time to ferret things out. Steve is still a powerful man. The prosecutor will want everything set before he leaves you alone and turns on Steve."

"But he will?"

"I promise."

She wove her fingers through his and laid her head on his shoulder. The familiar snuggle gave her the security she needed to believe the court might someday untangle the mess the Samson brothers had made. And the touch of Luke's skin against hers took the final edge off her frazzled nerves.

His sling rested against his stomach. She skimmed her fingers over it, careful not to press too hard. She had inflicted enough damage and didn't want to be responsible for one drop more.

"What did the doctor say?" she asked.

"He thinks I got shot in the shoulder."

She squeezed Luke's hand. "I meant the prognosis."

"It's fine."

She heard the edge to his voice and stared up at him, really looked into those intelligent green eyes. His smile looked forced.

She knew he had fallen back on old habits. "Tell me the truth."

"I guess I can't convince you this isn't important."

"The fact you're trying so hard not to answer is my first clue that it is."

He blew out a long breath. "Well, it would appear that running around with a shoulder injury and hanging off the side of a building are not good things. Who knew?"

"You did." She played with his hair where it curled at his ear.

"It was worth the risk."

"I'm not convinced that's true."

He shifted until she could see every inch of his handsome face. "So that we're clear, I would do it all again if it meant that you lived. That was my only goal."

A chorus of *ahhh*s sounded from behind them, but Claire tuned them out.

"Funny, but I had a similar goal."

"Then we agree."

She saw the tactic and blocked it. "You're stalling. Tell me what this injury means for your future."

"Even in jail I can't throw you off the scent."

"No."

"It's nothing serious." He toyed with her fingers. "Some physical therapy."

There was more. With them there was always more. "And?"

"There's a possibility of some loss of use. Slight."

"Oh, Luke." An unexpected sadness surged through her. He hadn't taken care of himself, hadn't thought his injury was a big deal, because he'd been too busy taking care of her.

"No, it's okay."

But it wasn't. "I'm so sorry."

She felt the apology with every cell of her body. If she could give him back a whole shoulder, she would.

He frowned at her. "Don't do that."

His change of tone to something harsh and unbending surprised her. "What?"

"Take the blame." He lifted their joined hands to his mouth and kissed her fingers. "I was where I wanted to be."

"You didn't ask to be shot."

"You didn't ask to be framed, so we're even."

He just kept giving and she didn't know how to accept it. "How can you say that?"

"Because the injury doesn't matter."

That wasn't true. His job defined and motivated him. She remembered the day he'd started this position. Their dating had moved from casual to something much more, and then his work life fell into place. At the time she thought it was a desk job in antiques and couldn't understand why shuffling papers filled him with such energy. Now that she knew his real job, she knew the real man needed the thrill and the rush.

"The job, my shoulder, none of that is really about my future."

"What do you mean?"

He rolled his eyes. "You really don't know?"

"Apparently not."

"*You* are my future." He said it emphatically, as if daring her to test him.

She could feel the force of his will. See the determination in his eyes and hear it in his rough voice. This promise meant more than the proposal and the beautiful diamond he'd once slipped on her finger.

Now she needed him to understand. "When I apologized, it was for everything."

"I know."

"For leaving."

He shook his head. "I pushed you away. I grew up with a certain set of rules and understandings. My dad did his work and I didn't question it. I thought that's the way it should be."

"I could have kept trying."

"I wanted to blame you for all of it, but we both messed up. We both need to own that and learn from it."

"Then I apologize for coming back and dragging you into this huge mess of a life of mine."

"No, you're wrong on that one. Returning to me is the best thing you ever did."

She gnawed on her bottom lip, trying to find the right words. When they didn't come, she went with what lived in her heart. "I can't promise that the nerves won't come again, that I won't get angry and demand you give me more. The need for trust and stability is ingrained in me. For so long I was denied both. I just don't want to live like that again."

There. She'd said it. She knew what she needed to stay grounded. Now *he* knew.

He gave her a blank stare. Seconds ticked by as she waited for him to say something. Anything.

"Will you leave me when I act like a jerk?" he asked.

The breath she was holding burst out of her lungs. "No. Never."

"That's all that matters."

Wave after wave of happiness crashed over her. "So you're willing to wait until I break out of here to start something special?"

"We already have something special."

When his lips met hers and the women in the cells cheered, she lost the last tethers to her control. Playing it cool didn't suit her. She wanted him to feel how much she loved him.

She wrapped her arms around his neck and kissed him back. Kissed him with all the feeling and joy she had bottled up for the two years they'd been apart. Kissed him for all they would have and for the hurts of the past. Kissed him in a promise of forever.

When she eased back, letting their mouths gently pull apart as their breaths still mixed, she whispered her vow. "I love you.

He brushed his thumb over her lips. "I've always loved you. I'll love you forever. When you act smart or stupid, when you yell or we make love, I'm going to keep on loving you."

She couldn't stop the huge smile that formed on her face. "I think we found something else we agree on."

He pressed a second, less heated kiss against her

mouth before coming back up for air again. "And now I'm going to take you home and show you."

"I can leave?" She hated to hope just in case the police officer in charge said no. But Luke's smile told her he had worked out every angle. "What did you do?"

"Didn't I tell you?" He brushed her hair out of her face. "In addition to the bail decrease, the prosecutor released you into my custody."

She loved how that sounded. "So I'm your responsibility now."

"That's what they told me."

"You think you can handle that?"

Luke winked at her. "With you I can do anything."

"Then take me home."

* * * * *

TEXAS LAW: UNDERCOVER JUSTICE

JENNIFER D. BOKAL

To John, Always.

Prologue

Decker Newcombe was very good at one thing. Delivering death.

Sitting in the passenger's seat, he stared through the dusty windshield at the front doors of the Pleasant Pines County office building. A month earlier, he'd registered at the Pleasant Pines Inn. Using an alias, he'd spent a week in Wyoming conducting reconnaissance. Playing the part of a developer interested in a tract of land, he'd gained access to the offices and had even managed to wander about the place freely while "researching" the deed.

From his time in town earlier, he knew that the building was closed for the evening, leaving only an elderly guard on duty.

Decker held a photograph of his latest target—Chloe

Ryder, the local district attorney. Months ago, she'd indicted all the members of the Transgressors, a local motorcycle club, on charges of trafficking—both drugs and humans. Everyone ended up in jail and the DA had been targeted by the national motorcycle club for termination. Decker had been given the kill contract.

To date, Decker had killed over seventeen people and never been charged with a single murder. As a rule, he never took contracts on public officials—the risk was always higher than the reward. Yet, this hit was worth so much cash—a cool 500K—he was on board. After his contact took his commission and the getaway driver was paid, Decker would still make $415,000—the biggest haul of his career.

His plan was a simple drive-by shooting, catching Chloe on the street as she left work. Afterward, the driver would take them to another car that was stashed a few miles outside of town. Before the district attorney was even pronounced dead, Decker would be gone.

The driver, a guy named Paolo, lifted a cigarette to his lips and inhaled. The tip of the cigarette burned to ash. With an exhale, he filled the car with smog.

"What time is it?" Paolo asked for what seemed like the hundredth time.

Decker glanced at the other man from the corner of his eye. "What do you care? You got some place better to be?"

"No, man. It's just, well, you said she left work every day at six thirty. It's almost seven now."

During his scouting trip, Chloe had followed a strict schedule. He didn't like that she hadn't come out of her office—forcing him to wait close to thirty minutes. "Maybe she's working late."

Paolo took another drag from the cigarette. "What are we supposed to do now?"

Decker was loaded with pent-up energy—a spring, ready to explode. It was always like this before he carried out a kill. The adrenaline enabled him to act on his violent impulses, without thought or care. It made him feel powerful, invincible—and it made him incredibly dangerous.

Decker never took his eyes from the door. "It's her time to die."

Paolo shook his head. "How're we supposed to do the job if she doesn't come out of the building?"

"Well, I guess we'll go and get her." Decker decided on the next move in an instant. From his earlier visit, he knew that the DA's offices were on the first floor in the back of the building. He knew that the sheriff had her offices on the second floor, but at this time of the evening all three deputies were either on patrol or at home. He knew that the door was left unlocked until 10:00 p.m. and that a single guard stood watch. He also knew that none of the zoned alarms were set until the guard went home. "The way I figure it, we have five minutes to get the job done. More than that and we'll be trapped by the local law."

"Five minutes," Paolo echoed. "Got it."

"You ready?"

Paolo held a handgun in his lap. Pulling back on the slide, he chambered a round. "Yeah, man. I'm ready."

Decker's gun was tucked into the small of his back, the hard metal biting his flesh. He reveled in the pain.

It kept him focused. Vaulting from the car, he sprinted up the steps. Paolo left the car's ignition running and was right behind him.

Pulling open the unlocked doors, he rushed into the dim lobby.

The guard, a man with a white mustache and a brown uniform, sat behind a desk. He stood as Decker and Paolo entered. "Hey, it's after hours. You can't be here."

Decker lifted the gun and fired once, its blast echoing in the cavernous space. The bullet struck the man in the chest. The guard slammed into the wall at his back, then pitched forward, falling face-first onto the desk.

Decker raced down the hall.

The DA's workspace took up a quarter of the ground level, with Chloe's personal office in the back corner. Sweat dampened Decker's back, and his shirt stuck to his skin. Standing in the reception area, he pressed himself against the wall. Paolo stood beside a door.

Holding up his hand, Decker lifted his fingers, signaling to his partner.

One. Two. Three.

Decker kicked the door open. Gun already aimed, he crossed the threshold.

A man with a comb-over and round glasses sat behind the desk, holding a phone to his ear.

His skin, already pale, turned the color of spoiled milk.

Decker asked, "Who are you?"

"I'm Jake Loeb, the district attorney."

Paolo snorted. "That's a lie. Chloe Ryder, she's the DA."

"Chloe works for the Attorney General's office now,"

said Jake, a tremor in his voice. "She left Pleasant Pines last week."

"Last week?" Decker echoed. His face flushed with anger.

It was the first time that his intel had ever failed him—and just maybe, the worst mistake he'd ever made, too. All the recon he'd done. All the days he'd gotten coffee at that crappy Main Street diner, hoping he'd remain unrecognized—and gloating a little when his disguises kept the locals from seeing him for the killer he was.

But not hearing the gossip about Chloe Ryder's promotion had cost him, huge. It would be a blow to his reputation for sure—and now, thanks to the screwup, he had a mess on his hands. The objective, always, was to get in and out without detection. Now, he'd be forced to leave a trail of bodies.

But there was no other way. Not if he wanted to survive.

Jake swallowed. "What do you want?"

The words brought him back into focus—and amplified his rage even more. "Not you," said Decker, he lifted the gun.

"Please. No. What do you want?" the attorney begged. "I can help you with anything…"

What he wanted was to kill Chloe Ryder. What he couldn't have were witnesses. He pulled the trigger. The bullet ripped a hole in the guy's neck and painted the back wall with red. The report boomed, rattling the window. Moving to the door, Decker said, "The clock's ticking, man."

They raced down the hallway and their footfalls rang

out in the empty corridor. Paolo was at his side. The car idled at the curb, a cloud of exhaust billowing around it.

They hadn't killed Chloe Ryder, but they'd assassinated the district attorney. The job—sort of—was done. Now, the Transgressors had to pay up.

Decker pushed the door open as a clap of thunder ricocheted off the walls. He glanced over his shoulder. Stumbling, Paolo held his middle. A red stain bloomed on his abdomen.

Paolo had been shot. But by who?

Turning his head, Derek saw the security guard was once again on his feet. His white mustache was wet with spit and stained red by blood. A tendril of smoke rose from the barrel of his gun. His hand shaking with pain, he raised it again to shoot, but Decker turned—fired once—and blew off the top of the old man's skull. The guard's weapon clattered to the floor.

"C'mon, man." Decker slipped his shoulder under Paolo's arm. "The guard definitely called the cops. We have to get the hell out of here."

Dragging the other man to the car, Decker shoved Paolo into the back seat. After stripping off the flannel shirt he wore, he tossed it to the injured man. "Put this on the wound. Press down hard."

Slipping behind the steering wheel, he slammed the car door shut and pulled away. His mind raced as he drove. Paolo's injury looked bad. There was a lot of blood and no exit wound. He needed to find someone who'd treat a gunshot wound and not call the cops.

Fat snowflakes fell as he sped into the gathering darkness. What they needed was to get out of Wyoming and disappear. With the money they'd just earned, they could go just about any place. Maybe Mexico. South America.

Anywhere was better than here.

"Hey, Paolo?" Decker called over his shoulder. "First, you get patched up and then we'll go south of the border while you recuperate. How's that sound? Tequila's the best medicine in the world."

There was no response.

According to the information he'd been given, the extra car was hidden behind an old barn. He followed the digital map along a narrow lane off the main highway until he spotted the structure, looming in the night. He parked, pulling in close and glanced at the bac seat. Paolo's hand rested on his middle, his eyes stared at nothing. The upholstery was soaked with blood. Reaching for Paolo's wrist, Decker felt for a pulse.

He found nothing.

This job was different from all the ones before. Most of his other victims were criminals already. The police investigation into those deaths were perfunctory, at best. This time, he had killed a DA. The cops wouldn't stop until someone was charged with the murder.

What now?

Decker knew that, once again, he had to act.

He found a couple of gallon jugs filled with gasoline stashed in the trunk of the getaway car. He pulled away from the barn, threw it into Park and left the ignition running before returning to Paolo. Decker dumped gas on the front seat and then fished Paolo's lighter from his pocket. Fumes leaked from the car, burning his nose and eyes. Standing at a distance, he flicked the lighter and a flame sprung to life. He tossed it into the car. The driver's seat erupted with a whoosh of heat and fire.

He didn't wait around to watch the car burn.

After sliding behind the wheel of the second car and pulling onto the road, a tendril of sweat snaked down the side of his neck. Burning the car to destroy all the evidence would damn well stall the authorities for a while—but he knew it wasn't a foolproof solution. Because of that, he had to disappear—and not just for a few days or even a couple of weeks. Decker had to lay low for months, a year. Maybe longer. Only when the case was considered cold, could he resurface.

He quit thinking about tomorrow, or next week, or even next year and let his mind go blank.

As he drove south through the night, Decker knew it was no use fighting it. Destruction was his nature.

Chapter 1

One Year Later

Clare Chamberlain looked at the dashboard and sighed. The gas gauge was almost flat. Her worldly wealth—a crumpled $100 bill—was shoved into her pocket. It was enough for half a tank of the premium gas her car needed, with change left over for a soda and a sandwich.

And then?

Then, she'd be flat-ass broke.

The dusty plains of south Texas stretched out in all directions, disappearing over the horizon. She hadn't seen a car for miles. In the distance, the sun winked—glinting off glass and metal.

She leaned forward, her chest pressing into the steering wheel.

What was it? A town? A mirage?

Clare continued to drive. A sign on a metal post stood at the roadside. "Welcome to Mercy, Texas."

Mercy, Texas, was little more than a wide spot in the road. At an intersection, a single light flashed red in all directions. There was a gas station/convenience store. A post office inhabited a trailer that was the same dust-brown as the landscape. Across the street from the post office was the Mercy Motel—something her father would have called a motor inn. A wide parking lot separated the motel from a long cinderblock building with a bar named House of Steele. There was also a tattoo parlor called Gettin' Ink'd. More than a dozen motorcycles filled the parking lot.

Clare turned into the gas station. Parking the car next to the pump, she tried not to stare at the topless neon woman flashing atop the bar/tattoo parlor. As she got out of the car, her knees ached. Her head throbbed. Her hands had gone numb from hours of driving. It felt good to stand, but this was no place for a respite.

She fished the money from her pocket, the bill damp with perspiration.

Damn. It was only $50.

Had she really spent all her money?

Fine, then. It was half a tank and a coffee.

After that... Well, Clare didn't know what came after now.

She stopped her fill-up at $40, jiggling the handle to get the last drops of gasoline into the tank.

In the convenience store, a tinsel garland was taped to the front of the counter. "Silver Bells" played softly, although she could see neither radio nor speaker.

Was it really almost Christmas? A wooden-block calendar sat next to the cash register.

December 20.

There was no way she could go home. Which meant that Clare was about to spend her first Christmas alone.

An old man with a stained baseball cap looked up from a gun magazine. "Afternoon," he said. "You lost?"

Truer words had never been spoken. "Just passing through."

She poured herself a coffee, took a long drink and topped off the cup. There went a dollar. She grabbed a bag of chips for $1 as well. Setting the money on the counter, Clare slid the bill toward the man.

He made change.

"Thanks." She scooped up the money and shoved it into her pocket.

"Uh-huh." His eyes were already back on the magazine.

On the way to the car, she ripped open the bag of chips and shoved several in her mouth. It had been more than a day since she'd last eaten. And now the change she got from the gas station had to pay for her next meal—and the one after that.

Clare had left her home because staying meant she'd be risking her life. She knew that to be a fact.

But starving wouldn't be better.

She looked back at the bar. On the door, she could make out a red-and-white help-wanted sign. From her side of the road, she couldn't tell what position they had open. But she wasn't sure it mattered.

It brought up another question, though.

What kind of people lived and worked in a town like

Mercy? From the looks of the place, Clare could only imagine they were people who had fallen so far from grace they had no other options. People who were alone in the world.

Then again, what was Clare?

Driving across the street, she parked at the back of the lot. The building with House of Steele and Gettin' Ink'd was a squat rectangle. There were no windows, only two doors. One word was scrawled on the help-wanted sign. *Bartender.*

That was the first bit of good luck she'd had since leaving home.

In grad school, she'd tended bar for a semester. Of course, that had been more than fifteen years ago. And yeah, it was at a trendy nightspot in a university town, not a seedy biker bar. But wasn't pouring beer the same all over the world?

For a moment, she realized that she could be walking into anything—exposing herself to anyone. She wiped her damp palms over the thighs of her jeans. At this point, she had no other options.

She opened the car door and slipped her tote bag over her shoulder.

Clare Chamberlain was certain of one thing and one thing only. If she wanted to live, she needed to disappear.

And she knew deep in her soul that Mercy, Texas, was the last place that anyone would ever come looking.

Isaac Patton stood beside a row of taps and wiped down the wooden bar. At the beginning of the op, it had all been so simple. Set out a trap for Decker Newcombe and wait.

Yet, waiting was all he'd done for nearly a year.

The life of a bartender in a backwater Texas town had swallowed him whole, and now felt more real than his old existence. Some days, the memory of his job as a member of San Antonio's SWAT team or a private security operative felt more like a dream than real life. What had given him the audacity to think he could start his own firm?

He glanced around the bar. A handful of round tables were filled with members of the Transgressors, the local motorcycle club who used the bar as their clubhouse. Most played cards. A few stared at their illuminated phone screens. Ryan Steele, his business partner—in a manner of speaking—was texting furiously at a table in the corner.

A black-and-white Christmas movie played on one big-screen TV with the sound muted, while another displayed a replay of the previous night's college football game. A set of red and green lights outlined a large mirror that hung behind the bar.

Isaac caught his reflection in the glass. He almost didn't recognize himself. The eyes that looked back at him had a hollow, defeated quality. He'd let his blond hair grow out of his usual crewcut. His cheeks and chin were covered in stubble. Though he'd kept up a fitness routine while undercover—pushups, sit-ups, and running—even that had gotten old.

The outside door opened, and a wedge of sunlight cut across the cement floor. Silhouetted in the light was a female form. Long legs, long golden hair, curvy hips. The woman's face was hidden in the shadow, but he imagined that she was pretty. His shoulders tensed and the immediate reaction left him unsettled.

Isaac straightened his spine. He had to ignore the rising emotions—no matter what. Because if there was one thing he'd learned during his life, it was that feelings of any kind were best avoided.

Tossing the rag into a bin of soapy water, he asked, "Can I help you?"

The woman stepped inside, her eyes darting to the tables and the dozen or so rough men. He'd seen wary glances cast at the gang members more than once. This bar was the first stop on a quick descent into hell. Yet, this woman seemed different from the others. She wore a pair of jeans and a silk tank top. Both were rumpled, but Isaac guessed they were good quality. The large tan and brown tote bag she had slung over her shoulder was expensive, too. He looked for jewelry—specifically a wedding ring. She wore none.

"Can I help you?" he asked again.

"I was wondering," the woman said, chewing on her bottom lip. "I saw your help-wanted sign. I'm here for the job." She cast a glance at the bikers, who all stared back. She returned her gaze to Isaac. "I can tend bar."

He asked, "Do you really want to work in a place like this?"

She shrugged one shoulder. "At the moment, I don't have a whole lot of other choices. I do have experience."

"What's your name?" Isaac asked.

"Clare," she said.

"Clare what?"

"Just Clare."

"I'll take it from here," Ryan cut in. Setting his phone aside, he rose to his feet.

If Isaac was forced to describe his relationship with Ryan in a word, he'd pick *complicated*. The biker was an integral part of the plan to catch Decker. As the hitman's former business manager, Steele was brought in by Isaac and his federal partners. As part of the bargain made with Ryan, he was set up as the owner of the bar, tattoo parlor and motel. Even though Decker had gone to ground months ago, after the disastrous hit gone wrong in Pleasant Pines, once the hitman needed his money, he'd come looking for Ryan.

And when that happened, Isaac would be ready.

His attention on the new arrival, Ryan continued, "Let's see what you can do, Just Clare. Can you draw a beer from the tap?"

Clare met Isaac's gaze. "Can I?"

Keeping up the cover story, he said, "That guy owns this place. I just work here." Stepping away from the taps, he continued, "It's all yours."

Ryan lifted his chin. "Go on."

After setting her bag on the bar, she made her way to Isaac's side. Taking a glass from a stack, she pulled back on the tap. She kept the glass tilted to prevent a foam head from forming. Once the glass was filled with golden liquid, she set the beer on the bar.

"Not bad." Ryan lifted the beer and took a sip. Setting it back down, he smirked. "Do you know what's in a Long Island Iced Tea?"

She lifted her chin. "Do you?"

The members of the MC chuckled. Narrowing his eyes, Ryan glared at Clare.

"She got you on that one," a man from the crowd called out.

"Besides," Clare continued, "at a place like this, it's mostly beer and shots. I can obviously pull a beer, and anyone can pour a shot." She met his gaze and held it steadily. "What about it? Am I hired?"

At six-two, Ryan Steele was every bit as tall as Isaac. He wore his dark hair long, but his temper was short. He was the kind of guy people avoided. Yet, Clare had stood up to him. Isaac admired her for that courage.

Maybe she did have the spine to work in this place.

"You?" Ryan scratched at the stubble on his chin and shook his head. "Naw, Isaac is right. You're all wrong for our place. If you want to stay, order a drink. If not, get the hell out."

He shouldn't care about what happened to Clare but for some reason, he did. A filmy mirror hung behind the bottles of liquor. His reflection—light brown hair, gray eyes—filled a corner of the glass. He watched Clare as she bit her bottom lip hard.

She let out a long breath. "Look, I need this job. Just give me another chance."

Watching in the mirror, Isaac held his breath.

Ryan returned to his seat. Stretching his legs in front of him, he folded his arms over his chest. "I don't think if I gave you twenty chances, you'd be any better."

"Really, I can do it," she insisted.

Picking up his phone, Ryan turned his attention to the screen. Clare and her troubles were already forgotten as far as he was concerned.

Isaac exhaled as Clare rounded the bar. She went to grab her tote bag, but accidentally knocked it from the counter. The contents spilled all over the floor. A small black flash drive. A wallet. Lipstick. Sunglasses. Cell phone. With a curse, she shoved her belongings back into the bag. Eyes straight ahead, she strode toward the door.

Then, Clare was gone.

"Look," said one of the bikers. He picked up a car's fob from the floor. Hooking a finger through a metal ring, he let it dangle from his finger. "She forgot her keys. How long do you think it'll take for her to work up the nerve to come back and get them?"

The crowd roared with laughter.

His hand instinctively made a fist. The need to take care of Clare, inexplicable as it was, clouded his vision. He rounded the bar. Standing before the gang member, he held out his hand. "I'll take them out to her."

"You're ruining the fun," said Ryan. "We could take bets. I'll ante up a Benjamin that it takes her more than twenty minutes."

Isaac didn't move. "Hand them over."

"Whatever, man." The guy slapped the keys into Isaac's outstretched hand.

From his last days on the San Antonio SWAT team, Isaac had made it a point to never build relationships at work. As he walked to the door, he reminded himself that doing the decent thing wasn't the same as making a personal connection. He'd return the keys and head back into the bar. It'd take him two minutes—no more.

Pushing the door open, he stepped into the afternoon sun. The light left him momentarily dazed. Yet, Clare was impossible to miss. Standing next to a black luxury sedan, she dug through her tote bag with a look of panic on her face.

"You dropped these." Holding up the fob, he approached her.

"Oh," said Clare, with an exhale. "You found them." She hesitated. "Thank you for bringing them out. I hated the idea of going back inside."

Clare held out her hand and Isaac pressed the keys into her palm. Her skin was soft and warm. Up close, he could see that her eyes were a deep shade of blue.

"I don't think that you're the type to turn your back on a challenge." Isaac withdrew his hand.

She gripped the keys. "Thanks again."

"If you don't mind me saying, you aren't like most of the women who work at the bar."

"What's that supposed to mean?" she asked.

"You have a nice car. Nice clothes. Nice bag. Seems like someone's been taking care of you."

"I can take care of myself," she said, unlocking the car door with the push of a button.

"Why go into a place like that?" Isaac hooked his thumb toward the bar. "And ask for a job."

"Because, like I said, I'm taking care of myself." Clare worked her jaw back and forth. "I'd better go."

"Where are you headed?"

She pulled the car door open. From where he stood, he could see a pillow and blanket. Fast-food wrappers. A small suitcase. She was on the run. Who was she running from and why?

"Why do you care?" she asked.

He lifted a shoulder. "Just making conversation."

"Well, don't," said Clare.

Isaac knew everyone had a past. But it was obvious that he'd pushed Clare for more information than she wanted to give. It was time to let her get back on the road. He should just walk away. Instead, he remained in his spot.

Fishing a wad of cash from his pocket, he pulled off two Benjamins. "You seem down on your luck. I hope this helps you get to someplace better."

"I don't want your charity," she said stiffly, ignoring his outstretched hand.

He reached over and set the bills on the hood of her car. "Suit yourself."

A hint of anger flashed in her eyes. "Keep your money. I don't need it."

Isaac knew that was a lie. He also knew that Clare would keep the cash if he refused to take it back. He turned toward the bar.

"Hey," she called out. "What's your name?"

He stopped walking and turned to face the woman. She held the bills in her hand, the afternoon sun turning her hair golden. "Isaac Patton."

"Thank you, Isaac."

"For what?"

"For bringing out the keys. For giving me—" she looked at the bills flapping in the wind and her eyes widened "—two-hundred dollars. For being the first truly nice person I've spoken to in weeks."

He nodded. "Take care, Just Clare."

She didn't move.

Neither did he.

Maybe it was the heat from the Texas sun that turned him a little crazy. Maybe it was that Clare had called him nice—something he hadn't heard in quite a while. Maybe it was the fact that Christmas was just a few days away and he felt like doing the right thing. Whatever the reason, Isaac asked, "You really want a job at the bar?"

"Define want," she said, with a short laugh. "I need to make some money."

Sure, Ryan told her to pound sand, but Isaac definitely had his thumb on all the owner's pressure points. What's more, Isaac knew how to squeeze. If he said that Clare was hired, Ryan had no choice but to agree. "I only need help through the New Year. All the jobs are off the books, so don't expect a paycheck or anything. Whatever tips you earn are yours to keep. There're a few rooms at the motel that are rented long-term. I know one with a free bed. You'd have a roommate, but it's better than sleeping in your car."

Clare's eyes flashed again—with anger, pride and something else. What had it been? Hurt? Shame? She slammed the car door shut. "Who says I'm sleeping in my car?"

"If you aren't, why you got a bed set up in your back seat? Why all the food wrappers?"

"Maybe I like to keep my pillow and blanket with me."

Isaac had to admit that he liked Clare's moxie. Maybe that was his problem.

She was a mystery that needed solving. After months of waiting for Decker Newcombe to surface with no luck, finding someone with a story to unravel, someone who, just maybe, could use his help, left him feeling like, well, he'd washed the grit of the world off his hands. "Look around you. Everyone here is down on their luck. Or worse, they got no luck at all. Do you want the job or not?"

"I don't think the owner likes me much. Who says he won't fire me as soon as I show up for a shift?"

"Me. I say so."

"And who are you?"

That was a question Isaac would never answer—not honestly, at least. He'd never tell her about his time with the San Antonio PD SWAT or why he'd left. He definitely wouldn't share that he was working undercover with the FBI's San Antonio office to catch a hitman who'd been on the lam for a year.

After a beat, he said, "I'm just a guy who's trying to make a living. You look like you need a break. You want the job or not?"

Clare scraped her bottom lip with her teeth. It was a gesture he'd already seen once. It was clearly a sign of nerves and something he found sexy as hell.

"Can I ask you a question?" She didn't wait for his answer. "Why are you being so nice to me?"

"Honestly?"

"Absolutely," she said.

"I have no idea." He paused. "The job. Yes, or no?"

"Yes," she said, breathless. "Of course, yes."

"Park in front of room seven. You'll have to move your car later, but for now you can unload your stuff."

He watched as she slid into her sedan and started the engine. She pulled into a space as he walked across the parking lot. Clare turned off the engine as he stepped on the sidewalk. She got out of the car, and he wrapped his knuckles on the door. "Trinity. It's me, Isaac."

The door opened a moment later. Trinity, a tall redhead, was wearing a threadbare T-shirt and baggy shorts. Tattoos covered much of her exposed flesh. A tiger lounged on one bicep. A pink python with eyes like emeralds was coiled around her calf and thigh. Eye makeup was smeared across her cheeks. "Hey, handsome. What can I do for you?"

"You got a new roommate." He stepped aside. "This is Just Clare. She's the new bartender."

"Don't worry, honey," said Trinity, reading the discomfort in Clare's expression. "Most of us don't use last names neither." She looked Clare over from the top of her head to the tips of her shoes. "What're you doing here? You look a little too well-off for a town like this."

Isaac answered the question. "She's tending bar with me. Starts tonight."

"I'm one of the tattoo artists," said Trinity, opening the door farther. "Come in, honey."

Clutching the tote bag to her chest, Clare said, "Thanks."

"Trinity, I'm putting you in charge. Make sure Clare looks right."

Trinity placed her palm on Patton's chest. "I'd do anything for you, you know that. Right?"

Stepping back, he let Trinity's touch slip away. "I'm counting on you," he said, stilling her with a look.

Walking away, Isaac could feel the women standing at the door, watching his back. In all his time undercover, Isaac had vowed never to get involved with anyone associated with any case he was working on. After a few short minutes with Clare, he'd already violated that rule by offering her assistance. And the thing was, he felt there were other rules which wouldn't matter too much to Isaac as far as Clare was concerned.

Maybe Ryan was right, and she had to go.

No. He'd never send Clare away. Not when she clearly needed protection from something. Or some*one*.

Which meant that she'd stay. And become a distraction that he couldn't afford.

Chapter 2

At 7:45 p.m., Clare sat in a wooden chair covered with a worn blue velour. The motel room was like many of the nondescript ones she'd seen before. Two full-size beds were separated by a small nightstand with a lamp. There was also a chest of drawers against the wall, along with a desk and a mirror.

There were differences, though. The room was obviously lived in—Trinity's clothes and makeup covered most every surface. She had also taken the time to decorate the drab space for the holiday, which gave it a bit of cheer. She'd set up a small Christmas tree in the corner near the single window. The artificial tree was four feet tall and covered in white lights and decorations in every shade of blue.

Clare couldn't explain it—the cluttered room and the

Christmas tree felt homey. After she'd gotten settled, she returned to the gas station and purchased a raspberry cereal bar. For tonight, it was her dinner. It left her almost no money, but she hoped that it was temporary. For the first time in months, she actually felt like she could relax. Then again, it'd be a mistake to let her guard down.

Her new roommate had offered to do her makeup for the first shift. It was an offer that Clare accepted. The other woman swiped a makeup brush through a palette of bright blue eyeshadow. She tapped off the excess.

"Close your eyes." Trinity wore a light pink robe. Her red wavy hair was pulled into a ponytail. A silver locket hung around her neck.

Clare hesitated a moment before letting her lids shut.

"I know this color seems like a bit much," Trinity said, applying the shadow. "But you'd be surprised how it looks when the lights are low."

Eyes still shut, Clare said, "I'm just pouring beers. Nobody will care how I look."

"That's what you think." She applied shadow to the other lid. "If you're behind the bar looking fine, you'll make more in tips." Trinity grabbed another brush, filling it with bright white shadow. "This is the highlighter. Keep your eyes closed."

Clare squeezed her lids shut again.

"Can I ask you a question?" Trinity asked.

"Sure."

"You ever work at a place like this?"

"I tended bar when I was in grad school near campus." She paused, trying to find a way to show that she belonged. "It was a popular hangout. On the weekends, there'd be a line at the bar that was five or six deep."

"Open your eyes." Clare did as she was told as Trinity examined her handiwork. "Filling pitchers of beer for frat guys is a lot different than working at this bar."

A jolt ran through her body, and she sat up straighter. "Why's that?"

"All those bikers hang out here. It can get pretty wild some nights. Violent. They do some business and it's not exactly legal."

She probably shouldn't be shocked. What's more, she was on the run because she'd learned that nothing—and nobody—were ever what they seemed.

Then again, here nobody wanted her dead. Memories swirled around Clare, threatening to pull her under and drown her with regrets.

She cleared her throat and tried to think of a way to change the subject. She asked about the first thing that came to her thoughts. "Tell me about Isaac." Huh. Apparently, the muscular bartender was still on her mind. "He seems nice."

"Isaac is probably the only decent guy around here, but he keeps to himself. Far as I can tell, he's never dated anyone. Never takes anyone back to his room. Never even flirts." She shrugged as if that was everything to know about Isaac Patton.

Honestly, Clare shouldn't be giving the guy a second thought, and yet, she was curious. "You said he doesn't date anyone here. Why not?"

Trinity smeared glue on a set of false eyelashes. "It's not an issue of liking or disliking—he just keeps his distance, that's all. I don't know really why. We like him, that's for sure. Isaac's handsome. He's tall. Built. Has the most amazing gray eyes that look like cracked glass. What's not to like?" She reached for Clare's lids. "Look up. Don't move."

Clare stared at the ceiling as Trinity applied the false lashes. As she waited, Clare knew she'd never stay in Mercy, Texas, long enough to find out more about Isaac. She just needed to make enough money to get to Mexico. From there, who knew? Maybe she'd try Costa Rica or Argentina. Someplace she could never be found.

Trinity applied red lipstick to Clare's mouth. "The bar opens at eight o'clock and closes at two in the morning. The first and last hours can be dead, but in between you'll be busy."

"This town is so small, though. Where do all the people come from?" From what Clare could tell, there wasn't another town for miles and miles.

"There are several ranches in the area and all the hands and sometimes the foremen show up after work. San Antonio is only a couple of hours away. Encantador is about twenty miles from here. But people come from Austin and Dallas, too. South of the border. Even as far away as Houston."

Clare felt as if she'd stepped through the proverbial looking glass, and everything she thought to be real was just an illusion. "People come from hours away for what? How crazy is the party?"

"This is a biker bar. It can get really crazy." Trinity drew her brows together. "Oh, honey, you really don't know what you've wandered into, do you?"

Clare didn't answer, but her expression clearly gave her away.

The other woman continued, "Isaac asked me to take care of you, so I'm going to give you some advice. Get back into that fancy car of yours and go. Whatever you left behind is better than where you are now."

Her throat began to close, making it nearly impossible to breathe "I'm never going back."

Shrugging, Trinity said, "Suit yourself." While applying blush to Clare's cheeks, the other woman ran her tongue over her teeth. "I'm done. What do you think?"

She glanced in a wall-mounted mirror. The woman who looked back was almost unrecognizable. She certainly had on more makeup than Clare would have ever worn, even to go out to a formal event, but Trinity was right—despite the wild colors, the overall effect made her eyes stand out more. The shirt—on loan from Trinity—was low and tight. It was all so very unlike her, and yet, Clare noticed something in her reflection that she hadn't seen in a long time. There was a spark in her eyes. What was it? Defiance? Confidence? Resolve?

In the end, she decided that it didn't matter. Whatever it was, it had given her the ability to strike out on her own. Certainly, her rediscovered self-assurance would help her to survive.

And if not? Her shoulders slumped. Well, then she'd fake it as long as she could.

Isaac stood behind the bar and kept his eye on the front door. Sure, he was always vigilant about who entered the House of Steele but tonight was different. Tonight, he was watching for Clare.

He'd told himself that it was stupid to shave and control his hair with a little gel. But he'd done it anyway. When he glanced in the mirror behind the bar, his own reflection was at least familiar. He turned back to the room.

A rock 'n' roll version of "Santa Claus is Comin' to Town" blared from the speakers. Spotlights swept erratically around the darkened room. A disco ball hung from the ceiling, scattering multicolored reflections across the floor. A few patrons sat at the bar and sipped drinks.

"Another one?" A ranch hand from the nearby Double S lifted his beer. The cattle ranch was one of the few in the area that actually turned a profit. The agricultural market had taken a hit in recent years with the rise of the corporate run–farms and unpredictable weather. Many of the small family ranches had sold their land, or simply folded.

Not the Double S. Run by the Sauter family for generations it was managed by Sage Sauter currently. The ranch started producing grass-fed beef before it was in demand and that toehold in the organic beef market kept them in business.

"Sure thing." Isaac grabbed a cold can from the fridge and popped the top. "How's Sage?" he asked, mentioning the only female ranch owner for miles.

"Same as always."

"Tough and fair?" Isaac asked.

"'Bout sums it up." The ranch hand gulped his beer. "You got plans for the holidays?"

"Does pouring beers count?" When he'd first started working the case, he'd been certain that Decker would quickly resurface for his money. All Isaac had to do was wait. Nearly a year later, he'd grown tired despite his dedication to nailing the bastard. He couldn't stop thinking about the life that was going on without him.

Was he about to miss visiting with family in San Antonio? The thought of spending Christmas alone burned a hole inside his chest. Yet, he wondered about Clare. He'd told her that she could stay through the New Year. But would she?

He pointed to beer. "You want that on your tab?"

Wiping his mouth with the back of his hand, the ranch hand said, "If you don't mind."

As Isaac marked the drink on the bill, the door opened. He looked up as Clare stepped into the room. He swallowed and dropped his gaze. Yet, he couldn't help but look at her again. Her shirt hugged her breasts like a second skin. The neckline dipped low, revealing likely more of her cleavage than she realized. He averted his gaze, reminding himself of his rule not to get involved with anyone—and to focus on his singular goal.

Approaching the bar, she gave a tight smile. "Trinity told me that the shift started at eight o'clock. I'm ready to get started. What do you want me to do?" She paused. "And did you talk to your boss? You're sure I won't get kicked out?"

Isaac had yet to speak to Ryan. Then again, tonight it didn't matter. He'd left Mercy and wouldn't be back before last call. He said simply, "The owner's not here tonight. I'll talk to him when he gets back."

"Okay, then," she said.

Isaac cleared his throat. "When was the last time you tended bar?"

"Grad school. About fifteen years ago."

"You still remember how to work a tap, so that's a

start," said Isaac. "Come back here and I'll show you where we keep everything."

She rounded the bar and stood at Isaac's side. The scent of her perfume—both floral and musky—washed over him. He held his breath for a moment, distracted by her scent. Shaking his head, he tried to focus. There would be a full house tonight. If she couldn't handle the crowd, things could get ugly.

Pointing to a small refrigerator, he began, "We keep the bottled beer in there. Beer glasses are under the taps. Shot glasses are under the liquor." He paused, distracted again by the brush of her arm on his as she leaned over to look at the layout of glasses beneath the counter.

Isaac forced himself to return to his instructions. "There are several cocktail waitresses and guys like to buy them drinks. If one of them orders a shot for herself, give her this." He held up a whiskey bottle. "It's filled with weak iced tea. They'll know what they're getting, so don't be worried about that."

She took the bottle from him. Her fingertips grazed the back of his hand, and again, that electric charge surged up his arm. She examined the amber liquid. "Smart idea, to make sure that the servers can stay sober."

It was exactly why they drank tea, yet he was surprised by her reaction. Had he expected her to be disapproving? Maybe because of the expensive bag and the luxurious car, he'd thought she wouldn't understand. But she did. For a moment, he was disappointed, and Isaac knew why. At least if she'd been judgmental, he'd have a reason to dislike her.

Isaac made it a point to never ask anyone about their

personal life. Having to answer questions put people on guard—and suspicions were the last thing he wanted. Yet, he couldn't keep himself from asking, "So, what'd you study?"

"In grad school?" she asked, before answering his question, but not saying too much. "Environmental engineering."

"Not many engineers around here." Still, he knew that education meant little. People's lives could take almost any kind of turn, up or down. He really should go back to minding his own business. But Clare had piqued his interest. "You ever work as an engineer?"

Clare lifted one shoulder and let it drop. "For a while at the EPA."

"I've never met anyone from the Environmental Protection Agency. What did you do when you worked there?"

She picked up a cocktail napkin and wiped down the bar. "Nothing interesting. Regulations and stuff."

It wasn't much of an answer. But his first impression of Clare was right. She was well educated and came from a financially comfortable background. Now he was certain there was more to her story.

Sure, he shouldn't care where Clare came from or where she was going. But he did.

He said, "Looks like you got settled and that Trinity's treating you right."

Clare gave a quick nod. "Thanks for setting me up in her room. She's been really helpful."

"She's been at Gettin' Ink'd since before I started working in Mercy. She's good people."

"So." Clare drew out the single word. "How'd *you* end up in Mercy?"

"I was in a Wyoming jail because a bar fight got out of hand," he began his well-practiced cover story. In fact, he'd told the lie so many times, it almost felt like the truth. "Ryan was my cellmate for a few weeks. He told me to look him up when I got out. I had no intention of ever contacting him." He shrugged. "But with my record, it was tough to find work. I remembered him mentioning this bar, so I made the call and Ryan offered me a job." He shrugged. "And here I am."

She nodded, seemingly buying his story without hesitation.

"Do you live in the motel, too?"

He nodded. "Room three."

"Anyone with you?" She discreetly placed a bottle of water for herself underneath the bar, then glanced back at him. "Wife? Kids?"

"This is hardly a place for a child to grow up," he said. "But no, I'm not married. Divorced once. No kids, and I haven't spoken to my ex in years."

She watched him for a minute. "Aren't you going to ask me if I'm married or have kids?"

"Don't need to. You aren't wearing a wedding band, so you aren't married. If you had kids, then you'd home with them—not tending bar in the desert a few days before Christmas."

"You can be married and not wear a wedding ring," she said, challenging him.

"People do it all the time—but not someone like you." He paused. "Tell me I'm wrong."

Clare hesitated, then shook her head. "You aren't wrong. What you are is perceptive."

"It's a blessing and a curse," he joked. Christ, when had he become so comfortable with Clare?

One of the patrons tapped his empty glass on the wooden top. Clare set the whisky bottle back in its place and moved down the bar. "What are you drinking?" she asked.

The electric charge still surged through his veins as he watched her go. It didn't matter if her scent teased his senses, or if her touch made his body go rock-hard. If he wanted sex, that was something he could find. Easily. But he was in this hellhole to serve a higher purpose. He'd sacrificed almost a year of his life working undercover and now wasn't the time to get sidetracked.

As Isaac watched Clare begin to serve customers, he reminded himself that she was on the run, from someone or something. Whatever she was tangled up in meant danger to his case. And he couldn't—hell, wouldn't—risk temptation when there was so much more at stake.

By 2:15 a.m., the bar was empty save for Clare and Isaac. She couldn't remember a time when her back or her feet hurt worse. For almost six hours straight, she'd served beers and shots to a growing crowd of rowdy—and increasingly drunk—patrons. But she welcomed the pain. It meant she had worked hard and earned some money—money that put her closer to the escape she desperately needed.

Or so she hoped, anyway.

"You did good." Isaac placed a stack of cash on the

bar. "It's half of the tips," he continued, then lowered his voice. "But don't count it here. Wait until you're alone."

Stuffing the wad into the front pocket of her jeans, Clare nodded. "Understood."

"You earned it." He took a bottle of beer from the small fridge. "You want something a little stronger than that water you were sipping all night?"

What she wanted was to sleep for hours. Since leaving her home in Columbus, Clare hadn't dozed for more than a few hours at a time. Afterward, she woke in the clutches of the same nightmare, and somehow more tired than when she closed her eyes. Maybe a beer—along with the fatigue from working—was the right mix for her to get some decent sleep. She reached for the bottle. "That'd be nice."

While opening his own beer, Isaac said, "Must've been hard standing on your feet, after being behind the wheel for so long."

She guessed that he was digging for information about her, but it would be a mistake to share too much with a guy as observant and discerning as Isaac. "I'm okay," she said, not giving away anything about her past. Yet, that didn't mean she wasn't curious about the House of Steele. "It seemed busy tonight."

He took a long swallow from the bottle. Setting it on the bar, he said, "It's always busy."

She nodded and took a drink. The beer landed in her stomach like an explosion. She really should've eaten something more than the gas station chips and the cereal bar. Honestly, she'd been nervous about her shift. The roll of bills was heavy in her pocket. How much had she made? Or maybe she should be asking a different question. How much did it cost to start a new life?

"There were a lot more people here than I expected to see. I mean, this place definitely is in the middle of nowhere..." She let her final word unravel into an unspoken question.

Isaac said nothing, just sipped his beer.

Clare tried again. "Why is this place so popular?"

"Let me give you some advice. Don't ask questions. You won't like the answers."

Like a boulder had been dropped on her shoulders, Clare felt a weight pressing her down. "Got it."

He eyed her carefully. "Are you going to be able to work here for the next few weeks? I really need the help through New Year's Eve. It's a good time to make a lot of tips. Bad time to be short staffed."

"How much are you talking about?" she asked.

He shrugged. "Over a thousand bucks, easy."

"I'll be here," she promised. Hell, she thought, for that much cash, she could stand it. At least, she thought she could.

"We're closed on Christmas Day if you want to visit family or whatever."

Christmas in Mercy. Now that was a joyless thought. She had no place else to go. Nobody else to see. "I'll be here then, too."

His gaze skimmed her expression. "You look exhausted."

She tried to make a joke. "I must look better than I feel."

He gave a quick laugh. "Let's call it a night." Isaac moved from behind the bar. "Come on. I gotta lock up."

Isaac punched a code into a keypad near the door. The alarm beeped three times. He opened the door for Clare.

After tossing the bottle into the trash, she walked to the front door and stepped outside. Isaac pulled the door closed. Using a key that he carried in his pants pocket, he locked the dead bolt. Only then did he give the handle a hard pull. Satisfied that the bar was secure, he shoved the key back into his pocket and gave a sigh that Clare could only describe as weary.

Night stretched over the open landscape, replacing the blinding sun and furnace-like midday heat with a sky of velvety black, along with a cold that bit into Clare's flesh and chilled her to her bones.

The motel was on the far side of the parking lot, an ocean of darkness between two islands of light. It wasn't that far away. Still, her pulse raced at the thought of walking alone. Clare wondered if she'd always been this afraid of the dark. Some days, it was all but impossible to remember who she'd been before her final night in Ohio.

Folding her arms across her chest, she stood on the cracked sidewalk and shivered.

"Damn," Isaac cursed. "It's cold."

"I didn't expect it to be this chilly." She rubbed her hands over her shoulders.

"I'll walk you back to the motel," he said, before quickly adding, "Just to make sure you get back to the room. It may look quiet here, but you never know who might show up around closing time."

As they walked through the night, she realized it was the first time in months that she'd actually felt…safe. It was more than finding a temporary place to live. It was Isaac and the fact that he'd seen her need and offered help. Cash. Shelter. A job.

There was more to his story—more to his life—than just a guy who threw beers at a roadside bar in Mercy, Texas. She was sure of that.

Who was Isaac Patton, really?

They stood in front of room seven. A single bulb hung over the door, buzzing loudly. Trinity had given Clare a spare key, which was in the same pocket as her money. She pulled it out, careful to leave the tips in place.

"Well," she began, key in hand. "I better—"

"Yeah, I should probably—" He spoke at the same time, then hooked his thumb over his shoulder. "You know, get going."

"Thanks, again." She turned for the door and tried to slide the key home. Metal scraped against metal, and it stopped. Clare jiggled the key and tried to tug it free. It was no good—the key was stuck. "Dammit," she cursed.

"Here," said Isaac, reaching around her. "Let me."

His hand covered her own and Clare's pulse spiked. His breath warmed her shoulder. She knew that she should move away, but she was rooted to the spot.

"Sometimes, you just have to ease it in," Isaac said, his voice dark and seductive.

He pushed her hand and the key slid home. For a moment, they stood with his palm on the back of her hand. Her pulse raced and her skin tingled. Clare let herself take in the moment. This was the first time in a long while that she'd felt a physical connection to another person.

To a man.

Then again, whatever she felt didn't matter. Mercy was only a temporary pit stop. As soon as she had enough money to disappear, she'd leave—and never look back.

Chapter 3

There was a rattling noise an instant before the door opened. Clare stumbled forward as the key slid from her grip.

Trinity stood on the threshold. Her face was clean, and her auburn hair was wound into a messy bun at the top of her head. "There you are," she said. "I heard something and thought maybe you couldn't work the lock." She paused. "It sticks sometimes."

"I warned her," said Isaac. He'd stepped away from the door and was already part of the shadows. "I have to go." He lifted a hand. "Good night."

"Good night," she called after him. Her voice cracked. It didn't matter. Isaac was already gone and blending with the darkness.

"Jeeze, it's freezing out here." Trinity stepped away from the door. "Come on in. This is your place, after all."

Following Trinity into the room, she closed the door. The lights on the tree twinkled and a *Friends* rerun played on a boxy TV. After standing outside, the room was hot—almost stifling. Or maybe it was having Isaac's hand on hers that left Clare flushed.

"How was your night?" Trinity asked. "From the tattoo parlor, it looked like you were busy."

"We were." Clare slumped onto the bed. The mattress sagged in the middle, yet she didn't care. After weeks of fitful naps in the back seat of her car, any bed was a luxury.

"I was just about to change," said Trinity. "But I'll go to the bathroom and give us both some privacy."

Clare took the moment of solitude to count her haul. The wad of bills was thick. Isaac had taken the time to organize the money. There were more $1 and $5 bills than $10s or $20s. Even so, she was surprised to discover she'd made $482. Along with the $200 he'd given her, she had almost $700. After almost two weeks of working at the House of Steele, she might save thousands of dollars.

For the first time since leaving her old life, she thanked her lucky stars. After slipping out of her sneakers, Clare rolled the bills into two separate piles and shoved each into the toe of a shoe. That was followed by a sweaty sock. She stashed her shoes in her suitcase and engaged the combination lock. Her roommate seemed nice, but she wasn't about to trust anyone.

Trinity exited the bathroom.

"You hungry? I know how I get after working a long shift."

The last thing she'd eaten was that cereal bar, hours ago. "Starved."

Trinity opened the top drawer of the dresser. "I always stock up on snacks whenever I can get a ride to the grocery store in Encantador. Help yourself." She removed an oatmeal cream pie and took a bite. "Really, I don't mind sharing."

Rising from the bed, Clare moved to the dresser. The drawer was filled with individually wrapped cookies, chips, pretzels and crackers. At the sight of the food, her stomach grumbled loudly. She took a pack of crackers with peanut butter and sat back on the bed. "Thanks."

After opening the crackers, she shoved one into her mouth. Chewing, she closed her eyes. Sure, it was silly to think that a stale peanut butter cracker was good, much less delicious. But to her, it was the best thing she'd eaten in a while. She swallowed and sighed. "That's tasty."

"Don't be shy. I can tell you weren't lying when you said that you were starving." Trinity tossed pretzels and chocolate chip cookies—both in bags—at Clare. The snacks hit the mattress. "Out here, we gotta take care of each other. Nobody else gives a crap about what happens in Mercy."

Scooping the bags closer, she gave a mirthless laugh. "This is more than I've eaten all week."

"Help yourself to the food whenever you want. You hear me?"

She nodded and ate another cracker. "I do."

Trinity remained on her feet and finished her oatmeal cream pie. She threw the wrapper in the garbage and held out her hand for Clare's trash. "The only problem with food in the room is you can't leave anything out. It attracts bugs. Big bugs." She circled her fingers, presumably showing the size of insect invaders.

Clare shivered. "I guess everything is bigger in Texas." She opened the pretzels and shoved several into her mouth.

"In the mood for a glass of vino?" her roommate asked, filling a paper cup with red wine. "A little holiday cheer in a cup."

Clare wasn't, especially after the beer, but she said, "Sure."

Trinity filled a second cup. Holding out the drink, she said, "Here you go."

"Thanks." Clare sipped the wine. The alcohol slid through her veins, relaxing her further. Although she had to wonder if chasing a beer with wine was really the best idea in her exhausted condition.

"Not often that I get a GWN."

"GWN?" Clare repeated.

"Girls' Wine Night," said Trinity. "You probably go to cocktail parties and have fun all of the time."

"I used to." When Clare married into a family filled with old Ohio money, she'd understood that there would be lots of expected socializing. But... "And I hated every minute."

Trinity barked with a laugh. "Damn, you're funny."

"Maybe Isaac would let me do a comedy night. What do you think?" Clare teased, finishing the last of her pretzels.

"Maybe..." Trinity sipped her wine, grinning.

At one time in her life, making small talk had been

easy. Now, she couldn't think of anything else to say. "What about your night? Did you have any customers?"

Sitting on her own bed, Trinity took a swallow of wine. "Oh, sure. Someone always wants a new tat. Mostly, I'm paid to keep my mouth shut about how the Transgressors use the bar as a place to do business."

"Oh." Clare's face was hot. She'd been warned more than once not to ask questions. And she'd been working so hard to keep up with the pace as the night went on that she hadn't had time to really pay attention to the goings-on among the customers. "I didn't mean to pry… I'm sorry…"

"Don't be sorry." Trinity held up a necklace that was around her neck. It was the locket Clare had noticed earlier. Slowly, she opened the front. Instead of a picture, fine strands of hair were tied with a tiny pink ribbon.

"I have a daughter," said Trinity. "Right now, she's with her father. One day soon, I'll save enough money to hire a fancy lawyer and get my visitation rights back."

"What…" she began, before deciding better than to snoop. Trinity was her first ally since leaving Columbus. She didn't want to alienate the woman who had taken her in and been so nice to her. She gave a quick smile. "I'm sure you will."

Trinity eyed her shrewdly. "Go ahead and ask."

She shook her head, wanting to do nothing more than sleep. "Doesn't matter."

Letting the necklace dangle between her fingers, Trinity took a sip of wine. "You want to know what happened? Right? As in why don't I have custody of my child?"

It's exactly what Clare wanted to know. "Like I said, it doesn't matter to me. Everyone has a story." Hadn't

Isaac said something like that earlier? Maybe there was a good bit of wisdom in his words. Just thinking about him brought a smile to her lips. Must be the wine. She took another sip.

"I don't mind you asking. It helps to talk it out. My ex-husband is an alright guy. And he is a good dad. When we got together, we both partied a little. That stopped when I got pregnant. But after I had the baby..." She paused. "You got kids?"

Clare shook her head. "No kids."

"Well, being a mom is the hardest thing ever. You actually work twenty-four/seven. If the kid's awake, you gotta take care of them. Even when they're asleep, there's stuff to do. And I was trying so hard to quit drinking. I really was. But sometimes, when I couldn't handle anything, I guess..." She sighed. "I guess sometimes I just gave in to that need. It caused a lot of problems.

"One day in our apartment complex's laundry room, I complained to a neighbor about being tired. He seemed so understanding and we started off as friends. Things progressed, and you know." Trinity shrugged. "The affair led to a divorce. The bastard I'd fallen for didn't want kids. Because I was young, dumb and in love, I didn't sue for custody. I was struggling with my own addictions. I missed several visits, and my ex-husband took me to court to terminate my parental rights. I didn't fight him. Not long after, the guy I was with left me. I took up with another guy—worse than the first. Seems like I dated every lousy man in Texas before I figured out what was important. Now I'm trying to get my life straightened out." Trinity placed her palm over the locket, pressing both into her chest. "Until then, this is all I have of my baby girl."

Clare sipped her wine and thought of her family. Her father died of cancer years before. Her mom was still alive and had relocated to Hawaii. She hadn't called her mom in all these months, too afraid that someone might be tracing those calls. By now, she could only imagine how worried her mother would be. Her throat tightened with guilt. "Must be hard to be away from your daughter during the holidays."

"It's hard every day, but yeah—Christmas is the worst. I mailed presents already. Her dad will let her call in the morning, and we'll talk. It's nice, but it's not enough." She sipped her wine. "What about you? What's your life story?"

"Just one lousy guy. And yeah, I married him." Clare chewed on the inside of her lip. She shouldn't have shared so much about her past. Maybe the beer and wine were making her a chatty…and reckless.

Trinity lifted her paper cup. "To lousy men. May we learn to avoid them."

Touching her cup to Trinity's, Clare said, "Cheers."

Exhaustion began to set into her limbs. Stretching out on the mattress, Clare pulled the comforter over her legs and chest.

Trinity settled onto her own bed. "No kids. No husband. What about siblings? Parents?"

Clare knew enough to not give away too many details. Still, she couldn't ignore Trinity's question. "No siblings. Lost my dad to cancer, but my mom is still around," she said, giving a true but vague answer.

"You close to your mom?"

After everything that had happened, she thought every day of calling her mother. Then again, what could her mom do from the other side of an ocean?

"We talk now and again." Clare folded the pillow and relaxed into the mattress.

"Well, speaking for all moms everywhere, we always want to hear from our kids." She paused a beat. "How'd you end up here, then?"

"This is where life led me," said Clare with a shrug.

"You drive a fancy car. You have expensive clothes and bags. That means you came from a life of privilege. It also means you have choices beyond pouring beers at some bar in the back-ass of beyond." Trinity's gaze hardened a little. "No one just chooses to be here. But you did, Clare."

Trinity wasn't wrong. But she wasn't completely right, either.

She sighed, not sure how much she could—or should—reveal. "Something bad happened. It was...where I used to work. If I stayed, there would've been trouble. For a lot of people," said Clare, skirting the truth as closely as she dared. "I had to get out. And I had to leave everything behind. Just get up and...go." Clare took a big sip of her wine, hoping she'd be able to choke it down along with the emotion clogging her throat.

"I thought my job was hard." Taking the last swallow of her wine, Trinity nodded. "You know, Clare, you're okay." She held up a hand. "No, I mean it. When Isaac showed up with you, I wasn't sure what to think. But you're alright. Not many I'd call a friend around here, so I'm glad you're my roommate." Trinity picked up the empty glasses and threw them both in the trash can.

Clare gave a quiet laugh. She couldn't help but recall her monied acquaintances in Columbus. In all those years, she'd never felt at ease with any of them. But Trinity was different in a good way. "I'm glad that I'm your roommate, too."

Trinity picked up a phone from the nightstand. "What's your number? Then we can text each other if things get boring at work."

Clare hesitated. "Oh, I really don't use my phone for much."

"I get it—a phone bill can be expensive. I'll just get your number for emergencies."

In all honesty, Clare hadn't bothered to memorize the number to the new cell phone. She took it from her bag and turned on the power. After creating a new contact, she handed the phone to Trinity. "You put in your information."

She typed on the screen. "I'll send myself a message from your phone."

She handed the phone back to Clare. The message read Hey sis.

"So, what happened to your lousy husband?" Trinity stretched out on the bed.

Had Clare said too much? She'd stopped in Mercy to disappear, not to bring up her past. "Divorced. I haven't spoken to him since I signed the papers."

Maybe she was starving for more than food but actual human contact. Besides, Clare had only agreed to stay until New Year's. She'd be long gone before she was asked any questions that she didn't want to answer.

"That's the best way to do it. No loose ends."

She gave a sleepy nod. Yet, for her ex-husband, Clare

was someone who knew too much. That made her more of a live wire than merely a loose end. Her eyes drifted closed.

"Hey, aren't you going to change?"

"No," Clare mumbled, knowing that sleep was close to claiming her. In her dreams, there were strobing lights and pulsing music. A shadow moved at the edge of the lights. The figure had no face, yet she knew it was her ex-husband.

Kyle.

Even embroiled in the dream, Clare was haunted by fear. Where was he? And what would he do if he ever tracked her down?

Decker needed two things. Information and his money. The search for both led him to Encantador, Texas. It was a town of just 2,800 souls that sat thirty miles north of the Mexican border.

Turning off the headlights, he drove down Main Street. All the storefronts were dark. Then again, at this hour nothing would be open. A flashing yellow light hung above an intersection, and he slowed his approach. The last thing he wanted was to get stopped by a local cop. After a year in hiding, Decker followed all the traffic laws like they were his religion. On the corner, a brown sign was affixed to a post. *Library, two blocks.*

With a smile, he followed the sign. Set at the end of a dead-end street, the library was in the perfect location. It was made of golden brick and a red sign was staked to the lawn. *Protected by South Texas Alarm System, San Antonio.* After a slow drive around the block, he was confident that his initial guess was right.

There were no cameras. Certain that the security was basic—and no match for him—he parked his car next to the building. After slipping on a pair of old gloves, he picked the lock. Next, he found the alarm's keypad and quickly circumvented the system. It would take several minutes for the security company in San Antonio to realize that the library was off-line. Then several more minutes would pass as they ran diagnostics. A few minutes more before they called the police. Then, how long until the police came to check?

His best guess was that he had ten to fifteen minutes. By then, he would have to be gone without a trace.

Standing on the threshold, he took a moment to get the layout. There was a single large room. Shelves with books ringed the perimeter and stood in rows. The back of the space was filled with round tables and partitioned desks. To his left was a smaller room. Through the door, he could see a mural of a beach and smaller tables. Decker assumed that was the children's area.

In the back corner, he found what he needed. A dozen computer monitors sat at individual workstations. Moving to a computer, he hit the power button. The screen blinked to life. A helpful card was taped to the monitor with the computer's password and internet login. After entering the keystrokes, he was on the internet.

He found the site for the Wyoming State Police. It took two minutes to hack into the database and another forty-five seconds to find his file.

Pinned to the top of the e-file was an old mug shot of Decker holding a placard with his ID. His blond hair was long, and his beard was shaggy.

There was a report about the murder of Jacob Loeb,

District Attorney of Pleasant Pines. Decker's DNA and fingerprints had been found in the getaway car, along with Paolo's body. Apparently, the fire hadn't been as total as Decker had hoped. Video footage from a doorbell camera showed Decker's car as he drove from Pleasant Pines.

The state had all the evidence they needed to throw him in jail for the rest of his life. Or worse, give him the death penalty. Then again, they had to find him first.

He continued to read the report. The case was assigned to a detective with the state police. The last entry was more than six months ago, when someone who resembled Decker had been seen at a local grocery store. Since then, there was nothing.

It meant his evasion tactics seemed to be working. Still...he couldn't afford unnecessary risks.

He entered the name of another person with Wyoming's DOC. Ryan Steele. Ryan's file was thinner than his own, but he had to find out if his old buddy had been caught up in the murder investigation of the DA. If Ryan was in jail, it'd be hard for Decker to get his cash. But if he was a free man...

It looked like Ryan had been remanded to custody for questioning following the death of Loeb and then released. Decker smiled. He couldn't wait to hear how his pal had gotten out of that mess. Knowing Ryan, it was quite a story. He closed the report.

His file still filled the screen. Moving the cursor to the *X* at the top of the page, he stopped. At the bottom of the file was a link. *DNA analysis, Newcombe, Decker.*

He paused. He still had a lot to do. First, he had to change his appearance—maybe he should create a more conservative, boring look. To do that, he'd need a haircut and presentable clothes. The library had to have scissors somewhere. Plus, if he were lucky, there'd be something that fit him in the Lost and Found. Once he was done, he still had to clean away every trace that he'd been in the library at all.

Did he have time to read another report?

He knew the answer was a definite *no*.

Then again, had the cops linked him to other crimes through his DNA? Decker needed to find out. He clicked the link.

The report gave genetic makeup as being mostly from the United Kingdom. There was a list of names that went back for generations and meant nothing. Decker had heard that the police used DNA taken from genealogy tests to link people to unsolved crimes, but this was different. They'd analyzed his family history. But why?

One name, Jeremiah Newcombe, was highlighted. A notation had been added: *genetic link to sociopathy?*

He closed the file but remained in his seat. His pulse pounded, resonating in his ears. He should just leave it alone and walk away, but he couldn't. Decker opened a new search and entered the name *Jeremiah Newcombe*.

In seconds, over one-hundred thousand hits appeared on the screen.

Leaning closer to the computer, he whispered, "What in the actual hell."

A headline from an article posted seven years ago was at the top of the search. "Identity of Jack the Ripper discovered through DNA."

The article read:

During the fall of 1888, London's eastside neighborhood of Whitechapel was gripped in terror. One of England's first documented serial killers, Jack the Ripper, was thought to be responsible for the murder and mutilation of five female prostitutes. Despite Scotland Yard's theories about the killer's identity, the actual name of Jack the Ripper has been a mystery for more than a century.

That is, until now.

In late 2007, it was discovered that the clothing of Jack the Ripper's second victim—Annie Chapman—had been saved in storage. Through analysis, two samples of DNA were taken from the dress. The first sample belonged to Chapman herself. The second sample belonged to an unknown male.

Recent discoveries have linked the second DNA sample to a Whitechapel baker, Jeremiah Newcombe. At the time of the killings, Newcombe was questioned by detectives but there was never enough evidence to bring charges. In the late 1890s, Newcombe emigrated to America and his name faded into obscurity.

Decker stared at the computer. His heart hammered against his chest. It couldn't be true.

"Jack the Ripper?" His voice was loud in the silent library. "I'm related to Jack the Ripper?"

He closed the file and conducted one final search. A shoebox lid, filled with stubby pencils and scraps of paper, sat next to the computer. Using a pencil and slip of paper, he wrote down a title and catalog number.

Decker cleared the history from the computer. Sure, any investigator would be able to pull up the search history from this particular hard drive. But if he left no trace that he'd been in the library, nobody would ever care to look.

A container of antibacterial wipes sat on the table's edge. A handwritten note was taped to the tube. *Kill the germs. Wipe down the keyboard and mouse after each use.* For once, Decker found a rule that he was happy to follow. With the computer and table free of prints, he pocketed the wipe—no sense in leaving behind evidence.

Taking the slip of paper with him, he walked through the history section and scanned the titles. He stopped and pulled a book from the shelf. *The Complete Guide to Jack the Ripper.*

Was he really related to the world's most notorious serial killer? It was a stunning—if kind of ridiculous—idea to wrap his brain around. Then again, Decker had always been drawn to death. He knew the desire to kill was a part of him.

Maybe those DNA results were right. Murder was literally in his blood.

Chapter 4

Arms tucked behind his head, Isaac lay on the bed and stared at the ceiling. He had yet to strip out of his clothes, but it didn't matter. He was too keyed up to sleep, and after pacing the room, he'd finally forced himself to stop, knowing he'd have to find another way to calm his restless mind. Certainly, staring at his four walls wasn't going to help.

Not tonight, anyway.

For the past year, he'd lived in the single room at the hotel. In all that time, he'd tried to make the place, if not homey, at least livable.

The small space was divided into three parts. A recliner, a footlocker that doubled as a coffee table, and lamp and four-tiered bookshelf sat near the door. The middle of the room held a bed, along with a dresser and TV. On the side farthest from the door was a dorm-sized fridge, small microwave and another set of shelves with dishes, food and a single-serve coffee maker on top.

He'd turned the TV to a twenty-four-hour sports channel. Nothing the overnight commentators said about a severe storm warning in Texas canceling upcoming games caught or kept his attention. What's worse, the constant drone wasn't enough to bore him to sleep, either.

He didn't have to wonder why he was lying in bed and awake. It was Clare.

What would've happened if they hadn't been interrupted by Trinity? He would have kissed her. But, then what? Would he have asked her to come to his room?

Would she have said yes?

The thought of Clare's naked body beneath him came to Isaac with a painful clarity. The image left him hard. He gritted his teeth and exhaled slowly. Was now the time to take matters in hand? Although he suspected the fantasy would be nothing compared to the reality of having Clare in his arms, in his bed.

His thoughts were suddenly interrupted by his phone, which sat on the bedside table and pinged with an incoming message. Sure, getting a text in the middle of the night was rarely because of good news. Still, Isaac was happy for the distraction. Sitting up, he scrubbed his face with hands and reached for the phone.

The message was from Jason Jones.

"Dammit," he muttered. The Supervisory Special Agent was the last person Isaac wanted to hear from—especially at this hour.

I need something to report back to DC by the end of the year.

"Bureaucracy," he grunted, while reaching for the TV remote. He turned off the sports channel. "The boring side of police work."

Another text followed.

I can't justify spending all this money if there are no results. Otherwise, it looks like I'm paying you for a yearlong vacation.

A vacation? Really? Clearly, Jason had never been to Mercy.

This is what he was going to hit him with at 3:00 a.m? Threats of closing the op? Isaac sent his own text: Trust me This is no vacation.

Then again, he understood that the SSA's problem was professional—and personal.

Decker had killed Jacob Loeb, but his actual target had been Chloe Ryder. She was now the AG, but she was also married to Jason's older brother, Marcus, and the mother to Jason's only niece. At the time of the hit, Isaac was working for Rocky Mountain Justice in Denver. Marcus was a colleague from the Wyoming branch. It was Isaac who came up with the idea to lay a trap for Decker. Ryan was on board—and the money owed to the hitman was bait. It was an audacious play—something the FBI loathed.

For Jason, getting Decker was personal. Until the hitman was in custody, the Jones family wouldn't be safe.

That's why the SSA agreed to the plan. He placed

Isaac as a single undercover operative in Texas. And what did Isaac get out of the bargain? Once Decker was in custody, Isaac would be his own boss.

For a split second, his mind returned to that old op. It had been four years ago already when he entered that dank hallway. And yet, as he sat in his room, he could still smell the stink of gunpowder. He could still hear the gurgling sound—like a clogged pipe. His hands were still hot with blood that sprayed like a fountain. Sure, the debacle hadn't been Isaac's fault. Since that fateful night, everything changed, and his old life was like an ill-fitting suit. He'd left the San Antonio PD within a month.

He'd gotten a job with Rocky Mountain Justice. But the job in private security was a bad match, too. The owner promoted teamwork too much. After San Antonio, the last thing Isaac wanted was to be part of a team. While he knew that he needed Jason to continue his one-man operation, Isaac resented the interruption to his solitude. He sent another text. What do you need?

Jason's reply was immediate. Something to take to my supervisors. Anything at all.

That was going to be a trick, because right now what Isaac had was absolutely freaking *nothing*.

Jason's next text read, Proof of life. Better yet, get me a location for Newcombe.

Isaac replied: Here I thought you were going to ask me for something hard. Sure, he knew better than to be sarcastic with Jason. But what the hell did he care?

He sent another text immediately.

If I knew that Newcombe was alive and his whereabouts, this case would be closed.

Jason sent another text.

Actionable intel by the end of the year. Or your op will be closed.

Isaac cursed. He knew what would happen if the Newcombe operation failed. It'd be more than a waste of money for the government—Isaac's reputation would be ruined.

Decker spent less than ten minutes changing his appearance. Using the scissors he found at the checkout desk, he gave himself a quick haircut and shave. He changed into a blazer and T-shirt he found in the Lost and Found. He quickly cleaned everything he touched as best he could on his way out of the building.

He left Encantador, putting a few miles between himself and the small town before pulling a burner phone from his pocket. Powering it up, he waited as the screen blinked to life, then entered a number that he'd memorized years earlier and listened as it rang.

The call was answered. "This better be good. Calling me from an unlisted number in the middle of the freaking night."

The gruff voice was almost as familiar to Decker as his own. "Ryan, man. Good to hear you."

Across the miles, he could hear the hiss as Ryan sucked in a breath. "Decker, what the… It's been a year, man. I thought you were in South America—or dead."

"I had a safe house about eight miles south of the border. Just a shack on a bluff. A well for water. Generator for power. An extra set of everything I'd ever need. An old lady who lived nearby delivered food twice a month."

"A safe house?" Ryan sounded equal parts impressed and perturbed. "I never heard anything about you having a safe house."

"If everyone knows, then it's not safe. Is it? I set it up years ago in case I needed to disappear for a few weeks."

"A few weeks? You've been gone for a whole damned year." Ryan's tone had risen. When he spoke again, he lowered his voice. "What do you want?"

"I need some information, man. Where are you?"

"Ever heard of a place called Mercy, Texas?"

Now that was an interesting twist. Based on the dust road signs he'd seen, Mercy was less than thirty miles from Encantador. Did he want Ryan to know he was that close? No, not yet. "Never been. Is it nice?"

"It's the exact opposite of nice."

Decker guffawed. "What are you doing there?"

"Got my own place." Pride was evident in Ryan's tone. "Bar. Tattoo parlor. Motel."

How'd Ryan come up with all the cash he'd need to start three businesses? Lip curling in anger, he realized Ryan must have used all the money from Decker's hit in Wyoming to set himself up.

The one person he thought he could trust was a self-serving piece of garbage.

Anger roared through him like a locomotive. Gripping the steering wheel tighter, he stared into the night as he drove.

Now wasn't the time to lose his cool. He still needed Ryan for whatever cash was left and information. The crazy notation about Jack the Ripper came to mind. "Did you ever hear anything about the cops doing DNA testing?"

"DNA? What kind of whacked-out question is that?"

"Nothing," he said quickly. "Never mind." Then, he was all business. "You know why I'm calling you, right?"

"You called 'cause you missed me, Decker."

He laughed again. "No, numb nuts. I need my money."

Silence stretched out as he drove.

After a full minute, Ryan spoke. "That might be a problem, Decker."

Ice crept into his voice. "You better find a solution, man. I need to get my butt into a country with no extradition to the US. And fast. I can't live in hiding anymore."

"Like I said, that's going to be a problem..."

Before Ryan could say more, he interrupted, "I don't want to hear excuses. I want my damn money. You got businesses, that means you got cash."

"I've got employees. Overhead. Hell, being legit means I gotta pay taxes and insurance and crap like that."

One word stuck with Decker. *Employees.* His vision went red. He could feel blood, silky and hot, wash over his hands. A bead of sweat dotted his upper lip. He licked it away, tasting the salt of his own skin. "It'd be a shame for something to happen to one of them people you gotta pay."

"You wouldn't do that, man. These are my people. My responsibility..."

Before Ryan could say anything else, he hung up. His friend had always been the smart one. It was no wonder that he owned a place of his own—even if it was in the middle of nowhere. He threw the phone out the window and glanced in the sideview mirror as it bounced across the pavement. Then again, if Ryan really was smart, he wouldn't have stolen from Decker.

After the text exchange with Jason, there was no way Isaac would get any shut-eye now. After shoving the phone into his pocket and grabbing the key to his room, Isaac stepped into the night. The motel consisted of twelve rooms, all on a single level. Three lights had been installed in the roof's overhang, and they lit up the walkway. He leaned against the brick wall, cooled by the night air.

Isaac refused to fail.

But he couldn't think of a way to succeed.

He stared into the night. Near the bar, a shadow moved, and Isaac froze. It was a person, but who?

Silently, he shifted to the end of the motel, and let his eyes adjust to the darkness. The figure was male; he could tell that by the height and broad shoulders. A second later, the flame of a lighter came to life as a cigarette was lit. Even at a distance, he could see a face. It was Ryan Steele.

He needed to pass on Jones's warning about the op being closed. Now was the perfect time.

Quickly and quietly, he crossed the parking lot. While still shrouded in shadows, he spoke. "What're you doing out here?"

Ryan pressed a hand to his chest. "Christ Almighty.

You scared the crap outta me. What the hell are you doing?"

Isaac stepped closer. Even in the dark, he could see the other man clearly. The pulse on his neck raced. His skin was pale. Ryan had been more than startled—as he'd said—but he was scared. Sure, Isaac had caught him unawares. But it wasn't enough of a surprise to cause the extreme reaction. The man also held his phone. Maybe he was expecting a call. Or maybe he'd just received one.

Isaac bet on the latter. "Who was on the phone?"

"You know, in a lot of ways, the real world is worse than jail. At least in lockup, I didn't have a personal guard. Here, I got you for a shadow."

"Cry me a freakin' river. You're out of jail. You have a chance to expunge your record. This is a sweetheart of a deal for you—especially since you've delivered two things. Jack and shit."

Ryan took a final inhale from his cigarette before flicking the butt into the night. "I heard that you let the blonde stay. What's her name? Clare?"

He could see Ryan's tactics from a mile away. He wanted to change the subject, challenge his authority and get Isaac rattled. The thing was, Clare did leave Isaac shook. He refused to bring her into the conversation.

Ryan continued, "She work for you at... What's your agency called? Texas Law? Is she a fed, or something?"

Shaking his head, he said, "I always work alone."

"Then, she's got to go. She made me look like an ass with her Long Island Iced Tea comment. Besides, this is my business, and you got no right—" Ryan began.

Isaac's temper flared. Poking his finger into the other man's chest, he growled, "I've got every right. The federal government owns this property. Unless you want to go back to jail, you'd best remember one thing. I own you." He paused a beat, glancing over his shoulder at the darkened hotel windows behind them, then lowered his voice. "We gotta talk about something else."

"Like what? You want my Christmas list?"

If Ryan Steele weren't such a jerk, Isaac might think he was funny. "We have to talk about Decker Newcombe."

Ryan smirked, "Too bad. I was hoping for a new gaming system."

"Cut the crap. Where's your pal?"

"Dunno." He fished a pack of smokes from his pocket and tapped out a filtered end. He caught it between his lips and shoved the pack back in his pocket. With the unlit cigarette in his mouth, he continued, "But if I knew, I'd tell you. I understand why I'm here."

"You turn over Decker and you get your criminal record expunged." Isaac didn't need to repeat the deal. They both understood the roles they played. Then again, he needed Ryan to be more than mere bait. If Decker was out there, he'd have to be lured into the trap. "I need you to call around. Ask questions. See if there are rumors, at least."

"Rumors, at least?" Ryan repeated. "What's going on? You sound pretty freakin' desperate, pal."

Isaac was, but he'd never admit as much to the likes of Ryan. Still, in giving the new order, he'd shown too much of his hand. Too bad it couldn't be helped. "I need something to give to the feds. And I'm not your pal."

Ryan took a lighter from his pocket. One handed, he flicked the flame to life and touched the fire to the tip of his cigarette. "What if there's nothing new to give?"

"By the end of the year all this—" he opened his arms, taking in the motel, bar and tattoo parlor "—will go away. You, too."

Ryan inhaled deeply. "I hate this, you know." He spoke words that were filled with smoke. It was akin to talking to a dragon. "This life isn't fun anymore. Drinking makes me sick. I've never gone for drugs— seen them mess up too many people. I like the women, but only if they like me first." He tapped ash from the end of his cigarette. "I want that second chance."

Isaac studied his face. "You really want to start over? Then you gotta earn it. Get me something." Isaac clamped his jaw shut. He was walking a pretty thin line between leaning on Ryan and begging the guy for his help. He'd be damned before he let the ex-con know just how bad the investigation was going.

Exhaustion flattened him in an instant, like being hit by a runaway eighteen-wheeler. His legs ached. His head pounded. His eyes were gritty. Isaac pinched the bridge of his nose. "We'll talk tomorrow."

"Isaac." Ryan's voice was harsh. "I want the blonde gone by morning."

Damn. Isaac wasn't in the mood for a fight. Then again, he wasn't going to make Clare leave—not now, at least. "No."

"You saw what happened in the bar today. I told her to get lost, but she's still here. How am I supposed to look like the boss with you undermining me?"

It was a reasonable question. He sighed. "Anyone asks, tell 'em it's a Christmas present for me."

"You think you deserve a Christmas present?" Ryan scratched his cheek with his middle finger. "Let me think."

Isaac wasn't sure if he should laugh or punch the guy in the mouth. "Say what you want, but Clare stays."

He turned for his room.

"Hey. Isaac." The words rang out like a shot.

Now what? He was too damn tired to think. He faced Ryan. "Yeah?"

"Just remember, I want a gaming system for Christmas—and a nice one, too."

The word *game* hit Isaac like a punch. "Let me see your phone."

"No way, man. I'm not giving you my phone."

He took a step toward Ryan. "Give me your phone or I'm taking it from you."

Placing his hand over his pocket, he asked, "Why do you need my phone? You have one of your own."

"I want to see what game you were playing, that's why." Even in the dark, he could see Ryan go pale. He'd found a nerve—now all he had to do was squeeze. "If you're lying to me, I'll have you back in jail tonight. You'll be charged with a dozen crimes. Accessory to murder. Money laundering. The feds will bring you up on RICO charges." He held out his hand.

With a curse, Ryan fished the phone from his pocket. He pressed it into Isaac's hand. "Fine. He called just now. I was going to tell you, I swear. I just had to get my head on straight… Besides, the number's blocked. It won't help you at all."

Isaac was too astonished to be furious. "Tonight? Now? What'd he say?"

"He said he's been hiding out in Mexico for a year at a safe house."

"Where in Mexico?" he asked, his pulse racing with excitement. There'd be time to answer questions later. But not here in the middle of the parking lot where they might be overheard. "Come with me."

This was the moment he'd been waiting for—and he wasn't about to waste another second.

Chapter 5

As they walked back to Isaac's room, each step was filled with a certainty that he hadn't felt in a long, long time. He worked the key into the lock and opened the door. After turning on the light, he gestured to the single chair. "Have a seat," he said to Ryan.

Isaac stayed on his feet and took out his phone. He placed a call to SSA Jones. The phone began to ring, and he turned on the speaker function.

Jason answered. "This better be good."

"Decker Newcombe called." Isaac tried to keep the excitement from his voice, but it was damn near impossible. He was a kid at Christmas, getting the best present ever. "Just now, Ryan Steele heard from him." He paused a beat and added, "He's here now and you're on speaker."

"This better not be some prank. Because if it is, I'm not amused."

He ignored the comment, though it did dampen his enthusiasm. "Decker's been hiding in a Mexican safe house. I didn't waste time with a debrief before contacting you."

"I'm listening."

Ryan took several minutes to share what had happened. He started with receiving a call from a blocked number—it was Decker, who was looking for his money. He had more information about the safe house. There was a well. A generator. It was located eight miles from the border. He ended his debriefing by saying, "He asked a real crazy question about DNA testing. Either of you know anything about that?"

Isaac shook his head. "I don't. What about you, Jason?"

"Nothing on my end. But local law enforcement agencies have been more aggressive in testing unknown DNA found at crime scenes against what the FBI has collected in CODIS." He turned the conversation from the Combined DNA Index System, and back to Decker's whereabouts. "What else can you tell me about the safe house?"

"Nothing, man," said Ryan, before repeating, "Just that it was eight miles south of the border."

Jason sighed. "The US–Mexican border is nearly two-thousand miles. That's a lot of ground to cover. Decker could be anywhere."

Isaac's temper flared. "You wanted intel, you got intel."

"Actionable intel," Jason corrected, then sighed. "At least we know he's close to the US and not planning on leaving without his money. Looks like the trap is finally working. I'll see what we can do with satellite images. Have you gotten the number?"

"Not yet." Isaac still had Ryan's phone. If he was lucky—and good—he'd be able to access the phone's memory and access the call log. The phone was locked. He held it up to Ryan's face. The biker stared back at him before realization hit his expression.

"Hey, man. You can't do that."

Isaac glared before looking back at the unlocked phone. It took him only minutes to find the most recent call and entered a code to circumvent the block. He repeated the number for Jason while writing on a scrap of paper. Then, he tossed the phone to Ryan. "There you go."

Ryan stared at the phone. "You got a number for Decker? How, man? The call was blocked."

Jason was the one who answered. "Everything received by a phone is stored in the memory somewhere. All you need to do is know where to look."

"So, how does a number help us?" Ryan asked.

"If Decker's phone is still on, we should be able to find him." He knelt in front of the footlocker and entered the combination into the padlock. Opening the lid, he removed a computer. He closed the lid once again and used the metal crate as a seat. With the laptop balanced on his knees, he powered up the device. "I subscribed to a service that will let me access information from cell towers."

It was Ryan again who spoke. "Can anyone get that information?"

Isaac tilted his head from side to side as he typed. "It's

not for the public, but law enforcement agencies can get access. Me, too. Jason would have no problem getting the information, but I imagine he'd have to go to the office to access the server."

"Confirmed," said Jason. "But I'm headed to the office now, anyway."

Once inside the server, Isaac entered the number and hit the return key. It took only minutes for a map to appear on the screen, along with a red flashing dot. "We got a hit," he said for the sake of Jason, who was still waiting on the other line.

"Is that really Decker?" Ryan asked, leaning toward the computer.

"It's the phone that called your number," said Jason, clarifying. "But if the cell is attached to the man, then yeah, we got Decker." He asked, "You got a location for me?"

Isaac read off a set of GPS coordinates. Then, he worked the map's aspect. The picture went fuzzy as the program was recalibrated.

"Holy crap," Ryan whispered as the picture became clear. "That's just down the road—right outside of Encantador."

Isaac was already on his feet. "I've got to go and check that out."

"Be careful," said Jason. "And report back with anything you find."

With a beep, the call was ended by the agent.

"I'm going with you." Ryan stood as well.

Isaac slipped on his coat but didn't argue. He could use the extra set of hands. Besides, Ryan had just as much at stake in finding Decker.

Ryan opened the door and impatiently swept his arm toward the night. The gesture was an unmistakable invitation for Isaac to exit his own room. "C'mon, man. We know where Decker was, but we don't know where he's going."

"Give me a second." From the footlocker, Isaac removed three more items. A translucent evidence bag, a box of surgical gloves and a Glock 19 with ammo.

Without another word, they left his room. As they walked away from the motel, his pulse was still racing. Decker Newcombe was close, and Isaac was going to bring him to justice.

Clare wasn't sure what woke her, but she lay on the sagging mattress and stared into the dark. The outline of the Christmas tree was visible from the light filtering in through the seam of the curtains.

There it was again. Male voices. Was it Kyle? Had he finally found her? She froze, not daring to breathe. There was something about the timbre of the voice that was familiar. Definitely not Kyle, though. She rose from the bed and crossed the room, careful not to bump into Trinity's bed. She stood at the side of the window and looked out into the night.

Just as she had heard, two men were outside and talking.

The lights were on under the roof's overhang, making it easy to see Isaac and Ryan.

"You think we'll find him?" Ryan asked.

"We can only hope," said Isaac. "I've got my Glock in the glove box in case we do meet your old buddy."

Ryan said, "I need something from the bar. It'll only take a second."

"Hurry up," Isaac called, his tone sharp.

They walked away from the motel, their shadows blending with the night.

What the hell?

"Hey." The single word was whispered, and Clare started. She spun around. Trinity was sitting up in bed, her form darker in the shadowy room. "You okay?"

Clare gulped down a breath. "Yeah. You startled me, that's all."

"Everything okay out there?"

"Sorry for waking you. I thought I heard voices."

"Is someone outside?"

"No." Clare wasn't sure why she lied. She maneuvered through the dark back to her own bed. She peeled back the covers and slipped between the sheets. "It must've been a bad dream or something."

"Try to get some rest. You've had a long day."

Even in the dark, Clare smiled. Finding a friend in Trinity really had been the first good thing to happen in months. "Thanks. I appreciate it."

Trinity's breathing became slow and rhythmic within minutes. Yet, Clare was still awake. She stared at the window, the sliver of light and the outline of the tree—all the while, hoping that sleep would reclaim her. Isaac and Ryan were obviously looking for someone. But who were they looking for? And why did they need guns?

Isaac unlocked the truck and Ryan slipped into the passenger seat. As Isaac settled in behind the steering wheel, Ryan laid a Heckler and Koch across his lap.

So, that's what he had to grab. He shook his head.

If Ryan noticed the gesture, he said nothing. "All this time, man. And here we are."

Isaac turned the key in the ignition and let the engine run. "What are you talking about?"

Ryan gazed at the bar. "How long have we been working this cover together now? Almost a year? And finally, Decker's back. I'll be honest with you, I thought your plan was out there from the beginning, but it worked."

Isaac pulled out of the parking lot and for the first time, he wondered if tonight was a setup. Was the phone call a ploy to get Isaac into the desert so he could be murdered by Ryan and Decker? A chill ran down his spine.

If that were the case, why now?

No, he had to trust Ryan—even if he didn't really trust anyone at all.

Ryan kept talking, "I still can't figure out how you worked that deal. Hell, I can't understand why you'd convince the feds to clear my record. I'm not the kind of guy people should help out."

Isaac stared into the night as he drove "Is that a Freudian slip?" He glanced at the gun on Ryan's lap. "You're suddenly making me regret that I okayed letting you carry a weapon—even if it's for a good cause."

Ryan stilled. "Why would you say that?"

He shrugged. "I'm just saying that you've been a very good boy, Ryan—as far as I know. Don't go giving me a reason to think otherwise. Especially if we're riding off into the desert alone together." He tightened his grip on the steering wheel. "Besides, I'm a better—and faster—shot than you."

Ryan snorted. "A cop? Never."

Isaac smiled, but his gaze was cold. "You'd be surprised what we ex-cops can do, partner."

The headlights cut through the darkness. As they approached the phone's location, he knew that they weren't going to find Decker. The stretch of road was empty for miles.

Isaac parked on the road's shoulder, his thoughts racing.

Ryan looked out the window. "What the hell was he doing out here? Think he's still around?"

From the beginning, Isaac knew they might not find the hitman. "We've only got an approximate location on his phone—not him." He turned off the engine, the night suddenly filled with silence. "But the phone's around here somewhere. If we find it, there's a lot we might learn about Decker."

Ryan unfastened his seat belt and opened the door. "Sure, let's look for a phone on the side of the road in the middle of the night. Sounds like fun. Easy, too."

Sometimes the dumb jokes were slightly amusing, but not tonight. Could the guy not keep his mouth shut? Isaac thought not. From the glove box he removed a flashlight. He held it out to Ryan. "You need this?"

"I'll use the light on my phone."

The ease with which Ryan handled the situation reminded him of his last partner at San Antonio SWAT. Miguel had been the kind of guy who rolled with the punches as well. He also told corny dad jokes. A feeling of affinity for Miguel squeezed his chest. For a moment, Ryan wasn't as annoying.

"Take these." He held out a pair of latex gloves. "Put these on before you pick up anything important."

"Yeah, I know. I've been arrested a few times. I've seen how you cops do things."

Isaac ignored the comment. Jumping from the truck, Isaac swept the flashlight's beam across the ground. He walked to the road's edge and looked into the night. In the distance, a coyote howled.

"What's the range of your tracker?" Ryan asked.

"One-hundred yards." Isaac stepped off the shoulder and onto the plains that stretched out for miles. "And please don't complain that one-hundred yards in any direction is a lot of space to cover. You offered to come along."

He grumbled, "Yeah, I remember."

For a few minutes, they searched in silence. Isaac turned back to the road and that's when he saw it. Hidden under a clump of tumbleweed was the reflective face of a phone. "I got it."

Isaac donned a pair of gloves to keep from transferring fingerprints before picking up the phone. He pulled the evidence bag from his pocket and placed the phone inside.

Without comment, they walked to his truck. As his tires hit the pavement, a line of pink showed on the eastern horizon.

He placed a call to Jason. "I have the phone," said Isaac as the SSA answered. "He must have tossed it from the car after he made the call." San Antonio was only a few hours away. "I'll bring it to you now." And after that, he could drop Ryan off at a restaurant or something for a few hours. Then he'd have time to stop by his parents' house for a preholiday visit.

"Negative on you coming to the office. Decker is

close and I don't want anything to appear out of the ordinary—like a long-time employee disappearing. Or my undercover operative not being on the property if the subject shows up." Jason sighed and Isaac imagined that he was weighing his options.

Ryan offered a solution. "There's a delivery place in Encantador. They can get packages to San Antonio within a few hours."

"Done. Deliver the phone but get back to Mercy as soon as possible. From there, it's business as usual."

Isaac asked, "What about the satellites? Have you gotten anything that can scan the area?"

"The request is moving up the chain of command at DOJ. With it being so close to Christmas, not everyone's in the office. They're being tracked down. We'll have to use satellites from Defense and that's going to be a whole different approval process. I have no doubt it'll get done. But it's taking some time. What makes it all worse is that there's a storm coming up from the Gulf of Mexico." Jason continued, "Get me the phone. Business as usual." He ended the call.

"Wow," said Ryan. "Your buddy is a real prince of a guy."

Isaac laughed. "Let's invite him to the bar. Have a beer. Watch a game."

"Did you just make a joke? After a whole year of knowing you, I thought you lacked the sense of humor gene." He paused a beat. "There was something else that Decker said last night. When I told him that I was in business for myself, he made a comment like, 'It'd be a shame for something to happen to one of them people you gotta pay.' You think we should call back Jason and tell him?"

A threat from a man like Decker should be taken seriously. But it left Isaac with a single question. "I'm not sure how much the feds care. Don't get me wrong, they don't want anyone to die. But would Jason intervene?" Actually, he knew the answer. The fed wouldn't change his plans. "We'll mention it to him next time with speak."

"Alright then." Leaning back in the seat, Ryan stretched his legs out and closed his eyes. Eyes still closed, he said, "Wake me when we get to Mercy."

Isaac shook his head and watched the sky. The horizon was filled with pink, rose and amber. *Red in the morning, sailor's warning.*

The new day promised to be long. Isaac still had to stay undercover and work the bar.

He would be beyond tired. This time, he didn't mind.

For the first time in a long while, his investigation seemed to be moving in the right direction. And the sooner he wrapped it up, the sooner he could get the hell out of Mercy.

Trinity wasn't used to having another person in her room. It wasn't that Clare was obnoxious or even that she snored. But the soft breathing of another human being in the opposite bed kept her from her usual deep sleep.

By 6:00 a.m., her head throbbed. She couldn't stand to toss and turn for another minute. She needed a cup of strong coffee. True, she had a coffee maker in her room, but it hissed and shook with every single-serve cup.

That'd wake Clare and honestly—Trinity was happy to be a considerate roommate. She took a moment to think and came up with a plan. She could grab them both drinks at the gas station.

Rising quietly, she stripped out of her T-shirt and shorts before donning a pair of jeans and sweatshirt.

True, Trinity wasn't used to thinking of other people. Yet, she liked Clare and figured she could use a treat. Picking up her phone, she sent a message.

Went to get us coffee. I can make a latte at the gas station. It's good. BRB.

Slipping out the door, Trinity pulled it closed behind her. The parking lot that stretched between the bar and motel was empty, save for a single car that sat near the road. Sunlight glinted off the windshield. Tucking her hands into her pockets, she strode across the pavement.

Nearing the road, she shaded her eyes and looked at the horizon for any traffic. There was nothing.

"Excuse me." The car's door opened, and a blond man stepped out.

Trinity staggered back, her heartbeat racing. "Holy crap." She pressed a palm to her chest. "You startled me."

To Trinity, the guy—with his short messy hair and thick-rimmed glasses—looked like an accountant after an all-night party. He smiled. "Sorry, I didn't mean to scare you. I'm a little turned around and was hoping you could help me figure out how to get back on the road."

Of course, the guy was lost. Nobody came to Mercy on purpose.

"Sure." She stepped closer. "You got a map on your phone, or something?"

"Yeah. It fell onto the floor but it's in here, somewhere." The guy ducked into the car. He called out, "Give me a second."

Trinity moved closer still. As she stood behind him, she noticed a rattlesnake tattoo on his neck that seemed out of character. And his hair was more than messy. The haircut was choppy, a total crap job.

Something wasn't right. She scanned the parking lot. It was still empty. A tinge of fear crept up the back of her neck. "You know, I can just give you directions."

The guy riffled through the junk on his seat. "What?"

Leaning down, she raised her voice to be heard. "Where are you headed? I can just give you—"

Then, he struck. The belt was around Trinity's neck before she even knew what was happening. The leather bit into her flesh. She clawed the strap, trying to pull it free. Her necklace broke. The chain slid from her throat. She saw the locket hit the pavement and she wanted to cry out. But every part of her body burned with the need for air. Her pulse echoed in her skull, like waves crashing on the shore.

The guy was close, his breath hot on her shoulder. Reaching behind her, Trinity punched, scratched, clawed. Her fingernails grazed flesh.

With a curse, the guy pulled the belt tighter. "Do that again and I'll kill you slow."

"What?" she said, gasping for air. "Why?"

Trinity's arms were too heavy to lift, and she could no longer fight. Her vision blurred and darkness crept in from the sides. For a single instant, as the pain melted away, she wondered what came next.

Then there was nothing.

For the first time in almost two months, Clare woke up feeling truly refreshed. Her mind was clear. Her muscles were relaxed, instead of aching and cramped from sleeping curled up in the back seat of the car. Stretching in the bed, she took in the hotel room. Trinity's bed was empty. Clothes were tossed into piles on the floor. Makeup and jewelry were scattered across the top of the nightstand and the chest of drawers. The little Christmas tree still stood next to the wall, its glossy ornaments glowing in the sunlight creeping around the window shades.

On the floor was Clare's tote. She rolled to her side and leaned over the edge of the bed. Peering into the bag, she exhaled. The flash drive and the phone, along with pictures of the documents, were both in the bag.

Clare knew that the time had come. She couldn't keep running forever, which meant that she had to do something.

She could contact the media.

Or maybe the local police.

What she really wanted was to call her mom—if for no other reason than to speak to a person who knew and loved her.

Trinity's wisdom from the night before rang loudly in her mind. *Speaking for moms everywhere, we always want to hear from our kids.*

In all this time on the run from Kyle, all those lonely nights on the road, she hadn't reached out, even though she knew her mom would be worried. Sharing what she'd found, or any hint of her location, would put her only parent at risk. But if she made a call, she didn't have to tell her mother anything important—just enough to let her mom know she was safe.

A digital clock sat on the nightstand, the numbers a darker gray on a smoky background. It was 7:12 a.m. In Kauai, it'd be the middle of the night. But if Clare didn't call now, she knew she'd lose her nerve.

The cell was a pay-by-the-month smartphone that had been purchased in Indiana. At the time, Clare paid cash for the device and six months of service. She'd entered no contact information but knew her mother's number by heart. She placed the call and waited as the phone began to ring. For an instant, Clare hoped to get voice mail.

"Hello?" The voice on the other end of the line was thick with sleep.

"Hi, Mom. It's me."

"Oh, Clare, honey. It is you! Where are you? How are you? I heard from Kyle and have been so worried..."

Clare tensed. She should've known that her ex would reach out to her mother.

Her mom was still talking. "I know what it's like to have a breakdown and need to get away. Really, I do. Are you back in Columbus? I'll book a flight. It might be a day or two. You know how hard it is to get to the mainland."

A breakdown? So that's what Kyle had been telling people. "No, Mom, I'm not in Ohio. And I want you to stay away from Kyle. He's a dangerous man, Mom."

"He said that was part of your breakdown, honey. That you'd been making up stories about him."

How had Clare ever loved such a manipulative son

of a bitch? "Mom, listen to me. I didn't have a breakdown. I'm not paranoid," she said, although the last part wasn't exactly true. "Kyle and his father, well, they've done some things. Trust me." Her voice had risen. She paused and breathed. "I just called to let you know that I'm okay."

"I love hearing your voice, but I want to see you. Where you are? I'll come to you."

Clare closed her eyes and let her mind fill with happy dreams of seeing her mother again. But those dreams would never become a reality—not with Kyle and his family still out there. "I can't see you right now." Her chest was tight, but she drew in a breath. "It might be a while, but I'll call when I can."

"Why won't you let me help, Clare?"

"Because it's better for us all if I take care of things myself."

Her mother made a small sound. Clare couldn't tell if it was a laugh or a cry. "You've always been so independent. Even as a little girl. *Me do.* That was your favorite phrase. *Can I get you cereal?* Same answer always. *No, me do.*"

Emotion clogged her throat, and she swallowed hard. Once she could speak, she made sure her tone was controlled. "I'm sorry, Mom. I really am. I called to let you know that I'm okay. I didn't have a breakdown. And Kyle isn't the guy we thought he was."

"Can you tell me anything?"

"I don't want to drag you into this." She rubbed her eyes and sighed. "Promise me one thing. Do not call Kyle or his dad. If they reach out to you, say nothing about talking to me, or where I am."

"I don't know where you are. Really you haven't told me anything…"

Love gripped her heart and squeezed hard. "One more thing. Merry Christmas."

"Merry Christmas, Clare. I love you."

"Love you, too."

Clare ended the call and stared at the phone. A hard kernel of regret was stuck in her throat. No. She wouldn't feel bad for calling her own mother. But she knew that reaching out hadn't been the best plan, either.

The phone pinged as a message notification appeared on the screen. The appearance of a text left her confused. Nobody had her contact information. She pressed her thumb onto the bubble.

It was from Trinity.

Went to get us coffee. I can make a latte at the gas station. It's good. BRB.

There was also a time stamp: 5:57 a.m.

She glanced at the clock again. It was 7:16 a.m. Trinity had been gone for over an hour. Or maybe, she'd been gone, come back and left again. Maybe to do her laundry or something…

Pulling her knees to her chest, Clare scanned the room once more. This time she looked for a take-out cup, filled with coffee that would be cool by now.

Nothing.

Sure, Clare didn't know Trinity well—or even at all, really. Just because her roommate had offered to grab an extra cup of joe, it didn't obligate her to bring one back.

For a moment, she was sucked back into memory,

to her darkened office at Chamberlain Plastics Manufacturing.

A cup of tepid coffee sat at her elbow. The computer's illuminated screen was the only light. She'd opened the file several minutes before and had read the contents twice, still unable to believe the words in front of her. Her pulse raced. Her chest was tight, and her lungs burned with each breath.

"Hey." Kyle's voice seemed to come from nowhere. He crossed the threshold, and the motion sensor clicked. Lights flooded the room. "What are you doing here, sitting all alone in the dark?"

Swallowing, Clare realized that she didn't know where—or how to begin. "Umm..."

"You look tense." Kyle wore a dark suit, white shirt and no tie. His blond hair was freshly cut, and just starting to show a touch of gray at the temples. Standing behind her, Kyle began to knead her shoulders. He continued, "Maybe all this volunteer nonsense is too much for you. You're working late and all the tension is settling in your shoulders."

Nonsense. The one word helped her find her voice. "I found a problem," she said. For the past several years, she'd worked with a non-profit that turned unused land into parks. She was researching a possible site owned by Chamberlain Enterprises. "With the tract of land."

"Problem?" he echoed. "What kind?"

She shifted to the side, so he could see the screen. "Look." She pointed to the internal memo written by her father-in-law, chairman of the company Kyle's family had owned for decades.

"So, it's a memorandum from my dad." He leaned

closer. His breath was hot on her neck. "Written, what, twenty-one years ago. So, what about it?"

"Kyle. Do you see what it says?" She pointed to the screen again.

His palms still rested on her shoulder and his grip tightened.

"Ow, Kyle. You're hurting me..."

He let his hands slip from her shoulder. "Sorry. It's just..." He paused. "Dammit. I just don't know what you expect me to do. He is my father, after all."

She turned in her seat to look up at her husband. "I don't expect you to do anything. It's us. We're in this together and we'll figure out what to do."

He looked down at her and smiled. "I'm glad I have you with me. I'd hate to face all this alone." He flicked his fingers at the computer and the document on the screen.

She stood. Kyle pulled her to him, wrapping her in a hug. His arms were stiff, trapping Clare next to his chest. Of course, her husband was shocked that the company his family had founded and run for years buried drums filled with toxic chemicals. Who wouldn't be? And yet, in that moment, she longed to escape from his embrace.

Now she knew that her marriage was already over. Yet, she hadn't realized that her life was altered forever as well.

Chapter 6

Clare knew that she needed to find a way to deal with her in-laws and put the past behind her. Rising from the bed, she headed into the adjacent bathroom. In the tub, she turned on the taps and stepped under the hot spray of the shower. Within minutes, she felt physically refreshed—but the tightness in her throat remained.

After stepping from the shower, she wrapped a towel around her torso and returned to the main room. As Clare dressed, she planned. She'd start by looking for Trinity at the gas station. After that, well, there wasn't much more she knew to do. For the day, she wore a white T-shirt, jeans and sneakers. Her money was still in her locked suitcase. She removed $40 from the hiding place in her shoe and relocked her bag.

Once she was ready, Clare grabbed her tote bag and

left the room. The door closed and automatically locked. The sun had risen, but the air was still cool. She folded her arms over her chest. The parking lot, a sea of asphalt, stretched out to the road. Beyond that was the gas station. From where she stood, the store looked like a child's toy.

She hustled across the parking lot and stopped at the edge of the road. She looked for any traffic but there were no cars. She took a step forward and stopped. She'd seen something—a flash of metal in the morning light. Turning, she looked back at the ground.

There, at the edge of the parking lot, lay a necklace. She lifted it from the ground. A locket spun in the air. Even before she opened the frame, she knew what she'd find. Instead of a picture, thin strands of hair were tied with a ribbon.

It was Trinity's locket. One of the links had snapped in two.

Clare didn't know why it was in the parking lot, or what had happened to Trinity. But she was determined to find out.

Running across the road, Clare pulled the gas station's door open and stepped inside. It was like nothing had changed since yesterday. The scent of stale coffee and used motor oil still hung in the air. The same shiny garland was still hung across the counter. The same man still stood next to the cash register.

The only change was the countdown calendar. Now it read four days 'til Christmas.

The old man who ran the gas station looked up. "Morning. What can I do you for?"

"I'm looking for Trinity," Clare began. "You know,

from the bar." She jerked her thumb vaguely in the direction of the roadhouse across the street. "Have you seen her?"

"This morning?" the man said. "Naw, she didn't stop by."

Her heartbeat thundered, echoing in her skull. "Where else could she go?"

The man's name was embroidered on the pocket of his shirt. Stu. "Not many places around here. If you want to go anywhere special, you need a car."

That was it. "You think Trinity drove somewhere to get coffee?"

"Not likely," said Stu. "She got no car. And she usually came in here, anyways."

Clare tried to swallow but her throat was tight. She looked out the window. There was nothing to see. Just the same old bar, tattoo parlor and motel. A truck, covered in faded paint, rust and primer, pulled into the convenience store parking lot and parked next to the pump. The driver opened his door and jumped to the ground.

It was Isaac. Her heart began to race again. This time, it was for a wholly different reason.

She turned for the door before she'd planned what to do next. He looked up as she stepped into the sunshine. "Morning," he said, already pumping gas. "You're up early."

Clare glanced in the truck and for the first time, noticed a passenger. It was Ryan. He glared at her from where he sat. Her shoulders tightened with tension. "I was looking for Trinity. She sent me a text saying she was going to get us coffee. That was over two hours ago. She hasn't come back, and Stu hasn't seen her, either."

Ryan opened the door to the truck and sat on the edge of the bench seat. "What'd you say about Trinity? That she's gone? I wouldn't worry about her too much. She might've called some guy and talked him into taking her out to breakfast."

Clare didn't think that was right. Pulling Trinity's necklace from the front pocket of her jeans, she held up the locket. "I found this in the parking lot right next to the road." She examined the chain. "I guess she could've been getting into a car when it broke..."

She looked up at Isaac. His brow was furrowed, and he was watching Ryan. Ryan's complexion turned ashen. It brought back the moment she stood at the window and watched as Isaac and Ryan crossed the parking lot in the middle of the night.

"You think we'll find him?" Ryan asked.

"We can only hope," said Isaac.

What had that been about?

"I have some stuff to mail from Encatador," said Isaac. "The overnight delivery place doesn't open for a few hours. I can go to town now and see if Trinity turns up." Then to Ryan, he said, "You should stay here. Business as usual, right?"

Jumping to the ground, he repeated, "That was the order. Business as usual."

Clare said nothing as Ryan sauntered to the road and then jogged across the street. "Well, I guess I better..." She pointed toward the motel. "You know, get back. Trinity might show up with that coffee she promised."

Isaac returned the nozzle to the pump. "Take care, Clare. And do me a favor. Keep your door locked, okay?"

"They lock automatically, you know that."

"Use the dead bolt and the chain."

His words left her chilled. "Is there something I should be worried about?"

Isaac removed a wad of cash from his front pocket. "Nothing. It's just that you can never be too careful."

Wasn't that the truth.

He stepped past her, his arm brushing against her shoulder. She couldn't explain what happened, but a shock went through her at the feel of his body against hers. She'd never felt anything like it—not even with Kyle.

Then he walked on, and the moment was over.

She watched him for a minute longer before looking back at the line of cinderblock buildings.

"Hey, Clare."

She turned. Isaac held the door to the gas station partially open. "Yeah?"

"You can come with me, if you want."

"To Encantador?" she asked. "Why?"

He shrugged. "It's better than sitting in your room all morning. There's a decent diner and we can grab breakfast. Also grocery store if you need to pick up any food. I have a few errands to take care of, but they won't take long."

"I don't know…" she began.

He pulled the door open the rest of the way. "No problem. Just thought I'd offer." He slipped into the store and let the door close behind him.

Clare walked to the side of the road. She wasn't sure why she'd turned down the offer to go into town. Maybe she'd spent so much time alone recently that she forgot what it was to be around another person. She glanced over her shoulder. Isaac was back in his truck.

There were a million reasons that she should just stay in Mercy. Trinity really might show up. Personally, Clare had secrets to keep. She's shared more with Trinity than she intended. In talking to Isaac, she might give some key detail away. There was also the fact that the more time she spent in public, the easier it became for Kyle to track her down.

Truthfully, there were only a few reasons for her go with Isaac. Clare now had money to purchase food of her own. Even better, she could replace the snacks Trinity had shared. Besides, it wouldn't be *that* bad to spend more time with Isaac—even if every time he looked it her, she felt a spark in her belly.

He turned on the engine and the truck's running lights glowed. Clare waved and he drove toward her. The truck idled as he pulled up at her side and lowered his window. "You need something?"

She swallowed. "Is that offer to ride along still open?"

Isaac had a list of things to do in Encantador, and bringing Clare with him was a distraction he didn't need. Yet, he'd be stupid to ignore the fact that Decker Newcombe had surfaced at the same time Trinity Jackson went missing. The hitman had even made threats towards those who worked for Ryan. Because of that, he didn't like the idea of Clare being alone.

She sat in the passenger seat as his truck rumbled down the road. The town of Mercy became a speck in his rearview mirror. One day soon, he hoped to leave the town for good. Before that, he had to find and catch a killer.

Clare stared out the windshield and he watched her in profile. The curve of her neck. The definition of her chin and nose and mouth.

Without looking in his direction, she asked, "Can I ask a question?"

"Shoot."

"What's the deal between you and Ryan? It just seems to me like…" She stopped and drew her bottom lip between her teeth. "Well, there's a vibe between you two. I know you say he's your boss, but it seems like Ryan's beholden to you."

He sat straighter. Gripping the steering wheel, he turned his eyes back to the road. Ryan Steele was more than beholden. Isaac was the only reason that Ryan was out of jail and without him, he'd go back to rotting in a cell.

He asked, "What makes you think that?"

"He's just, well… What's the word?" She paused to look out the window. "Deferential, I suppose."

Isaac's pulse began to race. He never should've brought Clare with him. She was too curious. Too astute.

"Ryan's a mean cuss," he said. "He's certainly never been respectful of anyone—me, included."

"It's just that he let you give me this job. You set the agenda for the day. It seems like he owes you." She glanced at Isaac. He made the mistake of looking in her direction. Their eyes met and she pinned him with her gaze. Desire, like a lightning strike, shot through him. She asked, "You know what I think?"

He looked back at the road—his jaw tight. "No. What do you think?"

"I think something happened in jail and you saved Ryan."

In a weird way, Clare was right and wrong at the same time. It was best to let her think what she wanted. With an exhale, he rolled his shoulders back. "It's not really something we talk about. So…"

"I won't say a word." Clare put a hand to her chest, as if taking a pledge.

He turned his attention back to the road. A bead of sweat trickled down his cheek. Wiping it away with the side of his hand, he glanced once more at Clare. She was looking out the window.

"What about you?" He glanced at Clare before turning his attention back to the road. "How'd you end up in Mercy?"

Without turning to look at Isaac, she said. "I took a wrong turn."

Isaac guffawed. He couldn't remember the last time he'd laughed out loud. With a shake of his head, he looked back at the road. Sure, Clare had a quick wit but there was more. She hadn't really told him anything about herself. Before he could think of the right questions to ask, he felt that same old shimmy in his seat a moment before the temperature gauge in his car started to climb.

"Damn." He slammed his hand on the steering wheel and eased his foot off the gas. A cloud of steam leaked out from under his hood.

"What's wrong?" asked Clare, a note of alarm in her voice.

He pulled to the side of the road, his tires kicking up a cloud of dust. "Truck's overheating." He should've known better than to take it out so soon after driving around all night. "It's hard to get parts for a vehicle this old. Plus, Mercy isn't exactly a shipping hub."

Clare's tote sat on the floorboards. She lifted it to her lap and looked inside. Pulling out a hair band, she wrapped her locks into a ponytail. "What can I do to help?"

"You? Help?"

"You sound surprised."

He shrugged.

"Why wouldn't I help? The quicker we get the truck fixed, the quicker we find Trinity. Besides, I don't want to sit on the side of the road all day, especially in this heat." She unlatched her seat belt and swiveled in her seat. The tote slipped from her lap and dumped the contents onto the grimy floor mat. He cataloged the contents. Sunglasses. Key fob. Cell phone. A flash drive. A water bottle.

Clare cursed. She bent to pick up her belongings.

Isaac leaned over in his seat. He scooped up the drive.

"Give that to me," said Clare, her voice hard as flint.

The change in her tone from amiable to threatening gave Isaac a jolt. "Sure," he said, holding up the slim metal drive. "Here you go."

She snatched it from his hand with the greedy speed of a thief with a jewel. He had to wonder what was on that drive that was so important?

Silently, she collected the rest of her belongings.

"You know," Isaac began, "that's the second time everything's fallen out of that bag of yours. Ever consider getting something with a zipper on top?"

"You know," she echoed both his words and tone, "I'm a little strapped for cash right now. Getting a bag with a zipper is low on my priority list."

"Maybe if you're a good girl, Santa will bring you a new purse."

She huffed out a small laugh. "Maybe."

"Besides, if you're low on cash, you can sell the bag. I don't know much about fashion designers, but that tote looks real to me. Probably worth something, even at resale."

Clare held the bag to her chest. "I thought about doing just that. Really, I have. Probably would've had no choice but to pawn off my tote if I hadn't gotten the job with you." She let out a long breath. "I've kept it because of what this bag means to me…"

Isaac could clearly imagine some monied dude giving Clare the expensive bag as a gift. Maybe that dude was why she was on the run. Or maybe, he was still out there, and she wanted to get back to him. It drove home the simple fact that he knew nothing of Clare or her life. He liked the way she looked. He liked her company. There was nothing more between them. Period. End of story. He swallowed down the sour taste of frustration. "You've kept it because it was a gift. I get it."

She shook her head. "It's not that at all. I bought this bag myself. At the time, it was more than my monthly rent." She shook her head. "It was a stupid splurge but being able to buy it made me feel like I was finally a success." Clare met his gaze. "Do you know what I mean?"

He recalled the moment that he'd gotten the buy-in from the feds for his plan to catch Decker Newcombe.

At a meeting that made the operation possible, Jason Jones had said, "You've got balls, my man. And you're either a genius or you're a fool." The agent shoved the contract across a wide conference table. The page's edge fluttered with the breeze of movement.

Isaac already had a pen in hand. "I'm a lot of things," he said, signing his name on the appropriate line. His chest was tight with pride. "But a fool isn't one of them. We'll get this bastard and soon."

He turned away from the memory and looked at Clare. The sun, just starting to creep higher in the sky, shone at her from behind. She was surrounded with a halo of light and her features were obscured with shadows.

"I know how you feel." He scratched at the stubble on his chin and let the moment pass.

Sure, he understood Clare's attachment to her expensive tote bag. But she was obviously protective of the flash drive. He imagined that it was part of the reason she was on the run. Even if he'd figured out a small part of her story, there was still so much more about her that he didn't know.

And that mystery was enough of a reason to keep his distance.

For Clare, stopping in Mercy had come with problems she hadn't anticipated. When she'd been by herself, she never had to worry about getting tripped up on a lie. Or worse, accidentally telling the truth.

Then, there was the flash drive. When she was alone in the car, she knew it was safe.

Now, she risked losing it—or worse, facing questions about it if anyone found out about it. If she left it in her car or the room, it might get stolen. Sure, keeping it in her bag wasn't ideal, either. But it was the best she could do for now at least.

Isaac was another problem altogether. He was too damn good-looking. Beyond the looks was the fact that he was charming, smart and insightful. It made him easy to like and easier to trust. But Clare had learned her lesson well. Everyone was capable of deception.

Still, she refused to let the current of life sweep her along. Hugging the bag to her chest, she glanced at Isaac. After weeks on the road, she'd figured out how to fix minor auto problems. "I can help with the car."

"We gotta wait for the engine to cool. Then, the reservoir needs to be refilled." He gave a frustrated sigh. "I can't wait to get rid of this heap of crap."

Sure, the vehicle was old. She patted the dashboard. "This truck is a classic. All it needs is some TLC."

"And that takes money, which I don't have."

She chewed on her bottom lip. Before she married Kyle, Clare hadn't been a wealthy woman. But she'd lived a comfortable life where money was available to cover all her needs, even if she couldn't buy everything she wanted. Life with Kyle had been opulent. Lavish. Excessive.

The minute she left Columbus, her circumstances

changed. Clare's thinking needed to change as well. "Sorry, I didn't mean to imply..." she began.

Isaac waved away her apology. "Just forget about it." He paused. "There's a jug behind your seat. If you want to help, you can grab it for me."

Clare folded the top of her bag over and carefully set it on the floorboard. She turned in her seat and came up on her knees. There, on the floor, was a plastic jug filled with water.

She looped two fingers through the handle and hoisted the water up and over the seat. "Here you go."

"Thanks." Isaac took the jug, not bothering to look her in the eye.

Had he been watching her? Then again, it'd been a while since Clare had gone for a run—much less taken a yoga class or worked out at the gym. Maybe he had taken a peek and hadn't liked what he saw.

Now, that was a humbling thought.

She dropped back to her knees. "You need anything else?"

"Naw, I'm just gonna get this in the reservoir and we can get going."

Isaac opened the door and stepped from the truck. She watched as he walked to the grille. His shirt clung to the muscles in his arms, shoulders and chest. He looked up, their gaze meeting through the windshield. Clare's cheeks warmed and she turned her gaze to the side window.

"Hey," Isaac called.

She looked at where he stood at the front fender.

"Can you pop the hood for me? It's the lever under the steering wheel. Left side."

Clare moved to the driver's seat and pulled back on the toggle. The hood unlatched with a pop. Isaac lifted the hood and braced it on the prop rod. He was hidden behind the hood but still she could hear his curse. "Aww. Dammit."

"You okay?"

"The radiator cap's too hot to touch. Can you grab me something?"

Clare scanned the inside of the truck. True, it was old, but it was clean. Not even a used napkin wedged into a door pocket. She opened the glove box and froze. Atop a pile of maps was a gun, along with a box of ammo.

She told herself that she shouldn't be surprised. It was Texas after all. Besides, given the nature...of business, she supposed, at the bar, it seemed only natural that Isaac might keep a weapon around.

Clare touched the handle with a finger. She expected the metal to be cold and smooth. The gun felt like nothing more than death.

But Isaac was a convicted felon. Weren't there laws about convicts not having weapons? She shook her head. A lifetime of living by the rules had given Clare a headful of thoughts that were ridiculously unhelpful now. Her world was now a dangerous place. In fact, she wondered why she'd never gotten a gun already. Or maybe she hadn't gotten a gun because she didn't know how to use one.

"I think there's a rag behind the seat. It's back where you got the milk jug."

Isaac's voice startled Clare. She closed the glove box.

"Just a sec." She turned and looked over the back of the seat. There, on the floor, was a red bandanna. She pinched the fabric with the tips of her fingers and sat in the seat. "Got it," she called out, while opening the door and stepping from the truck.

The cool air was already giving way to the heat of the day. Clare wondered what the weather was like in Ohio. Most likely rainy and cold. Or maybe there'd be a white Christmas in Columbus this year. Snow wasn't something she'd see in a place like Mercy.

"Here you go." She rounded the front of the truck and held out the bandanna.

Isaac took the cloth. "Thanks."

He bent under the hood and unscrewed the lid of his water reservoir. A hiss of steam escaped. "Damn. Still too hot. If I put in water now, it'll just boil off."

Clare leaned against the side of the truck, her mind returning to the gun in the glove box.

"We got no choice but to wait."

"I was wondering..." Whatever else she wanted to say was stuck in her throat. Maybe her mother had been right, and Clare hated asking for help. She shook her head.

Isaac shoved the bandanna in the front pocket of his jeans. "You were wondering what?"

Clare coughed to clear her throat. "Well, it's just that when I was looking for a rag, I opened your glove box." She paused a beat, forcing herself to speak. "I saw the gun."

"Okay." He narrowed his eyes and watched Clare

for a moment. She wasn't sure what to read in his gaze. Hesitancy? Curiosity? "What about it?"

Maybe asking for a lesson in firearms was a bad idea. Then again, she'd come too far to turn back. Her heart hammered against her chest. "Would you show me how to shoot?"

Chapter 7

When Isaac came to Mercy, he'd made it a rule to never get involved personally with anyone. He should be following that rule with Clare, but he already knew that it was too late to simply be indifferent with her. What's more, he wanted to know why she was hiding in Texas. He wanted to know why she was running.

Clare asking for a firearms lesson brought up a whole other interesting set of questions. Namely, who might she need to shoot—and why?

Even though Isaac did care, he gave an uninterested shrug. "Sure. Why not. We got some time." He walked to the end of the truck's bed. Clare followed. "The first rule of gun safety is this—every gun is loaded. I don't care if you know there aren't any bullets in the firearm. It's loaded." He lowered the tailgate.

Already, she sounded confused. "How can that be? If there are no bullets, then—"

"That's the mindset I want you to have. A gun is a dangerous and deadly tool, and it's key that you to respect that fact from the beginning. It'll help keep you safe when you're using one. Rule two." He climbed into the back of the truck. A metal box was wedged behind a wheel well. He lifted the lid and paused. "Never take out your gun if you don't intend to use it. Got it?"

She dutifully repeated the rules.

He nodded at her words and lifted the lid of the metal box. Taking a knee, he rooted around inside, tossing several empty soda bottles into the bed of the truck. Slamming the lid shut, Isaac collected the bottles and stood. He walked the edge of the truck and jumped to the ground. He landed right next to her, and a shiver of desire ran down his spine. Clare really was a beautiful woman. Her fingers were long and graceful. What would it be like to have her touch him? To explore her in return.

"Here, hold these." Laced between his fingers were the empty bottles. "We'll use these for target practice."

Clare took the bottles.

"Now," Isaac continued, "we need the gun and the ammo. What's the first rule of firearms?" Walking to the passenger side of his truck, he looked over his shoulder as he spoke. Her legs were firm, and the swell of her hips filled out her jeans nicely. Another image stole into his mind, one of arms and legs tangled in sheets. Or of her thighs parting as his hips drove forward. His mouth went dry, and he looked away.

She repeated his earlier warnings. "A gun is always

loaded. Followed by rule two and that's to never take out a gun unless you plan to use it."

He heard her words and nodded, but his mind was still filled with his fantasy. True, it'd been months since he'd last slept with a woman. Maybe it was a simple physical need that drew him to Clare.

Then again, he'd seen plenty of good-looking women pass through the bar in Mercy. And well, his pulse didn't race *veins around* any of them at all.

Isaac stood at her side. In one hand, he held the gun. In the other hand, a box of bullets. "I stowed your bag behind the seat. Hope that's okay."

"Yeah. That's fine."

He nodded and slipped the gun into the waistband of his jeans near the small of his back. After locking the truck's door he asked, "You ready for your first shooting lesson?"

Clare walked next to Isaac. It took less than five minutes for him to find a flat-topped rock, that was about three feet high.

"This will work," he said, setting the bottles in a row.

She watched him walk back to where she stood. "Now what?"

"I always want you to be cautious around guns. But if you take out a firearm, it's because you plan to eliminate a threat. Aim for the center mass." Isaac used his finger to outline a circle on his torso. All the while, he kept his gaze on Clare's face as he spoke. He was making sure that she was paying attention to what he said, and what's more had, absorbed the information. She didn't mind that he was being so careful while teaching her how to use a firearm. But again, his background as a convict didn't seem to meld with his caution. "Got it?"

"Got it." She paused. "Where'd you learn how to shoot?"

"Aww, darlin'," he said, his drawl becoming thick. "I learned how to handle a firearm from a young age."

Was that really true? Or was there more to his story? Before she could wonder, he held the gun on the flat of his hand. "This here is what's commonly called a handgun. Officially, this is a Glock 19. It's not a big gun, but it can punch a hole through a person at one-hundred paces. The magazine holds ten bullets and there's one in the chamber."

"Eleven shots," she said.

Isaac smiled. "Glad that you're paying attention." He pointed at the gun again, going over each part, from the grip to the magazine, making sure she could familiarize herself with each.

"If you're going to shoot, you're going to have to know how to reload a gun." He pointed to a black button on the left side of the firearm's grip. He pressed it with his thumb. The magazine slipped free. He handed it to Clare. "That's the magazine release." Next, he pulled back on the slide and bullet was ejected from the top of the gun. He handed that to her as well. "And that's the ejector port."

Next, he pulled back on the slide and exposed the ejector port once more. "This is the slide release lever, and it locks the slide into place and open. You can see into the magazine well." He held up the weapon so Clare could see daylight at the other end of the gun. As he spoke, Clare had to admit, that his precise lessons weren't what she expected from an ex-con. Isaac was definitely proving to be quite a puzzle—it's just that she didn't know how all of the pieces fit.

He concluded, "Now you know that the firearm is empty."

He spent a minute loading the firearm. The magazine was returned to the well. He released the slide and chambered a round. Then, he released the magazine a second time and took the extra bullet from Clare. "When you add the final bullet, it's called topping off." Holding the fiream by the grip, he held out the gun to her. "Now it's your turn."

She slipped her hand over his as he passed the gun on to her. Clare's breath caught in her chest. It was more than holding a deadly weapon. It was Isaac. He was large man—muscular and solid. His shoulders were broad, and his arms were well-defined. Having him so close both excited and intimidated her.

He let go of the gun and the weight of the firearm pulled her arm down. "It's heavier than I imagined."

"If you spend a lot of time handling weapons, you'll get used to it."

They spent the next few minutes working together to load and unload the gun. Eventually, Clare knew all the steps by heart.

Isaac said, "Firing a gun is easy. Point and shoot. Hitting a target, now that's the tricky part."

Clare turned to look at the bottles lined up in a row. They were impossibly small from this distance.

"See this." He pointed to a small piece of metal that stuck out from the barrel. "That's the sight. You line that up with your target and pull the trigger. Got it?"

"Line the sight up with the target. Pull the trigger. Got it."

Gripping the gun in one hand, he pointed the barrel to the ground. "Take it."

Isaac chuckled. "Unless you're using a gun all the time, your arm and wrist will fatigue quickly. In the end, it'll mess up your aim. So, you'll have to compensate."

"That's a lot to keep in mind."

"Sure, but using a gun is serious business." He pointed to the soda bottles. "Just remember what I told you and fire."

Clare lifted the gun. Her wrist wobbled.

"Tighten up everything." Isaac ran his hand over her forearm.

Her pulse raced at his touch, but she squeezed the muscles in both arms from wrist to shoulder. The gun steadied in her grip. The sight, a red piece of metal stuck up from the barrel. She touched the red tip to one of the bottles and pulled the trigger.

The blast of gunfire filled the silent desert. The scent of gunpowder wafted on the breeze. The gun bucked in Clare's hand, sending a shock wave through her body that she felt in her chest and her teeth. A cloud of dust erupted in front of the rock.

The dust settled and all the bottles were still standing.

"Damn," she cursed, passing the gun from one hand to the other. Her palm throbbed and she shook it out. "What'd I do wrong?"

"You can't expect to be an expert after firing one bullet."

"Is that another rule for me to remember?"

"Life advice," Isaac said. "There was this one time I

was teaching a young man how to shoot..." His words trailed off and he scratched the side of his ear. "Anyway, everyone always thinks it's easier to be a marksman than it really is." He paused a beat. "Try again."

Clare lifted the gun, taking care to line up the sight with a bottle. Inhale. Exhale. Pull. Fire. Once again, a cloud of dirt and gravel shot up into the air. As the dust settled, she saw that the bottles still stood in a row. Sure, she wasn't surprised, but she was still disappointed. "Dammit. What am I doing wrong?"

"You aren't doing anything wrong, but I can help you get a little closer to right. Lift your gun and aim at the last bottle."

She did.

Isaac moved in behind her, close enough that his chest touched her back. He bent down so his cheek was next to hers and she could hear his breath. "Lift your arm a little." He placed his hand near her wrist and applied the whisper of pressure. "You want the sight on top of the target, not beneath it."

The bottle was hidden behind the sight. Yet, with Isaac so close, it was hard to concentrate on anything beyond the feeling of his body next to hers.

"See what I mean?" he asked.

She looked at the sight and covered the bottle with the red metal line. "I think so."

He put pressure on her arm from the bottom. "Make sure you keep the gun level. Now fire."

Hooking her finger around the trigger, she pulled back. The gun jumped in her hand as the rock exploded into bits of dust. The bottle still stood upright. She lowered the gun, letting the weight of the weapon pull down on her shoulder. "I missed again."

He squeezed her arm. "Not too shabby for only firing a gun three times." He stepped back. "Try again."

Clare rolled her shoulders up, back and around. She stared at the bottle, imagined the bullet punching a hole through the plastic. Lifting the gun, she covered the target with the sight. Inhale. Exhale. She squeezed the trigger. The boom of the gun's blast rolled out over the plains as the bottle shot up into the air.

"You did it," he whooped. "I knew you could. Try again. See if you can hit another bottle."

She aimed and pulled the trigger. The crack of a whip echoed over the plains as the bullet kicked up a cloud of dust. The bottle still stood. She inhaled. Exhaled. Setting the sight on the target again, she fired. Shredded plastic jumped off the rock as the bullet ripped through the empty bottle.

"Great job," said Isaac. His enthusiasm made her smile. "You're a great natural shot, but make sure to practice whenever you get a chance."

"That was a combination of excellent teaching and beginner's luck." She held out the firearm. "I want to see you shoot."

Isaac took the gun from her hand and worked his jaw back and forth. "The engines probably cooled enough that I can add water by now. You ready? Or you want to try and shoot again?" He offered her the butt-end of the gun.

She waved the firearm. "I'm good."

Isaac nodded toward the rock. "I'm gonna get the bottles. No sense leaving garbage out here."

"No littering. Now, that makes you a man after my own heart."

He stared at her. "Huh?"

"You won't litter. I went to school for environmental engineering. Just a little conservation joke." *And apparently not a very good one.* Her face burned. "I can help." She hustled past Isaac and scooped up the bottles that were still standing.

Isaac had shoved the gun into the waistband of his jeans again. She leaned her hip on the rock and watched as he gathered the bottles that had been shot. He looked up at her and smiled. Just seeing that smile warmed her insides.

Then again, he never answered her question about where he'd learned to shoot. It wasn't an accident. He'd obviously ignored her. She was determined to find out more about the man who it her up like a freaking Christmas tree.

They began to walk. "You never answered my question earlier, about where you learned to shoot so well. Why's that?"

He leveled his gaze at her. "Why's it matter?"

She swallowed, not sure what to say next. "It's just that I'm out here in the middle of nowhere with a guy I don't know anything about. Suddenly, I learn that he's a master marksman. I have a right to be curious."

Isaac continued to stare at Clare. "No, you don't. Besides, you were the one who wanted the shooting lesson."

He was right. She had asked for his help. In the distance, sunlight winked off the truck's windshield. Clare trudged toward the waiting vehicle. Isaac walked at her side.

At the truck, he lowered the tailgate and jumped into the bed. "Hand me those bottles."

She did. He placed all the plastic back into the metal box and shut the lid. Then, he jumped to the ground. "Imani Omar." Isaac slammed the tailgate closed.

"Who's that?" Clare asked. "The person who taught you how to shoot?"

"Nope. She's the first girl I ever kissed. Prettiest girl in the seventh grade. Beautiful, brown eyes. Long nails that she kept pained bright pink. She smelled like vanilla and tasted like strawberry syrup. I think it was her lip gloss."

"Why're you telling me about a girl you kissed when you were a kid?"

"No, Imani wasn't a girl. She was *the* girl. I'm not telling you about how I learned how to shoot because that's not a story you need to hear." He rested his hand on the top of the tailgate and shrugged. "When you asked me about my firearms instructor and I wouldn't answer, you started to worry that I was untrustworthy."

He wasn't wrong. She shrugged. "So instead…"

"Instead, I decided to tell you about Imani. She's more important, anyway."

"Because she was your first girlfriend?"

Isaac shook his head. "Girlfriend? No. Especially not after the kiss."

"Why's that?"

"I'd rather not say."

"You were the one who brought her up. You can't start a story without finishing. It's not fair."

"Well, I was an inexperienced kisser."

Clare asked, "Isn't everyone inexperienced at that age?"

"Trust me, I was bad."

Isaac slapped the back of the truck and walked to the front grille. Clare followed. The hood was still up. The jug filled with water sat on the ground. "Now you've got me hooked on your story. How bad were you at kissing?"

"Let's just say I didn't have an understanding of technique." He lifted the jug from the ground and took off the lid, pouring water into the reservoir. "I definitely didn't know how to French kiss, and she taught me everything I needed to know. At that age, anyway."

Clare laughed out loud. "I think I get it."

She waited as he screwed the lid back in place and slammed the hood shut. "Let's get out of here."

Clare stepped away from the truck at the same moment Isaac turned. They collided and she pitched back. She knew she was going to fall. Before she went down, Isaac caught her in his arms.

Her hands were pressed against his chest. His heartbeat was strong under her palms. Without thinking, she brushed her mouth against his. His lips were strong, and he tasted of citrus.

Then, Clare started thinking too much. She stepped back. "I shouldn't have done that. I don't know why. I mean, I do. You're handsome, and you were holding me, and it just seemed like the thing to do. If you're offended, I'm so sorry…"

"I'm not offended. You don't need to be sorry. It was nice."

Well, nice was something. "Okay, so long as we understand each other." What kind of understanding they had, she wasn't sure.

"Hey, Clare?" He reached for her. His touch was alluring, and she didn't move away. He pulled gently on her hand. She let herself be drawn closer, and as his forehead touched hers, their gazes met. "Okay?" he muttered, his lips nearly against hers.

It felt like torture, when all she wanted was his kiss. Again. "Okay," she whispered as his mouth took hers.

This time, it felt less gentle and more like an exploration. He pressed his tongue into the seam between her lips and she sighed, opening herself to him. Pressing her body against his, she melted into the embrace. Isaac wrapped his strong arms around her waist and held her tighter. The kiss became hungrier and deeper. His hands traced her side, her stomach, her breasts. She ran her fingers through the short hair at the nape of his neck and the heat of his skin scalded her hotter than the Texas sun.

"Oh, Isaac." Clare was dizzy with lust and longing. But she needed to stop now because in a minute she'd lack the fortitude to walk away.

Breathless, she pushed Isaac's chest. "You've obviously gotten better at kissing since the seventh grade."

He gave a quiet chuckle. "That's good to know at least."

Her head still swam and her legs were weak. She reached for the door handle to keep herself steady. "We better get going. You have errands and I'd like to look for Trinity." After pulling open the door, she climbed onto the seat and got settled. Yet, her mind raced as she wondered what the hell should happen next…

Get a hold of yourself, Clare. You're a grown woman.

Sure, she wanted to believe that. But she knew that she was lying—because that had been a hell of a lot more than *just a kiss*.

And if she didn't forget it—and remember why she was in Mercy—it could only lead to trouble.

Decker Newcombe drove through the side streets of Encantador, one hand holding the steering wheel and the other resting on the book he'd stolen from the library. *The Complete Guide to Jack the Ripper*.

He'd killed the redhead to send a message to Ryan Steele. As life leaked out of the woman, he knew that the money wasn't as important as his legacy. His heritage was murder and terror. But he didn't want to die in obscurity, like his infamous ancestor.

Hell no, that wouldn't do for him.

He'd never settle for the hollow notoriety that came with being an unknown killer. He wasn't a shadowy bogeyman. If it weren't for DNA found on the clothing of a victim, Jack's true identity would've forever remained a mystery.

Wrapping his hand tighter around the steering wheel, Decker looked for the perfect place to watch and wait. He found it in an abandoned municipal lot that was surrounded by the rear entrance to a strip mall. It was 10:15 a.m. A dollar store sat between a laundromat and an Asian restaurant that was only open for dinner. There was also a grocery store that wouldn't open for another forty-five minutes. He scanned the roofline of the buildings and above each door for cameras.

There were none.

Slumping low in the seat, he reached for his book. After opening the covers, he scanned the table of contents. "Chapter Three: Victims of Jack." Page 87.

He read:

Throughout the fall of 1888, Jack the Ripper was believed to have committed five grisly murders. Also known as the Canonical Five, there were eerie similarities between each of the killings. First, all the victims were women. Second, they all worked as prostitutes in London's Whitechapel neighborhood. Finally, each woman was disemboweled after her death.

Their entrails were never found.

Decker set the book on the passenger seat. Pulse pounding against his skull, he gripped the steering wheel tight. His mouth was dry. What would it have been like all those years ago? London streets so dark that it'd be impossible to see a hand in front of a face. Or a knife at a neck. Had his ancestor hidden in shadows and waited for his prey?

Or had he spoken to his victim before slitting her throat?

Drawing in a deep breath, he finally knew what he wanted.

The scent of decay and death already filled the car. Turning his gaze to the rearview mirror, he glanced at his closed trunk. Even though he couldn't see it, he knew that the body of the redhead was still there, waiting for Decker to make his mark.

One day soon, the world would fear his name, too.

Chapter 8

Clare glanced out the window as the truck passed a large wooden sign. In blue script were the words *Welcome to Encantador: A Charming Place to Live. Population 2,872.*

A single street led through the middle of town. Both sides of the road were lined with businesses. A doctor's office. A post office. A diner that served breakfast and lunch sat across the street from a bar that only served dinner and alcohol. Like arteries off a vein, side roads led to and from neighborhoods. Houses, surrounded by green lawns, sat behind picket fences.

"Looks like a nice town," said Clare, as Isaac pulled the truck next to the curb.

Isaac gave a noncommittal grunt. "Guess so." After turning off the engine, he pocketed the keys. Pointing, he said, "That's the best place to look for Trinity."

The diner, Over Easy, sat in the middle of the block. The picture of a snowy field and happy snowmen had been painted across three windowpanes that overlooked the street. A paper cutout of Santa hung from the front door.

Following Isaac, she stepped into the diner. The dark and nutty aroma of coffee greeted her, along with the spicy-sweet scent of baking cinnamon. Her stomach gurgled, a painful reminder that she'd skipped more than her morning coffee—but breakfast as well.

She was also developing one hell of a headache, the result of no coffee—which she'd basically lived on for months on the road—and the burning Texas heat. Now that she thought about it, she hadn't even had much water this morning. No wonder this place smelled so good.

He stopped on the threshold and scanned the room. "Trinity's not here."

She followed his gaze. Half a dozen booths lined one wall. A narrow counter with fifteen stools sat between the booths and the kitchen. All the stools were vacant, and only half the tables were filled. Trinity was definitely not one of the customers.

Swallowing, she asked, "If she's not here, where else could she be?"

"Maybe she stopped by earlier and left. Let's grab a seat," said Isaac, leading the way to the counter. "The server might know."

Clare sat on a stool. Isaac took the seat beside her. Both places were already set with silverware wrapped in a paper napkin. An upside-down coffee cup rested in a saucer.

An older woman with short gray hair stood behind the counter and approached as they sat. "Morning, folks." Her name tag read Mae. Flipping over the coffee cups, she continued, "Want a fill up?"

"Please," said Isaac.

"High-test or low-octane?" the server asked, comparing coffee to gasoline.

Isaac looked to Clare, waiting for her order.

"I'll take caffeinated," she said.

"Make that two."

"Anything else?" Mae asked.

"The cinnamon rolls smell good," said Isaac before asking, "They fresh?"

Mae filled Clare's cup with coffee from a glass pot. "Of course, they are. Came out of the oven a few minutes ago." She filled Isaac's cup.

Once again, he looked to Clare. How long had it been since someone actually showed her any consideration, even if it was just to let her order first? Obviously, there were the two months since she left Columbus. But honestly, it had been longer.

Sure, on paper, Kyle had been the perfect husband. Smart. Good-looking. Successful. But when it came down to it, there were problems in the marriage even before everything went to hell.

"Hon? Y'all want a cinnamon roll?" Mae asked, drawing Clare from her thoughts.

Clare's stomach growled again. "Yes." After a beat, she added, "Please."

Isaac said, "Make that two."

Mae nodded and turned toward the glass and chrome pastry cabinet. Clare reached for a bowl filled with packets of sweeteners. After emptying two sugars into her coffee, she stirred and then sipped. The drink warmed her from within and she gave a contented sigh as the caffeine hit her brain.

"The first sip is always the best." Isaac held his own cup, lifting it slightly as if they were toasting with champagne flutes.

"You think the coffee's good, wait 'til you try these," said Mae, setting two plates on the counter. Fat cinnamon rolls, covered in icing, filled each plate. "Enjoy."

Clare reached for her silverware and unwrapped the napkin. After cutting off a piece, she stabbed it with her fork and took a bite. Spicy sweetness filled her mouth. "Wow," she said around her bite. "That's delicious."

Mae beamed. "Glad you like it. It's my momma's recipe."

Isaac had already finished half his cinnamon roll. "Compliments to your mom," he said, taking another bite.

"Well, she's been gone for nearly thirty years, but I'll tell her when I see her in Heaven." Mae filled Isaac's cup with fresh coffee. "What brings you two to town? You folks visiting family for the holidays?"

Isaac took the last bite of his roll and scraped his fork through the icing on the plate. "We're looking for a friend of ours. We think she might've stopped by this morning."

"Maybe I can help. What's she look like?"

"Redhead," said Clare, a bite halfway to her mouth. "She's tall, too."

"A tall woman with red hair," Mae echoed as she shook her head. "Can't say that I've seen someone like that, but the breakfast rush was especially busy today. Maybe she was here, and I just don't recall."

"Oh, trust me." Isaac pushed his plate back. "You'd remember Trinity. She's got a few pretty elaborate tattoos. One like a tiger on her arm. A pink python on her leg."

Mae shook her head. "I definitely didn't see anyone like that."

"Any place else that might've been open around half-past seven?" Clare cupped her hands around her mug of coffee.

"Just us." She glanced over her shoulder. A wall clock sat above the door to the kitchen. It was almost eleven o'clock. "The grocery store opens soon. She might be headed over there."

Isaac nodded. "Thanks."

With a coffeepot in hand, the server came from behind the counter and moved to a table.

"So..." Clare wasn't sure where to lead the conversation. She refused to bring up the kiss, even though her lips still tingled. Still, she was curious about Isaac. "What's your story? You met Ryan in jail. Then came looking for a job when you got out. What was going on in your life before all that happened?"

He gave her that smile. "Me? I thought I told you. I'm a Texas boy, born and raised."

Clare ignored the fluttering in her chest. "How long have you been in Mercy?"

"About a year."

"A whole year?" Clare couldn't imagine spending that much time in a place like Mercy, Texas. Then again, she might not have another choice. She took a bite of her cinnamon roll and thought about her future. Before she could plan for anything beyond today, she needed to deal with her past—Kyle and her in-laws included.

Mae returned. "Anything else I can get for you two?"

Clare had eaten the entire roll. "I'm good."

Isaac got to his feet. "Thanks for your help." He pulled a roll of cash from his front pocket and set a bill on the counter. "That should cover everything," he said.

"You don't have to pay for me," Clare began.

He stopped her words with his smile. "It's not every day I get to take a beautiful woman out for coffee." His Texas drawl was thick, and his voice made her toes tingle. "Come on." He held the door open for Clare to pass. "Let's see if the grocery store is open and ask about Trinity before it gets too busy."

As she walked past, her shoulder brushed against his chest in the cramped doorway. At least by now she'd had enough accidental physical contact with Isaac that she knew what to expect. The little hiccup to her pulse as her heart began to race. The warming of her skin at the exact point of contact. She also knew that she'd be able to feel his touch on her skin for hours more.

The grocery store looked as though it had been built not long after World War II ended. It consisted of one level—all red brick, glass and metal—and filled half the block. Wide windows looked onto the street and held posters advertising weekly specials. A set of glass doors opened automatically. A wave of frigid air washed over Clare. She hugged herself tighter and followed Isaac inside.

A teenaged girl in a blue smock stood next to the entrance. "Morning. My name's Adeline." She held out a paper flier. "Care to see our specials?"

"We're actually looking for someone," said Isaac. "A friend of ours. Tall woman. Red hair, lots of tattoos."

"When would she have stopped by?" Adeline asked.

"This morning," said Clare.

The teenaged greeter's smile faded as she shook her head. "Nobody's been in the store who looks like that."

"You sure?" Isaac pressed.

"Sure, I'm sure. I've been right here since we opened."

Clare couldn't help it; her shoulders slumped with disappointment.

An older man with silver hair and a thin mustache approached Adeline. He wore a tie in the same shade of blue as the smock, black trousers and a white button-up shirt with short sleeves.

"Adeline, I need you to help Greg in the back. I'll take care of handing out today's ad."

"Yes, Mr. Yoshida." Adeline handed over the stack of papers, then glanced at Clare and Isaac. "Uh, these people could use some help, I think." She quickly headed to the back of the store.

Mr. Yoshida tapped the sheets on a window ledge, until all edges were in a line. "Morning, folks." He smiled. "Anything I can help you with?"

"We're here looking for a friend of ours. Female. Tall. Red hair," said Isaac. "She would've come in right as you opened."

"Hmm," hummed Mr. Yoshida. "I haven't seen anyone like that in the store. Or in town all morning, really." He paused. "Why are you looking for her, anyway?"

"She's my roommate," said Clare. "This morning she

went out, texted that she'd be back within a few minutes and hasn't come back for hours." Her words trailed off. "Well, I'm just worried is all."

Mr. Yoshida kept the same smile on his face, but his brows came together in a look that was both friendly and troubled. "I can see why you'd be concerned. Tell you what, I'll keep an eye out for your friend."

"Trinity," Isaac said.

"Okay. Trinity. If she shows up, I'll tell her that you've been by and ask that she call to tell you she's okay. How's that sound?"

"Much obliged," said Isaac, his Texas drawl thick once more.

The doors opened. A woman, carrying a dark-haired toddler, walked through the door.

"Ms. Erikson," said the store manager. "Nice to see you this morning. Here's a flier with all our specials..."

Clare, Isaac and their search for Trinity was all but forgotten.

The scent of cooking meat filled the air. It was so much like what she'd smelled the last night she's spent in Columbus with Kyle. After her discovery of the memo outlining the secret burial of toxic chemical, they'd walked from the corporate offices of Chamberlain Plastics Manufacturing to the Dublin Link. The pedestrian bridge connected both sides of the Scioto River. Each bank was filled with newly erected luxury apartments, chic boutiques and restaurants.

Clare leaned against the railing as the wind whipped through her hair. She held her tresses in one hand and watched her husband. Kyle stood at her side and stared at the water as it flowed. Kyle was the first to speak. "I guess it'd be wrong of me to ask..." He blew out a breath and shook his head. "Never mind. It'd be wrong."

Even then, she knew what he wanted. Yet, she'd said, "Ask."

"Is there any way we can just ignore the whole thing? I mean, it was years ago. Laws were different back then, weren't they? Besides, I bet my dad didn't even know how toxic those chemicals were."

She'd read the memo. She understood—same as Kyle—that his father knew he'd broken the law by burying the drums of toxic sludge. And worse, he knew the chemicals were dangerous, knew the damage they could cause. "We can't," she said. "And you know why."

Kyle scoffed, showing a side she'd almost never seen before—especially not directed at her work. "You can't really think one report will make a difference in a decades' old mistake that nobody seems to know about."

"First, it's morally wrong to ignore this. People are going to get sick if they haven't already, and part of my job is to look into that. And second, we know. To ignore the problem makes us complicit, Kyle."

"This will kill my dad. It'll ruin his reputation. Destroy the family business." Kyle shook his head. "He's going to hate me."

Clare couldn't help but feel sorry for Kyle. True, her father-in-law was a tough bastard. She placed her hand on his arm. "We'll get through this, together. Besides, I used to work for the EPA. If the company comes forward now, the government will go easier on the business." Finally, she had a way to be useful to Kyle and his family. "I know how to best negotiate a settlement. Your dad might not get that much time in jail..."

"My dad in jail?" he spit. *"There's no way I'm going to let me dad get arrested."* He drew in a shaking breath. *"I'm sure this is hard for you to understand, Clare, since you don't have a family name to protect."*

A family name? *"Don't you dare make this about me. What I'm talking about is taking responsibility and protecting the community."*

"No, you're right." His tone was conciliatory. Kyle stepped away from the railing, letting her hand from his arm. Without looking in her direction, he began to walk. *"Let's go. I have a lot of thinking to do."*

The memory faded. Clare's stomach cramped painfully as her breakfast roiled. "I gotta get out of here," she said, bolting for the door.

Turning, she jogged outside. The sun was bright, and her head began to pound.

Isaac stood at her side. "You looked a little sick in there."

"I'm fine." She tried to smile.

The thing was Clare was far from fine. Her last day in Columbus haunted her even now. Yet, she had to do more than escape from the ghosts of her past. She needed to decide how to deal with her problem. Because until she did that, Clare would never have a future.

Clare and Isaac stood on the street. The queasy feeling that gripped her in the grocery store had passed, yet she was exhausted. Maybe she shouldn't have been so quick to come with Isaac to find Trinity.

Isaac said, "I need to send a package by express mail to San Antonio. You can come with me if you want. Or hang out for a bit."

"You go. I'm fine." But was she? After months of being by herself, she loathed the idea of being alone. "I promise, I'll be okay on my own."

"I know you'll be okay. In fact, you might be one of the most capable women I've ever met." He lifted his hands in surrender.

She smiled again. The expression was starting to fit once more. Drawn like a magnet to steel, she took a step toward him. His scent—musky and male—enveloped her. "That's a nice compliment."

"You need to quit calling me that," he said, his tone teasing.

"If you aren't nice, then what are you?" she asked. "A hero?"

"To tell the truth, I'm nobody's idea of a hero."

His voice was dark and smoky, like a good wine, and she was drunk on his words.

"I..." she began, not sure what to say next. She'd kissed him once and she wanted to kiss him again. "I..."

Her words were cut off as a scream pierced the quiet morning. The sound was almost feral, and full of terror. Clare froze as her blood turned cold. The scream continued, echoing off the buildings.

Isaac scanned the street. "What the hell?"

"I think it's coming from over there." She pointed a shaking finger at the narrow alleyway that ran alongside the grocery store.

Squeezing her shoulders once, Isaac said, "You stay here."

"What? Why? Where are you going?" Her words didn't matter. He'd sprinted toward the sound. Then, the screaming stopped. The silence was worse than the noise.

She glanced up and down the street. Doors to businesses and offices were opening. People stood on the sidewalk, shading their eyes with their hands. They looked to one another, all confused about the scream that had shattered the silence.

"What was that racket?"

"Where'd all the noise come from?"

"Everyone okay?"

"Did anyone call Sheriff Cafferty?"

Clare looked toward the gap between the two buildings, her eyes retracing the path Isaac had taken. He still hadn't returned.

Indecision pinned her to the concrete. Yet, she forced herself to move, one step at a time, toward the alleyway.

From where she stood, Clare could see Isaac. The muscles in his neck were tight. His back was damp with sweat—she could tell because the fabric of his shirt stuck to his skin. Isaac cursed and ran a hand through his hair. Even from the end of the alleyway, she could tell that he was looking at something on the ground.

Mr. Yoshida, the grocery store manager, stood near the grocery store's rear door that led to the alleyway. Next to him, Adeline sobbed.

"What is it?" a man asked.

Clare took another step. "I'm not sure."

She made it to the end of the alleyway and finally got a look at the scene—and immediately regretted it. At Isaac's feet lay a body—or what was left of it. The first thing Clare saw was red hair, matted with blood. The eyes stared at nothing. The mouth was open as if death came in the moment of a scream. She sucked in a breath. Isaac turned and the look in his eyes said it all. He rushed to her side, trying to put himself between her and the gory scene.

She began to tremble.

"Don't look," he said. He took her face in his hands and met her gaze. "Clare, *please*. Just...don't look!"

It was too late. Clare had seen enough to know the truth. The pile of bone and blood and gore lying in the alleyway was Trinity. Or rather, it had been Trinity.

"Isaac... I... I don't understand." Clare was suddenly freezing, and she began to tremble. Her eyes were dry. Her throat was tight. She wanted to cry, but the tears refused to come. "What in the hell happened? She was fine when she left this morning!"

Isaac's expression was grim. "I have no idea. But we're damn well going to find out."

Chapter 9

Sheriff Maurice "Mooky" Cafferty dropped his foot onto the accelerator and his police cruiser shot down the road. Lifting the mic from his in-car radio, Mooky pressed the talk button. "Dispatch, this is Sheriff Cafferty." He drew in a deep breath. "Repeat what you just said."

"Shane Yoshida, down at the grocery store, found a body in the alley, next to the dumpsters." The 9-1-1 operator's voice broke on the last word. She continued, "It's a woman, and he says that she's a bloody mess."

The single word rattled around in his mind. *Body*.

There'd been a killing in his town. His stomach started to burn. Reaching between the seats, he found the bottle of antacids and flipped open the top. There were only three tablets left, and he poured them all into his mouth. Chewing furiously, he swallowed and tossed the empty bottle aside. Bringing the mic back to his mouth, he depressed the talk button. "He say anything else? Did he recognize the victim?"

"Don't think so, Sheriff."

"Anyone there?"

"I called in Todd and Kathryn," said the dispatch operator, mentioning the names of the two deputies on duty. "They're on their way. ETA is two minutes."

"Ten-four," he said. "I'm right behind them."

After hooking the mic back onto the radio, Mooky flipped two switches. Immediately, the lights atop his car began to flash and the siren started to wail. He dropped his foot onto the accelerator. The car shot down the road, pressing him into his seat. Ahead, he saw the grocery store and the road—clogged with onlookers. The burning in his stomach combusted into an inferno.

Laying the heel of his hand on the center of the steering wheel, he let out two quick bursts from his horn. The crowd slowly parted. Mooky turned off the siren as he parked his cruiser across the end of the alleyway.

Todd Travers, the newest addition to the department, came up to the cruiser. As Mooky opened the door, he asked, "What've we got?"

"It's bad, Sheriff. Real bad." He worked his fingers through the belt loops on the uniform trousers. "I ain't seen nothing like it."

Kathryn Glass, a ten-year veteran of the department and the chief undersheriff, stood in the middle of the alleyway. She wore dark sunglasses. The lens reflected the swirling lights on the roof of his car. Her arms were folded and her shoulders stiff. Behind her, a tarp lay on the ground.

"That her under the canvas?" he asked Todd. "The victim?"

The younger officer pulled on the belt loops so hard that Mooky feared the seams might rip. "Uh-huh."

Mooky had been with the department for almost twenty-years, and half of those as the sheriff. He'd seen a lot—but he also knew how violent deaths could affect police officers. He'd speak to Todd later and remind him that counseling was available if the images stayed with him awhile. Hooking the arm of his sunglasses to the front of his shirt, he said, "Secure this location. Get everyone off the street and set up a barricade at each end of the block. Barricade the other end of the alley, too. Can you do that?"

The young deputy swallowed. "Yes, sir."

He gave a quick squeeze to Todd's shoulder. Turning, he scanned the crowd again. He recognized most every face—except two. There was a big guy and a blonde woman, who was crying.

He strode down the alley. From twenty paces, the stench of decay hit him like a brick wall. Hand covering his mouth, he called out, "What've we got, Kathryn?"

"A mess." She hitched her chin toward the heap on the ground. "Come see for yourself."

Mooky knelt next to the tarp and lifted the corner. One glance was all he needed. Bile rose in the back of his throat. But he'd be damned before he puked at a crime scene. Coughing, he looked away. He cataloged everything he'd seen. Red hair. Blue lips. Exposed and sliced flesh. Eyes that saw nothing. And yet, in her frozen gaze, he'd seen terror.

He shuddered to think of the last thing she'd witnessed.

"You recognize her?" Mooky asked as he stood.

"Never seen her before in my life."

He dusted his hands together and looked back at the end of the alleyway. His car was still parked but the crowd was no longer visible. At least Todd was doing his job. "Who found the body? Dispatch said that Shane Yoshida called in."

"One of the employees found her when she brought out some trash. A college student home for the holidays. Her name is Adeline." Kathryn paused. "They're all inside. Adeline was pretty shook up by what she saw."

"I can imagine." Mooky had been shaken as well. "I'll go interview them. You call the medical center and have them pick the body up."

A metal door was set into the wall at the back of the store. It'd been propped open with a brick and Mooky stepped into the stock room. To his right, he saw the office. The door was open and from where he stood, he could see a metal desk, two filing cabinets and three chairs—all filled. The store manager came out to greet the sheriff, clearly shaken. "Thanks for getting here so fast, Sheriff."

"Sorry to see you under these circumstances, Shane." Mooky paused at the threshold. Aside from the manager, there were two females. One was Shane's wife, who was also the bakery manager. Mrs. Yoshida held the younger woman's hand, trying to comfort the shaken teenager. He turned to the girl now. "I haven't seen you since you were just a kid, Adeline, but I played football with your daddy." He took a small notebook and pen from the front pocket of his uniform. "Can you tell me what happened? How'd you find the body?"

Adeline drew in a shaking breath. "Well, Mr. Yoshida told me to help in the back. The stock workers needed the broken-down boxes put in recycling and I went to take them out. I saw her as soon as I opened the door." She let out a shuddering breath. "I guess I just started screaming and everyone came running."

"Did you get a good look at the woman?"

Adeline shook her head. "I just saw the body and the cuts and that's all." Her voice began to tremble.

"Who covered her with a tarp?" Mooky asked.

"That was me," said Shane. "It seemed like the decent thing to do. Plus, a crowd was gathering." He lifted his shoulders and let them drop, his face pale.

"Then what about you? Did you get a good look at the woman's face? You ever see her before?"

"No. Never." He paused. "But…"

"What?" Mooky coaxed.

"There were two people looking for someone that matched the woman's description. A man and woman. He's a big guy. She's a blonde."

The acid in Mooky's gut spewed like a volcano. He'd seen those two himself, standing at the edge of the alleyway. Now all he could hope is that he could find them before it was too late.

Clare pressed her eyes closed, but the image of Trinity's flayed body, sprawled on the ground, was burned into her brain. Purple bruises circled Trinity's neck. Her clothes were torn and covered in gore. The flesh in her chest and abdomen were cut.

She drew in a shaking breath and counted. One. Two. Three. As she exhaled, a sob escaped.

A sheriff's deputy had cleared the street and she now stood behind a wooden sawhorse at the end of the block. Isaac still held her shoulder. "It'll be okay," he whispered into her hair. "I promise."

How was that even possible, though? After what she'd seen, Clare found it hard to believe Isaac's words.

Clare groaned. "Her poor daughter. Does anyone even know how to get a hold of her ex?"

Isaac said, "I can get a number."

"Excuse me." A man with a brown crew cut and a tan sheriff's uniform strode down the street. A pair of sunglasses covered his eyes, yet she had the uncanny feeling that he was looking directly at Clare. "Can I speak to you for a minute?"

Pressing a hand to her chest, Clare mouthed the word. "Me?"

"Yes, ma'am," said the cop. He maneuvered around the end of the barricade. "I'd like to speak to both of you."

Clare's hands began to tremble. Shoving her palms under her armpits, she nodded. "Sure."

The man removed a business card from his pocket and held it out. "My name's Maurice Cafferty. I'm the sheriff for this county."

Clare accepted the card. Numbers for both his office and cell phone were listed. She handed it to Isaac.

Isaac asked, "What can we do for you, Sheriff Cafferty?"

"The folks in the grocery store said you came in this morning."

"So, what if we did?" Isaac asked. "Nothing illegal about going to a grocery store."

Isaac was avoiding answering the sheriff's questions. Was it because he'd been incarcerated? Or was there more? She hadn't asked him about his midnight road trip with Ryan. Yet, she suspected there was more to Isaac's story than the few details he'd shared so far.

The sheriff said, "Listen, I don't want to play games with you. We can either have a friendly chat here. Or you can come to my office and answer my questions more formal-like."

Isaac sighed. "What can we help you with?"

"Just answer the question," said the sheriff. "What were you doing in the grocery store?"

Trinity deserved justice. If Isaac wouldn't tell the sheriff what they were doing, she would. "We're in town, looking for a friend."

"That friend have a name?" The sheriff removed a small notepad from the breast pocket of his uniform, along with a pen.

"Trinity," said Clare.

"Trinity what?" the sheriff asked, his pen pressed against the paper.

Isaac said, "Her name was Trinity Jackson."

The sheriff wrote it down, then looked back to Clare. "What about the two of you? You have names?"

She could hardly ignore the investigation of anyone's murder. It didn't matter whether she knew her last name or not. Yet, she didn't want to get involved with the police—not while her ex-husband was still out there, somewhere.

Had the past several weeks of running just come to

nothing? Because if Kyle could find her in a place like Mercy, where else could she hide?

The sheriff ask for Clare's driver's license. She wanted to refuse. The minute he scanned the bar code on the back, her name would end up in a computer system. From there, it was just a matter of time before Kyle figured out that she was in Texas.

Her eyes burned. She loathed the idea of running again, but she had no choice. As soon as she could, she had to get back on the road. But if Clare could be found in a place like Mercy, where else could she hide?

"A report will show up in my office," Sheriff Cafferty said. "Until then, let's start over with the person you're looking for." Pen perched on his notepad, he asked, "Description of your friend?"

"Female," Isaac began as he listed the basics. "Tall, maybe five feet ten inches. Red hair. Lots of tattoos. There's a tat of a pink python on her leg."

The sheriff scribbled on his notepad. "Now we're getting somewhere. Why were you looking for her?"

She felt the pull to flee, like a tether around her middle pulling her toward the open road. But she couldn't leave now, even if she wanted to go. Besides, Trinity had been kind and Clare owed her for the kindness. She answered the sheriff's question. "She's been missing."

The sheriff lifted his brows as he wrote. "How long had she been gone?"

Clare swallowed, already knowing how her answer was going to sound. "Since a little before six o'clock."

The sheriff jotted a note in his book. "That's last night, right? Or, do you mean yesterday morning?"

"No." Clare shook her head. "This morning."

Sheriff Cafferty stopped writing. "She's been gone since six o'clock this morning," he repeated, his tone filled with incredulity. He checked his watch. "Well, that's only a few hours. Did you have reason to think she was in trouble?"

"She texted me that she was going to grab us a cup of coffee. When she hadn't showed up after a while, I went looking. I found a necklace—one that she loves—near the road." She paused. "One of the links was broken."

"I assume you know that the body of a redheaded female was found in the alleyway behind the grocery store. I've reason to believe that she's your missing friend. I need someone to identify the body and for now, you two are the best I've got."

Clare had already seen the corpse, yet a wave of emotion washed over her. Her eyes burned and her throat was tight. She tried to speak but the words were caught. She could only manage to nod her head.

The sheriff put the notepad and pen back in his pocket. Rocking back on his heels, he continued. "I'd also like for you both to answer some questions at my office."

"What kind of questions?" Isaac asked.

"I want you to help me understand why two people show up in my town and start looking for a woman who really wasn't missing but was already dead."

Clare took a step back. "Are you saying that you think we're involved with what happened?"

She didn't need to ask the question because she already knew the answer. What's worse, this wasn't Columbus, Ohio. There were no traffic cameras on every corner to chart their drive from Mercy to Encantador. Hell, there were barely traffic lights at all. They had no way to prove when they actually arrived in town or even to prove that they had nothing to do with Trinity's murder.

The floor-to-ceiling windows of Chamberlain Plastics Manufacturing overlooked downtown Columbus. Kyle Chamberlain sat in his corner office. The Scioto River, almost serpentine in its movement, shimmered with the light.

Walking to the sideboard, he picked up a bottle of fine Tennessee whiskey. The same questions he'd been asking himself for months occupied his thoughts. Where was Clare? What happened to the flash drive? And what did she plan to do with the evidence? Two months of hearing nothing and waiting for a story to break in the media, putting their family business—indeed, their family—in the harshest of spotlights was starting to show on Kyle. He'd lost hair and gained weight. What's worse, his father's fury hadn't faded.

After pouring two fingers from the bottle, he tossed back the drink in a single swallow. The liquor exploded in his gut like a bomb, and Kyle's limbs began to relax.

A voice came from the door. "A bit early in the day for a drink, don't you think?"

Kyle glanced at his father. It was hard to look at the old man and not see his own future. "My wife is gone. And we have no idea when she might use the information that she took to expose the company. Days like today are why God invented alcohol." Kyle poured another drink.

"She's your ex-wife." His father lifted a single brow. "And you know that."

Kyle certainly did know that Clare had left him. Divorced him. Guilt hit him like a fist to the gut. In the tug-of-war on whether to release the memo or keep it hidden, he'd chosen his father over his wife. Sure, Kyle had been raised to believe that family loyalty was supreme. But with Clare gone, he wasn't so sure. He threw back his second drink.

His father asked, "Any news from the private detective?"

"Nothing. Apparently, she disabled the GPS tracking on her car, turned off her phone and hasn't used a credit card since the day she left." His father knew all those facts, as well as that the family had spent a small fortune trying to locate her. Kyle's phone pinged with an incoming text. He glanced at the screen, blinked, refocused. "I'll be damned."

"What is it?"

"The PI just send a message. He said that Clare's name was run through a police database."

"She's back in Columbus?"

"I don't think so." Kyle scrolled through the message. "The search took place in a town called Encantador, Texas." He poured another drink. "I'll pass this along to the PI."

"That's the problem with you." Taking the glass from Kyle's hand, his father dumped the whiskey into the wastebasket. The medicinal scent of booze wafted through the room. "You never do anything on your own."

"You can't be suggesting that I waste my time following up on this myself."

"Suggesting? No. Telling? Yes."

Kyle mentally scrambled for a way to avoid the task. "What if she just got a flat tire and has already moved on?"

"Then you better find her before she disappears again."

"Me?" Kyle asked. "What am I supposed to say to Clare?"

"You force her to see things our way. And you get the evidence back."

"And if she refuses?"

His father met Kyle's gaze. The look sent a chill down his spine. "Make sure that she can't."

The Sheriff's Department sat at the edge of town in a converted warehouse. The whole property was surrounded by a chain-link fence and topped with coils of razor wire, so Isaac guessed that beyond the office space for the sheriff and his deputies, there were facilities to hold prisoners as well.

Isaac sat in a windowless interrogation room that was barely big enough to hold the wooden table and four seats. Isaac sat in one of the chairs, with Clare at his side.

Back when he was a cop, he never would have put two suspects into the same room and let them wait. It gave people a chance to talk and decide on the story they planned to tell. He couldn't help but wonder about Sheriff Cafferty. He could be playing a game with Isaac and Clare. The room might be filled with electronic surveillance. At this moment, was the sheriff watching them both while waiting to see what they said to one another?

Or was the small-town sheriff not used to investigating serious crimes, and therefore had no idea how to deal with serious criminals?

For the sake of Trinity, Isaac hoped it was the first but feared it was the latter.

Either way, he didn't need to worry about Clare saying anything incriminating. They'd been settled in the interview room for more than ten minutes. In all that time, she'd done nothing but stare at her hands.

"Say something," he said, his voice low. Then again, if the room were bugged or a camera was hidden in a vent, there was no reason to whisper.

She shrugged. "What is it you want to hear?"

He tried again. "It'll be okay."

"If you say so," she said, unconvinced.

After shaking her head, she looked back at Isaac. "What's going on in Mercy?"

Now, that was a loaded question and something that Isaac couldn't answer. Yet, it was impossible to miss the challenge in her tone.

"I don't know what you're talking about," he lied.

"Can you cut the crap, just for a minute?"

"Excuse me?" he asked, his anger flaring.

For a split second, Isaac realized that Sheriff Cafferty might be a genius to have left Clare and Isaac alone for so long. With tensions high, people began to turn on each other. Vengeful subjects might be more willing to talk to the police than ones who were simply scared.

Clare gritted her teeth. "Stop lying to me. I know there's more going on in Mercy. I know there's more to your story as well. So, don't pretend like you care about me or how I'm doing. You're in this up to your neck."

"What makes you so damned certain?"

"I saw you leave the motel last night. You and Ryan. Where'd you go? Is that what got Trinity killed?"

Clare thought he was somehow responsible for Trinity's death. Was his growing attraction—hell, his desire—for Clare enough for him to care what she thought of him?

The answer came to him quick and clean. *Yes.*

But was he willing to blow his cover, just to prove that he had nothing to do with a murder?

That answer wasn't as easy to find. In his own indecision, there was a danger to both himself and his case. "You've been asking me a lot of questions. Maybe it's time for you to answer a few of your own. Who are you, really?"

"Transferring your anger will change nothing," said Clare. "You can accuse me all you want, but you've been lying to me from the beginning." She went back to silently staring at her hands.

The sheriff and a female deputy slipped into the small room. Without preamble, they sat on the opposite side of the table. Both set pads of paper and pens before them.

"Mind if I record this interview?" Sheriff Cafferty asked.

A younger deputy, a male, squeezed into the tight space. He held a small video camera. A tripod was tucked under his arm.

"Be my guest," said Isaac.

The deputy set up the video equipment and left. The green record light glowed on the camera.

How many times had Isaac been in a room like this? It was too many to count.

Yet, today was different. Now he was the one being questioned.

The sheriff ran down the basics of the case and asked them to state their names for the record.

Isaac paused just long enough to wonder how much he'd be forced to share. He glanced at the camera before looking at the sheriff. "My name is Isaac Patton." At least he hadn't used an alias in his cover story. Then again, one of the rules of working undercover was to make it real life as much as possible. It made the operative less likely to make a mistake. To keep Isaac's past with the San Antonio PD secret, much of his personal history had been removed from the internet.

"And you?" The sheriff pointed to Clare with his pen.

"Clare." She paused and cleared her throat. "My name is Clare Chamberlain."

"Where you from?" Sheriff Cafferty paused as he wrote on his notepad. "Originally?"

"San Antonio," said Isaac, again thankful that his cover story matched as much of his actual background as it did.

"And you?" The sheriff pointed to Clare.

Clare shifted in her seat. "Columbus, Ohio," she said, her voice a whisper.

The sheriff made a note. Setting the pen aside, he leaned back in his seat. With a loud exhale, he folded his arms across his chest. "Encantador is a peaceful town. The folks who live here mostly abide by the law." He pinched the bridge of his nose, inhaled and started again. "We're not used to seeing this kind of crime committed in our town. So, I'm gonna level with you both. I don't like what I see."

Clare asked, "What is that you see, and don't you like?"

"The few facts you've given me don't pass the smell test. You both say that you came from Mercy this morning because you're worried about this missing friend. Yet, she'd really only been gone for a few hours, which, to be honest, isn't legally considered missing. Then she turns up here, deader than a doornail." He paused again. "Here's what I'm thinking. You two had something to do with her death and you left her body in that alleyway. Then, you come back to town and start asking questions." He hooked air quotes around the last two words. "You're thinking is probably something like this—nobody'd suspect the concerned friends." He reached for the pen and pressed the nib into the pad of paper. Ink leeched into the fibers. "Care to tell me if I'm wrong?"

Sure, the sheriff was wrong. Which left Isaac with a decision to make. Did he stick to his cover story or did he tell truth?

Chapter 10

Sheriff Cafferty had all but accused Clare and Isaac of killing Trinity. He cast a glance at Clare. Her eyes were wide. Her brows were drawn together, and her lips were pressed into a colorless line. He knew she was worried, and she should be.

"There're a few problems with your theory, Sheriff," said Isaac.

"Enlighten me."

"There's not a lot to the town of Mercy. It wasn't hard to figure out that Trinity was gone." He sat back in his chair. "Clare found her broken necklace in a parking lot. It was enough to make us concerned, because Trinity never took it off. Ever." Isaac leaned forward. "You've been up front about your suspicions. But I gotta tell you. You're wrong to make up your mind already."

"Okay, so if I shouldn't make you two my prime suspects, who should I have in mind?"

The notion of giving away a year's worth of work left him ill—especially since Newcombe had finally made contact. Yet, Isaac couldn't exactly hinder a murder investigation. And finally, there was Clare. He still didn't know much about her situation, but she was obviously running from something.

Or someone.

He couldn't—no, make that wouldn't—let her be suspected of murder. "For the past year, I've been working undercover in Mercy. I'm on assignment trying to find Decker Newcombe. He's a hitman who killed a district attorney in Wyoming."

The sheriff gave a grunt of disbelief. "I'm supposed to believe that you're working undercover?"

"It's the truth."

"Now, you know I'm not going to take you at your word."

"I figured as much." He exhaled. "Go ahead and do a search for Decker Newcombe. You'll see that he's wanted for the murder of Jacob Loeb, the DA from Pleasant Pines, Wyoming." Isaac paused as the sheriff removed his phone from a holster on his hip. As the sheriff typed with his thumbs, Isaac continued, "My gut told me that Newcombe would reach out to Ryan Steele at some point. Steele is one of his old contacts. I came up with a plan. The feds bankrolled all of Steele's businesses, including the bar he owns in Mercy. Then, I posed as an employee at the bar, hoping Newcombe would make contact."

The undersheriff leaned forward. "Everything you said about Newcombe's past checks out. Still, it don't mean I can verify a word you say. You could've done an internet search, same as me."

Now was the time for Isaac to prove his bona fides. "Who do you know with the FBI? Anyone out of the San Antonio office?"

Glass and Cafferty exchanged glanced.

"We can find a name if you give me some time," she said.

Isaac said, "Take all the time you need. I'm not going anywhere soon."

"Damn right, you won't. This door locks from the outside." The sheriff rose to his feet. Undersheriff Glass stood as well. "You both just wait here. I'll be back in a minute."

Without another word, both officers left the room.

Then, the room was silent. He kept his gaze on the table, yet he could feel Clare watching him.

He glanced at her from the side of his eye.

The single look was all the invitation that Clare needed to speak up. "You lied to me."

Whatever he'd expected her to say, *that* had definitely not been it.

He wasn't going to be chastised—especially since she was part of the calculus to blow his cover. "What was I supposed to say to you? Someone who, oh, by the way, is a complete stranger. And who is clearly carrying some big secrets of her own."

"I'm not saying that your investigation isn't important." Clare inhaled. Exhaled. "Or even that I have a right to know everything—or anything—about you. It's just that after we found Trinity's body, you owed me the truth."

Did he? Isaac wasn't ready to admit to anything—at least, not yet.

"What about you?" he countered.

"What about me?"

"You've been far from honest with me about your past. What really happened in Columbus?"

She hesitated. "Nothing."

She was lying and they both knew it. Then again, why should she trust him? He'd hardly been forthright with her. He supposed now was the time for all the BS to end.

"Alright," he said with a sigh. "After college, I joined the San Antonio PD. They figured out I was a good shot and put me on SWAT. My training agent was a guy named Miguel. He was the one who honed my sharpshooting abilities. He drove home all the rules of firearm safety. We ran together every morning. He invited me over for cookouts on the weekend and his kids called me Uncle Isaac." A stab of emotion struck him in the chest. The severity of the residual pain surprised him. Clearing his throat, he continued, "One night the team got tasked with a raid in an apartment complex. Our subject was the member of a street gang. He got a tip that we were coming. The rest of the gang members turned the complex into a shooting gallery." The memory crashed down and he slumped in his seat. "Anyway, Miguel and I were close to the subject's apartment. Just a short hallway between us and them. We were told to wait for backup. The funny thing was—Miguel wanted to rush in. I insisted that we wait. Those few minutes gave the gang time to regroup." He cleared his throat. "We went in, and Miguel caught a bullet in his throat. He bled out on the floor as I applied pressure to his wound."

"Oh, Isaac." Clare drew her lip through her teeth. Before she could say anything else, the door opened. Sheriff Cafferty stepped into the room. He held a small square of yellow paper, the sticky strip on the back was adhered to his finger. "I got a name and number for the SSA at the San Antonio Field Office."

"Jason Jones."

"That's the one."

"Call him. Ask about me. Tell him there's been a homicide and you want to know if I'm a guy you can trust."

After dropping into one of the seats, the sheriff placed his phone on the table and entered the number. He turned on the speaker function and the call went through.

A familiar voice answered after the third ring. "This is Agent Jones."

The sheriff leaned toward the phone. "Hi. This is Maurice Cafferty, sheriff out of Encantador in Texas. I've had a recent homicide and a name has come up. Isaac Patton."

Jason cursed. "Is he your victim?"

"No. In fact, he's alive, well and sitting right across from me. I've got you on speakerphone."

"What've you gotten yourself into?" he asked.

Isaac smothered a grimace behind his hand. "Nice to hear your voice, too."

"Glad that you're on this side of the grave. But you didn't answer my question. What's going on?"

"There's not much that would get me to break my

cover, but one of Steele's employees was murdered this morning."

Jones asked, "Any suspects?"

"Aside from me?" Isaac looked the sheriff dead in the eye. The other man had the decency to look away. "Not really."

"Murder isn't a federal offense," said Agent Jones. "Why bring me into the case?"

"It's more to verify Mr. Patton's identity," the sheriff added. "Is he someone I can trust?"

"He's a pain in the butt," said Jason. "But yeah, he's trustworthy." The fed continued, "Is my package on the way? IT is ready."

"I haven't had a chance yet." Isaac tamped down his annoyance. What part of *he'd gotten involved in a murder investigation* didn't Jason understand?

"Get it done," said Jason and then, "You need anything else from me, Sheriff?"

"Thank you, Special Agent. I'm set for now." Reaching for the phone, the sheriff ended the call.

"Satisfied?" Isaac asked.

Leaning back in his chair, the sheriff cradled his head in his hands. "I suppose so."

Turning to Clare, Isaac said, "Like you heard, I still have some business to take care of here. After that, I can give you a ride back to Mercy."

"You forget something?" the sheriff asked.

Was the guy really still going to threaten Isaac and Clare with a murder charge?

Gritting his teeth, he asked, "What's that?"

The sheriff sat forward "The body. I need someone to identify the victim."

* * *

The Encantador Medical Center was a two-story building of redbrick located a few blocks from the sheriff's office. The main floor contained a walk-in medical clinic. A hospital with six beds was located on the upper level. The morgue, located in the basement, was a windowless room with the same tile on the floor and three of the four walls. A metal counter bisected one wall. An empty stainless steel table sat in the middle of the room. The sheriff stood next to the sink and scrolled through his phone.

The fourth wall, on the far side of the room, was filled with large stainless steel doors—four across and three, top to bottom. Clare had seen enough movies to recognize them as coolers where bodies were stored. Trinity was certainly behind one of the doors.

A sudden chill gripped her, and she gave an involuntary shiver.

Isaac stood at her side and leaned in close, the heat from his body was warm and soothing. "You don't have to be here," he whispered, his words washing over her shoulder. "I can do this by myself."

Glancing at the door, Clare had a momentary fantasy of sprinting from the room. There was no shame in not wanting to look at a dead person. Yet, she shook her head. "I owe it to Trinity to see this through."

"You've done plenty for her, you know. If you hadn't found her broken necklace, neither one of us would have come here. It would've taken weeks to identify her body."

Was Isaac right? Clare thought not. First, there'd be media reports about the murder and the unknown victim. Someone from Mercy would've recognized Trinity from the news. "I bet that you would've nosed around the investigation." She gave a quick smile to show that she was teasing.

She still wasn't sure how she felt about Isaac after confessing that he was a cop and not a criminal. Did she like him more—or less? At least with the old Isaac, she thought she knew him. This new guy was filled with secrets.

The door opened and a dark-haired woman in a white lab coat crossed the threshold. Embroidered above the breast pocket were the words: Shelia Garcia, MD

"Thanks for coming over, Sheriff," said the doctor. "I haven't had time to do anything other than scan the report." She grimaced. "Sounds pretty gruesome."

"Worst damn thing I've ever seen," said the sheriff.

Dr. Garcia approached the sink. Using pedals on the floor, she turned on the water and began to wash her hands. Looking over her shoulder, she made eye contact with both Clare and Isaac.

"This is Isaac Patton and Clare Chamberlain," said the sheriff, obviously understanding the doctor's glance as a question that needed answering. "They both knew the victim and are here to do an ID."

"Alright, then." Moving to the end cooler on the middle row, the doctor opened the door. She pulled out a drawer, along with a blue sheet that was draped over a form. "If you both can come here?" Dr. Garcia asked.

Clare and Isaac took up places on the opposite side of the drawer.

The doctor folded the sheet down, just so the head, neck and shoulders were visible. The skin was white. The lips blue. The eyes were closed, yet one was swollen and bruised. The tail from a tiger tattoo was visible on the upper arm. The features were unmistakable. Clare swallowed. "It's her."

"You sure?" the sheriff asked.

Isaac answered, "Positive."

"Do you have contact information for her next of kin?" The sheriff held his pad of paper and a pen.

Isaac shook his head. "I can find the information once I get back to Mercy. Or I can call Ryan now."

"Give it a minute before making the call," said Sheriff Cafferty.

Clare's chest hurt as she thought about Trinity's daughter and the sad fact that the little girl would never get to know her mother.

"Okay, then." The doctor reached for the sheet, ready to cover the face once more.

"Wait," said Clare, not even sure of why she'd spoken. Something was wrong. What was it?

The doctor froze, cloth in hand.

Moving closer to the body, Clare pointed to the throat. An ugly dark line ran straight across her neck. "Bruises? Is that the cause of death?" she asked. "Strangulation? I only saw a little bit of Trinity in the alley, but it looked like she'd be stabbed, too."

Isaac said, "There wasn't a lot of blood on her clothes. That means that she was cut postmortem."

The doctor drew her brows together and pulled the sheet to Trinity's ankles. A jagged seam ran through her sweatshirt and the front of her jeans. They had been pulled back together for transport, but the fabric had black stains and was stiff with dried gore.

"But there's blood..." Clare began.

Dr. Garcia spoke as Clare's words trailed off. "Not as much as I'd expect to see if her heart was beating when she sustained these injuries."

Clare's confusion must've shown on her face because the sheriff picked up where the physician left off. "If she still had a pulse, blood would've gotten everywhere. Think of a fountain."

The image of a blood fountain left Clare lightheaded. Yet, she tried to put the pieces together to form a timeline for Trinity's death. "You think that she was strangled, then stabbed and cut after she was dead?"

"I have to do an autopsy first," the doctor began. "But that'd be my initial assessment, yes."

"What'd you think the killer used to strangle her?" Sheriff Cafferty asked. "His own hands?"

The doctor bent closer to Trinity. "Not his hands. The bruises are uniform all the way around. With fingers, there's different amounts of pressure, so the bruising isn't consistent all the way through."

The sheriff asked, "She strangled with a cord?"

It was Isaac who answered. "Cords are thin. This was something wider—maybe a belt."

The doctor looked at Trinity's hands. She used a pen to point to the ring finger. "See that?" The nail was ripped away. "She fought. If we're lucky, we'll get some of the killer's DNA." She swiped around the nail with a swab before sealing the swab inside a vial. "Since this is a definite homicide, I'll let you send this to the crime lab." She set it on the counter. "They can at least identify DNA that doesn't belong to the victim."

The doctor continued talking. "Let's see what else we have." She slipped on a pair of surgical gloves and held out a box of surgical masks for everyone to put on. After putting on a pair protective glasses, she continued, "Of course, anything I note here might not jive with my final findings." She peeled back the sweatshirt and jeans, exposing Trinity's chest, torso and hips. There was a deep gash that ran from under her rib cage downward to her pelvis. Several other lacerations bisected the first. The flaps of flesh exposed muscle and bone.

The floor under Clare's feet seemed to tilt. She feared that she'd lose her footing—or worse yet, her breakfast.

Yet, there had been something about Trinity's wounds. Something almost…familiar.

Isaac's cover was blown and there was no going back. Since he couldn't retreat, that left only one direction—forward.

The sheriff wasn't a bad guy, per se. To Isaac, he seemed like a good cop who genuinely cared about his community. Moreover, he took his duty to protect and serve seriously—even if there was a bit more bluster in his personality than Isaac actually liked.

The doctor continued to examine the wounds. "The blade is smooth—as in, not serrated—and about five inches long."

"A hunting knife?" Isaac suggested.

The doctor shrugged. "Possibly. Or even a strong kitchen knife." She paused and bent closer to Trinity's middle. "What's going on here?"

"What's going on where?" Clare echoed, her voice an octave higher.

"The abdomen doesn't look right." Dr. Garcia drew her brows together. "It's almost concave." She picked up a set of surgical clamps and held on to a flap of skin. Pulling up and back gently, she exposed organs and tissue. The doctor gasped and jumped back as if the clamps had become hot to the touch. They hit the floor with a clatter.

The doctor drew in several long breaths. She picked up the discarded clamps from the floor and tossed them into the sink with a clang. For a moment, the room was silent. With a shake of her head, the doctor continued, "This woman has been more than cut open, but several of her organs have been removed."

"Removed?" the sheriff echoed.

Dr. Garcia confirmed the worst. "Trinity was disemboweled."

Isaac went cold. "You have more than a murderer in your town—but a deranged killer." From everything he knew of Decker Newcombe, the hitman only killed for profit, not pleasure. Still, what were the chances that two killers were in the same area? He had to get in touch with Jason and pressure the fed to get more resources on the case.

"Now, if you don't mind, I have an autopsy to perform." The doctor slipped the swab and tube into an evidence bag as she spoke. After a beat, she held out the vial with the DNA sample. "Go straight to the lab, Cafferty, and drop this off for me."

"Yes ma'am," said the sheriff, taking the evidence bag.

That was their cue to leave.

The hallway—floor and wall, both—were covered in the same white tiles as the morgue. The sheriff leaned against the wall and shoved his hand into his uniform pocket. "Where are those damned antacids," he mumbled before continuing, "You said you could get me a name and number for a next of kin?"

Taking out his phone, Isaac placed a call to Ryan. He actuated the speaker function as the phone began to ring.

Ryan answered, "Hey, pal."

There was no way to soften the news of a murder. He said simply, "We found Trinity's body."

"Aww, hell. What happened?"

"I'll save you all the details, but it was bad. I've got you on speaker. The sheriff and Clare are here with me." He paused. "I need a name and number for Trinity's ex. The sheriff's gotta let him know."

"Give me a minute." In the background, Isaac could hear the clicking of fingers on a keyboard. He imagined that Ryan was accessing an employee database. Despite the fact that Steele was only running a bar and tattoo parlor as bait, he was actually a decent businessman. "I got it here. You ready?"

The sheriff had a pad of paper and pen in his hand. He said, "Go ahead." Ryan gave the information, which Cafferty wrote down. "Thank you so much."

Ryan said, "Let me know if you need anything else. And, Isaac, is this connected to our other *friend*?"

Decker Newcombe was no friend of Isaac's, yet he understood the cryptic question. "We might have a lead. I'll keep you posted." He ended the call as another thought came to him. He said to Cafferty, "You have some DNA from the killer found under Trinity's nails."

"Possibly," said the sheriff, clarifying. "We'll know in a day or two once the tests have been run."

"Let me know what you find." Isaac gave the sheriff his cell phone number. If Decker was responsible for Trinity's death, they'd connect him by his DNA. It was the kind of information that Jason would need to keep Isaac's case open.

"One more thing," said Clare. From the front pocket of her jeans, she pulled out Trinity's locket. "This was hers." She nodded her head to the door of the morgue. "I think she'd want it given to her daughter. Can you pass it on for me when you talk to her ex-husband?"

"I'm happy to oblige." Cafferty took the necklace and placed it the breast pocket of his uniform. "How much longer are you staying in town?"

Isaac had to send the phone to the FBI's office in San Antonio. All the same, he didn't want to be away from Mercy for too long. Decker was close, and Isaac was determined to find him. "We'll be here for a little longer."

"I'd like it if you can stay for a few hours. I'm going to call in the state police. They might have questions about the victim that only you can answer."

He wanted to argue. But what was the point? The sheriff could order Clare and Isaac to stay in town. Besides, staying in Encantador would give Isaac a chance to ask a few questions himself—like if anyone had seen Decker. Maybe he'd get lucky, and someone had noticed something important. And if not? Well, then his luck had run out.

Chapter 11

After spending time in the dark basement, the midday sun was blinding. Heat rolled off the pavement. Clare stopped at top of the steps, suddenly lightheaded.

If Clare had just gone with Trinity, maybe her friend would be alive. Or maybe Clare's body would've been dumped in the alleyway. She gripped the railing to keep herself steady.

Isaac's hand was on her elbow. "What's going on?"

"I'm fine." His touch left her breathless and her flesh tingling.

"You're probably just hungry." He looked at his phone. "We didn't have much of a breakfast and we missed lunch."

Clare hadn't noticed her empty stomach until Isaac mentioned food. Her middle gave a grumble. "Maybe."

Isaac gave her that smile that left Clare weak in the

knees. "C'mon. I'm know that I'm starved. You look like if you don't eat soon, you'll pass out."

"Gee, you really know how to flatter a girl."

"Being blunt seems to be a side effect from working undercover for so long." He shrugged. "Let me take you out to lunch because honestly, you aren't going to find food this good in Mercy, even though the bar is the only place to eat—or any place else nearby."

The short walk to Isaac's truck gave her time to think. She needed to eat, but more than that, she realized, Trinity's murder was a turning point for her.

Sure, she'd been running for months, always thinking she had to solve her problem on her own. Clare recalled what her mother had said this morning. *You've always been so independent. Even as a little girl. Me do. That was your favorite phrase.*

Maybe that had been her problem from the beginning. Clare never let anyone help.

They reached the truck, and without a word, Isaac unlocked the door, collecting an evidence bag with a phone inside from under the driver's seat. He tucked that into a paper bag that was stashed with the evidence bag. He was obviously working on something big if he had a direct line to a supervisory special agent with the FBI. He'd been working undercover for a year. Isaac was the perfect person to ask for ways to deal with her former in-laws.

If she could work up the nerve.

He slipped his Glock 19 from the glove box and tucked it into the waistband at his back. Untucking his shirt, he covered his firearm with the hem.

"The delivery service is over there." He held the bag

and pointed across the street. They waited for traffic to pass before crossing the road.

Clare paused on the sidewalk. "I'll wait here."

It took Isaac only a few minutes to send his package and return to where she waited. By then, she'd made a decision. "Can we talk?"

"Let's go to the restaurant." Isaac started walking down the sidewalk. Clare stayed at his side. "We can find a corner table and talk there."

He stopped in front of barbecue place. A cartoon cow and pig were painted on a large set of windows. Stenciled beneath were the words *Phil's. Best Damn BBQ in the Lone Star State.*

Next door, the Saddle Up Inn, sat behind a parking lot. On the other side of the restaurant was a florist.

Isaac pulled the door open, and she crossed the threshold. After everything that happened over the past few hours, Clare shouldn't have been hungry. Yet, her mouth began to water as the savory scent of roasted meat rolled out of the restaurant. "Smells better than good."

"Just wait till you taste the food."

A man with a mustache, beard and a bald head stood behind a cash register and looked up as Clare approached. He wore a bolo tie, white shirt and a name tag that read Phil. "Howdy, folks," he said. "Just the two of you?"

"Yes," said Clare.

Phil took two menus from beneath the counter. "Right this way."

Wood, gray with age and weathered, covered the walls. More than a dozen tables, with red-and-white-checked cloths, filled the middle of the room. Thankfully, there were no other patrons.

As Clare sat, Phil said, "Heck of a day. Did you hear that a body was found in the alley behind the supermarket?"

Clare and Isaac glanced at each other as Isaac took a seat and asked, "Really? What happened?"

Clare assumed he was looking for news being churned through the town's rumor mill.

"Well, I've been hearing that it was a pretty grisly scene. They didn't just die. They were slaugh—" Phil stopped himself. "But don't let me put you off your meal. Care for some tea?"

Of course, Phil meant sweetened iced tea—the only thing that was served in the South. But that was fine with Clare. It was the perfect cool drink that would also give her a jolt of energy, which she lacked. "Please," she said.

Isaac added, "Make that two."

The proprietor disappeared into the kitchen to fetch their drinks.

Eyes on the menu, Isaac began, "You said we needed to chat. What about?"

Looking down at the menu, she saw nothing. "It's about what happened to me in Columbus."

For a minute, he was silent. Finally, he said, "Okay. I'm listening."

Her throat tightened like a fist, making it hard to speak or even breathe. "I found something I shouldn't have. Something so damning that people would kill to keep me quiet."

"Who?"

"My ex-husband." Sure, she'd decided to trust Isaac. But she needed more than a confidant. "I need help." She paused, choosing her words carefully. "And you have certain knowledge. Skills."

"I'll do what I can," said Isaac. "But you need to tell me everything."

Without another thought, she found the burner phone that she'd picked up after leaving Ohio. Holding it to her chest, she said, "My husband's family is wealthy. Seriously rich, and powerful. They have connections in state government and even in DC. They own a company that manufactures plastics. When we met, I was with the EPA in Northern Virginia working on the hazardous waste compliance program. When we got married, I tried to get an interagency transfer, but my position was already filled in Ohio. I taught some classes at the university part-time. Budget cuts reduced my department, and I was let go. For the first time in my adult life, I didn't have a job. But I didn't need money, either. Since I'd worked hard my whole life, being able to relax seemed, well, nice."

"I'm guessing it didn't last long," said Isaac.

Before she could say more, the kitchen door opened.

Phil approached with two glasses of tea on a tray. "Here you go." He set both on the table, along with small paper napkins. "I just checked with the cook. Jorge recommends the brisket sandwich."

"Sold," said Isaac. "Give me fries and a side salad."

"I'll take the same," said Clare, thankful for the easy decision. "No fries for me."

"Are you sure?" Phil asked. "They're pretty darn good, if I do say so myself."

"I'll steal a few from him." Using the end of the menu, she pointed to Isaac.

"Alrighty, then. Be back in a jiff with those sandwiches." He didn't bother to write down the order.

She waited until Phil was in the kitchen to pick up the narrative where she'd left off. "It wasn't long before I got bored and offered to help at the family business. After all, they manufacture plastic and there's a lot of environmental regulations to follow. I'd never worked for industry, but after years of working on hazardous waste regulations with the EPA, I definitely knew how to keep the company in compliance." She gave a quick laugh at her own ignorance, although it hadn't been funny how she completely trusted her ex-husband. "Kyle turned down my offer. He said they already had an internal department that handled environmental compliance."

"That wasn't true?"

"He was being honest to a point. I also think he realized how dangerous it was to let someone from the EPA have access to all the company's files." She sighed. After powering up the phone, she opened the photo app. "He encouraged me to volunteer in the community. I got involved with an organization that turned unused plots of land into parks. It was fulfilling, until I found these."

She opened the first picture and handed the phone to Isaac. "This is a form from about twenty years ago. Two-dozen containers of cadmium and chromium, heavy metals that are used in manufacturing plastics, needed to be disposed of properly. Chromium needs to be incinerated. Cadmium has to be mixed with hydrochloric acid, sulfuric acid and nitric acid to break it down. That's the law, but it's expensive." She took back the phone and opened the next photo. "Then, there's this." The trail of memos was easy to follow. They all outlined the decision by Kyle's father to bury the chemicals on a plot of undeveloped land. "That piece of land was where we wanted to build the next park."

Isaac leaned back and cursed. "That's pretty damning evidence."

"I agree. I showed Kyle. I assumed that he'd want to make it right."

"He didn't."

Clare shook her head. Her eyes burned but she refused to cry anymore. She'd made her choice when she stole the documents and left Ohio, knowing what her fate could be. But the risk was worth it if it meant she could find a way to expose the company—and protect herself. "Those heavy metals will eventually burn through the drums and leech into the soil. Once the water is contaminated, there would be an elevated risk for issues like increased renal failure and other kidney diseases in the population, especially children. Cancer rates—especially kidney and liver—would be likely to rise. I said that the authorities had to be notified. Kyle said it would ruin his father and the company." She let out a long breath and shuddered. "In the end, he agreed with me. I went to bed that night thinking everything was okay. But something woke me, and I overheard him talking to his father on the phone."

The tile was cold beneath her feet. The hallway was dark, save for a seam of light at the bottom of the door to Kyle's office. Clare, clad in her robe, held her breath and listened as Kyle spoke to his dad.

Her father-in-law said, "I told you from the begin-

ning that marrying one of those environmental types was a bad idea." The words wounded Clare. Kyle Sr. always seemed to like her. Obviously, it was just an act. "I told you that she was going to cause us problems and that you shouldn't defy me. But you swore her love for you was strong and that you could handle her. And here I am now, having to say 'I told you so' but it's our livelihood and reputation on the line."

"It's a little late to chastise me now." Beyond the voices in the room, Clare could hear the tinkling of ice on crystal. She imagined that her husband had poured himself a whiskey. "The proverbial cat is out of the bag. We have no choice but the deal with the situation."

"The hell we don't have any choices," her father-in-law said, his voice colder than the ice in Kyle's drink. "By tomorrow afternoon a tragic accident will solve all our problems..."

Back in the restaurant, with the bright Texas sun beating down on the sidewalk, Clare spoke. "I listened while Kyle and his dad planned my murder to keep me quiet. After Kyle left for work that morning, I printed off the documents and saved them to a flash drive as well. Then, I packed a bag. I took nine-thousand dollars from the checking and savings accounts I shared with Kyle. Finally, I maxed out several credit cards to pay for a no-fault divorce." She turned the power off on the phone and stuck it back in her bag. "I was worried about the paper copies getting lost or ruined, so I bought a phone and took pictures, just to make sure that I had as many copies as possible of the evidence. I've been on the run ever since."

"Clare, I need to ask you an important question. What's the outcome you want?"

"Ah. That's the question I've been asking myself every hour of every day for the past two months. I know I can't ignore the buried chemicals." She ran down a long list of possible solutions, along with why they'd never work. "I knew right away that I couldn't go to the police. My former in-laws are in tight with the local law enforcement, and they have connections in government, too. The press is another possibility. But once I hand over the information, would the story become big enough to keep me safe? My former coworkers at EPA were definitely people I could reach out to, but my last boss retired a few years ago." Clare let her words trail off until she felt as if she were drowning in futility.

Isaac placed his hand on hers. "Clare—do you trust me? I can help you, but I need you to trust me."

She let him work his fingers between hers. The warmth of his touch was delicious, yet she had to stay focused, not get distracted by her attraction to him. Distraction could be dangerous—maybe deadly.

She moved her hand from beneath his. "So, what's your plan?"

Staying in Encantador was reckless, there was no doubt about it. But Decker was fascinated by the investigation. He'd watched the young girl discover the body and the chaos that followed.

The sheriff had been easy to spot. He'd spoken to a man and woman, taking them with him from the crime scene. But who were the people? Suspects? Cops in street clothes? Even for Decker, it was hard to tell.

But the couple—especially the woman—was intriguing.

Now he was a ghost—able to pass through town all but unseen. It gave him a sense of invincibility, yet he wanted more. He wanted people to fear him, to fear his name—to fear the very idea of him.

Just as they had his famous ancestor, Jack the Ripper.

Lifting the book that he'd stolen from the library, he scanned the table of contents.

Chapter 9: Defining a Serial Killer

He read: *By modern standards, a serial killer is a person who kills three or more people with a similar profile and/or commit the murders in a similar manner. Therefore, serial killing, as in a series of murders, are connected.*

Yet, in the late summer and early fall of 1888 that concept had yet to be defined or explored. All of that changed with Jack the Ripper. Even though death was everywhere in the crowded and impoverished neighborhood of Whitechapel, the gruesome nature of the first murder caught the attention of Metropolitan Police's Criminal Investigative Division straight away.

Decker set the book aside and started the engine. He pulled onto the street and turned left at the end of the block. A barbecue restaurant sat next to a motel. A large window allowed him a full view of the eatery's interior. He saw her and automatically Decker stepped on the brakes. The tires squealed as a cloud of burned rubber wafted over his vehicle.

Gripping the steering wheel, he cursed his reaction.

Slamming on the brakes in the middle of the road was sure to call attention to the car—and to Decker himself. He eased his foot onto the gas and drove away, thinking only of the woman. She was the one he'd seen with the sheriff. He turned right at the corner and then turned right again. He could circle the block a time or two—all the while deciding on his best move.

Then again, he already knew what he was going to do. He'd found his next victim.

Isaac's list of problems had just grown by one. Technically, he was still undercover, searching for a lead on Decker Newcombe. Now, though, he'd promised to help Clare. To protect her.

Well, it was a promise he intended to keep.

He sipped his tea. "There's really only one way to battle your ex and his family and that's to go after them—and hard. First thing I suggest is talking to the FBI. I'll introduce you to my contact in San Antonio."

"Is he the guy you called today?"

Isaac nodded. "Jason's a hard-ass, that's for sure. And that's what we want. Because from what you told me, there's enough evidence to start a criminal investigation. The FBI's office in Columbus will take over."

"How do I know that the Columbus FBI won't be influenced by my in-laws?" she asked. "They really are a big deal in Ohio. Friends with their congressperson. Both US senators attend their annual holiday party."

He understood why Clare had gone on the run. Nobody wanted enemies, but powerful enemies were hard to fight. Still, an influential family presented a different set of opportunities. "The press will be your best ally. The fact that the Chamberlains are well connected will make the story even more irresistible to the media. I have some regional contacts—San Antonio, Dallas, Denver. But my acquaintances will have friends at the networks. Cable news. National papers." His pulse was strong. His heartbeat was steady. He knew how to help Clare, and he was going to do whatever it took to keep her safe.

"How will this help me?"

"Once the world knows about the chemicals your father-in-law buried, Chamberlain Plastics Manufacturing will go on the defensive. They'll try and make plenty of counterarguments, defend themselves, and just to prepare you, they may go as low as an attempt at character assassination. I've seen it. But you have the evidence. Plus, you'll have set the narrative."

Clare sipped her tea. "They'll claim I had a breakdown."

"What if they do? You found out some pretty damning information about your husband's family. Then you overheard your husband and father-in-law discussing your murder. What you heard will go a long way in both the court of public opinion and the court of law."

Smiling, she wiped a bead of sweat from the side of her glass. "But you won't be with me for most of this, right? You'll be here working on the other case." She paused. "Decker Newcombe."

The thing was she was right. Isaac couldn't abandon the search for the hitman.

That was the moment when Isaac realized that somewhere in the back corner of his mind he'd allowed himself the luxury of asking the most dangerous question of all—what if?

He was saved from trying to put his thoughts and feelings into words by the opening of the kitchen door.

Phil, a tray of food balanced on his forearm, approached. Even from twenty paces, Isaac could see the steam rising from the plates. The salty, spicy scent of barbecue hung in the air and Isaac's stomach contracted painfully.

"Here you go." Phil set the plates on the table, along with sets of silverware and paper napkins. "How's that look?"

"Amazing," said Isaac.

"Enjoy," said the restaurant owner as he retreated to counter behind the cash register. The man was on the other side of the room and certainly far enough away that it'd be difficult to overhear any conversation.

Clare picked a fry off his plate and took a bite. As she chewed, Isaac couldn't help but feel... Well, he really couldn't categorize his emotion. But he definitely liked sharing his meal with her.

Finally, she spoke. "I'm not sure that I'll ever be safe." Sitting back, she folded her arms across her chest. "I've worked on cases like this before for the EPA. There's a battle on the horizon, but it'll be a legal one. There will be wrangling over fines and how much responsibility Chamberlain Plastics Manufacturing is forced to accept." She shook her head. "In the end, the only thing that Kyle and his family will lose is money. When it's all said and done, they won't be chastised—they'll be furious." Letting out a long sigh, Clare shook her head. "Then, they'll really want revenge."

It wasn't in Isaac's nature to give up or give in. "Eat." He pointed to her plate. "You need food for energy."

Reaching for her plate, she took a bite of the sandwich. She chewed and washed down her food with a swig of tea. "This is good."

They spent several minutes saying nothing and focusing only on their meals. When Isaac's brisket was gone, he cleared his throat. "I can start making calls for you tonight…"

His words trailed off as a car drove slowly past. The driver looked into the restaurant and ice shot down Isaac's spine.

He no longer had a beard or long hair. The face was thinner—gaunt, even—but the eyes were unmistakably the same.

Decker Newcombe.

Now what? Going to get his truck would waste time that he didn't have. Calling the sheriff was a must, but that'd take time, too. Decker was already in a car, so who knew where he would go? He had to know he'd been recognized. Isaac had to find and follow the car as best he could. Decision made, he stood abruptly.

"Isaac?" Clare spoke, alarm evident in her voice.

He moved to the window and watched the car as it drove slowly down the street. "I'd swear that was Decker Newcombe."

"Are you sure that was him?"

That was the exact question Isaac intended to answer. Sure, chasing the killer on foot was less than ideal, but he didn't have any other choices. Letting Decker get away was unacceptable. "Call the sheriff and tell him that Newcombe is in town."

"Where are you going?" Clare asked.

He squared his shoulders, ready for the fight of his life. "I'm going to catch that bastard."

Chapter 12

Decker drove, his hands already warm with the very thought of the woman's yet-to-be-spilled blood. He made several rapid turns, checking his tail after each one. After several minutes of driving, he slowly steered down an alleyway that ran behind the barbecue restaurant. He backed the car into a delivery bay at the rear of the eatery. After turning off the engine, he pulled two large trash cans next to the grille. It wasn't exactly camouflage, but maybe it was good enough for someone to overlook his car.

The restaurant's back door was propped open with a cinder block. Decker picked up the large brick while guiding the door to silently shut. The cook, his dark hair held back by a headband, stood at a stainless steel counter. He hummed along to music that played through wireless earbuds.

Moving silently, he came up from behind the man, who turned suddenly to grab a tub of onions from the storage rack behind him. Shock barely had the chance to register before Decker swung the cinder block as hard as he could. Concrete connected with the cook's chin, an arc of blood spewing from his mouth. Decker hit him with the cinder block again and again. There was the crunch of concrete on bone and the man slumped down, dead before he even hit the floor.

One of the earbuds came loose and a Huichol song came out of the small speaker. Decker stepped on the white plastic device, silencing the music forever. A block of kitchen utensils sat at the back of the counter. Decker selected a carving knife and stood next to the door, listening.

Clare stood next to the cash register, the acrid taste of panic in the back of her throat. Phil, the restaurant's owner, pressed the phone to his ear. "Yes, Undersheriff Glass, I need to speak to Sheriff Cafferty now."

As he spoke, Clare scanned the street. It was empty, save for a few cars parked at the curb. Where was Isaac? Had he found Decker? Where was the killer?

Speaking into the receiver, Phil said, "Yes, I know you said he's on a call with the highway patrol. But what do you think he'll do if you don't tell him that there's a dangerous criminal in town?" His voice was full of the same frustration that Clare felt. "Well then, why don't you pass him the message while I wait." Phone still at his ear, Phil let out a long sigh and shook his head.

"You think we should lock the front door?" Clare suggested.

"Good idea." Phil pulled a set of keys from his pocket and held them up. "The key to the front door is on the blue ring."

After finding the correct key, Clare locked the door. Just to be safe, she jiggled the handle to make sure it was secure.

When she returned, Phil was speaking into the phone. "Yes, we'll wait here. Glad to hear that he's on the way." He hung up and turned to Clare. "Well, you heard that."

"I did."

"You hungry?" Phil pointed to her half-eaten lunch. "You didn't finish your meal." He strode to the table, picked up her plate. "We can heat that barbecue right up for you."

Clare was too nervous to eat another bite. "You don't have to," she said, trying to be polite.

"Don't worry. It's no trouble whatsoever. Jorge!" he yelled. "Come here and get this plate. We got to get the food good and warm. Add French fries to the dish this time, too." For a moment, they stared at the kitchen door. It remained shut. "He loves loud music so he can't hear a darn thing I say."

Slowly the door opened. A man stood on the threshold. He was covered in blood. In one hand, he held a knife. In the other was a cinder block stained red. True, Clare had never seen a picture of the hitman. But she knew that the person before her had to be Decker Newcombe.

"What the…" Phil's voice trailed off, the plate falling from his hand, bread and meat tumbling to the floor.

"What do you want?" she asked, her body frozen with fear.

"You," he said, smiling. "I'm here for you."

* * *

Isaac scanned the street left and right. The sedan was gone.

He cursed in frustration as his phone began to ring. After fishing the cell from his pocket, he swiped the call open. "Yeah?"

"Is it true?" At once, Isaac recognized Sheriff Cafferty's voice. "Did you really see Decker Newcombe?"

Isaac mentally reviewed everything he'd seen. The guy in the car looked nothing like any of Decker's pictures, but there was something about the eyes. Something he just couldn't dismiss. Still, he had to at least ask himself if his mind was playing a trick. Just in case.

Deep down, though, he knew his instincts were on target. "Let's say that I'm ninety percent sure."

"I'd like it to be a certainty before we move on this," said the sheriff.

"Me and you both." Wherever Decker had gone, Isaac wasn't going to be able to find him on foot. He turned back toward the restaurant. "But ninety percent is a whole hell of a lot better than what we had before—which was nothing."

"I'm coming over to Phil's now. I'll have Glass send out an APB."

"Meet you in a minute."

Isaac jogged to the restaurant's rear entrance. Two trash cans were set at the end of a delivery bay. Behind them sat a sedan. Isaac's instincts jolted again. It was the car he'd noticed earlier. Quickly, he snapped a photo of the license plate.

Still, he stepped around the green plastic bins and

placed his hand on the hood. It was hot, but not from the sun. The engine was still warm.

That meant only one thing: Decker Newcombe had gone into the restaurant.

And looking toward door, Isaac realized Clare was facing the monster alone.

Decker watched the woman as her eyes filled with terror.

"Hey, you." A man in a bolo tie stepped forward. "You can't be here. Jorge!"

Decker cocked his head. "That your cook? Hmm. I don't think he'll be much help."

"What'd you do to Jorge?" panic tinged his voice.

Smiling, he held the cinder block higher. The corner was stained with blood. "I'll let you guess what happened to Jorge."

The man turned the color of used paste. He walked to the counter. There, he pushed a button on the cash register and a drawer opened. "It's all yours, just take it and leave."

"It's not money that I'm after." Energy coursed through Decker's system.

He looked at the woman. She stood near the door, a set of keys in hand. It was then that he understood—she'd locked the front door to keep herself safe from him. He wanted to laugh.

Instead, she'd created a trap.

"You need to get the hell out of here," said the man behind the counter. His voice held a defiant edge, but his hands shook. "Before I get rough."

Decker was on the man in a heartbeat, bringing the

cinder block down like a club on his skull. The impact sounded like a ripe melon hitting the pavement. The man's knees gave out and he crumpled to the ground. A pool of blood—so thick it looked black—seeped out of the head wound, slowly surrounding his prone form.

Keeping his gaze connected with the woman's, he moved from behind the counter. He pointed at her with a knife. She drew in a shaking breath and his chest warmed with satisfaction. "Bring those keys to me. Now."

In moments like this, when people were about to die, Decker had seen it all.

People soiled themselves. They cried. Pleaded. Made promises they'd never keep.

Some did all of that and more.

Yet, whatever it was that Decker had expected to see, it sure as hell wasn't a challenge from a woman radiating fear. "You want these keys? Come and take them."

Twin emotions—annoyance and amusement—fought for supremacy, with amusement winning out.

"You think you can take me on?"

She said nothing, only lifted her chin in defiance.

He dropped the brick at his feet and lifted the knife. He was a predator, ready to pounce. "Alright then, let's dance."

Sunlight glinted off the knife's edge and Clare's stomach dropped to her shoes. Her mind raced as fear gripped her body. What the hell did she know about dodging a murderer?

Newcombe blocked the door to the kitchen and the rear exit. The front door, just a few yards away, was now bolted. She'd never be able to unlock the door and escape in time.

That meant if Clare wanted to live, she was going to have to fight.

She scanned the room for a weapon.

"What do you want from me?" Even she could hear the fear in her voice. The last thing she wanted was to expose her raw nerves to a killer, but she was in uncharted territory. "How's Phil? Is he alive?"

Decker looked at the body behind the counter. "He's breathing, for now." Pause. "Why do you care?"

"Because nobody else needs to lose their life, Decker."

As if slapped, the killer's head snapped back. "How do you know my name?"

Well, there was no reason for her to lie. "I work at a bar where a lot of bikers hang out. Your name's been mentioned and put two and two together." She paused. "You've been missing for a year. You're on the run and wanted for the murder of some district attorney in Wyoming."

She glanced at the table and came up with a plan. Hesitating for only a moment, she took a step closer to the table.

"What're you doing?" The knife in Decker's hand twitched as he rolled his wrist. "Stop right there."

"I just want a drink of tea," she said, making her voice a hoarse whisper. She took walked slowly toward the table. Laying her hand on the back of a chair, she stopped. "Then I can tell you everything the police know."

"Just pick up the glass and nothing else." Decker was

clearly enjoying himself. Yet was his perverse happiness enough of a distraction?

She reached for the tea and brought it to her lips. After taking the last sip, she flung the glass at Decker's face. He lifted an arm to block the flying object. It bounced off his wrist and shattered on the floor. Next, she threw the plate at him, whirling it through the air. It connected with his hairline and a seam of blood opened on his forehead.

He growled. "You'll pay for that."

Clare ran for the kitchen. She pushed open the door and sprinted forward. Her feet slid out from beneath her. She landed hard on her back. The impact drove all the air from her lungs. Her head hit the floor. For a moment, everything went black.

A pinprick of light broke through the darkness and Clare touched the back of her skull. Her hand was wet. Sticky. Blinking hard, she looked at her palm. It was red with blood.

But it wasn't hers.

She looked around and swallowed a scream. A man lay in a pool of gore. His black hair was wet and matted. His eye socket was crushed. His nose, gone. His white t-shirt was scarlet. His black pants were wet with gore. She tried to scoot away. A spike of pain shot from the back of her head until she saw stars.

Then her vision returned. Standing above her was Decker Newcombe.

"You should've listened to me from the beginning. If you had, I would've been gentle and let you die easy-like. But not now," he said, grinning. "Now, I'm gonna kill you slow."

* * *

Isaac rushed to the restaurant's rear entrance and pushed on the handle. It didn't budge. He pushed again and once more. He had to get inside. But how?

He examined the door. The handle was a typical touch bar, and most likely the lock automatically engaged to the outside when closed. It meant that the mechanism was controlled by a roller strike. He could try to pick the lock, sure. But even with the right equipment, it could take hours—time he didn't have.

From inside the room, he heard metal crashing. A woman's scream. "Clare?"

He pounded on the door with the side of his fist. "Clare, can you hear me?" He waited, listening, for an answer.

There was nothing.

The silence fueled his worst fears. He slammed his fist against the door. "Clare, I'm coming. Just hold on."

Isaac ran back down the alley. Pulling the phone from his pocket, he placed the call.

The phone rang once. Twice. Three times.

"Come on. Come on. Answer your damn phone," he cursed as he ran.

On the fifth ring, the call was answered. "This is Cafferty."

"He's here. Decker Newcombe's at Phil's." His voice was a breathless wheeze.

Isaac had worried that Decker was responsible for Trinity's murder from the beginning, even though he had no proof. Now he was sure that the hitman was responsible for the first killing. And if he didn't get that door open, Clare would become the next victim.

"I'm on my way. You wait for me to get there before you try to go inside," said the sheriff. "You hear me?"

Isaac had heard, yet he had no intention of following the sheriff's orders.

He rounded the corner and sprinted for the front of the building. But would he get there in time to save Clare?

Somehow, Clare had kept the keys wedged between her fingers. Decker straddled her torso, keeping her pinned to the ground. He pressed one of her arms to the ground, but her hand with the keys was still free. She struck out with the sharp keys, focusing on his face. His arm. His hand. Any place she could do damage.

A long set of gashes on his forearm wept blood. Still, she wasn't going to be able to fight forever. Decker was stronger. Faster. Meaner. He'd killed more than once. And he was clearly determined to do it again.

Leaning forward, Decker pressed her chest down with his own. The stench of body odor surrounded her. She tried not to gag or worse, retch. Grabbing her wrists, Decker pinned her to the floor.

Clare's mind went blank with terror. If she wanted to live, she had to focus.

She was unable to move her arms to fight off his attack, but instinct took over.

She slammed the keys into his cheek. The ends punctured Decker's flesh. He roared with pain and pitched backward. Clare scrambled from beneath the killer. He grabbed her hair.

Decker drew back his fist and hit Clare in the temple. Pain erupted in her skull as her vision filled with a thousand tiny floating dots. She sprawled across the floor as the keys fell from her hand. They hit the tiles with a clatter and slid under a metal table. "Dammit."

Rolling to all fours, she scrambled to her feet. She was grabbed from behind again and spun around. She dug her heels into the floor, but Decker forced her toward the stove, where all six burners were lit. He grabbed the back of her hair. A sharp pain filled her scalp.

She reached back, slapping, hitting, clawing. Decker grabbed her wrists, pinning them to the back of her head. Her shoulders ached with the strain of being held at such an odd angle. Yet, that was the least of her worries. With his hand pressing the back of her head, Decker shoved her face toward a burner. The flame's heat danced along her skin. She closed her eyes. Yet, the fire still wavered behind her lids.

Clare refused to die. She tried to pull her hands free. His grip tightened, his fingers digging into her flesh. She screamed in pain, and he pushed her closer to the lit burner.

Clare refused to die. But what could she do to escape from the killer?

"Why are you doing this?" she asked, her voice trembling.

"Because." His breath washed over her ear as he spoke. "Being a killer is in my blood."

"You don't have to do this, you know. You can stop now." Clare was dangerously close to begging for her life. It was one thing she refused to do. "Let me go," she said, her tone flinty.

"Letting you go is one thing I won't do. It started generations ago with Old Jack. It's why I killed the redhead, too."

Clare couldn't believe how easily he'd just admitted he'd murdered Trinity. She knew he had no qualms about killing her, but what was she supposed to say to get more out of him—not to mention to hold him off at least until the sheriff arrived?

Without thought, she said, "She was a mom, you know. Now her daughter will grow up without a mother. And you took away her life. Why?"

Decker snarled, "Shut up."

He pushed her down harder, closer to the flame. Clare pushed her feet into the floor harder. It did her no good. The tile was too slick with grease and blood to gain any purchase.

Then again, maybe that was what she needed. She pressed her back into Decker's chest and brought back her skull, smashing his face with the back of her head. At the same moment, she lifted her feet, and pushed off the stove. The momentum sent them both tumbling to the ground. Clare was the first to regain her footing.

A knife lay on the prep table. Clare reached for the blade. Her hand found the hilt and she swung it toward Decker as he rose to his feet. The knife sliced open his shirt and the flesh beneath—but the cut wasn't deep enough to stop the killer. With a curse, he jumped to his feet and lunged at her. She brought the knife up and around, the blade catching his arm. With roar, Decker grabbed her wrist and wrenched her arm to the side. She screamed as her hand went numb. The knife slipped from her grip at the same moment she heard the sound of breaking glass.

Chapter 13

Isaac charged at the glass door, shoulder first. The pane shattered on impact, and he rushed into the restaurant, ignoring the shards of glass clinging to his flesh. The dining area was empty. Plates and glasses were strewn across the floor.

He'd heard Clare's scream and realized Decker had her in the kitchen. Pulling his gun from the waistband at his back, he ran toward the set of double doors.

A pool of blood was spread over the floor. A dead man, his face crushed, lay on the tile. Decker had Clare by the shoulders on the floor, where they struggled over a kitchen knife. Isaac lifted the firearm. "Let her go, Newcombe."

Decker held Clare to him and ducked down until she was a human shield. A knife was pressed to her throat. Isaac tried to get the killer in his sights, but it was impossible. There were no shots to take without the risk of killing Clare. But he didn't lower the gun. "Let her go," Isaac ordered.

"Why? So, you can shoot me?"

"You let her go and I won't shoot." Isaac hated to negotiate with the hitman. Yet, he'd do anything to save Clare's life.

"So, you can arrest me, then. No thanks."

Speaking to Clare, he said, "It'll be okay. I'll get you out of this."

Isaac remained by the doors to the dining area. But Decker was maneuvering toward the rear of the kitchen and the exit. Isaac couldn't let them escape. He aimed and pulled the trigger. The bullet punched a hole in the wall as the acrid scent of gunpowder mixed with the salty smell of grease and the coppery stench of blood.

"Don't move," Isaac warned. "I will shoot you."

The killer sneered. "I don't think so. If you had it in you to shoot your friend to get to me, you would have by now." He pressed the blade into Clare's shoulder. The wound wept blood.

Then, Decker kicked over a stainless steel table. It toppled to the ground, pinning Isaac next to the door.

With Clare still screaming, Decker pulled her by the arm and ran for the exit.

To follow, Isaac was forced to climb over the table, but Decker had already made it to his car and was speeding down the alleyway. Heart pounding and feet slapping the pavement, he gave chase.

The car turned the corner and the door opened. Clare tumbled from the driver's seat. Then, Decker punched the gas. Smoke rose from the tires and the smell of burning rubber filled the air.

Isaac ran to Clare's side. She lay on the ground, covered in blood.

Terror seized him, turning his hands icy.

Was she dead?

Dropping to her side, he smoothed her tangled hair from her face. She stared at him, her breath coming in short gasps. His eyes stung and he blinked hard. "You're alive. You got away."

"He didn't say anything. I don't know why he threw me from the car." She pushed herself up. Her palms were scraped and raw. Blood streamed down one arm from a cut to her elbow. There was a bruise on her cheek. He wanted to pull her into his arms and ease the fear and shock she must be feeling. Let the feel of her body pressed close to his ease his own disappointment at once again losing sight of his prey. Instead, he asked, "How bad are you hurt? I've got a med kit in the truck. We should get you to a doctor, Clare."

In leaving her at the scene, Isaac had been forced to decide—tend to Clare or continue to follow the killer. It was a brilliant decision on Decker's part, but Isaac hadn't even thought twice. He'd found Decker once, and he was sure that the killer would get careless now, making it easier to locate him again.

Because he was sure to come after Clare again, meaning she was in more danger than she'd been before. And while Isaac wanted to nail Decker, he was laser-focused on keeping Clare safe at all costs.

"I'm okay, I think." She reached for his arm. "Help me up."

"No, you just sit. I'll call an ambulance. You really should be seen by a doctor—you could be in shock, Clare."

"It's Phil." Clare used Isaac's shoulder as leverage to stand. He stood as well. "He's hurt bad."

Whatever Isaac wanted to say next was cut short by the shriek of a siren. Sheriff Cafferty slammed on the brakes, parking his cruiser in the middle of the alleyway. With the lights still flashing, he stepped from the car.

Holding on to Clare, Isaac called, "You need to call for backup. Newcombe was here, but got away." He gave a quick description of the car, along with the license plate number.

It took Mooky only a few seconds to send out another APB from the cruiser's radio. Stepping from the car, he asked, "What the hell happened?"

Isaac recalled the chaos in the restaurant. Sure, the restaurant was a crime scene, and anyone who entered would contaminate evidence. But Phil might be alive, and he'd be damned before he'd stand around and wait while a man needed savings. "Call an ambulance and follow me inside." He turned to Clare. "I know it's probably ridiculous to ask you to wait here."

Defiantly, she stared him down. "No way," she said. "I'm coming."

The sheriff made the call, then joined Isaac. The lawmen entered through the back door, Clare at Isaac's side. The dead cook lay on the floor. The room was still in shambles. Clare leaned heavily on his shoulder. "Phil's behind the counter."

The sheriff rushed into the dining area and Clare and

Isaac followed. Phil lay on the floor. An ugly purple bruise ran the length of his swollen jaw. Blood splatter covered the walls. A cinder block, the edge red with blood, sat on the ground.

Phil's breathing was shallow, although the bleeding seemed to have slowed. If he survived, it'd be nothing more than luck.

The sheriff applied a bandage to the head wound. He glanced at Clare. "How about you? Looks like you've been to hell and back."

She looked at her bloody elbow. "I think I'll be okay."

"And what about you?" The sheriff nodded to Isaac. "You've got glass all over your arms."

He picked a shard loose. "I'll survive."

Another siren could be heard in the distance. The sheriff looked up from Phil's side. "That's the EMTs now."

The ambulance parked in the back alley and the EMTs came in through the kitchen. Between them, they carried a medical kit and collapsible stretcher. Isaac pointed. "We have one victim behind the counter. He's alive but unconscious. There's another man in the kitchen. Deceased."

The sheriff and Clare moved into the dining area, giving the EMTs room to treat Phil's wounds. Isaac met them at a table. "Sit here," said Isaac to Clare. "This is a lot to take in, I know. You want a glass of water?"

She dropped into a chair, feeling the unsteadiness in her limbs, in her mind, as the adrenaline began to fade from her body. "Sure."

A stack of glasses and a water pitcher were stored on a table in the corner. Isaac retrieved three glasses, along with the pitcher and returned to the table. He poured water into a glass and handed it to Clare. "Here. It's not much, but maybe it'll help you feel better. For the moment, anyway."

She took a sip and gave him a wan smile. "Thanks."

He sat next to her and pulled another piece of glass from his arm. Sheriff Cafferty remained on his feet. Isaac spoke to the sheriff. "You have to go, I'm sure, and lead the search for Decker."

"I called the highway patrol. They got helicopters and airplanes looking for Newcombe's car. He might've gotten out of town, but he won't get far. For now, I need to know what happened here."

Clare spoke, her voice a whisper. "He told me that he killed Trinity."

"He said those words exactly?" asked the sheriff, his tone filled with incredulity.

"Not exactly, no. He said it's why he killed the redhead, too."

"That's a pretty compelling confession." The sheriff ran a hand down his face. "But why would he kill Ms. Jackson? You said he was a hitman and only killed for money."

Clare asked, "And why eviscerate her that way?"

"From what I can tell, nothing Decker Newcombe does makes sense." The sheriff folded his arms across his chest.

"It's wrong to think he's out of control. He's been nothing if not deliberate. Hiding for a year. Taking Trinity in Mercy and dumping her body in Encantador," Isaac said, just mentioning a few of Decker's recent crimes. "But his mode and motivation for killing has changed."

"Why?" asked the sheriff.

That was the most important question of all. He turned to Clare. "What else did he say? Even if it doesn't seem like a clue to you, it might be significant to the investigation."

Shaking her head, she said, "It's all such a blur. He came in through the kitchen. Then he attacked Phil. I'd locked the front door and knew I was trapped." Her voice broke on the last word. She picked up the glass. Her hand trembled and water sloshed over the rim. She took a sip and set the glass back on the table. "Like I said, it's all a damn blur. I wish I could remember but I don't."

She was frustrated. He could see that in the lines of worry between her brow and set of her jaw. He gave her arm a squeeze to show his support.

For now, he had no choice but to wait and see if Clare regained all her memories. Even if she did, Decker might not have shared anything germane to Trinity's murder or his plans. But Isaac had to get back to work. "Sheriff, I'd like to ask a favor of you."

"I'll help if I can."

Isaac was thankful for Cafferty's cooperation. "I need a private place to make a few phone calls. And a place for Clare to shower and a clean set of clothes for her."

"I can get you the clothes and a place to make calls." He paused. "Are you going to check in with SSA Jones? I could surely use the FBI's help."

Jason was the first person who Isaac planned to contact. "I imagine he'll be in touch with you soon."

He nodded his thanks. "I have just the place for you, then."

First, Isaac was forced to work with Ryan. Now the sheriff's office was involved in Newcombe's case as well. It was a hell of a way to be a singleton. But for the first time in a long while, he didn't mind having a team.

At Phil's, EMTs had examined Clare. Like she thought, all her injuries were minor. Her scrapes were cleaned, and her cuts were bandaged. They offered to take her to the emergency room, but she refused further treatment. With Phil so badly wounded, the doctor didn't need to worry about Clare.

Deputy Travers had scraped beneath her fingernails for evidence. He also gave her an Encantador Sheriff's Office T-shirt in exchange for her blood-soaked T-shirt, which was taken into evidence as well.

Likewise, the EMTs treated Isaac at the scene. The shards of glass were removed from his arm and all the cuts were treated and bandaged.

Then, Isaac and Clare were directed to the motel next to the restaurant. The Saddle Up Inn was a single-level motor inn that sat at the back of a parking lot. Half a dozen cars were parked in spots for a dozen rooms. The building was adobe, painted pink, with a roof of terracotta tiles. A sign on the street showed a lone saddle hanging on a peg, along with the words *Saddle Up*.

At the bottom of the sign, the word *VACANCY* was painted in red. There was a hook next to the vacancy sign and Clare guessed that in the motel office was the word *NO*, which was put out when all the rooms were filled.

Half a whiskey barrel had been converted into a fountain. It bubbled happily next to the front door.

"Looks like this is the place." Standing on the sidewalk, Isaac shaded his eyes. "I thought for sure that Cafferty would just put us back in the conference room at the sheriff's office."

"I just want to get out of these clothes and take a long hot shower," said Clare. She tried to ignore the image of holding Isaac's naked body next to hers beneath the spray of hot water. Yet, the fantasy left an indelible mark.

Without saying another word, they walked across the parking lot. Isaac pulled open the office door and a wave of air-conditioning crashed over Clare, leaving her instantly chilled. The desk clerk, a man with round glasses, looked up as they entered. Stockings of red and white hung in a line on the counter.

A radio played in the background. The announcer said, "You all know that last song was 'Jingle Bells'—and I hope that you sang along. Be sure to run all your holiday errands early today. A storm is moving into our area…" The clerk turned down the volume and smiled at Isaac and Clare. "You two must be the folks from the sheriff's office who need a room."

"We are."

"I've got your keys." He held up two worn plastic cards with a black magnetic strip. "Here you go."

Isaac took the cards and handed one to Clare.

The man continued, "That's for room ten. Turn right when you go back outside. Number ten is the third door from the end."

"And what about me?" Clare asked.

"That key will work on the lock, too."

"No," said Clare, clarifying her question. "What room am I supposed to be in?"

"Room ten."

"You don't understand," said Clare. "I need my own room."

Isaac removed his wallet from his back pocket. "I'll pay for another room," he said, a stack of bills in hand.

"Sorry, I can't help with that," said the desk clerk. "Three of our rooms are being renovated. The other ones are rented."

Clare glanced at Isaac, her face suddenly hot.

Then again, Decker Newcombe was still at large. If he showed back up, she didn't want to be alone. She nodded at the desk clerk. "Thanks."

They made their way down the walkway to number ten, and Clare waited as Isaac unlocked the hotel door. She crossed the threshold. The room was clean and comfortable. The Western motif that was popular around town was on full display. A barn door headboard sat at the top of a single full-size bed. Prints featuring riderless saddles hung on three of the four walls. The TV stand was an old wagon wheel with a glass top. A sign hung on the bathroom door as a joke: Outhouse.

"It's not the Ritz," said Isaac. "That's for sure."

A combo heat/air-conditioning unit clung to the wall beneath a window and blew a weak stream of almost-cool air. Clare adjusted the temperature and fan speed. The unit rattled the pane and icy cold wind gusted from the vents. She lifted her hair, letting the air-conditioner dry the sweat at the nape of her neck. "It's perfect," she said, dropping her bag on the TV table.

"Really?" Isaac sat on the end of one bed. "Look at these blankets. Cowboy-hat print? I haven't seen this since I was a kid."

The mention of his childhood left Clare wondering about Isaac. "Growing up, was your bedroom decorated with lots of cowboy stuff? After all, you did grow up in Texas."

"Me? Cowboys? No, I was more of a race-car kid." He laughed. "The more I look, the surer I am that this room is tacky."

"Cute," said Clare. Every part of her ached or hurt. "Enthusiastic," she added, rubbing the back of her neck.

"Which is a polite way to say tacky."

She laughed and her neck twinged. Clare didn't recall making a face, but she must've. Isaac's hand rested on her elbow. "Do you want me to call the hospital?"

She wanted to lean into him. To feel his hands on her, massaging the soreness, soothing the pain. Touching. Stroking. Stoking the heat in her veins.

She wanted him. It was that simple.

Then again, any kind of relationship with Isaac would create more issues than it fixed. "Phil's going to need a lot of care. I won't bother the doctor for a few bumps and bruises."

"I imagine that Phil has already been airlifted to a bigger hospital. Besides, I'm worried about you—and until you get examined, you won't know what's wrong."

She understood the wisdom of Isaac's words. But she ignored his comment altogether. "So, who gets the shower first? Me or you?"

"You go first. I'll call Jones." He took the phone from his pocket and sat on the edge of the bed.

"Alright, then."

She slipped into the bathroom and stripped out of her clothes. Turning on the cold tap in the tub, she plunged her pants into the stream. Clare waited as the runoff water turned from red to pink to clear.

Good enough. She twisted her jeans, wringing out the excess water, and then hung them on a towel hook to dry.

She adjusted the water temperature from cold to scalding and stepped under the spray. She closed her eyes and let the water sluice over her body. At the edge of her imagination, she sensed that memories of Decker Newcombe wanted to sneak into her mind.

She refused to think of him.

A complimentary bottle of body wash sat on the edge of the tub. Clare poured a dab into her palm and worked it into a lather. She ran her hand over her stomach, her chest, her breasts.

Isaac's face came to mind. What would it feel like to have his hands on her body? He would be a gentle but powerful lover, she decided, with her hands between her thighs.

Her own touch did nothing to excite her passions or ease the ache for Isaac's touch. Then she remembered the kiss. The power of his lips on hers. The sensual feel of his tongue in her mouth. Clare leaned against the tiles and explored her body. But it wasn't a fantasy that left her breathless and trembling. It was the memory of being touched by Isaac. Held by him, kissed by him.

She stood under the shower and turned her face to the spray. Isaac had come into her life at the exact wrong time. And that meant only one thing. There could be nothing between them beyond longing and unfulfilled desire.

Chapter 14

Isaac placed the call to Jason. The SSA answered after the first ring. "Have you got news for me?"

He filled his boss in quickly. "His intended victim is a woman named Clare Chamberlain." He hesitated. "One more thing. Decker's seen me. He knows that the police are looking for him. My cover's been blown."

To his credit, Jason remained calm. "I'm not pulling you off the case, yet. Tonight, I'll send in a team to Mercy and get more eyes at the bar."

Even though he was on the phone, Isaac nodded. "Solid plan." But there was more. "Decker admitted to Clare that he killed Trinity—the murder victim from this morning. A DNA swab was taken from the body. Soon, we'll know if it's a match with Decker, but I have no doubts."

"Interesting." Jason drew out the single word. "Why'd

a hitman who only killed for money start targeting women? And in such a brazen way that he's willing to attack others to gain access to his victim, no less?"

"I was hoping you had some insights."

After letting out a long breath, Jason said, "I'll run this by the behavioral sciences unit. They'll have a theory. For now, I want you to stay out of Mercy. The last thing we want is for you to be spotted by Decker."

A hard knot dropped into the middle of Isaac's chest. He hated to give up the case. But Jason was right. If Decker spotted him again, the hitman would know that Mercy was a trap and disappear. "What about Ryan?"

"He's still the bait," said Jason. "The undercover agents will be at the bar before it opens. If Decker shows up, we'll get him."

It didn't seem right to leave Ryan without protection. Then again, Jason had promised that backup was on the way. "I'll let him know. By the way, the local sheriff is looking for some federal help. Call me if you hear anything else."

"There is one other thing. I've finally gotten the authorization from DoD to task a satellite eight miles into Mexico. We're starting near where you found that phone. If all goes well, we'll have a location for the safe house by evening."

That would be good news. Then again... "Why would he go back to the place he's been holed up for a year? He told Ryan about it—I imagine Decker will find someplace else to hide."

"We have to follow every lead," said Jason, annoyance evident in his tone. "You know that."

"Yeah, I know. No stone, and all." He paused, wondering if now was the time to bring up Clare and the buried chemicals. "There's something else that needs you attention. I've seen some evidence that a company in Columbus, Ohio has buried some pretty toxic chemicals."

"You have a name for the company?"

"Chamberlain Enterprises," he said.

"I'm not making any promises, but my people will look into." Jason paused. "Anything else?"

"I'm keeping Decker's intended victim—the women he attacked—with me. We're staying in a motel in Encantador for now. If you need to talk to her, let me know."

"Eventually, I will. For now, my focus is on the DoD satellite. I'm hoping that we can get some images before the storm hits." Jason ended the call.

Isaac held his phone. Truly, he hated that he'd been told to stay away from Mercy for a variety of reasons. From the beginning, this had been his plan. He'd worked the case for months. It didn't seem fair that he'd given up a year of his life. Then, a team of undercover agents were going to show up and make the arrest.

He also loathed leaving Ryan on his own. It didn't take a gifted psychologist to help Isaac understand why he wanted to work as a singleton. For years, he'd carried Miguel's death around like a shield. It was meant to protect Isaac, but it also kept people away and it was exhausting.

He knew now that he'd never given Ryan enough credit. At great personal risk, he was trying to do the right thing. He wanted to bring Decker to justice and, at the same time, start over. True, Ryan would never replace Miguel, but he wouldn't have been a bad choice as a friend.

But if he had to lay low, as Jason said, there were worse places to be than a hotel room with Clare. He listened to the shower running in the bathroom. He imagined Clare's body, slick with soap, as water sluiced over her breasts.

He wanted to think that if he let himself into the bathroom, she'd welcome him with open arms and open thighs. But they'd only kissed once. And even he knew that hardly gave him the right to expect more. Still, it didn't stop him from wanting her.

He ignored his growing desire. Now wasn't the time to get drawn into adult fantasies. He had one more call to make. He pulled up his contacts and selected Ryan's number.

He answered the phone after the third ring. "I never thought I'd say this, but I'm glad to hear from you."

"Hey, man," said Isaac. "I have news. You alone?"

"I am. Go ahead."

"Decker's in the area." Isaac gave a simple recounting of the events after Trinity's body was discovered. He ended with, "The FBI will be sending several undercover agents to stake out your bar. I don't know who or how many, but enough that when Decker shows up, they'll be ready."

"Plus, I'll have you here."

Did Ryan already suspect that Isaac was being sidelined? "I'm staying in Encantador for now. Decker's seen me. If I show up in Mercy, he'll know there's a trap. Before he can be taken into custody, he'll take off. After that, we'll never find him."

On the other end of the line, Isaac could hear Ryan sigh. "There's not many people in the world I trust. Without you around..."

After a year of working together, he supposed they'd developed a respectful relationship of sorts. "The agents will keep you safe, man. They'll get Decker when he shows. Soon, all this will be over."

"I guess this is goodbye, then."

Isaac hadn't really thought about it that way, but Ryan was right. He was done with his time in Mercy. Despite the fact he'd hated the place, to know that he'd never go back was shocking, like ice water to the face. "I guess it is."

"I'll make good on that second chance, Isaac. I promise," said Ryan.

"I hope so," said Isaac. "You've earned it, man. And, Ryan—"

"Yeah?"

"Nothing. Just...be careful. And—good luck."

Then he ended the call.

Clare stayed in the bathroom to dry and redress. Thankfully, the sheriff's office T-shirt came to her thighs, and she need not put on her wet jeans. She and Isaac traded places, muttering polite nothings as they slipped past each other, Clare into the room and Isaac to the shower. Laying on the bed, she flipped through the TV channels, watching a local news station as it tracked a line of storms up from the Gulf of Mexico. The news anchor promised high winds, hail, rain and an unseasonable tornado watch.

Isaac exited the bathroom and Clare looked up from

the TV. His hair was still damp. He wore his jeans, no shirt.

After spending time with him, she knew that he was muscular and well-built. Yet, she was wholly unprepared for how he looked without his shirt. His arms were powerful, the lines of muscles were unmistakable. A dark sprinkling of hair covered his chest and abdomen.

Just seeing him left her breathless.

He ran a towel over his hair. "How're you holding up?"

She shrugged. "Sore. Tired. Worried."

"About Decker or your ex?"

"Both, I suppose." Using the remote, Clare turned off the TV. True, there hadn't been a lot of time to consider Isaac's suggestions for dealing with her in-laws, but she knew there were some flaws to his plan. She sat up, resting her back on the headboard. "As far as my ex, I have lots of concerns."

"Well, we'll be here for a while. Let's figure out how to ease them, if we can."

"Well, you mentioned bringing in the media and law enforcement. I agree that once the story becomes news, the Chamberlains will have to leave me alone. But how long will the world be fixated on some buried chemicals? Weeks? A month, maybe." She shrugged. "The investigation will eventually end, too. And then, who will be around to care what happens to me?"

"Me," said Isaac. "I'll care." He sat beside her, and their shoulders touched. Clare didn't bother to move away. "You could be my second client at Texas Law."

"I don't have money to pay you." She paused a beat before adding, "Except what I earned last night."

Smiling, he shook his head. "You can keep that cash. I won't charge you a dime."

"Really? Don't you need paying clients?"

"Sure, just not you." His thigh pressed against hers and she shivered with yearning. "For you, I just want to do the right thing."

Clare gave in to her longing to touch Isaac. Placing her hand on his cheek, she said, "Then I was right from the beginning."

"About what?"

"You really are kind."

"I don't know about that," he drawled. He leaned closer, so close that his mouth nearly touched hers. "Would a nice guy kiss you?" he asked.

"Only if I wanted a kiss," she said.

"Is that what you want, Clare?"

Without a word, she placed her lips on his. His mouth was strong. He reached around her waist, pulling her to him. Her breasts pressed against his chest. She sighed with the closeness, and he slipped his tongue into her mouth.

Winding her fingers through Isaac's hair, Clare pulled him closer. At first, the kiss was tentative—almost timid. As if he were reining in his passion. Or giving Clare a chance to retreat. Yet, she was done with running. She'd spent the past two months avoiding thoughts and feelings. Hell, she'd survived the hands of a killer.

Clare was ready to embrace her emotions again. She wanted to do more than simply survive. She wanted to claim this moment for her own and live.

She ran her palm over the muscles of his chest, a silent invitation. Holding her tighter, Isaac growled with pleasure.

His palm skimmed her side until Isaac found the hem of the T-shirt. He gently pulled it up, his fingertips branding her skin, traveling from her belly to her chest.

She began to burn, from the heat of his skin, from her own wanting. "Touch me," she whispered into the kiss. "Please, Isaac."

"Where?" he asked, slipping his finger inside her bra.

"Everywhere."

He rolled her nipple between finger and thumb, and she gasped with longing. Liquid heat settled low in her belly, and she ached for Isaac to explore every part of her. What's more, she wanted him inside her.

She couldn't recall ever feeling such intense desire—for any man. She'd never acted on her feelings so quickly before, ever. Sure, these were extenuating circumstances—to say the least!—but who knew what they faced in the coming days, or even hours? No matter which way she turned, she was being hunted.

So would it be such a crime to steal this moment for herself? Why should she deny herself the pleasure, the man, she'd been longing for?

Clare lay back on the bed. Isaac knelt on the mattress next her. She studied him—examining his shoulders, arms, chin, lips and eyes. How long had it been since she'd been so drawn to a man? For a moment, she couldn't remember. Then again, maybe she'd never been so attracted to anyone before now.

He ran his hand up her calf. Desire rushed through her veins.

"What're you looking at?" he asked, a small smile on his lips.

"You."

Isaac hovered over her. His fingers grazed the flesh of her stomach. "Tell me what you want."

Clare's blood buzzed and she gasped in anticipation as his fingers traced the silky fabric of her panties.

His voice low and husky, he asked, "Here?"

"Lower."

He gave her that smile she was starting to love. "I was hoping you'd say that."

Clare was already wet, swollen with want and desperate to have him inside her. Isaac slipped his hand into her underwear and ran a finger down the middle of her slit. She lifted her hips, and he slid a finger inside her. He began to move, and she drew in a short and shaking inhalation. He slipped another finger inside and she moaned with desire.

"Is this where you want to be touched?"

"Yes," she said, sighing. "Oh, yes."

He moved his fingers inside her as his thumb traced a circle over the top of her sex. She was still sensitive from her time in the shower. But having Isaac's touch was so different from her own. And really, it had been too long since she'd been properly stroked—or loved. The orgasm came on hard and fast. She cried out and clung to his shoulders. He smothered her cries with his kisses. Her heartbeat raced and every part of her body thrummed with ecstasy.

"Isaac," she whispered. "Oh, Isaac."

He kissed her again; deep and slow. Then, he moved his mouth to her neck, her shoulder, her chest. She stripped out of her T-shirt and dropped it to the floor. Next, she removed her bra.

He kissed her deeply. "You're perfect."

Clare wasn't sure that she believed him. Kyle had gone from being indifferent to planning her murder. And he certainly never called her perfect—or anything close. Yet, the look in his eyes told Clare that he saw her as beautiful and desirable.

"Better than perfect," he continued. "Clare, you're gorgeous."

Isaac lowered his mouth to her breast and took her nipple between his teeth. He bit gently. She hissed with the pleasure and the pain. He reached for her other breast and ran his thumb over her areola, until both of her nipples were hard.

Running her hands through Isaac's hair, she let the silky strands slip between her fingers. But she wanted— no, she needed—to feel more of him. She ran her hands down his chest, to his abs. To his hips. She traced his length through the fabric of his jeans.

"Oh, Clare," he moaned.

She worked the top button of his pants free.

"What're you doing?"

"Fair is fair," she said, pulling down on the zipper. Clare ran her hand inside his pants. He was hard and thick. She traced the head, moving her hand up and down his shaft.

Isaac kissed her hard. "Dammit, that feels good."

He got harder with her touch, but swiftly put a stop to her plans.

"Hold up." He held on to her wrist. "You gotta hold up."

"You don't like it?"

"Hell, I love it. It's just that I'll lose it unless you stop." He kissed her hard, gave her a wicked smile. "Take off those panties."

Clare did as she was told. While she disrobed, Isaac took off his jeans and underwear. She lay back on the bed and he stood, naked before her.

He bent down to kiss Clare and reached between her legs. He kissed her neck. Her shoulder. Her breasts. Lower still. Her stomach. Her hip. Then, his mouth was on her sex. He slid one finger inside her and then another.

The sensations were too much. Yet, she wanted more than to take her pleasure from Isaac—but to give him pleasure as well.

"Come here," she gasped, pulling him by the shoulders. "Lay on your back."

He rolled to the middle of the mattress and lay on his back. She was on his chest, with her rear toward his face. Clare studied Isaac's body. There was a scar on his chest and mole on his thigh. She wanted to investigate the map of his life and know everything she could about this man.

At the same time, she knew that any relationship between them—beyond the here and now—was impossible. So, Clare decided to drink in the moment until she was drunk with bliss. She ran her tongue around his tip and then, took him into her mouth. His tongue and fingers inside her. The pressure of ecstasy began to build, yet she'd never be able to climax again—not without Isaac inside her.

She swirled her tongue over him once more and nipped the inside of his thigh.

"Wait a second." Isaac rose from the bed and picked up his discarded jeans. From his back pocket, he took out his wallet. "Success." He held up a square foil packet.

Clare lay back as Isaac unrolled the translucent condom.

He knelt between her thighs. "So sexy," he murmured. He entered her slowly. "You are so freaking sexy."

She cried out as he drove hard at the very end. Isaac adopted the rhythm—a delicious torture—slow, slow, hard.

Clare's passion swelled. For her release, though, she needed more. Clare ran her tongue over Isaac's neck, savoring the salt on his skin. "Harder," she whispered into his ear. "I want you to take me harder. Faster. Now."

Isaac complied. His strokes carried the same urgency she felt. The wave of passion grew until it towered over Clare, threatening to drown her in her own pleasure. She cried out as she came. "Isaac. Isaac. Oh, Isaac."

The headboard slapped against the wall as he drove into her one final time. With a growl, he climaxed.

Heartbeat racing, he flopped down on Clare. He placed a kiss on her neck and gently bit the lob of her ear. "I like to hear you say my name like that."

"Like what?"

"Like when you come." He kissed her once more.

Her eyelids were heavy, yet Clare rolled to her side to watch Isaac. "That was really good."

He gave her a wide smile. "We are really good together."

Wrapping his arms around her middle, Isaac pulled Clare to him. They fit together perfectly, as if made for one another. Clare wanted to say or do something, but she was more than exhausted, and sleep came to claim her. As the last bit of consciousness faded, one word led her to her dreams. *Safe.*

Chapter 15

Filtered sunlight shone through the curtains, turning her hair that shade of gold that always made Isaac smile.

Was it wrong to want to hold on to the moment just a little bit longer? Was it horrible to create a place where it was just Clare and Isaac—and the rest of the world could keep spinning outside of their door? The condom began to leak, and Isaac supposed that he'd gotten his answer.

Slipping from the bed, he pulled the cowboy hat comforter over Clare. After placing a kiss on her head, he scooped up the pile of discarded clothes and doubled-timed it to the small bathroom. Isaac redressed in his boxers and jeans.

He wasn't sure what he noticed first. Was it that the air in the stuffy bathroom had grown softer? Or had he heard a breath? Seen a movement in the small mirror?

Lifting his eyes, he met her gaze through the mirror. Clare stood on the threshold, watching him. Her hair was tousled. Her lips were swollen from his kisses. She was clad only in the comforter and, honestly, Isaac had never seen anyone look more beautiful. He dropped his gaze.

Throughout the day, he'd come to realize one important truth. He was drawn to Clare. Yet, it was more than her looks or her mind or her sense of nobility. It was that being with Clare let Isaac be a decent man once again.

He wanted to tell her all that and more. He said, "You need to use the bathroom? I can get out of here, if you do."

Use the bathroom? Great way to woo a lady, Patton. Was there a less romantic phrase ever evented?

"I'm okay," she said.

They'd just had sex—no, that didn't do justice to the passion and pleasure that had passed between them. He really should say something. But what? Especially since his opening salvo for romance was all about using the loo.

He tried to find the right way to tell her how he felt. That after months of pretending to be someone who didn't care, Isaac had become apathetic. What's worse, he worried that his apathy had made him a lesser person. "The fact that you saw me as nice or kind gave me back a piece of myself that I thought was gone forever."

He let the fabric of his sentence unravel and hoped that she would pick up the thread.

Mutely, she watched him.

"Say something."

Clare stepped forward and placed her hand on the side of his face. "You are a good man. I know."

She let the blanket slip from her body. The fabric pooled around her feet. How had he gotten so lucky?

Isaac moved to Clare and placed his mouth on hers. They backed up into the wall. The kiss was hard and meant to claim. Hell, he was hard again as well. And what it wanted was Clare. He broke the embrace and found another condom—his last—in his wallet. With his mouth on hers again, he unbuttoned the fly of his jeans. He rolled on the condom and gripped Clare's rear.

She wrapped her legs around his hips, gloriously opening herself to him. He entered her in one deep stroke.

"Oh, Isaac," she moaned.

God, he loved hearing her say his name. Or to feel her breath on his shoulder. He remembered where and how she liked to be touched and reached between their bodies. He found the top of her sex and rubbed. Her muscles contracted around him as she neared another climax.

Isaac knew he wasn't far behind.

He pumped his hips, driving into Clare, as her moans of ecstasy echoed in the small room. She raked her nails over his back as she came.

He was close, so close. Pressing his lips on hers again, Isaac slipped his tongue into her mouth. They kissed and his world shrank until it contained only him and her.

As he came, Isaac realized that for months he'd been pretending to be something that he wasn't—until all that was left of Isaac was the shell of his former self. Yet, Clare had somehow filled him. Or maybe, she'd revived a part of him that had long been dormant. For the first time in months, Isaac found himself.

If Decker believed in anything beyond his own superiority, he'd have seen the past few hours as being fueled by sheer luck. Since leaving Encantador, he'd stolen and ditched three different vehicles. The last one was a pickup truck parked in the lot of a bar. He'd driven that truck to a secluded house at the end of a mile-long driveway. He now stood in the bathroom of that house with the shades drawn. Nearby, several flies droned in the late afternoon.

There were no neighbors, just an old dog that had been chained to the porch. The woman of the house must've been the vain sort. Her medicine cabinet was filled with dark brown hair dye and more cosmetics than a typical drugstore.

Not only had there been enough color for Decker's hair, but there was enough dye leftover to color the stubble on his cheeks and chin. True, he didn't have a full set of whiskers, but the skin beneath was stained and gave a passing appearance of a dark beard and mustache. A brown cosmetic pencil gave him a thick brow, and he decided to take it with him. Surely, he'd find a use for it along the way.

He donned a large flannel shirt and pants that were several sizes too big. He tucked a bed pillow into both. The added girth changed his body shape. He slipped on a set of reading glasses, before adding a baseball cap in blaze orange as the finishing touch. Standing in the bathroom, he examined himself in the mirror.

"Damn." Decker admired his disguise. He was a whole new man.

From the bathroom, he walked down a short hallway to the kitchen. With each step, he tried to adopt the stride of one who was heavier and older. A crockpot filled with chili sat on the counter. He found a box of crackers in the cabinet and a block of cheese in the refrigerator.

Whoever had made the chili was a good cook—and that was actually lucky. He finished one bowl of chili and then started on another. While eating, he planned and reflected.

Decker was surprised that the police knew all about him. And now, they knew he'd killed the woman in Mercy.

The blonde woman he'd attacked today was another problem. Certainly, she'd spoken to the police, and even now, every cop in southern Texas was looking for Decker—and likely had some half-assed ID for him, too. Although it didn't matter. He was done with this part of Texas—or he would be soon.

To stay one step ahead of the police, Decker needed funds—specifically the money Ryan owed to him. After one last stop in Mercy, he'd disappear.

Placing his empty bowl in the sink, Decker returned to the master bedroom. From the closet, he took two more pairs of pants and several button-up shirts. Certainly, the man—whoever he was—wouldn't mind lending his clothes to Decker.

He walked by the bathroom and pulled back the shower curtain. The couple lay in the tub, arms and legs tangled. Their life's blood now black. A spider crawled over the husband's face before disappearing into his hair.

Pulling the curtain shut, he thought of how the man had begged Decker not to do anything depraved to the woman he loved. As if Decker would ever find an old sow like that appealing. In the end, Decker was merciful. Two shots—both between the brows. The couple died within seconds of one another. He pulled the door closed.

In the kitchen once more, Decker slipped his newly acquired clothes into a plastic bag. Thank goodness the stove was gas. Then again, it's exactly what he expected this far from the main electrical grid. He turned on all the burners and the stink of rotten eggs filled the room. He also opened the gas valve for the oven. He picked up yesterday's newspaper and long-necked lighter. The last thing he did was grab a set of car keys from a pegboard on the wall.

With the fumes of natural gas filling the small house, Decker left through the front door. The old dog growled, showing a mouthful of discolored teeth. Decker crumpled up the newspaper, set it alight and let the bundle burn for a moment. Then, he threw the ball of flames into the house and pulled the door shut.

Keys in hand, he walked to the truck and started the engine. From the porch, the dog watched him with wide eyes—obviously aware that something was wrong.

For a moment, Decker was back at a similarly small house and a dog on a chain. To him, a young boy, the dog had been nothing but teeth and claws, and a dangerous beast on its best day. He hadn't understood that his fourth stepfather kept the dog hungry enough to be mean. Putting the car into Drive, he looked toward the road, but he couldn't take his foot off the brake.

A rawhide chew sat on the truck's floorboard. Decker slammed his fist in the steering wheel. "Dammit all to hell."

He shoved the gearshift into Park, grabbed the rawhide chew and opened the door. Striding up to the porch, he unwound the dog's chain and picked up a tin bowl filled with grimy water. "Come on." He gave the lead a tug.

The dog looked back at the house and dug his paws into the porch.

"They left you out here in the sun with only dirty water. That's no way to be treated. They didn't deserve you." Decker wasn't sorry that he'd killed the couple, but in hindsight a little bit of suffering might have been warranted. He tugged on the chain a second time and lifted the rawhide for the dog to see. "C'mon."

Head down, the dog ambled to the truck and jumped into the passenger seat. Decker slammed the door shut before rounding to the driver's side. He slid behind the steering wheel and pulled his own door closed. This time, when he put the gearshift into Drive, he let off the brake and drove down the road.

Tossing the chew into the passenger seat, he asked the dog, "What's your name, fella?" A round tag hung from a worn collar. "Old Blue," Decker read out loud. "It's an odd name for a brown dog."

Old Blue sighed in agreement.

There was a *whoosh* and Decker glanced into the rearview mirror. The house had caught fire and the windows exploded, black smoke billowing out into the gray light of the approaching storm. By the time the fire department arrived, Decker and Old Blue would be long gone.

Clare was in the thin space between sleep and wakefulness. In her dream, she was in London, encased in thick fog. Voices came to her. First was that of Dr. Garcia. *This woman has been disemboweled.*

And then, the tail end of the doctor's words were those of a killer. Decker said, *Being a killer is in my blood... It started generations ago with Old Jack. It's why I killed the redhead, too.*

She sat up, heartbeat racing. She knew why Trinity's wounds seemed so familiar—because they were. Clare looked around. She was still in the small hotel room with the saddle prints hanging on the wall. Outside, the wind howled—must be the storms promised by the TV news. She glanced at the bedside clock—5:17 p.m.

By her side, Isaac slept. With his head cradled in his arms, he snored softly. She knew that he'd been out the night before and imagined he was exhausted, but her revelation was too important to ignore.

She placed her hand on his arm. "Isaac. Wake up. I remembered something about Decker. I think it's important."

He opened his eyes with a sharp intake of breath. "What do you remember?"

"When we were in the kitchen." Clare could still feel the flames from the stove on her face. She inhaled and pushed the horror aside, focusing only on what was useful. With an exhale, she started over. "He said to me, *being a killer is in my blood... It started generations ago with Old Jack. It's why I killed the redhead, too."*

Isaac sat up and rubbed his face. *"Being a killer is in my blood,"* he repeated. "What's that supposed to mean?"

"I think I know."

"You know?" he asked, his tone incredulous.

Maybe knowing was too strong a term. "Let's say I have a hunch." Now what she needed was proof—and that meant getting her phone. Her tote bag sat on the table next to the TV. After the second round of lovemaking, Clare hadn't bothered to get dressed. She held the blanket under her arms, but her clothes were scattered across the floor.

Well, now wasn't the time for modesty. Naked, she rose from the bed and crossed the room to get her bag. Back at the bed, she slipped between the covers again. Inside her tote, she found her phone and pressed her thumb to the power button. The screen winked to life, and she accessed the motel's free Wi-Fi.

"Are you going to tell me about your hunch?" Isaac asked.

She entered several words into the search bar as she spoke. "It wasn't just what Decker said, but what he did to Trinity. The disemboweling, I mean." She pressed the spyglass icon. It took only minutes for over one-hundred thousand hits to appear. It was just as she'd suspected—and feared. Holding up the screen for Isaac to see, she said, "This is what he's doing."

He reached for the phone, his hand covering her own. He read the text, then met her gaze. "Everything you found is about Jack the Ripper. What does any of this have to do with Decker?"

"Trinity was killed and then disemboweled after her death." The more she spoke, the more certain she became of her hunch. "It's the same thing Jack the Ripper did to his victims."

"How do you know that?"

"A few years ago, Kyle and I went to England. When we were in London, we went on one of those Ripper tours. You know, you shlep all over Whitechapel, a guide shows people where crimes took place or bodies were found."

He considered her words, looking a little skeptical. "There are lots of other killings with postmortem mutilation. What makes you connect Jack the Ripper and Decker?"

"When we were…" The kitchen of the barbecue restaurant was the place that forever would be the source of Clare's nightmares. "Well, Decker told me he was like *Old Jack*. What other famous killer do you know of named Jack besides Jack the Ripper?"

Scrolling through her phone, he said nothing for a moment. "I'm not saying that the connection you've found is wrong. But I'm going to need more before I try to convince the FBI that Decker's started committing copycat killings based on murderer from Victorian England."

Was Isaac playing the devil's advocate in asking her for more facts? Or did he really not think her argument was compelling?

He continued, "Maybe a year of being alone was too much for Decker and he completely lost it. But it would explain why he's suddenly targeting women and not killing for a profit." Isaac paused. "I'll pass the information onto the Bureau. But I'll be honest, I hope that you're wrong."

Clare couldn't help it. She was offended by his remark. Sitting up taller, she gave him a side-eye. "Why's that?"

He held up her phone; the screen was filled with an article about the victims. "I'm no expert on Jack the Ripper but says here that his Autumn of Terror claimed the lives of five women. It means if Decker's copying the murders, then Trinity's death is just the beginning."

Isaac had to get in touch with Jason. Sure, the FBI would have to analyze Clare's theory. Even he agreed with her that Decker was copying Jack the Ripper's killing. After rising from the bed, he slipped into his boxer shorts. From there, he found his phone and sat back on the mattress.

He placed the call. His phone blared with three tones and a prerecorded message. *We're sorry but your call cannot go through.*

Looking over his shoulder, he glanced at Clare. She shrugged. "Weird. Try again."

He placed the call for the second time. It began to ring, the line filled with static.

Jason answered. "Isaac? Can you hear me?" In the background was a rushing noise. Immediately, Isaac pictured a locomotive rumbling past.

"I can hear you. Where are you?"

"I'm heading to the basement at my office building. Listen, San Antonio is under a state of emergency. Several tornados have touched down in the area. I'm not going to be able to send undercover agents to Mercy. Did you hear me? If you can get in touch with Ryan, you need to let him know."

"I can hear you," Isaac yelled into the phone. His chest tightened at the notion that Ryan would be left alone to deal with Decker.

"And one more thing," said Jason, his words breaking up as he spoke. "We found the safe house. It was just like he said, eight miles south of the border by where he dumped the phone. A team's ready to raid the place as soon as we can get there."

Isaac opened the drawer in the nightstand. There was a Bible, along with a pad of paper and a pen. "You got those coordinates for me?"

The phone beeped once. And the line went dead.

Isaac gripped the phone in his hand and cursed. "Dammit."

What was he supposed to do now? Did he stick with the original plan and stay in Encantador? Or did he go to Mercy and provide reinforcements for Ryan if—and when—Decker showed? Actually, Isaac didn't need to ask himself the question. He already knew what needed to be done.

"I'm going to Mercy." He stood and picked his pants up off the floor.

"Now?" Clare asked.

True, he wanted to be gone in the next few seconds—a minute at most. But Isaac had to think the scenario through. He needed to keep Clare safe and hidden. But where? He could leave her in Encantador and under the protection of the sheriff. Or did he take her with him to Mercy?

Or maybe it wasn't his decision to make.

"You heard what Jason said. I can't leave Ryan to deal with Decker alone. You still need protection. I can call Cafferty and request a deputy be placed on the street."

"Don't bother." Clare reached to the floor for her underwear. "I'm going with you."

Chapter 16

If Isaac's thinking about Decker's plans was right, the killer would still go to the House of Steele for his money. It meant that obviously Isaac couldn't work the bar, but would have to stay out of sight. If he waited in Ryan's office, he could arrest the killer when he arrived. As complicated as taking a hitman into custody would be, that was the easy part.

To Clare, he said, "In order to apprehend Decker, I'm going to hole up in Ryan's office. If you're in Mercy, I can't keep you with me. Newcombe has tried to kill you once. If he knows you're there, he'll try again."

"I can stay in your room," Clare suggested. "If the door's locked and the curtains are closed, he'd never even know that I was in town."

The situation was suboptimal, but her plan was decent. He nodded. "Let's get our stuff together and get out of here."

He redressed, putting on his jeans and shirt. Clare got her jeans from where they'd hung this whole time on a hook in the bathroom. She emerged a moment later, rubbing her hands on the front of her legs. "They're still damp, but they'll work."

"Don't forget your bag. Make sure you have the phone and the flash drive."

She picked up her tote bag and looked inside. "I've kept both of those safe for so long, it'd be a pity to lose them now." She looked at Isaac and met his gaze. "Now's not the time, I know. But I like your plan—law enforcement and media. It's better than what I have been doing. Which is basically hide and hope Kyle and his family never find me."

"We'll talk about this later." Maybe once the FBI agents arrived in Mercy, Isaac would take Clare back to San Antonio with him. Hell, he might bring her home for Christmas. He had no right to think about the holidays, or what sort of changes Clare might bring to his life—or he to hers. Not yet.

Not until the job was done.

Both keycards lay on the end table. He grabbed those along with the scant notes from his phone call with Jason. "Let's get out of here."

He pulled the door open. A gust of wind swirled through the room. The first thing Isaac noticed was the sky. It had gone from clear blue to roiling with clouds of gray-green. As every good Texan knew, a sky like that was a problem. "We might not have to worry about Decker showing up. Those are tornado clouds."

"I didn't think it was tornado season," said Clare, raising her voice to be heard over the wind.

"There's no season for anything anymore. Best to get back to Mercy and hunker down." He reached for Clare's hand. She slipped her palm into his and squeezed. Head down and shoulder into the gale, he moved down the walkway to the motel's office. He pulled the door open. The wind jerked it hard from his grasp and it slammed into the wall.

He waited for Clare to enter the building before following and pulling the door shut.

"Quite a night out there," said the desk clerk. "Although it's just wind now, but a storm's coming up from Mexico." A radio sat on a desk and blared the Emergency Broadcasting System's signal. A mechanized voice announced severe weather for the listening area. The clerk watched the radio as the warning played. He turned back to Isaac and Clare. "See?"

"We're getting out of here." He set the room keys on the counter. "Much obliged."

"You sure? It's much too risky to be out on the roads now." He gestured to the radio. "There's likely going to be shelter sirens going pretty soon."

Isaac couldn't leave Ryan to face Decker alone. If they left now and he drove fast, they'd be in Mercy before the worst of the weather hit. "I'm positive. What do I owe you?"

"Nothing. The room was covered by the sheriff's department." Isaac opened the door and the clerk called out, "Merry Christmas."

"Happy holidays," said Clare as they stepped back into the coming storm.

True, downtown Encantador wasn't big. But Isaac had left his truck parked in front of the diner. What had been an easy walk this morning was now treacherous. The street was empty, and all the businesses were closed. A plastic garbage can tumbled down the middle of the road. A streetlight hung above an intersection and swayed drunkenly in the brutal winds.

A fat raindrop hit the sidewalk as a fork of lightning illuminated the sky. A minute later, thunder sounded. Isaac gripped Clare's hand harder. "Can you run?"

She took off sprinting, pulling him along. The rain began to fall harder and faster. They came up next to the truck on the passenger side. He worked the key into the lock and pulled the door open for Clare. She slipped inside and slammed the door shut. Rainwater dripped from Isaac's hair. He wiped his face with a damp hand and moved to the driver's side. Once inside the car, he started the engine and backed out of the parking space.

He didn't know what waited for them in Mercy. And now he had to pray they'd make it there.

Kyle Chamberlain pulled into an empty parking spot at the Saddle Up Inn as the dark gray sky turned black. Pulling the phone from his pocket, he sent his father a one-word text. Here.

It had been a horrendous day of travel. Booking his flight from John Glenn International last minute, meant he had fly coach the whole way. From Ohio he made it to San Antonio in under five hours—even with a plane change in Atlanta. Once in Texas, he'd rented a car. While driving to Encantador, he'd fought deteriorating weather the whole way.

After turning off the engine, he stepped into the parking lot. His hands were sore. His knees ached. His head hurt and he could use a drink. The wind blew and a cold rain fell, a rivulet snaking down his back.

He ran for the office and pulled the door open.

A man with a round face and glasses to match stood behind the counter. "Good evening. You need a room?" he asked Kyle. "You're in luck. A couple just left."

What Kyle needed was information. He opened his phone and found a photo of Clare. He looked at her picture, his chest tightening with emotion. "I'm looking for my wife. Have you seen her?"

The man leaned forward to get a closer look at the phone. He sniffed. "I really can't talk about our guests."

I'll take that as a yes. "I'm sure you're very good at your job." He shoved the phone into his pocket and removed a wad of bills he kept secured with a money clip. Kyle peeled off $300. "It's important that I talk to my wife." He held up his hands like he was surrendering—it was just a happy coincidence that the man could see the money. "Her father had a heart attack," Kyle lied. Clare's dad had been gone for years. "I knew Clare would be here and it's important to me that I tell her myself."

"Well." The man put a book on the counter.

Was Kyle supposed to slip the money under the book? He shrugged and placed the cash under the novel.

"She's not here anymore, but you missed her by less than fifteen minutes."

Damn. "Where was she headed?"

"That I don't know."

But there was something else the man had said. *A couple just left.* Was Clare with another man? Kyle ground his back teeth together. Not only had his wife left him, but she was with a guy. Sure, he'd been upset before but now, he was furious.

He turned from the desk and walked across the small lobby. He jerked the door open.

"Merry Christmas," the clerk called after Kyle.

"Yeah, yeah. Merry freaking Christmas to you, too."

He ran through the deluge to his car and pulled open the door. He slid inside and cursed. What was he supposed to tell his father now? That not only had Clare stolen vital information about the company, but she had already had sex with some other guy?

He slammed his palm onto the steering wheel. Pain radiated from the heel of his hand and into his wrist. According to the desk clerk, he'd only missed her by minutes, but those minutes were valuable. By now, Clare could be in a hundred different places.

Or could she?

It wasn't like there were highways and roads all over the place. In truth, Clare could have gone anywhere but he doubted that she'd go far with the weather getting worse by the second.

He took out his phone. After opening a mapping app, he looked for towns within fifty miles. He counted seven, with the closest being a hamlet called Mercy—only thirty miles away.

It made sense to start his search in Mercy. Once he found his ex-wife, he'd convince her to come back to Columbus and let life be good—like it was before she found the damn memos. He'd talk nice to her and convince her of his love. He'd have to convince his father that Clare was loyal to the Chamberlain name—and it might mean cleaning up the contaminated soil without involving the government. But Kyle was sure that both his father and Clare would come around.

Unless Clare really was with another guy—and then, there'd be hell for her to pay.

Decker Newcombe found a secluded spot off the road that gave him a complete view of Mercy. The wind buffeted the truck, rocking it from side to side. Rain fell in sheets. Yet, from his vantage point, he could see everything. The plan was simple—find Ryan. Get the money. But one lesson he'd learned from the hit in Pleasant Pines was that even the simplest plans could get jacked up. Best to watch and wait. Settling back against the seat, Decker knew that it was going to be a long night.

Old Blue lifted a paw. A box of dog biscuits that Decker'd found behind the truck's bench seats sat between Decker's knees.

"You hungry, boy?" He held up a biscuit and the dog whined and nosed the treat but didn't take it. Decker set it on the seat and the dog gobbled up the food.

Another thing he had found stowed behind the seat was a set of binoculars. He held those as well and brought them to his eyes. Decker scanned the parking lot between the motel and the bar. Only a few cars were parked near the lot, which suited him just fine. The fewer people around meant fewer variables.

A set of headlights cut through the storm and Decker watched as a truck pulled into the lot. From the shadows in the truck, he could tell there was a driver and a passenger. They parked not by the bar but the motel. He lifted the binoculars to his eyes again. A man opened the driver's door and jumped from the truck.

Pulling the ocular from his eyes, Decker looked again.

He knew the guy. It was the man from Encantador with the gun—he was the one who stopped Decker from killing the woman. That must mean...

He turned his attention to the passenger side and watched as the blonde exited the truck. With a bag held tight to her chest, she ran to the motel's overhang. There, she smoothed her sodden hair from her face and spoke to the man. She pointed to a room but walked to another. The man produced a key and opened the door.

The woman stepped inside, and the man followed.

"Old Blue, looks like were in luck."

True, the man was most likely a cop—and if the cops were in Mercy, then Decker wouldn't get his cash. But in Encantador, he'd had no choice but to let the blonde woman go. She was unfinished business—and Decker hated unfinished business.

Now, though, he had a second chance. And this time, he'd take care of the blonde—for good.

The money could wait.

Isaac's room was the same exact size as the one where Clare had stayed the previous night. Yet, the dimensions were where the similarities ended. For starters, Isaac's room wasn't furnished like a hotel. And she was thankful that Isaac's living conditions were a little more, well, livable.

An unmade bed sat against the far wall. Next to it was a dresser. A recliner was tucked into the corner near the air-conditioning unit. Next to both was a metal footlocker that doubled as a table with a lamp. In the opposite corner sat a kitchen cart with a microwave and a coffee maker. A small refrigerator—the kind Clare had used in her college dorm room all those years ago—was beside the cart.

"It's cozy," she said, sitting in the chair. "I like it."

"I hate to just leave you here, but I need to let Ryan know that I'm back and that no reinforcements will show up tonight."

Lines of worry creased the corner of Isaac's eyes. She could guess what was bothering him. Without the FBI's help, the people of Mercy were on their own. "Don't worry, I know the plan. I stay put in the room. You'll go to the bar and watch from the office."

"Correct," said Isaac. "I want to do a little more research on Decker, too. See if there's something in his file linking him to Jack the Ripper that I might have overlooked before." He opened the footlocker and removed a sleek metallic laptop.

"You wouldn't happen to have another of those, would you?" she asked. "When I worked for the EPA, I wrote a few press releases. Since the media is where we'll start, I should...well, get started."

The lid to the footlocker was still open. "I don't have another laptop, but I have a tablet computer. It has a word-processing program." He rummaged through the trunk for a moment and then handed the device to Clare. "It should have a full charge."

Clare wasn't sure how to act in this situation. Part of her wanted to bawl and beg that Isaac stay with her. The other part—she supposed that independent streak that always wanted to do things on her own—wanted to remain calm. Yet, it would be stupid to be casual about a man as dangerous and deadly as Decker. "One more thing," she said, her mouth suddenly dry. "Do you have a gun I can keep with me?"

Isaac said nothing. Yet, from the trunk he removed a black metal safe with a fingerprint scanner. Isaac placed his thumb on the pad and the lock clicked open. "This isn't the same model we used earlier today, but the concept is the same."

"All guns are always loaded," she said, paraphrasing Isaac's first rule of firearm safety. "Put the sight over the target—which is the center mass. Pull the trigger. Shoot."

"And..." he encouraged.

"And never take a gun out unless you plan to use it."

"Correct." He set the gun on the nightstand. "You have your phone, right? There's no landline in this place, but if you need me, call. That is, if you can get a signal in this weather. I'll be at the bar and can get to you in seconds." He paused. "Are you sure that you're okay with this? I can stay here. Ryan can wait with us."

The offer of company was tempting.

She lifted the computer. "I've got a project. That'll help keep my mind off what happened. Besides, once the storm passes, it won't take long for the FBI to get here, right? I only need to wait a few hours." Then again, she knew that it took only seconds to change a life forever.

Isaac slipped the laptop into a backpack, also stored in the footlocker.

"What all do you keep in there?" she asked, half joking, half curious. "So far, there's been a laptop, a tablet, a gun and now a backpack."

"Let's just say this is my whole office in a box. I have lots of goodies. I'll show you—"

"Tomorrow. I will be fine, honestly."

"Honestly?"

After everything that had happened today, she suspected that she wouldn't actually be *fine* for a long while. Still, she said, "Now go."

"Do you need anything else?" He pointed to the kitchen area. "There's food. Water. Beer and juice in the fridge."

"I'll help myself if I get hungry." But did she need anything? Her suitcase was still in Trinity's room. Right now, Clare would love to get out of her clothes and change into something more comfortable. She was supposed to stay in the room and hidden, but surely she could walk down three doors and get her stuff.

"But..."

"But, what? I didn't say but?"

"I can see it on your face. You want to ask for something, so ask."

"My suitcase is in the other room," she began.

Isaac held out his palm. "Give me the key. I won't be gone for a minute."

She found the key and her cell phone in her tote. After handing the key to Isaac, she set the phone next to the handgun. As her fingertips grazed his palm, her hand filled with that same electric energy. It traveled up her arm and around to her chest until her heart skipped a beat. Yet, this time it was different. She now knew what his lips felt like on hers. She'd touch him and been touched by him in return. She knew that he fit inside her perfectly and that he gave a primal growl the moment he came. It was more than the raw sexuality of their coupling. Or even that Clare had come to Mercy lonely and alone. In Isaac, she'd found someone she could trust.

Clare had stood far too long while holding on to the key. She withdrew her hand. "Thanks."

"Lock the dead bolt and the chain when I leave. Don't open it for anyone but me."

"Got it." Clare stood by the door and held the handle as Isaac stepped out into the rain. She closed and locked the door. Her chest tightened and she could barely draw a breath. Pressing her forehead into the door, she forced an inhale. One, two, three. Exhale. One, two, three. On her tenth round of breathing, there was a rapping sound on the door.

"It's me. Let me in."

She recognized Isaac's voice. Her fingers trembled as she fought with the chain lock. "Just a second." Once that was free, she unlocked the dead bolt and pulled the door open.

He wheeled her suitcase into the room. "Here you go. Can you hand me my backpack?"

She maneuvered the suitcase into the room and moved onto the bed, where she picked up Isaac's computer bag. She held it out to him, and he took it from her hand.

Isaac stood at the door. Behind him, wind blew the rain sideways. Lightning flashed, illuminating an empty parking lot. He pulled her to him, placing his lips on hers. "Take care of yourself, Clare," he said, speaking into the kiss.

"You, too."

She locked the door behind him and then watched through a crack in the curtain as Isaac ran to his truck. There, he removed his gun from the glove box. He slipped it into the waistband at the back of his jeans and then sprinted into the rain. She stayed at the curtain and watched as his form blended with the darkness, realizing that she felt more for Isaac than simple lust. She liked his company. He was a good man who always did the right thing.

Had she come to care for him?

Then again, she shouldn't torture herself with wanting a relationship, especially since she had problems beyond Decker Newcombe. And he was a problem enough. If she took Isaac's advice, she was about to go to war with her former husband and his family. Even though the Chamberlains weren't as bloody as Decker, they were no less brutal and dangerous.

She had to get ready for the battle to come.

Chapter 17

Kyle stood at the gas pump and seethed. Across the road was a rattrap of a motel. Despite the storm, he'd seen it all so clearly. Clare stood at the door to a room and kissed another man. The guy had run to the bar, leaving her alone. After paying for his gas, he drove across the street and parked. Oblivious of the rain, he strode to the door and knocked.

"Clare? You in there? It's me. Kyle."

There was a window next to the door. He waited and watched. The curtains twitched. She'd peeked out and seen him.

He waited a minute. Then a minute more.

"Clare?"

Nothing. Not a sound. Kyle reached for the knob. It was stuck. He jiggled the handle. He tried to keep his temper in check, but he could feel the heat rising from his middle. Despite the cold rain, he started to perspire. Her new friend couldn't buy her all the things that Kyle could afford. So, what was she doing with some oaf who probably smelled like chewing tobacco and motor oil?

Slamming his palm on the door, he spit, "Open the damn door, right this freaking minute."

Nothing, still.

Well, Kyle refused to be ignored. He was going to get into that room one way or another—and then, he'd make Clare sorry.

There were no customers at the House of Steele. The weather kept everyone at home, even though the bar, tattoo parlor and motel were made of cinderblock and would withstand high winds and blowing debris. In truth, Isaac would have preferred a packed house to an empty room. With witnesses, Decker would have to be cautious. Without anyone around, Isaac would be forced to face the killer alone.

No, that wasn't necessarily true. He had Ryan and Clare.

Having people who he could rely on was a forgotten notion. For so long, he'd wanted to be a loner. But now? Well, he couldn't worry about now—not when the killer was still out there, somewhere.

At the moment, Isaac and Ryan were in Ryan's office at the back of the bar. And office was a generous term for the converted closet where the legitimate businesses were run. A filing cabinet sat in the back corner. In the middle of the room was a desk, along with a computer. The monitor was on. The screen was filled with four different pictures from security cameras. The bar's front door, exterior and interior. There was also a camera above the entrance to the tattoo parlor and one that gave a panoramic view of the parking lot. It was difficult to see anything other than rain, but if someone approached the building, they'd have time to react.

The light from a single lamp illuminated a pool in the middle of the desk. The rest of the room was shrouded in shadows. Isaac's gun was still tucked into the back of his jeans. Ryan held a shotgun, taken from behind the bar, across his lap.

Isaac's laptop was also on the desk and was connecting to the internet.

"You came back," said Ryan. From his mocking tone, he could tell that a joke was on the horizon. "You miss me?"

He'd already given the other man a rundown of the most recent events—including the hard truth that reinforcements couldn't get to Mercy. He also told him of the possible connection between Decker's most recent murders and Jack the Ripper. Instead of repeating the facts, he said, "Yeah, I missed you." And then, "You've known Decker for a long time. You ever notice a fascination with Jack the Ripper?"

"The only person who fascinates Decker is Decker."

The computer finally connected with the internet and Isaac was able to access his remote server for Texas Law. Isaac entered the secure site. "I get updates if anything's added to Decker's file. There hasn't been much recently, but let's start there. We might find something that was missed before."

Decker's mug shot was pinned to the top of an electronic document. It listed the crimes for which he'd been charged, and any time served. Isaac couldn't see anything in his criminal past that connected him to the Victorian era serial killer.

"You know Decker better than anyone," said Isaac. "When he attacked Clare in the restaurant, he said *being a killer is in my blood. First, there was the Old Jack. It's why I killed the redhead, too.* That mean anything to you?"

Ryan scratched the stubble on his chin. "When he called the other night, he asked if I knew anything about DNA testing. It made no sense to me then, but maybe there's a genetic predisposition to violence."

"You two grew up together. What were his parents like?"

"For a while, we lived near each other. We were kids and the same age, so we played together. As far as his parents…" Ryan shook his head. "His mom worked odd jobs to make ends meet. She had a tendency to get involved with guys who got violent with her and with Decker. I never met his real dad."

Isaac continued to scan through the file. He stopped. A new document had been attached. He only had a moment to wonder why there'd been no notification. Then again, it wasn't really an update to the case and therefore hadn't been flagged. *DNA Analysis, Newcombe, Decker.*

Ryan was reading the screen, too. "What the hell?"

Hell might be right. He clicked the link. It was a DNA profile, much like those done for a genealogy service. It listed places where genetic makeup originated, along with a list of ancestors. One name, Jeremiah Newcombe, was highlighted and an additional notation was attached. *Genetic link to sociopathy?*

Ryan already had out his phone. "This answers the question as to why Decker's become a copycat killer." He'd done his own internet search for the name Jeremiah Newcombe. The first hit came from an article published several years prior. *Identity of Jack the Ripper discovered through DNA.* "I wonder how he found out. Do you think he hacked into a computer system, or does he have a mole in Wyoming who's feeding him information?"

Both were interesting scenarios. But in reality, the *how* didn't matter nearly as much as the *why*. Decker was undoubtedly still out there. It was only a matter of time before he killed again—unless Isaac found him first and brought the murderer to justice.

Clare looked at the dark screen on her phone, not sure if she wanted to curse or cry. She'd left the device on with the internet connected for hours. Now there was no battery left and she couldn't call Isaac.

Outside, Kyle slammed his fist against the door. The frame rattled. "I saw you with him, you know. I saw you kiss that guy."

She found the charger in her bag and plugged in the phone. The screen winked to life. A message, gray words on a gray screen, appeared.

No service available.

"Come on," she urged the phone.

Kyle's voice came from the window. "Is that why you ran off, Clare. To be with that bastard? I loved you. I still do."

Clare might not know everything about love, but she did know that whatever possessiveness Kyle felt for her was the opposite of caring. She couldn't help but speak up after that baseless accusation. "You know why I left. I heard you on the phone with your father while talking about the little *accident* you two were planning for me."

"And to think, I came all this way to try and work things out with you." He gave a mirthless laugh. "My dad was right about you from the beginning. You are more trouble than you're worth."

"Why'd you track me down, then? You didn't need to come and find me."

Her words were followed by the crack of lightning and rumble of thunder. Was Kyle thinking about what she'd said? Had he left? She wanted to look outside—just to see where he'd gone. She moved slowly to the window and reached for the curtain. She pulled it away from the wall at the same moment the glass shattered. A brick skittered across the floor, bouncing off the footlocker.

Kyle shoved his hand through the broken pane, reaching for Clare. She dove toward the nightstand and snatched up the gun. She turned back to the window as Kyle pulled back the curtains. A long gash was open on the back of his hand, and it dripped blood onto the sill.

Clare remembered her brief shooting lessons. Isaac's words came back to her. If you take out a firearm, it's because you plan to *eliminate a threat. Aim for the center mass.* She lined up the sights with Kyle's chest.

"Get back in your car, Kyle, and go. I'm not leaving with you now or ever."

"That's where you're wrong," he began, lifting his foot to climb in through the broken window.

She fired once, striking the wall next to his head. "That's your warning. Come any closer and the next bullet will go through you."

His eyes went wide. "You wouldn't dare," he said, perching himself on the sill.

She fired again. A bullet struck Kyle in the shoulder. The impact shoved him back. With a curse, he tumbled out onto the sidewalk. Clare rushed for the window.

On the ground, her ex-husband held an arm across his abdomen and wheezed. "Christ! You shot me. You really shot me! Damn. I'm bleeding."

Her hand began to tremble. Yet, she pointed the barrel to the floor—just like Isaac had that morning. For a moment, Clare's ears buzzed and her eyesight went blurry. She blinked hard and forced herself to focus.

A large man in a hunter's cap lumbered across the parking lot. The rain fell and he seemed to materialize from the water. "I seen it all," he shouted to be heard above the wind. "I saw him break that window and you shoot." He had a phone in his hand. "I'll call 9-1-1."

Clare moved closer to the window. Without the pane, wind and rain blew into the room. "Go to the bar. Tell Isaac to come here." Lighting danced along the horizon.

The man placed a finger to his ear. "What'd you say? I'm hard of hearing. Speak up."

A rumble of thunder filled the night. She moved closer, leaning toward the man. "Go to the bar. Tell Isaac to come here."

It was then that he struck. Reaching for her arm, the

man pulled Clare through the window. A shard of glass caught her arm and she cried out in pain and anger.

Wrenching back, she held the gun by her free hand and lifted her arm. The man gripped the gun's barrel and flipped the firearm to face Clare.

"Who are you?" she asked, but she saw his eyes and knew.

"Miss me much?" he asked.

Before she could answer or even scream, he brought the butt end of the gun down on her head. For a minute, Clare saw nothing other than a blinding flash of white. The darkness encroached from all sides. She slipped down, down, down into oblivion.

Isaac looked up from his laptop and stared at Ryan. "Was that gunfire?"

Ryan was looking at the computer monitor and the stream coming from the safety cameras. "Three thunderclaps in a row? Unlikely. But I don't see anything." He tapped on the keyboard and brought up another set of cameras. There, on the feed from the front of the motel, was a big guy standing outside of Isaac's room. On the ground was a body. The guy lifted a gun. The picture was grainy, but there was enough detail for Isaac to know—the guy on the ground had been shot. His body went limp, and a pool of blood spread from behind his head.

Isaac was on his feet and sprinting from the office and across the empty bar before he even realized that he'd moved. He ran into the night in time to see a set of taillights swerving out of the parking lot and onto the road. It skidded on the wet pavement and disappeared, as if swallowed by the storm.

He kept running and slid to a stop on the sidewalk next to his room. The person who'd been shot was male. Isaac had never seen him before. There was a bullet wound to his shoulder and another through the center of his forehead. The curtains from Isaac's room billowed, blown by the wind. The glass pane was broken.

And Clare was missing.

The door was still closed and locked. At the window, he grabbed a handful of fabric and pulled the curtains and the rod out of the wall. The room was empty. He turned to the road. The car that had sped away was long gone.

Ryan, shotgun held tight to his chest, ran through the rain. "I saw it all on the camera." After placing the gun on the ground, muzzle pointed toward the parking lot, he knelt next to the body. In the dead guy's pocket, he found a wallet. "His name is Kyle Chamberlain from Columbus, Ohio." He looked up at Isaac. "He must be related to Clare."

How Kyle had found Clare was definitely a mystery. But the one he wanted to solve was where she'd gone. Ryan continued, "The big guy climbed in through the window and got Clare. She wasn't moving, but I don't know if she's dead or not."

Isaac threw a curtain panel over Clare's ex. Eventually, he'd call the sheriff and let him know about the homicide. "He's changed his look again, but we both know who took Clare." His throat was raw with terror and dread.

Ryan stood. "You think it's Decker?"

"You don't?" Isaac fished his keys from his pocket. "I'm going to get her back. You can come if you want. Or stay and call the cops. Tell them everything we know."

Reaching for his shotgun, Ryan stood. "You gotta be kidding me. I'm coming with."

Isaac held out the keys. "Start my truck. I need something from my room."

He hated wasting precious time in the search for Clare. But without his equipment, he'd never find her. Climbing through the broken window, he opened his footlocker. It really was what he'd told Clare—his workplace in a box. Instead of office equipment—printers, monitors and pens—Isaac had a sleek black drone that was controlled by an app on his phone. He also had a Smith and Wesson 500, along with an entire box of ammo.

He grabbed two bulletproof vests and a pair of dark jackets. Not bothering with the window, he unlatched each of the door's locks and walked to his truck. Ryan sat in the passenger seat, and he opened the door as he approached. "What's that?"

Isaac handed over the gear. Wiping the rain from his face, he jogged around the grille to the driver's side.

He backed out of the parking lot and followed the truck. His wipers moved back and forth across the windshield at top speed, but it did little to keep the rain off the glass. "That is a military-grade drone." He continued, "This can go twenty miles per hour and is whisper-silent. Two cameras—one in the front and one in the rear. It has a range of ten miles and a battery life of ninety minutes." He started the dual propellers and the drone lifted from the back of the truck. "It sends back pictures in real time to my phone." He held out the screen for Ryan to see.

"I changed my mind," said Ryan. "I don't want a gaming system for Christmas—I want that."

Isaac wasn't in the mood for jokes.

"How're we going to find Decker? For the drone to be effective, we have to be close to our target."

"We'll be close." He shared what Jason had said about Decker's possible safe house being eight miles from where they'd discovered the phone. He ignored the aching in his chest and the gritty burning in his eyes. "We'll find Clare and bring Decker to justice in the process."

Yet, his words weren't entirely true. Isaac wasn't interested in cold and impartial justice anymore. What he was looking for was closer to vengeance. Decker had harmed the woman he loved more than once—now it was personal.

He tightened his grip on the steering wheel. Did he really love Clare?

Maybe he did. All he could do now is hope that he found her before it was too late to tell her.

Clare's eyes were still closed and yet her head throbbed with each beat of her heart. Her arms and legs were stiff and sore. Then, she recalled those harrowing seconds outside of Isaac's room and the terror came back. Her heart began to hammer against her chest and Clare struggled to sit up.

That's when she realized that she was bound—wrist and ankle—to something hard. A table?

"Oh, you're awake."

Clare looked to the left. Decker stood next to a shelf and smiled. His cheerful tone and friendly manner made her shiver.

"What do you want?" Her tongue was thick.

"You seem like a smart woman. I'm sure you've figured it out."

She had. "You're going to kill me. But why?" She bit back a sob. Clare refused to let this animal break her will.

Her arms and legs were tied to a table with worn rope. They were in a small room. A single electric bulb hung from a wire. Behind Decker was a counter. Upon the counter were several knives. Clare swallowed.

"There's more to your death than just murder." Decker picked up a knife. The razor-sharp edge glinted in the weak light. "Killing you will link my name with the most famous serial killer of all time. But I won't hide behind a pseudonym like he did."

Is that what motivated him? "So you're doing this for what? Fame? You want notoriety?"

Decker chuckled. "Fame is fleeting. I plan to be a legend. In a way, you're lucky. People will remember your name, too. So, I gotta ask you, Clare, are you ready for your death to make you immortal?"

Isaac drove through the storm to the exact place that he and Ryan had found Decker's phone. He parked on the side of the road.

"I'm going to call Jason once more." So far, his cell service had been disrupted by the storm. He placed the call. Immediately, three tones sounded. He didn't wait for the recorded voice to tell him that his call could not go through. He cursed and shoved his phone into his jacket pocket.

"Grab that drone," he said to Ryan. For the ride, it'd been stored on the passenger floorboard. "And come with me." He stepped out into the storm. Cold rain soaked his clothes and left his fingers stiff.

Carrying the drone, Ryan followed Isaac onto the empty road.

Black as a midnight sky, the drone was equipped with four rotors and two cameras. Isaac explained how the device worked. "It's controlled with an app on my phone." He continued, giving voice to his plan, "With the wind and the rain, these are crap conditions. But we'll send this bad boy up and see what we can. Best luck, we find the safe house. Worst luck, it gets blown to the ground and we find nothing." Which would mean that Isaac had no way to locate Clare.

After setting the unmanned craft on the asphalt, he opened the app. He tapped on the phone's screen and the propellers began to spin, their rotations a continual blur. Isaac entered the command and the device shot into the sky. After a few seconds, it blended with the endless sea of night.

The phone's screen was filled with an aerial picture taken in night-mode. Right now, there was nothing to see but rain and the ever-changing horizon as the drone fought against the wind to stay level. They went back to the truck and slid inside. Isaac adjusted the heat to the inferno setting and held out his phone so Ryan could watch the drone's progress.

Like many of his ideas, this one had been bold, brash, and there wasn't a guarantee of success. It's just that his resources were limited, and time was essential. Because if they didn't find Clare soon, she might not be alive for much longer.

"Wait," said Ryan, pointing at the screen. "Can you go back? I think I saw something."

"What?" Isaac reversed the drone's path midflight.

"It was a line. It looked like a fence."

From thirty feet above the ground, the fence did look like a black line had been drawn across the landscape. "Good catch," said Isaac. "Let's see where this leads. Left or right?"

"Right," said Ryan.

Isaac flew the drone along the fencing another quarter mile until they spotted a gate, and beyond that a road. He followed the road and found a small house sitting on a bluff. Next to the shack was a generator. A pickup truck was parked next to the door—it was the same one from the footage taken at the House of Steele.

Isaac exhaled a breath that he didn't know he'd been holding. Despite the odds, they'd found Decker's safe house. "Now," he said, "Let's go save Clare."

Chapter 18

Isaac was not a praying kind of guy. Still, he thanked whatever deity controlled the weather. Near the safe house, the storm was lessening. The rain still fell in a sheet, but the wind had calmed. From his truck, he was able to control the drone and survey the house.

There was a rickety front door with a cylinder lock. The rest of the wall was adobe. At the back of the house, there was a window with a cracked and dirty pane. The room beyond was dark, yet the camera captured the interior, along with a dirty mattress covered with blankets and lumpy pillows. At the edge of the house, the drone rounded another corner and passed the right wall. There were no windows. No doors.

On the final wall, there was a single window. Isaac maneuvered the camera to get a view inside and his hands began to shake with cold fury.

Clare was strapped to a table. Sure, he was thankful to see that she was alive. But that relief only lasted for a few seconds. Beside her, a small counter was cluttered with knives. Decker stood next to her, a blade in his hand.

"I've seen enough," said Isaac, his voice tight.

Ryan was right beside Isaac. "What's the plan?"

He hated that they couldn't drive right to the door. But if Decker heard an auto approaching, he'd kill Clare. "We get in close to the house. I take the front door. You cover the back of the house." Isaac put the truck into Drive. "And then, I finish this—even if it means finishing Decker Newcombe."

Sure, it was tough talk. But Isaac couldn't help but wonder if his plan would be enough to save Clare.

Clare stared at the knife in Decker's hand. Her limbs went rigid with fear. For the past two months, she'd had little to live for. But when she met Isaac, all of that changed. He'd offered her help and despite herself, she'd accepted. She'd finally found a potential way out of the danger that had sent her on the run from her life and everything, everyone in it.

Sure, she always wanted to be strong and independent. Yet with Isaac, she'd learned what it was to be a partner with another, rather than just dependent. She wanted to see him again and tell him that even though they hadn't known each other a long time, he'd brought her from the edges of existence and back to the possibility of living a real life.

So, she couldn't just lay on the table and die. Thrashing, she strained against her bindings and hoped the ropes would break. It was no use.

Or was it? She pulled her left arm, her muscles straining, her joints aching. Then she went limp. The rope had stretched but not enough. She needed time and that meant she had to keep Decker talking. What was she supposed to say, since she knew next to nothing about the man... Wait. That wasn't true.

Clare understood Decker's motivations.

She began. "The last time I was in London, I went on a Ripper Tour, you know."

The knife in his hand wobbled. "A what?"

"That's what they're called. Ripper Tours. A guide leads a group through London to visit all the places associated with Jack the Ripper." She developed a rhythm. Pull. Release. Pull. Release. The old rope gave a little with each motion. Clare twisted her wrist and tried to work out of the knot.

Decker regarded her for a moment, and she froze.

He asked, "What did you see?"

Her pulse raced and sweat snaked down her back. "What did I see where?"

He sighed. "On the tour. What places did you visit?"

She began to work her arm back and forth again, the movements smaller this time. "They go to all the places where the victims were found. I mean, the crimes took place more than a century ago, so every place is something different now. One of the crime scenes has been turned into a parking lot." Pull. Release. Pull. Release. "Kind of a letdown."

Decker stared at her. His blue eyes had turned black.

For the first time in her life, Clare knew what it felt like to look at pure evil. "Do you think," he began, "that one hundred years from now, people will visit this run-down old shack? Will they come to look at the place where you died?"

Isaac and Ryan made good time. Light from the house leaked out from beneath the door and made it visible from over a hundred yards away. Without a word, they donned the body armor and black jackets. Blending with the night, they approached the shack.

Then, Isaac heard a dog barking and froze.

Ryan heard it, too. Both men dropped into the mud.

"What the hell was that?" Ryan whispered. "He's got a dog now? Since when is he an animal lover?"

Isaac listened to the sound carefully. "Sounded like it came from the house."

Ryan turned to Isaac. "But that's impossible."

The barking started again, louder this time and more insistent.

Isaac didn't pretend to know anything about serial killers, but he knew a lot about Decker Newcombe. "He doesn't seem like the kind to keep a dog."

Ryan whispered, "He's not." Pause. "Is it a wild dog?"

Isaac shrugged. Maybe it was or maybe it wasn't. Then again, who cared? "All I know is that the dog has ruined the element of surprise and..."

"And what?"

"And we can't wait any longer. If we're going to get to Clare in time, we have to get in there right goddamn *now*."

* * *

To prevent Old Blue from being underfoot as he worked, Decker had put the dog in the bedroom and closed the door. If truth be told, he had wondered more than once if he'd been prudent to save the dog's life.

Yet, as Old Blue barked and scratched and howled, he knew he'd been right to take the canine in.

"Someone's outside." He stared at the door. *Who the hell could have found this place?*

Looking at Clare, he ran the knife down her lips, grinning as her eyes grew even wider in fear. "Not. One. Word." He couldn't imagine who'd hear her in the storm—or who was even out there in this weather—but he wasn't taking any chances.

Moving to the window, he peered into the darkness. It was hard to see anything through the constant rain. Yet, the dog continued to bellow.

For the first time in years, Decker felt exposed. His skin crawled as if a thousand ants covered his body. He'd learned to trust his instincts and his gut told him there was something wrong.

Could the feds have located him? After all this time? But how? He'd been so careful, even after killing that woman in Mercy. Still…something didn't feel right…

He slowly moved to the door. Turning the handle, he pulled it open. There was nothing to see—beyond the night and the continual rain. Then, a flash of light. A blaze of fire. And pain that stole his breath as the shape of a man bore down on him.

With Decker's back to the table, Clare struggled to break free, even as the dog's barking became more frenzied. *Where in the hell had a dog come from?* Finally, she pulled her wrist from the rope. Flipping to her side, she started working on the other knot, glancing back at the door, when the gunshot rang out.

It was like a thunderclap had exploded in the small room. Decker spun in a drunken circle, as a red bloodstain bloomed on his chest and shoulder. He fell to his back and stared at nothing.

Isaac rushed through the door, covered in mud as Clare struggled to pull her hand from the rope. Smoke wafted from the barrel of the gun in his hand. Her eyes watered in relief that they were both safe. She was overwhelmed with another feeling as well. It was a deeper emotion, more personal, and wholly connected to Isaac.

"You came! How did you even find me?"

"I did. Now, let's get you out of here." Grabbing one of the knives from the counter, Isaac cut through the ropes at Clare's ankles.

Ryan followed Isaac into the room. He was covered in mud as well. Decker lay on the floor, as a pool of blood spread across the floor.

She wondered if Decker was finally dead. The notion left her lightheaded with disbelief, after everything they'd been through. Ryan bent to Decker's prone form. He grabbed the killer's wrist—presumably to feel for a pulse.

Which was when everything went to hell.

For Isaac, the struggle erupted in slow motion. Decker must've been waiting for just the right moment to jump, and when Ryan reached for his wrist, the killer rolled to his side, knife in hand. Yanking Ryan to the floor, the two men struggled as blood and mud flew everywhere.

Isaac rushed forward as the dog began to howl, the sound taking on a hollow quality as if they were all lost in a cave. Ryan screamed in agony as Decker swung the blade into his side up and under the body armor. The handle protruded haphazardly.

Then, Decker rose to his feet and staggered into the night.

Isaac fell to the floor beside Ryan, who was clearly in agonizing pain. But Ryan gritted his teeth and held onto the wall for support, trying not to pass out. "I'll be fine. Just catch Decker, dammit. Don't let him get away after all this!"

Clare was at Ryan's side. "I'll stay with him."

Ryan grimaced, "We'll keep trying to get a hold of Jason."

He gave a terse nod and ran into the storm. Earlier, he'd set the drone down next to the house. Thankfully, it was still there. Pulling his phone from his pocket, he turned on the rotors. Rain still fell, but the wind no longer blew. The device lifted straight into the air. With the cameras on, he watched and searched for signs of Decker.

He found him within minutes.

The hitman staggered across the uneven ground, less than a quarter mile from the house. Water dripped from his hair, but the rain wasn't enough to wash away the blood that was coming from his chest. Isaac watched as Decker stumbled to the ground. He never got up. He wasn't sure if his truck would make it over the uneven terrain. The last thing he wanted was to break down.

Isaac had no choice but to go after the hitman on foot. He sprinted into the desert. Within minutes, Isaac was soaked with rain and sweat both. He found the spot where Decker had fallen. Yet, the hitman was gone.

Clare found little in the small shack that was helpful. As she'd guessed, a dog was locked in the bedroom. It shied away from Clare when she opened the door, but eventually came to stand at her side as she rifled through Decker's room.

There was a dirty blanket, which she used to stanch the bleeding, and a pillow, which she placed behind Ryan's back.

"Is that better?" she asked as he settled against the pillow. She knew enough to leave the knife alone. Once it was removed, he'd start to bleed again.

"A little," he grimaced. "Thanks." The dog stood in the doorway that separated the main room from the bedroom. "How'd Decker end up with a dog, do you think?"

She had no idea and simply shook her head. "We should call someone. Sheriff Cafferty, maybe? Or the feds that Isaac's been working with."

"The feds are stuck in San Antonio with the storm." He held out his phone. "Encantador isn't too far away. Call the sheriff."

Clare found the contact information and placed the call. "This is Clare Chamberlain," she began as Mooky answered the phone. "There's been an incident..."

As she spoke, Ryan patted the floor. "Come here, boy." Head down, the dog ambled to Ryan's side and lay down.

Having given the sheriff all the pertinent information, she ended the call. Turning to Ryan, she said, "I think the dog likes you."

He scratched the dog's ears. "I've always wanted a dog."

Ryan's shotgun stood against the wall. She picked it up and cradled it against her chest.

"You know how to use one of those things?" he asked.

Not really, but she said, "Isaac taught me how to shoot a handgun."

"Well, careful with that thing. It has a nasty kick when it's fired."

She took note of his warning. "If Decker comes back, I'll be ready."

It wasn't Decker who returned to the shack, but after some time, the sheriff arrived, leading a long line of county vehicles with sirens and lights.

Clare met them outside. The rain still fell, and the wind still blew. But the worst of the storm was over.

Cafferty's cruiser was the first to stop near the door. "Christ almighty," he said getting out of his car. "You either have the best or worst luck in the world to tangle with that son of a bitch twice."

A pair of EMTs rushed past Clare and into the shack. The rain from before had lessened and now the sky only spit drizzle. She watched for a moment as Ryan began to get treatment for the knife that was still stuck in his side.

"Decker kidnapped me from Mercy and brought me here. He was shot and I thought he was dead."

"But he wasn't."

"He stabbed Ryan and ran into the storm. Isaac is trying to find him." A hard kernel of worry clogged her throat. She had no idea if he'd found Decker, where he'd gone or even if he was okay.

As the storm lessened, Isaac deployed the drone for a second time. After searching, he had to admit that the killer had disappeared once again. What's more, he'd used the unmanned aircraft to view the safe house. On the app, he'd seen over a dozen different emergency vehicles at the shack. There were cars from both the sheriff's office, the highway patrol and the Mexican police—the Federales. With all those reinforcements, Decker was as sure as found—or so he had to believe.

He jogged back to the shack with the drone under his arm. He arrived as Ryan was being taken from the small house. Strapped to a gurney, an oxygen mask covered his face. As Isaac approached, he lowered the mask. "You find him?"

Isaac hated to admit the truth. "No."

"He won't get far—not this time." And then, "I need a favor. The dog needs someone to get it home. Old Blue's address is on his collar's tag."

"Sure, I'll take care of him."

"Thanks, man. I don't want to see him left on his own." He let out a pained, shuddering breath. "I appreciate everything, man. Thanks."

For the first time, he liked hearing Ryan saying those words.

An EMT placed the oxygen mask over Ryan's nose and mouth. "You have to keep the mask on, sir."

Ryan gave a thumbs-up as he was lifted into the back of the waiting ambulance. Once the doors were closed, they drove away. Isaac set the drone on the ground, near the sheriff's cruiser, and looked at all the gathered vehicles. Without the storm to interfere with the cellular service, he'd be able to call Jason soon.

The sky was lightening from ebony to soft gray. True, they didn't have Decker in custody or his corpse in a body bag. But they'd survived the night and that had to count for something.

It left Isaac with a single need. He wanted to see Clare.

He turned to see her standing on the threshold, speaking to Sheriff Cafferty.

"Clare." He whispered her name.

She turned and looked over her shoulder. Their eyes met and Isaac's pulse jumped. He moved across the ground, oblivious to anything but her. She held out her hand to him. He slipped his palm into hers and pulled her to him. He inhaled, breathing in her scent. She wrapped her arms around him, holding him to her.

There were so many things that he wanted to tell her—like that her embrace was the one place he wanted to claim for his own.

"Good to see you, buddy," said the sheriff, interrupting the moment. "What'd you find?"

"A lot of sand and rocks and rain," he said. "But no Decker."

The horizon was filled with a cloud of dust. "That must be the feds," said Cafferty. The look on Isaac's face must've asked what was on his mind because the sheriff continued, "He was already on his way when I called."

It took Jason only a few minutes to arrive. He introduced his team, which consisted of four special agents and a forensic pathologist, Michael O'Brien. Dr. O'Brien was with the team when they left San Antonio and tasked with the forensic examination of Trinity's body. But with Decker wounded and missing, the physician was asked to help with the search and to give his analysis of any trace evidence they managed to find. Jason mentioned that dogs and their handlers were on the way.

The first thing on the agenda was a video taken from the drone. Using the app, he found the moments when Decker was spotted, stumbling through the night. On the screen, the killer fell.

"Stop the video," said Michael. "Can I see your phone?"

Isaac liked the other guy's combination of command and courtesy. He handed him the cell. "Sure thing."

"Until we have a body, I won't proclaim anyone to be deceased," the doctor said.

"Patient. Surgery. I thought you were a forensic pathologist," said Jason. "Doesn't that mean you conduct tests on tissues or examine blood and urine for toxins? Besides, all your patients are already dead."

"True enough," said Michael. "But I did go to medical school. I can sew up a bullet wound if needed."

Yep, Isaac definitely liked Dr. Michael O'Brien.

If Jason were offended by the slight rebuff, he made no comment. Instead, he said, "We need to walk from here to where Decker was last seen. Everyone needs to be shoulder to shoulder. If you find something, stop and let us know. It'll get tagged and bagged for evidence. Understood?"

There were plenty of law enforcement officers for the job and Isaac need not volunteer. Yet, Decker was still his responsibility. "I'll go, too," he said as the line was forming.

"I'm coming, too," said Clare.

Jason shook his head. "No way."

"He attacked me twice," she said. "I'm done running away and hiding. Besides, I've spent time with him. I know how he thinks."

Jason glanced at Isaac. He shrugged. "She has a point."

The fed sighed. "I don't have time to argue. You can come along."

Clare stood next to Isaac as they walked into the desert. He took reassurance from her presence and longed for the moment when he could talk to her about everything that had gone down between them. About everything he'd started thinking and feeling about her, about them.

Still, this was hardly the place or time.

The line of people moved forward as one. With last night's storm, the typical hard-packed earth was silty. The wind continued to blow, sending dust devils skittering across the ground.

Using the coordinates taken from the drone's video, they returned to the place Decker was last seen. A detective from the Federales stopped. *"Tengo algo." I have something.*

Everyone broke ranks and formed a loose circle around the man. Partially buried in the sand was a bloody and torn shoe. The detective said what everyone had to be thinking. "He was attacked by an animal."

Jason marked the shoe with an evidence card *#1*. Another FBI agent began to take pictures.

Clare turned to the doctor. "I'm curious what you think. You saw Decker's wounds. You've seen this shoe. Is he even alive?"

Michael took a knee. "I need to get this to my lab. The teeth marks look canine, but I'd have to analyze the saliva for DNA. Likewise with the shoe. Sure, there's blood on the fabric but it might not have come from a human. And furthermore, we can't assume that shoe belongs to Decker."

"If it's not his, whose would it be?" Clare asked. Isaac thought it was a good question and he was curious for an answer.

The doctor said, "I can only deal with medically proven facts. If the blood on the shoe is Decker's, then I can tell you. And as far as his condition, until we have a body, medically speaking, we have to consider that he's possibly alive. And if he was attacked by an animal, then chances are that we'll find proof of that attack."

The search continued for several more hours. Mile after mile of desert was covered, one at a time. The sun climbed in the sky, and the heat along with it. By 11:00 a.m., nothing else had been found. The team reversed their search. It was midafternoon by the time they made it back to the shack and took a break.

It was Clare who broached the subject of procedures again. "The desert is a big place. How much longer will we search for Decker?"

Jason was handing out water bottles. "The simple answer is until he's found and in custody or the morgue. The more complicated answer is an active investigation can only continue for so long. Like the cop said, he might've encountered a wild animal who saw him as he was—wounded prey. The weather last night could have washed away any evidence there was to find, and now, the dust is covering anything left for us to find today. Basically, unless Mother Nature spits up his body, Decker may never be found."

"But you *do* think he's dead," Clare pressed.

"I didn't say that, either. Like the doctor said, until we have him in custody—or evidence of his death—the FBI will consider Decker Newcombe a fugitive."

"Fugitive?" Clare scoffed. She twisted the cap off her water bottle and took a drink. "That sounds like you'll quit looking." Isaac felt her frustration himself. It was born of the futility of finding a body in the desert, along with having survived a harrowing twenty-four hours. And in Clare's case, also being on the run for over two months.

"We'll never quit looking. But you're talking about an active search, and I can't tell you anything other than it's not over today." Jason finished the last swallow of water in the bottle. "Let's get this shack processed as a crime scene, and while we're at it, I'll bring in fixed wing air support."

Search aircraft had positives and drawbacks. On the plus side, they could cover a much larger area than individuals on foot. A huge minus—there were plenty of small clues on the ground that they'd never see. But either way, Isaac knew it was time to go.

"Hey, Jason. I need a minute of your time."

Isaac stepped away from the group. Both Clare and Jason followed. "If you need something more from us, we'll stay…"

"Go," said Jason. "It sounds like the past twenty-four hours have been traumatic."

"It was," said Isaac.

Clare just nodded.

"And about our agreement—you did a good job. Make sure you have your phone handy. The FBI will be reaching out for your services again—and soon."

"What about the other case I mentioned to you?" Isaac asked. "You remember, Chamberlain Enterprises."

Jason shook his head and chuckled. "Most people would be happy to have their plan to catch a killer work—even if the subject isn't in custody. But not you—you're ready to move on to the next case. You're a tenacious bastard, I'll give you that."

Tenacious bastard? He'd take it. "So have you heard anything?"

"Actually, I did. The CDC has a pocket of renal cancers in Columbus. The testing is just starting." Jason turned to Clare, "If you can get me all your information, we can see if there's a connection."

Clare gave him a quick nod. "I can get you those documents to you as soon as I get back to Mercy."

Jason nodded to them both. "I'll be in touch."

For Isaac, it was a good start. "You ready?" he asked Clare. They still had to walk back to his truck, and he was looking forward to a few minutes alone with her. There was so much he wanted to say... "Clare. Wait a minute."

He jogged back to the small house.

"Where are you going?" Clare shaded her eyes with a hand.

"I made a promise to a friend, and I have to keep it." He collected Old Blue and his water dish. In the truck Decker stole, he found a leash and the dog happily trotted at his side. "You walk him," said Isaac, holding out the lead to Clare. "I'll carry the drone."

With so many emergency vehicles having driven to the safe house, the road back to Isaac's truck was easy to follow.

"Why the dog?"

"Well, Ryan was worried about him. Besides, I couldn't just leave him there. I think he's been through a lot."

"See?" She gestured to the dog. "You might try to fight your nature, but you really are kind."

"Not always," he amended.

"Always with me," she said.

He gave her a small smile. "That's because you're special."

She glanced at him as they walked. "Oh?"

Only moments before, he'd struggled with what to say. Now he couldn't restrain himself from speaking. He stopped walking and reached for Clare's shoulders, turning her to face him. "Since Miguel died, I haven't cared about anyone or anything. Then, you walked into the bar and all that changed. I changed." He swallowed. "When we were driving—hoping to find Decker's safe house—and you, I realized. Well, I realized that I care deeply for you." Did he love Clare? He thought he might. Still, it was too early for him to be able to put those feelings into words. "I know we've only had a little more than a day together. But I want to see what a week would be like with you. A month."

He didn't add *a year or a lifetime*, though the words came to him.

She sighed. "When Decker had me in that room, I didn't want to die. But I wasn't sure what there was to live for, or to fight for, either. I'd been so alone for so long, fighting everything on my own, betrayed so badly by Kyle. But you, Isaac. You came to mind." She scratched Old Blue on the head and the dog leaned into her leg. "Just thinking about you gave me the strength to fight and survive." Clare shook her head and scanned the horizon. "I'm sorry about what happened to Kyle—although I'm thankful that he's not after me anymore. But I didn't want Decker to kill him, that's for sure."

"I'm sure Decker will be charged with his murder," said Isaac. With the crime being recorded by the cameras at the bar, a conviction would come easy—once they found the killer, that is. "Eventually, there will be justice for Kyle."

She didn't reply and he let the silence settle over them.

She spoke again. "He was my husband and I hate that everything turned out the way it did. One thing I don't regret, Isaac, is you. I'm not sure what comes next. But whatever it is, I'm glad that we're together."

Reaching for Clare, he pulled her to him and placed his lips on hers. He held her tight, pressing her body against his. God, it felt good just to hold her. As he kissed her deeply, he wasn't sure where the road would take them, but he would unquestionably enjoy the ride.

Epilogue

New Year's Eve
6:55 p.m. Hawaiian-Aleutian Standard Time

Clare wore a bikini and linen cover-up. She dug her toes into the sand and let the waves wash over her ankles. She looked out over the Pacific Ocean and sighed, not sure if she should really believe that her New Year was starting in paradise. This close to the equator, the sun was just starting to slip toward the horizon.

Before leaving to visit her mother in Hawaii, she and Isaac had paid a visit to Trinity's daughter and ex-husband. The little girl was eight years old and looked exactly like her mother in miniature. She assured the girl that she was very much loved by her mother—and as proof she gave her the locket that Trinity always wore.

The girl's father seemed to appreciate the visit, so Clare and Isaac hadn't felt unwelcome.

A phone pinged with an incoming message. She turned around to look at Isaac, who stood at her back in the surf. Since arriving in Kauai days earlier, he'd been getting messages and calls nonstop. Many were from well-wishers who'd seen the media coverage about Decker Newcombe, the modern era's Jack the Ripper. In fact, Clare had even been interviewed by various cable news networks more than once. Many others who reached out to Isaac were looking for his firm, Texas Law, to take on their cases.

It looked like his professional success was guaranteed.

He wore a set of swim trunks and a short-sleeved shirt, open at the chest. He pulled the phone from his pocket and glanced at the screen.

"Admirer or client?" she asked.

"Neither. It's Ryan." The day after Christmas, Ryan had been released from the San Antonio Area Medical Center. After getting out of the hospital, he'd met with the local US attorney and had his criminal record cleared, per his agreement with Isaac and the FBI. Then, he'd returned to Mercy, collected his clothes and personal belongings—along with Old Blue, whose family had been killed by Decker—and left. "He sent a link to a podcast. Same old stuff, theories about what happened to Newcombe." Using his thumbs, Isaac typed a reply. "I asked him if he heard anything useful in the episode."

Within seconds, Ryan sent a reply. "He says no. Unless space aliens are real."

Clare laughed. Everyone had their own conspiracy as

to what had happened to Decker. Some were absurd—like a Martian abduction. Others thought they could prove that he'd perished in the desert somewhere, while others knew just how he'd survived. But until the killer was actually found, Clare wouldn't rest easy.

No, that wasn't entirely true. Since surviving the day where the lines had blurred between hunter and the hunted, Clare found solace from her fears in Isaac's arms. The first few nights had been plagued by nightmares, but eventually, slowly, she began to recover from the trauma. Now, though her sleep was still far from peaceful, the bad dreams were finally starting to fade. Some of that was due to the therapist the FBI had referred her to, and some was because of Isaac. Leaning into his chest, she breathed in the salt air and his male scent. She wanted to stay here forever, but Clare knew that Isaac had a business to run in Texas.

He wrapped his arm around her and held her tighter. His phone pinged again.

"Give that thing to me. I'm going to throw it in the ocean," she said, joking. Or mostly joking, at least. Still, she grabbed it from his hand and noticed that the message came from Jason Jones. It began RE: Columbus Case. She handed back the device to Isaac. "It's about the Chamberlains."

He opened the message and held the screen so she could read as well.

DOJ opened a case into Chamberlain Plastics Manufacturing for both environmental crimes and conspiracy to commit murder. Target letters have been sent. Expect indictments soon.

"That's good news." Clare had worked at the EPA long enough to know that a DOJ case meant criminal charges. Chamberlain Plastics Manufacturing would have to pay a fine. But she didn't know if it was enough to put them out of business. Then again, it might not matter. The people who buried and hid the chemicals were certain to spend time in jail. "Now, turn off your phone already! I want to just enjoy the moment."

"Just a moment?" Isaac asked, powering down the device and slipping it into his pocket.

Clare pulled her to him and brushed her lips on his. "We can start with now and see how the rest of our story unfolds."

"Fine with me." Isaac enveloped her in his arms and together, they watched the sun set over the water.

* * * * *

COMING SOON!

We really hope you enjoyed reading this book. If you're looking for more romance be sure to head to the shops when new books are available on

Thursday 26th March

To see which titles are coming soon, please visit
millsandboon.co.uk/nextmonth

MILLS & BOON

FOUR BRAND NEW BOOKS FROM
MILLS & BOON MODERN

Indulge in desire, drama, and breathtaking romance – where passion knows no bounds!

OUT NOW

Eight Modern stories published every month, find them all at:

millsandboon.co.uk

TWO BRAND NEW BOOKS FROM
Love Always

Be prepared to be swept away to incredible worldwide destinations along with our strong, relatable heroines and intensely desirable heroes.

OUT NOW

Four Love Always stories published every month, find them all at:

millsandboon.co.uk

LET'S TALK
Romance

For exclusive extracts, competitions and special offers, find us online:

- **f** MillsandBoon
- **X** @MillsandBoon
- **◉** @MillsandBoonUK
- **♪** @MillsandBoonUK

Get in touch on 01413 063 232

For all the latest titles coming soon, visit
millsandboon.co.uk/nextmonth